REVELATION
& OTHER TALES
OF FANTASCIENCE

FIRST EDITION

2 4 6 8 10 9 7 5 3 1

ISBNs
978-1-786367-08-2
978-1-786367-09-9 [signed]

Design & Layout by Michael Smith
Printed and Bound in England by T.J. Books

PS PUBLISHING LTD
Grosvenor House, 1 New Road
Hornsea, HU18 1PG, England

editor@pspublishing.co.uk
www.pspublishing.co.uk

REVELATION

& OTHER TALES OF FANTASCIENCE

ALBERT E. COWDREY

Contents

INTRODUCTION

ATE IN **1996**, when I took the editorial reins of *The Magazine of Fantasy & Science Fiction* from Kris Rusch, I was barely familiar with the name Albert Cowdrey. He'd had a cover story a few months before I started, and there were three other stories in inventory that Kris had bought, but at that time, I could hardly distinguish his name from that of thousands of other writers submitting stories.

Obviously, that would change.

In fact, by the time I passed the editor's reins to Charlie Finlay in 2015, I had bought seventy Albert Cowdrey stories. The number of stories he sent me that I declined to publish was, if memory serves, one.

But I'm getting ahead of myself. Back to '97.

Those first months of editing *F&SF* were a blur for me, filled with manuscripts and more manuscripts. My tally for one month of 1997 showed that I received nine hundred-plus submissions in thirty days—and I read them all. (My one attempt at enlisting readers was dissatisfying enough to convince me I was better off handling the submissions myself.) So I can probably be forgiven if I don't have a vivid memory of receiving "Crux."

I do have strong memories of the story itself, as well as its sequels "Mosh" and "Ransom." They read like vintage science fiction: well plotted, ambitious, twisty time-travel tales concerning a future where Russian culture had won out globally. I still have a note in my file sent by a subscriber in Hollis, New Hampshire, who summed up my feelings when he said, "You should tie Albert E. Cowdrey to a chair in front of his word processor and not release him until he has finished his Ulanor tales . . . or at least the next installment for you to publish."

The novel that incorporated these stories—also called *Crux*—didn't enoy the commercial success I'd thought it would, but that's probably just as well: it meant that Bert Cowdrey continued to focus his efforts on short stories. Which means that we readers have this book to enjoy, plus enough material for several more volumes.

As the editor who was grateful to be on the receiving end when these stories were submitted for publication, I came to appreciate a great many things about Albert Cowdrey's fiction: the stories invariably are well told, vividly imagined, and they frequently allow the author's wit to shine. They manage the difficult trick of being both reliable and unpredictable, which means that a reader can pick up a Cowdrey tale and feel both comfortable and unsettled all at once.

Over time, I came to see Bert Cowdrey's stories as falling into one of three categories (usually):

One category is vintage SF: In "Poison Victory," "The Tribes of Bela," and "The Assassin," it's easy to see that Cowdrey cut his teeth on science fiction magazine stories of the '40s and '50s. These tales tend to feature hard-bitten characters with combat experience and understanding of diplomacy. They're worldly and cynical. One could easily imagine the likes of Poul Anderson, Eric Frank Russell, and Gordy Dickson gratefully viewing them as successors to their own work.

Another one of Cowdrey's modes is lighter fare: these stories tend to be fantasy, but they don't take their concepts very seriously—they're yarns like "Mister Sweetpants and the Living Dead" and "The Boy's Got Talent" that play with familiar fantasy figures like ghosts and zombies. Cowdrey gives them free rein while he celebrates the marvels of character and setting.

Then there are the weird tales: these are the stories that pay homage to Machen and Bloch, Bradbury and Dahl. Many of them, like "Twilight States" and "Grey Star," are set in Cowdrey's home turf—the American Southeast—and they seem to be the stories for which he's known best.

As I write this, and as I look at the book, it occurs to me that I might add a fourth category: historicals like "The Lord of Ragnarök" and "The Overseer" that draw on Cowdrey's strength and training as an historian and let him bring to life a particular period in time.

What amazes me is that the stories, regardless of how one categorizes them, are so consistently good. A reader may well favor the science fiction adventures or prefer the horror fables, but all of them—every last one—is crafted well. They're fully realized but without excess verbiage. What's more, Cowdrey's stories don't show the decline in quality that many writers exhibit. I suspect there are two reasons why this is so:

First, there's the maturity of the work. After publishing a novel and a story or two in the 1960s, Bert Cowdrey had a successful career writing nonfiction. When he returned in his sixties to writing fiction, he did so without facing the aflictions that bedevil many a writer who pursued the course of a professional writing career. (Do I need to name these afflictions? We've all seen and read histories of writers tormented by them: financial struggles, questionable choices in life and love, bitterness at how one's work is received, and so forth.)

The other reason is because the themes that Albert Cowdrey explores are timeless. He's interested in these odd creatures known as humans, interested in their foibles and their passions, in the things that truly make them what they are. But he's also interested in the monsters that torment them (whether external or internal) and he's interested in their settings, the times and places where their lives play out, whether these be another planet or somewhere in the great state of Louisiana.

The wells from which Cowdrey draws his inspiration are deep and never run dry. The hand with which he raises and lowers the bucket is steady and experienced. Small wonder, then, that each new serving is so very refreshing.

There's a school of thought that holds that an introduction such as this one should make reference to every story in the book, as though it somehow slights a story by not making mention of it. I have never belonged to that school, so the careful observer who has noted which four stories I have not alluded to should draw no conclusions in advance of reading them. In fact, one might well want to try those stories first, because they're all good.

Indeed, as I mentioned earlier, Albert Cowdrey has written stories enough for another book or three, and those volumes will also include some of my favorite works of his. But once again, I get ahead of myself. This book you hold in your hands is a grand assemblage of Albert Cowdrey's short stories, a sterling collection of fantastic tales, a delight both for readers new to his work and for those folks looking to read them anew, a cornucopia of Cowdreyana.

Enjoy.

—Gordon Van Gelder

To GVG

A sardonic tale that gives a nasty twist to the ancient query: what is the meaning of human life? Doctor Dread might well annotate it, "Addle that yolk!"

REVELATION

ORSHIN JOINED DREA at his usual table in the Federal City Wine Cellar, inhaled a dark red half-inch of Mondo Rosso Cabernet from a Walmart goblet, and began to denounce his patients.

"Phil, you don't know what it's like, having to listen to a bunch of goddamn nuts all day."

He had a bass-drum voice and a build to match. His drinking buddy was thin, waspish, and bitter as only an overage campus radical could be.

"I have to read the rubbish my students write," protested Drea, "and I get paid roughly ten percent of what you make."

Gorshin paid no attention. When soliloquizing he was as unstoppable as Hamlet.

"Even my favorite screwball is getting to be a pain in the butt. I mean, here I am, one of a tiny shrinking band of Freudians—no pun intended— encircled by the howling Indians of drug therapy. So I finally get the perfect patient, intelligent, good rapport, with a truly original paranoid delusional system and a huge bank account, but I can't seem to break through to him."

"What's original about paranoia?" Drea demanded. "All the paranoids I've ever known have been dreadful bores. They all think Monsanto's poisoning the water supply, or there's a Jewish plot to rule the galaxy, or the KGB's trying to control their brains by beaming radio broadcasts to the fillings in their teeth, or—"

"My patient thinks," said Gorshin slowly, "that the Earth is an egg."

That got Drea's attention. "The Earth is an *egg*?"

Involuntarily he raised his eyes and looked over the hump of Gorshin's left shoulder. At the opposite end of the Cellar a Sony HD was broadcasting the evening news to boozers at the bar. A picture sent back by the Mars Orbiter stared from the screen like an inflamed eye. *Okay*, thought Drea, finding a grain of logic in the fantasy, *planets are slightly ovate—and come to think of it, ovate means egg-shaped—*

"Yes, an egg," Gorshin rumbled on. "It was laid gazillions of years ago by a huge cosmic beast that my patient calls the Mother Dragon."

"Look, if a Freudian can't make something out of that, you ought to take down your shingle."

"All the inner planets are eggs," he continued, flattening Drea's interjection like a Hummer ironing out a motorbike. "That's why they're so different from the outer planets. Only one's hatched so far—that's where the Asteroid Belt is today. He thinks Mercury and Venus probably won't hatch at all, because they're too close to the sun and the embryo dragons—he calls them 'dragonets'—have gotten cooked inside their shells. But the Earth is sort of like the porridge in the Goldilocks story that wasn't too hot and wasn't too cold: it was just right."

"So if we're just right, why haven't we hatched yet?"

"That's why he's got acute anxiety symptoms. He thinks we're just about to. He says global warming is a sign. He says it's not caused by greenhouse gases at all, it's caused by the friction of our dragonet moving around inside its shell, preparing to bust out. Every time my patient hears about another earthquake or tsunami he thinks the dragonet's tapping the Earth's crust with its egg tooth."

"What's an egg tooth?"

"It's a bump that young crocs get on the ends of their noses to help them break out of their shells. I tell you, Phil, I love this guy. His delusional system is such a welcome break from the usual run of crap I have to listen to, it's almost a shame to cure him. But that's my job, and he really wants help, he wants to be freed from his crippling fear that the Earth will disintegrate when the dragonet breaks out at last. He's paying me a ton of money to help him shake it, and I feel like I'm failing in my duty, which, because of my anal-retentive upbringing, is a real issue with me."

"You drink enough red wine," Drea assured him, "and you won't be any kind of retentive, believe me."

A week had passed and the conversation at the Cellar had been forgotten when Drea greeted the first session of the new semester's seminar in Creative Writing.

In the English department of Aaron Burr University (Silver Spring Campus) he was known as Dr. Dread, a reputation he treasured because it kept his classes from becoming overcrowded. His current crop numbered nine, and he gazed at them with distaste.

Most were as grungy as Serbian Army conscripts. But not quite all. One black guy displayed precise cornrows, a sculpted goatee, and little pale blue expensive-looking shades; he had a touch of the lean dark Malcolm X look, as if he'd started life as an AK-47. Farther down the scarred seminar table sat a white guy looking neat and earnest as a Mormon stockbroker. A Brooks Brothers label was almost visible through the nubby cloth of his conservative jacket, and his well-scrubbed face shone limpidly fair, like an acolyte of some suburban preacher.

Briefly Drea fantasized having the two of them dipped in bronze and displayed in a campus chapel dedicated to the great god Diversity. Their names fit them neatly: when Drea, calling the meager roll, reached U. Pierson Clyde, the stockbroker made a strangled sound that might have been "here." When he reached Inshallah Jones, the AK-47 didn't answer at all—just raised one long beige hand about three inches off the tabletop and let it drop soundlessly back.

The students had been instructed to bring a sample of their work to the first class, and Drea watched gloomily as a growing heap of paper slid toward him along the table like a gathering wave. Most of the manuscripts were fat as American children in training for a diabetic future, and—Drea was willing to bet—florid with the acne of adolescent prose.

But U. Pierson Clyde, bless him, contributed a plastic-jacketed manuscript that was thin to the point of bulimia, while Inshallah Jones tossed down a tubular scroll secured by a rubber band. Drea conceived a faint hope that good things might come in small packages.

Well, he'd find out soon enough. Right now it was time to put the class through the get-acquainted ritual. One by one, they rose to mumble their names and backgrounds and longings for World Peace, while he, like an experienced teacher, dozed.

He woke twice. The first time when Jones revealed that he'd grown up in the Anacostia Project, which was truly impressive; in that neighborhood, a kid who contracted literacy was marked for almost certain death. Drea woke the second time when U. Pierson Clyde, his voice trembling yet under tense control, revealed that he'd joined the class at the urging of his shrink.

"Dr. Gorshin said that if I wrote things out, I might find it easier to objectify my fantasies and see them for what they are," U said.

This confession drew only bored glances from the other students, most of whom had been seeing therapists since they wore Huggies. But it enraged Drea.

That goddamn witch doctor, he thought, his small bloodshot eyes getting smaller and redder yet. *He's getting paid five hundred bucks an hour for curing this nut, and now he wants me to do his job for him!* Resentment rising inside him like acid reflux, he resolved to hit U's work with comments so scathing that he'd drop the course and join the queue at the lobotomy counter in Gorshin's clinic.

Fifteen minutes later, the class dismissed, Drea entered his musty office with its thrift-store furnishings, its odor of dead pipes that lingered though he hadn't smoked for a decade, its thousand or so dust-veiled volumes of literature and criticism and other rubbish he'd studied for his Ph.D. in 1971, and never opened since.

He sat down in a semi-defunct swivel chair, prepared to do execution, flicked back the neat plastic cover of U's work and gazed with remorseless eye at the title, "Revelation." The byline gave the author's full name—Uriel Pierson Clyde—and unexpectedly his rage began to abate.

A passionate liberal reformer in his youth, Drea had almost exhausted his lifetime supply of empathy before the age of forty. Yet a few tiny drops lingered in the dry chambers of his heart: racism still made him fume, and he still pitied people who had to go through the hell of childhood additionally burdened with an oddball name. The reason was his own: Philbert. His namesake, shrewd Aunt Philberta who'd founded a string of weight-control salons that successfully thinned bank accounts, was supposed to (but didn't) leave him a bunch of money. All she'd left him was the joy of being known as Filbert the Nut until he was old enough to vote.

Now, gazing at Uriel's paper, he tried to imagine what life must have been like for a kid who had to fight his way through school being addressed as Urinal Pee. Was this the root of the lad's psychiatric problems?

His tide of bile receding, Drea began to read "Revelation," now rather hoping that he would not have to flay its author alive.

The cosmic egg has an addled yolk—Henry Miller, read the epigraph. Drea liked that; he'd often thought the same thing.

Alas, the story itself was a mishmash. The hero, Jamie Cassandra, was a Poor Little Rich Boy with a menu of all the usual symptoms—sexual confusion, obscure phobias, chemical dependency—the sort of baffled youth without whom Gorshin wouldn't own his condo at Cozumel.

At unpredictable moments, however, Jamie morphed into an unrecognized prophet, trying to warn the human race about a danger only he could see: the Earth was going to hatch. After some pointless plot complications (inconclusive fondling by an elderly male relative, quarrels with a ditzy wife he'd married at seventeen to convince himself he wasn't gay) Jamie came to realize that warning the world was pointless. He couldn't save it, and it couldn't save itself. On that note the story didn't exactly end—it petered out.

Though tempted to live up to his Dr. Dread image by scrawling across U's paper *This is the most incoherent farrago of rubbish I have encountered during decades of scanning undergraduate drivel*, Drea put "Revelation" aside for mature consideration. And not only because of U's presumably miserable childhood. Despite its gross deficiencies, there was something about this battered torso of a tale. Some quality of... authentic... desperation? Something, anyway, that made it stick.

Among Drea's most deeply guarded secrets was the fact that he still hoped, sometime before he died, to find and nurture a real talent. U seemed a most unlikely candidate, but still he wanted to think "Revelation" over, and meanwhile went on to the other papers.

In general they covered a narrow range from babbling fluency to utter incoherence. Inshallah's was, as he'd hoped, an exception. The man actually could spell, though where he'd learned was a mystery to Drea, who like most residents of Montgomery County believed firmly that District of Columbia public schools taught only two things well, Shooting and Shooting Up.

Still more improbably, his student had been reading Kipling, from whom he filched his title, "The City of the Dreadful Night". Drea was dazzled by what followed. Inshallah's account of one stifling August night under the staring vapor lamps in the concrete-and-sooty-brick maze of the Anacostia Project was like listening to what rap might be if it lacked rhyme and possessed a soul. No wonder the man resembled an assault rifle; that was how he used language. Drea was able to write at the end of the paper the rarest of all professorial comments—"With minor changes, this ought to be publishable."

Finally, as the shadows of evening lengthened over Silver Spring—a traffic-throttled Maryland blurb conspicuous for its lack of either silver or springs—he got back to Uriel, or U as he'd begun to think of him. The basic problem, he concluded, was that U was mixing up his story with his analysis, thus creating a sort of chimera that was false as a confession and incoherent as a tale.

On the last page of "Revelation" Drea wrote, "Forget Jamie's damn sex problems and tell me why a rather banal young man with limited intelligence and an unlimited trust fund came to believe in the existence of a cosmic dragon."

See if that does any good.

Then Drea locked up, climbed into his battered Toyota, and headed south on Georgia Avenue to the Federal City Wine Cellar. Gorshin had left his office—appropriately located in Foggy Bottom—early, and was already overflowing his usual chair while glancing over his shoulder at the evening news. Tonight the Sony's screen exhibited a huge red valley tucked beneath the towering mountains of Mars.

"For some reason," he commented as Drea sat down, "that reminds me of Caitlin."

"Why don't you ever stay home with her?" Drea asked, inserting his lips into his first goblet of Mondo Rosso. "She is your wife, after all."

"Not anymore. She left me last year. Didn't I tell you?"

"No. You also didn't tell me you were sending U. Pierson Clyde to my class so I could do your job for you."

"He's an interesting guy, isn't he? I mean, as loons go."

"Don't evade the issue. You're the one being paid to shrink his head, not me. Then why do I have to read his stuff?"

"Look, I'll buy you a case of Mondo Rosso. Deal?"

"Deal."

Gorshin asked if he had any other interesting students this year, and Drea told him about Inshallah Jones, whom he described as "a remarkable young black man."

"Young male *African Americans*," Gorshin said reprovingly, because Drea hadn't used the currently okay designation, "have terrible castration issues. It's on account of those old African American women who raise them. That's why they explode in violence if you look at them crooked. Or even if you don't."

"Without those old women they'd all be dead before the age of one."

"Yes, and better off, too," said the Dr. Mengele of the Wine Cellar. "I'm just saying, keep an eye on him."

Drea sat gazing at Gorshin, noticing for the first time that despite the breadth of his fat face, his eyes were so close together that only his nose stopped them from overlapping.

Why did Drea associate with him? Had a mere busted marriage and a dead-end career and a grown son who preferred not to speak to him so completely emptied his life that he had to fill it with Gorshin and cheap wine? Was he that lonely?

Well, of course they had. And of course he was.

"Believe me," he said at last, "I intend to keep an eye on him."

If he'd been marking his own conversation, he'd have scrawled *Awfully weak* on this poor excuse for a comeback.

Like all members of the Academic Community, Drea filled his days by drinking coffee, a schedule interrupted only by occasional hours wasted in class and necessary trips to the bathroom.

The day after he returned the Creative Writing bunch their papers, Drea was in the student center drinking a cup of caffeine-and-saccharine-flavored mud at his favorite table overlooking the glassed-in swimming pool. He liked to sit there, eyeballing the sort of shapely young women who, perhaps warned by a website called gropingprofs.edu, never took his classes.

"Can I sit down?" asked a voice, and without waiting for an answer, U sat down.

He'd shed his young-broker attire and donned casual clothes, in which he appeared even more of a lank, flaxen-haired nonentity than before.

"Please do," Drea muttered, with what he thought was irony. It went unnoticed.

"You, uh, uh, asked me about the dragon, Dr. Dread," U said, and instantly turned scarlet.

"My name is Drea, Philbert Eugene Drea. Dr. Dread is merely what people call me."

U turned even brighter, a kind of neon, and for the moment appeared to be completely deprived of the power of speech. Drea sat there in silence, enjoying the discomfort of this blushing nut who'd invaded his private space.

"I consider the name a compliment," he said finally, and gave U a Dan Rather-type smile, stretching without elevating the corners of his mouth.

Uncertainly U smiled back. The flood of scarlet ebbed from his face and his tongue became functional.

"I, I, uh, uh, can't tell you where the dragon came from, Dr. Drea, because I really don't know. I've explained that over and over and over to my therapists, and every time I do they try to make me say something that just isn't true."

"I am not interested in true truth, I am interested in fictional truth—" Drea began. But U, like a Gorshin in training, promptly overwhelmed him with a flood of chatter.

"See, Dr. Drea, I used to do codeine."

"Just like Jamie Cassandra. What a surprise."

"It wasn't good for me."

"No, I don't suppose it was."

"It practically wrecked my life. My wife Brittany left me on account of it."

"You were married to a spaniel?" Drea jested. But U rushed on, unheeding.

"Even her leaving didn't make me stop. It was my toothbrush did it. I was standing in my bathroom one morning about six months ago, I guess I was there for a couple of hours, and *I couldn't find my toothbrush.* That was when I realized I needed help, and checked myself into rehab at Georgetown Hospital."

"A shocking experience."

"I mean, it was staring me in the face, yet I couldn't find it. Well, after they detoxed me, the people in rehab recommended long-term therapy and sent me to a lady shrink. She asked me just what you did, where did the dragon come from, and when I couldn't tell her she tried to make me admit that I invented it during a drug-induced psychotic episode. But she was wrong. It was thinking about the dragon that started me taking codeine. The addiction was the effect, not the cause."

"So you switched from the drug lady to Gorshin."

"Yeah, and at first I thought I'd found the right shrink at last. He agreed with me that drugs were just a symptom of deeper problems. He thought—"

"Castration," Drea muttered.

"What?"

"He thought the underlying cause was castration anxiety."

"How'd you know? He thinks I'm the dragonet, and the Earth is the womb—Mother Earth, you know—and in bursting through the shell I'd be escaping from the castrating influence of mother love. He says I want to escape and achieve autonomous phallic maturity, but at the same time I'm afraid to, and the conflict is what's causing my anxiety. But he's wrong too."

"Gorshin is right only at long intervals, when the laws of probability catch up with him. Did you know he's been married six times? Six. Most people become immune to the bug after one or two exposures, but with Gorshin it's like the flu, it comes back every February.... Why, specifically, is he wrong this time?"

"Well, Mama died when I was three hours old, and I don't see how she could've done much castrating in such a short amount of time."

"Who raised you?"

"Oh, a bunch of nannies, a Ukrainian au pair named Olga, Daddy until he died, some of his mistresses, my Uncle Uriel, two or three Catholic boarding schools, and whatnot."

To Drea that sounded about right as a breeding ground of lunacy. He asked if U would like a cup of coffee, but he said no, caffeine made him hyperventilate.

"The truth is," he went on, his eyes taking on the thousand-yard stare of introspection, "it really baffles me, not knowing where the dragon came from. As a kid I always liked scaly critters, because they were kind of outcasts and rejects, like me. I loved dinosaurs—wanted to be an Allosaurus when I grew up, and eat people. I used to keep pet snakes in a toilet at St. Mark's until the Prefect of Discipline found out and flushed them. Later on, when Brittany wanted us to get matching tattoos as a sign of eternal commitment, I suggested twining rattlers. But she insisted on the Sacred Heart of Jesus. Now she's gone, and I've got the Sacred Heart on my left deltoid and I'm not even a Catholic anymore."

In spite of himself, Drea had gotten interested in this naïve recital. He asked when the dragon business started.

"When? Whenever the Loma Prieta earthquake happened. Ninety-five? I don't remember. Anyway, they kept showing the scenes over and over and over on TV, and suddenly I just flashed on the fact that a dragon had caused it, a dragon down under the Earth. Of course, my first thought was *that's ridiculous*. But the idea kept coming back to me, and it kind of grew, because it seemed to explain so much—earthquakes and floods and global warming and the Asteroid Belt and so forth.

"I began to feel like for the first time in my life I'd discovered something terribly basic and terribly important. The existence of an embryo dragon implied a mother, so I started calling the little guy a dragonet, and I dreamed about him. I saw the dragonet coiled up inside the Earth like a baby snake in its egg, and from time to time it moved, and when it did, the Earth shook.

"When the big tsunami hit Asia the day after Christmas '04, that was when I went on codeine. Because on the twenty-fifth, Christ had his birthday, and on the twenty-sixth, Antichrist tapped the Earth with his egg tooth. I mean the real A.C., the one that's going to finish us all off. Then the next year global warming caused that big hurricane that wiped out New Orleans. That's what all those screwy old prophets of the Last Days dimly foresaw—devastation, the Four Horsemen, the dragon breaking out of the Earth. They thought God would bind him for a thousand years, as in Revelation 20:2, only there isn't any God. So all those dead people, they're just a down payment on what's going to happen."

After his outburst U sat in silence while the filmy cataracts of self-absorption slowly cleared from his eyes, which were grayish or bluish, it was hard to tell which. He finished sadly, "I guess now you think I'm insane, too, Dr. Drea."

"Yes. But that's your business and Gorshin's—who, by the way, you ought to ditch instantly. There *are* rational shrinks, you know. My business is with your story, about one percent of which is worth saving. Can I make a suggestion?"

"Sure."

"Go home. Dig your story out. Try to forget about yourself for half an hour—forty-five minutes, if possible. Your hero is Jamie Cassandra, not Uriel Pierson Clyde, and for the sake of the story you need to devise a plausible scenario to explain what made Jamie believe in his dragon. Not *your* dragon: *his*. I hate to tell you this, but fiction consists of making things up. So go home and make something up."

"I don't want to say anything unless it's absolutely true—"

Drea's temper was none too certain at the best of times, and at this he lost it.

"A storyteller has no more to do with truth than a lawyer has. The lawyer's business is advocacy; the storyteller's is plausibility. Now," Drea concluded, "go away. I'm getting old, and voyeurism is the only kind of sex I can really count on anymore. Will you look at that thong down there with the girl inside it?"

U got up, but seemed troubled. "I thought creative writing meant, you know, spilling your guts," he muttered. "That's why I joined your class."

"Nobody wants to look at a pile of guts except Gorshin, who makes a fortune doing it despite being crazier than you'll ever be. Now scram."

U did. The thong started practicing two-and-a-half backflips, or whatever the proper term was. Drea got himself another cup of mud and settled down to watch.

U was absent from the next class meeting, which was too bad because it contained some lively moments.

Drea passed xeroxes of Inshallah's "City of the Dreadful Night" to the other students as a model for their own work. Some gazed at the author with awe, others with hatred—such were the penalties of success. With Inshallah's permission, Drea had already sent the manuscript to an agent he knew, who didn't usually handle short fiction but might, he hoped, make an exception in this case.

"If you imitate Mr. Jones," Drea told the class, "I'll flunk you straight off. Don't imitate, emulate. He seems to have found his voice—what I want you to do is look around for yours."

That launched the kind of free-for-all teachers dream of. The students peppered Inshallah with questions, and he rapped back with a fluent mix of psychobabble and street language. This was a guy who could make two syllables out of a four-syllable obscenity, yet include in the same sentence words like "polymorphous" and "subliminal"—properly used, at that.

His story, he said, had been drawn directly from his life, and he told about his young days in the Project, dealing drugs, dodging bullets, visiting the fortified home of a big supplier in Potomac Estates where people were filling plastic garbage bags with money and weighing it because counting took too much time. About how he stopped dealing after his brother Shabazz got shot and bled to death in his arms. About how the raging need to memorialize him burst out at last in the struggle to write.

It was great stuff. Gazing dreamily at his prize pupil, Dr. Dread, terror of the English Department, who spent his life stewed in wine and cynicism, wondered whether this moment of—well, of epiphany—gave meaning to his otherwise wasted life as a teacher.

And then, without warning, his critical faculty came to life. *Inshallah was making it all up.*

"The City of the Dreadful Night" wasn't any more original than its title. It just seemed so because of that machine-gun style its author had probably caught—in the same sense that you catch a cold—by listening to rap, deleting the drums and rhymes and spilling it on a page as prose.

His glasses were too expensive, his beard too sculptural, his cornrows too neat, he could spell, he spouted polysyllables, he'd read Kipling—this was no child of the Project. Then why was he lying? Couldn't he just say, Hey, I grew up in a condo in the Watergate, and let the story stand by itself?

Before leaving the campus after class, Drea stopped at the registrar's office and looked up Inshallah's records. He'd graduated from Bunche-Mandela, a pricey private school that specialized in grooming the children of black professionals for success. He lived with his parents in the so-called Gold Coast on the edge of Rock Creek Park, where *café-au-lait* politicians, businessmen, city administrators, top-ranked bureaucrats and presidents of historically black colleges lamented racism while sipping double scotches beside their swimming pools.

By the time Drea reached the Cellar his sense of gallows humor had taken over. After all, he'd been right the first time: life really was a fraud. And so was literature. There was nothing to do but enjoy it, and of course drink.

Full of *Schadenfreude*, he was slurping down Mondo Rosso and grinning like a satanic Happy Face when Gorshin came in and sat down.

He was looking happy, too. "Can't stay long tonight," he said.

"Why not?"

"I'm getting married again. Marvelous woman named Leila or Delilah or something. Met her today in Georgetown Foods. In the meat department."

Drea congratulated him while Gorshin quaffed the single glass he said he would allow himself tonight. Then snapped his fingers.

"By the way. Almost forgot to tell you. Clyde's been hospitalized. At Georgetown. Mixed codeine and vodka, OD'd, almost died. Maybe a suicide attempt. What the hell did you say to him, anyway? He's out of the ER now and resting in the ICU. I'd look in on him, but Delilah and I are flying to Vegas tonight. Krishnamurti will cover for me."

"ER? ICU? Delilah? Vegas? Krishna—what the hell do you mean, what did I say to him?"

"Got to run," said Gorshin, and did.

Next day, Drea phoned the hospital and, after interminable delays, got to speak for thirty seconds to Dr. Krishnamurti. The news was good: U was out of intensive care, resting comfortably, and could see visitors in another day or two.

"It would be good if you came to see him," said the fluent accents of Mumbai. "I believe he is quite isolated, which is unfortunate in so young a man."

"I suppose he's driven all his friends away, talking about his dragon."

"Either that or talking about his analysis," said Krishnamurti dryly.

When Drea saw U again, he was wearing maroon PJs and a blue terrycloth robe and sitting on a bench in a solarium on the ninth floor of Georgetown Hospital. A ray of sunlight penetrating the dusty glass made him look almost translucent; like drugs, suicide had not agreed with him.

"How are you?" Drea asked, shaking his lax and nerveless hand.

"Oh... okay, I guess. Just don't ask me to coagulate."

"Er... all right."

"I'm better, but I can't coagulate yet. I can't coagulate my thoughts. It's my prescription. It's an anticoagulant. It's like I can think of A, or B, or J, but how they connect I don't know."

"I'm sure you'll be doing better soon."

"Jesus, I hope so. I feel like such a fool, almost losing my life worrying about a dragonet who may not even exist."

"You remember that, then."

"Oh hell, I remember everything—well, not your name, but everything else—only I can't coagulate. I can't draw conclusions. Why don't you sit down?"

It had been so long since Drea tried to comfort anyone that his machinery of empathy had frozen up. He was sitting at the end of the bench, trying to think of something to say, when U relieved him of the embarrassment of being nice by falling sleep.

Suddenly his head slumped to one side and he began to snore. Drea was used to having students nod off, so he just sat there for a while, resting. When a male nurse came by, wearing green scrubs and thick fur on his stumpy forearms, Drea stopped him and asked in a low voice if U was going to be all right.

"Yeah, until the next time he tries it," said the nurse, and headed through a door marked HOSPITAL PERSONNEL ONLY. From inside came the hum of a microwave and the odor of chicken-noodle soup.

Next day Drea got a call from his agent pal.

"Absolutely brilliant," he burbled. "That story by Allah whoever. Terrific! I won't make a dime on it, but I'll try sending it around anyway."

"Marvelous," murmured Drea.

"Just one thing. This guy is black, right?"

"Absolutely."

"I just wanted to make sure. Sometimes, people find out somebody writing about the black experience isn't black, they feel cheated."

"Good thing Shakespeare didn't know that when he wrote *Othello*."

"When who wrote what?"

"Nothing."

Just before the next class meeting, standing in a blank tiled hallway outside the seminar room, Drea told the news to Inshallah, whose blue shades grew misty with emotion.

"Awesome," he muttered. "Awesome, awesome."

On impulse, Drea also told him about his fellow student being hospitalized after a suicide attempt.

"I was thinking. Maybe if he could get off the dime with his story, it might help him with his other problems. And since you're a writer and young, and I'm not either one—"

"Oh man, I would be *so* happy to give this screwed-up dude a hand. You know, I been screwed up myself."

Next day they met at Georgetown and ascended to the ninth-floor solarium in an enormous elevator that also contained a fat man on a gurney and his gum-chewing attendant. Drea found U much improved. He could even coagulate again, and was proving it by working out a chess problem from *The Washington Post* in his head.

"How's it going?" asked Drea, and U said, "It starts Qh7 check. It's pretty easy."

He and Inshallah shook hands, and the latter immediately said, "Dr. Drea sold my story, and he says he could sell yours too, except you ran into some kind of a block."

The double lie acted on U like two swigs of Lourdes water.

"Really? You're not kidding me? He said that?" Apparently asking Drea, who was located about a yard distant, never occurred to him. He was staring at Inshallah like a wild pig at an anaconda, both fascinated and fearful.

"Yes, he did. Now what exactly is your story about?"

U told him, phrasing it to make it seem like nothing he would ever dream of actually believing himself.

"Jeeeeeeeeeeesus," breathed Inshallah, "that is such a treeemendous idea! Where'd you get it from?"

"It just came to me," said U modestly.

"Wow! I mean, look, all I do is—I'm like Tom Wolfe: I just report back what I hear on the streets. But you, man, you are like Edgar Allan Poe, wild stuff comes to you out the air. So what is your problem?"

"Well, Dr. Drea says I have to explain to the reader where Jamie Cassandra got his vision of the dragonet. That's not totally honest, because I really don't know where it came from—"

"No, no, no, no!" exclaimed Inshallah. "When you write, man, you invent a parallel universe. So you need an explanation to create a sense of 'reality,' a word Nabokov says means nothing unless it's between quotes."

Enlightenment spread over U's pale countenance. "Oh yeah, right. He said that in his essay 'On a Book Called *Lolita*.'"

"As for your problem, man, that is so simple. Just haul out the old ESP. I mean, you named this dude Jamie Cassandra, right? Maybe a little sexual ambivalence there, which is good in itself. But the point is that Cassandra was the prophet nobody would believe."

"Right. In the *Odyssey*."

"No, man. *The Iliad*."

They wrangled over this for a few minutes, then turned to Drea. Called upon for the first time to intrude on this astounding conversation, he muttered, "Actually, I think it was the *Aeneid*."

Both young men instantly dismissed this information. "Whatever," they exclaimed in chorus, and went back to their dialogue.

"Anyway, you start with one of those canned scenes, everybody been doing it for eons now, where Jamie learns he has visions like Haley Joel Osment in *The Sixth Sense*. I can see the trailer for the movie now. Then—"

"You know," U interrupted, "when I was little I really *did* see visions of things that weren't there. Like Daddy dropping dead in the lobby of the Metropolitan, or Uncle Uriel kissing the mailman behind the garden wall."

"Really? You had the gift? How'd you lose it?"

"Therapy. They started me on it when I was seven."

"Oh yeah, that'll do it. . . . But look, that means you got a personal experience to build on, and that's important, right, Dr. Drea?"

Drea, having learned his place, said nothing. Meanwhile Inshallah and U were shaking hands in various complicated ways and promising to see each other again real, real soon.

As he and Inshallah were leaving the hospital, Drea said something about a friendship maybe developing out of this. Inshallah shook his head.

"No man, I'm too busy. He's a sweet dude, but I got no time for him. Besides writing, I'm an intern in Senator Frist's office, I'm entering Georgetown Law, and my woman needs me at night. Oh, you mean what we said? No, that's just something you say. It don't mean anything."

Before they parted, Drea asked Inshallah if he'd ever actually been in the Anacostia Project. His reply was perfectly unembarrassed.

"Just once. To buy some dope. That was back when I was screwed up. Even then I didn't want to hang with those dudes. They're suicide bombers, man. They just want to die and take somebody with them."

"Then why'd you claim you were born there when you weren't?"

"It's bull," Inshallah explained patiently, as if to a child. "It takes bull to get along in this world. Everybody needs a legend. Life, man, is something you make up."

"I think you ought to be teaching the seminar, not me," said Drea in a burst of candor.

"No, I don't have time for that either," Inshallah replied, and drove off in a new pearl-gray BMW his Daddy had given him.

Gorshin returned from his Vegas marriage and honeymoon, played husband for a few weeks, then started visiting the Wine Cellar again.

At first he brought his wife, whose actual name was Delia; Drea thought her far too sensible a woman to be stuck with Gorshin. Then he began leaving her at home. Drea gathered that not all was well in the new menage.

"Phil, it's hard to listen to those goddamn nuts all day and her pointing out my flaws of character all night," Gorshin said, slurping down a goblet of Mondo Rosso in two gulps.

"You've got a lot of flaws for her to work on."

"She has a streak of violence, too. When we were shopping for groceries the other day, I told her she was the most blatant case of penis envy I've ever seen, and she started throwing canned goods at me."

"You should stay away from supermarkets. How are you and U getting along?"

"Me and who?"

"U. Pierson Clyde. The dragonet guy. He's out of the hospital and back in class, so—"

"Oh him. He quit me. He's going to Krishnamurti. Of course I respect a patient's right to choose his own physician, but I just don't think you can cross a cultural divide that wide in anything as personal as analysis."

"That's a nice way of saying Krishnamurti can't understand U's problems because Wog is Wog and White is White and never the twain shall meet."

"I have never, ever been a racist," declared Gorshin, believing it absolutely.

Meanwhile U's story was developing, not in the gentle quiet of the study, but under a withering barrage of criticism from his fellow students. The nine aspirants to literature read each other's work and, after some initial diffidence, began shredding it in a style which—if only they'd had a better grasp of English—would have been downright Oxfordian in ferocity.

Three people dropped out of class, unable to stand the gaff, and some (not all of them girls) went home in tears. But the survivors' work, if not exactly earth-shaking, became increasingly coherent and pointed.

Inshallah was especially fierce. Midway through the semester, a hip-hop magazine aggressively titled *In Yo Face* bought his story, made him cut it from 4,500 to 1,500 words, and renamed it "Nigga Project Rap." When his agent began shopping for a book deal, he became something of a terror at the seminar table, dispensing his opinions with a faith in his own infallibility that might have impressed His Holiness, Pope Benedict XVI.

Fortified by his new shrink, U survived and even throve in this bracing atmosphere. Gradually Jamie Cassandra took form as a true fictional hero—somebody who both was and wasn't his creator. Jamie became a man escaping from the chaos of his youth, while at the same time clinging fiercely to his ESP-inspired vision of disaster and trying to force it on an unbelieving world.

U's last problem was to find a bang-up ending. That came to him one night in a mysterious dream of vast, barren landscapes overlooked by a bloodshot sky. He jumped out of bed and almost wore out his PC, working until dawn. Drea, who knew how seldom night-time visions last into daylight, began reading the new coda with misgivings—which soon vanished.

Jamie Cassandra, giving up in despair his mission to alert humanity, decided to pursue his estranged wife Chelsea to California, where she'd taken refuge at an ashram run by her guru. Following the westward direction taken by the sun, the course of empire, and screwballs of all types, Jamie reached the Mojave Desert and checked into a tiny, rundown motel for the night.

U did a good job conveying the barren grandeur of Death Valley—the ringing silence; the insinuating whisper of windblown sand; the searing day when the world was half sun and half rock; the frigid night when Jamie's cabin seemed to rise and hover among the stars.

"That's not bad," Drea allowed after reading this far. "When were you in the desert?"

"Never," said U. "But it sounds so great, I might go."

There, in Death Valley, as Jamie strolled beneath the blazing panoply of the midnight sky, dreaming of a jewel that Chelsea wore in her navel and the greater jewel that she carried beneath it in what he termed her "moist and silken purse"—there, while Jamie's brain dreamed of love and his left hand tugged at his shorts—a sudden tremendous shock abruptly sent him sprawling on the gravel and dust of the desert floor.

He raised his head. Great dry swells, gray in the starlight, rose in the distance and rushed toward him like spreading waves before a storm. The motel went dark, then disintegrated into tincans and toothpicks. Jamie's car upended and plunged downward into the earth like a Frank Herbert sandworm.

Miles away in the depths of the valley, the shell of the planet burst open and a vast structure like a flattened Everest rose—and rose—and rose, a wedge of blackness driven into the Milky Way. Alone among the desert rats, sidewinders, and tarantulas witnessing the monstrous birth, Jamie knew what he was gazing upon: *the egg tooth of the dragonet!* Thunderously the earth continued to fracture, canyons spreading in a crazy weblike pattern, while out of them erupted fountains of fire.

Unheard by any living thing, Jamie cried out—his last words before his own extinction—*"You dumb bastards! Maybe you'll believe me now!"*

—.—

"It's an adequate finish," Drea admitted. "Melodrama is the comfort food of the soul. Go with it."

"Well, I still don't feel that it's really true, I mean there's…I don't know… something that's still a little off about it. But if you think this version works—"

"It does. Try sending it to *Fantasy & Science Fiction*. I'll give you a covering note to the editor, Gordon Van Gelder. I met him someplace or other, I think in a bar."

At semester's end, Drea gave U an A- for strenuous endeavor, Inshallah an A+ for triumphant mendacity, and everybody else who was still in class a C- for durable mediocrity. Those who had dropped out too late to be eligible for I's he flunked, despite their pleas for mercy. Dr. Dread had his reputation to think of.

The night after handing in the grades, he found Gorshin already seated in the Federal City Wine Cellar, looking grim.

"What's the matter with you?"

"Delia left me today. Somewhere, somewhere in this world there's a sane, balanced woman I can spend the rest of my life with. I keep looking for her, but I always wind up with the wackos."

"What'd she do?"

"It's what she was thinking of doing. I know the signs."

"What was she thinking of doing?"

"Cutting off my penis while I'm asleep. Like that poor Wayne Bobbit character. I was afraid to go to sleep, and I can't face that parade of nuts all day long without eight solid hours."

After gulping some wine, he added, "It's costing me three hundred dollars to get the locks changed so she can't sneak in at night and go for me with the blade from her Lady Elegance razor."

"Gorshin—"

"Don't try to comfort me," he said. "I'm feeling too lousy."

Drea wouldn't have dreamed of doing so. Instead, he sat sipping and musing on the events of the semester just past.

The more he thought about it, the more he respected U's fantasy. How satisfying it must be to believe that some magnificent primal beast laid the

Earth to contain and shelter its young—that this noble and simple act is the whole meaning and purpose of our world—and that human beings, with all their bizarre kinks, are only a kind of microorganism growing on the outside of the soon-to-be-discarded shell.

Obscurely comforted, he raised his eyes over Gorshin's defeated bulk and rested his gaze on the Sony across the room. The latest signals from the Mars Orbiter were being broadcast, just as they arrived via Houston. Thus Drea happened to be one among the millions privileged to look on as the red planet split open along the sutures of its great barren valleys, and began to hatch.

Much of Albert Cowdrey's work takes place in New Orleans and features a crew of characters as odd as anyone you'll find this side of A Confederacy of Dunces. *This story attempts to convince readers that he gets his material by shaking the branches of his family tree. Don't be deceived. Mr. Cowdrey is actually descended from John Collier on one side of the family and from François Rabelais on the other, which explains why so many of his stories are finely-crafted, witty, larger than life, and sometimes vulgar. It has also been rumored that Charles Addams and Albert Cowdrey were cousins, but no one knows if this is true. After all, you've got to take everything you hear about this guy with a large grain of salt.*

THE BOY'S GOT TALENT

A LL YESTERDAY AFTERNOON I struggled with a science fiction story, and the story won: the plot sprouted superfluous limbs like a sick frog; crumpled paper fluttered from my desk like the leaves of a dying ficus.

At five o'clock I gave up and settled in front of the TV to watch the evening news. Inevitably I fell asleep, only to be waked by the bleating of the phone.

Now, here was something odd: when I fumbled the phone to my ear, I heard the unmistakable squawky voice of my nephew Josh Bullard. At the same moment, his face seemed to be hovering on the TV screen.

"They're after me," he gasped. "I dunno what to do. I gotta talk to you, Uncle Bert."

Still feeling a bit disoriented, I suggested we meet at the Circus Lounge, and he agreed at once.

"Where are you going?" asked my wife, Alice, as I passed the living room on the way out.

"Josh Bullard wants to talk to me."

"You mean he wants money. If you give him any, you better not come home. Ever."

"If only, my dear, you'd use your talent for menace for some useful purpose, such as extortion."

"You'd better make that silly story come out," she warned. "The bank account's getting low. *And no money to Josh.*"

I slammed the front door.

The Circus Lounge is my favorite oasis, twenty-three floors above the hysterical traffic of Decatur Street in the French Quarter. Greeted by Jimmy the bartender and an impressionistic decor of painted clowns, elephants, acrobats, and dancing bears, I sat down at the revolving bar.

"How's the writing going?" Jimmy asked.

"Not. Sometimes I think I ought to give up. Nobody wants fiction anyway. I'd be better off doing a badminton column for the *Times-Picayune.*"

More than wife or therapist, Jimmy knows what I need in such moods. He opened a bottle of malt-rich Mexican XX beer, set it down beside a chilly glass, and tuned his boombox to a classic-rock station where the Grateful Dead were playing "Dark Star."

The circus creatures picked up the beat, spinning toward me and then away. The bar was revolving, Jimmy was revolving, I was revolving—kind of a planetary condition. I began to feel I was viewing the world from a great height. Or at any rate, from a tall barstool.

"Hello, Uncle Bert," somebody squawked at my elbow.

"Oh, hi, Josh."

Small, bony, ill-clad, dim of mind and obviously distraught, my nephew climbed onto the barstool next to mine. We shook hands, and I ordered him an XX.

Josh likes to begin conversations in midair, and only gradually let you in on what he's thinking about. Tonight his opener was, "It ain't easy on me, not being nobody."

"My boy, if there's one thing you are, it's nobody."

28

"That's nice of you to say, but things ain't been good. I tell you I got fired from Tastee Donuts? When I discovered my talent I figured my life'd improve, but it just got screwed-upper."

The last item was news to me. "You've got a talent, Josh? What is it?"

"Walking through walls."

The beer was good. The bar was balm to my spirit. If I went home, what would I do? Fight the goddamn story with the proliferating plot? Watch television? Listen to Alice complain about our finances?

"Tell me all about it, Joshua," I said.

Josh didn't know how he came by his talent. Maybe he'd always had it.

"Mama brung me up wrong. She was like, 'It can't be done.' And I believed her. *You* coulda helped me," he added accusingly. "You write science friction and crazy shit like that. Instead, I hadda find out for myself." He explained that a few weeks back he'd fallen desperately in love with a sophisticated older woman of twenty-four. Heather Crome possessed remarkable beauty, major-type hooters, and a virginal air of cool remoteness.

"The first time I saw her, she looked like a great big bottle of antiperspirant," he recalled, breathing heavily. "I figured, like, when she walks around in August her crouch don't even get damp."

But Heather was less than encouraging. "She's like, 'I got rich guys gimme nice stuff. So fuck off, Needle Dick.' She said it real sweet, but even so I felt discouraged."

Josh began to study her habits, stalking her not like a determined rapist but like a hopeful stray in search of a home. She lived in the Quarter and her favorite nightspot was My Blues Heaven. After work, Josh hung about her apartment, followed her to the bar and lurked in dark alleys, getting threatened by paranoid panhandlers and rained on by cloudbursts. Then he'd follow her home and fantasize about being invited inside.

But on the return trip she always had an escort with her. She favored a certain type, hulks with evident bulges on hip or in armpit. These must be the guys who gave her nice things. Josh gave them a collective name. They were all Kong.

Josh tried to cling to his original vision of Heather as cool and virginal, but he had suspicions. Thinking about what the Kong *du jour* might be doing with or to her almost drove him mad. Tortured by jealousy, he'd repair to some less than A-list saloon and drown his hopeless love in beer until his money ran out.

The Friday night after losing his job at Tastee Donuts, he had his final paycheck to ravage and got drunker than usual. About two A.M., with pockets empty even for him, he lurched away from the Up-Yours Club on Bourbon Street into the broad, dew-slick lamplit emptiness of Canal Street.

A gleaming jeweler's window lured him. Inside stood a papier-mâché pig draped with pearls. *Don't Cast Pearls Before Swine*, said a discreet sign. *Give Them to Someone You Love.*

Longing desperately to do just that, Josh lurched forward until his shiny red nose touched its image in the glass. He pressed his right palm against the glass and his hand slipped through and his stubby fingers grasped the string of pearls.

He jerked his hand back as if he had touched fire. The pearls rattled against the glass and fell inside. Josh stared at his right hand. It tingled, then ceased to tingle. Cautiously he rapped his knuckles against the shop window; it was hard and cold.

Behind him a party of crapulous tourists staggered by, singing "Louie Louie." A street-cleaning machine passed with a roar of surf. The pearls lay heaped against the inside of the glass. The pig looked naked without them.

Slowly Josh slipped to his knees and then, feeling incredibly weary, sprawled on the pavement. He closed his eyes and quietly, gently, like a weary child passed out. He woke to find the vast blush of dawn filling the sky over Canal Street.

Such was the essence of his story.

Of course, I've expressed it in English, not in Josh-speak. What with repetitions, circumlocutions and lousy grammar, he took over an hour to convey what I have briefly summarized above.

I wasn't complaining. To hear such a fantasy issue from Josh's mind was like finding a peony growing on an ash-heap.

Spawn of my sister Nat—an amiable, boozy slattern—Josh grew up in a succession of trailer parks scattered around the purlieus of New Orleans. Nat rarely fed him, and her parade of scruffy lovers beat him up as a form of calisthenics.

Josh had a lousy life and he escaped it by telling ridiculous lies. When he was six he had an invisible dog; when he was ten he enjoyed an intimate personal friendship with Batman; at eighteen he was accepted into the Navy Seals; at twenty he was abducted by aliens. Banal stuff—absolute rubbish.

Despite the wretched poverty of his imagination, I always had a soft spot for the boy. After all, we crawled onto life's verge from the same gene pool. The Gene of Prevarication that gave me a career writing fantastic fiction made him attempt to lie his way out of his miserable existence.

And now, suddenly, came this story about the pearls and the pig. All my science-frictional instincts were aroused. Four or five double-X's gurgled in my gut and I smiled blissfully.

Misreading my smile as mockery, Josh said, "I know you don't believe me, Uncle Bert. But—but this—this—this is real."

A strained, desperate honesty throbbed in his voice. That, I thought approvingly, is the right way to put over a big thumping lie. The boy had found his talent—for telling whoppers. After twenty-one years of nattering nonsense, he was at last ready to graduate from foolishness to fiction, from devising trashy falsehoods to inventing a finer reality.

I signaled once again for beer and said warmly, "Tell me more, my boy. I want to hear all about it."

Josh said that waking up on the marble-chip pavement of Canal Street was even tougher than most waking-ups.

Knees creaking, he clambered to his feet. His mouth tasted like refrigerator fungus smells and his bladder felt like a soccer ball full of BBs.

Yet he took time to check the window. The pearls were still lying where he'd dropped them. It hadn't been a dream.

"Shit fire," he muttered, inadequately.

He stumbled around the corner into Bourbon Street and peed on a wall. Standing there in the roseate dawn, he felt that a new day was beginning in every sense.

After years of wandering and confusion, of two-bit jobs and poverty and scorn, he'd discovered his unique talent, his shtick, the thing that he alone could do in all the world. He was downright blissful as he zipped his fly and started the four-mile walk to the Midcity slum where he lived.

"Jesus God," he thought. "I can walk right into Heather's place and see what's going on with her and Kong. And hey, she wants nice things, I can sneak into stores after hours and get great stuff to give her. I just need practice."

In the apartment he called, with good reason, "the Squat," Josh closed his eyes and fixed his mind on Heather's image—wasn't he developing his talent for her?—put his arm through the wall of his airless little bedroom and drew it back.

Next he tried his right foot, only to get something of a shock when his shoe fell off, thumping on the floor. Then he remembered the pearls. His shoe wasn't part of him and his singular power over his own body meant nothing to it.

By afternoon he'd gotten up courage enough to walk through a wall. It was a scary moment; he feared it might stop his heart. But the sheetrock pushed through him, driving his clothes ahead of it with a dry, gently rasping, ticklish feel. He found himself standing nude on the lino of the tiny fetid bath, facing a rusty tin shower stall.

He dressed and repaired to the living room, a thoughtful young man. He was still brooding when his roommate, a jackleg carpenter's helper named Archy Doss, came home.

Kicking his steel-toed shoes into a corner, Doss muttered, "Gimme a joint," and collapsed on the semi-defunct sofa.

Josh joined him. As smoke rose in an acrid ribbon and the shared joint shrank to a roach packed with cannabis residues, Josh stumbled into speech.

"Doss, listen. Real early this morning, you know? Something like totally awesome happened to me."

"Christ, you don't mean you finally fucked Heather."

"No. Something else."

"Well, if you jacked off like as usual that ain't nothing much, unless you used a handful of warm Noodle Roni like I told you to. *That's* kind of awesome."

"Watch this."

A moment later Josh emerged from the bathroom with an Econolodge towel wrapped around his middle. The look on Doss's face was the first real reward he'd had yet from his discovery of his talent.

A search of the fridge showed no food whatever in the Squat, so they went out for a giant pizza called the Emperor Nero at Tarantella's. Josh's pockets were empty, but for once Doss sprang for the meal without complaint.

"Dude," he said through a mouthful of red peppers, anchovies, mozzarella and crunchy crust, "you gotta talent. So what you gonna walk into first? That julery store?"

Josh blushed. "Nuh uh. First I wanna go inside Heather's apartment. There's something I just got to know. You help me," said Josh, "and later on, when I start stealing stuff, I'll split with you."

"Deal," said Doss, and the two examples of young American manhood shook pizza-stained hands.

In Doss's ancient rattletrap van, they arrived after dark at block-long Talleyrand Street in the French Quarter. The curbs were lined with parked cars and the sidewalks with high walls topped by razor wire and broken glass. Quarter dwellers agree with Robert Frost: good fences make good neighbors.

One streetlight illuminated the far corner. Doss slid into the only empty space, by a fire hydrant.

"So that's Heather's," he said, viewing a door set between stone pillars under an iron lamp. "She live downstairs or up?"

"Down."

"Whatta we do now?

"Wait."

Doss unstuck a wad of previously chewed gum from the steering column, inserted it into his mouth and made popping sounds until the door opened and Heather emerged. At that he swallowed the gum.

After choking briefly, he managed to gasp, "Christ, look at them hooters."

Four yearning eyes followed the firm-fleshed opulent young woman until she rounded the corner and disappeared in the direction of My Blues Heaven.

"Okay," said Josh. "Now you know what to do?"

"You gonna walk through the door. When your clothes fall off, I pick 'em up and put 'em in the van. You find you a place to hide inside, and when I see Heather coming back I knock on the door to warn you."

The two friends searched the shadows of Talleyrand Street, then stepped out of the van. The spring night was fragrant with the scent of secret gardens. From nearby houses came muted sounds of revelry; it was Saturday and parties were tuning up. Someplace nearby a dog barked; on the river, a ship brayed a warning.

Closing his eyes, Josh approached the lamplit door, eyes shut, hands out in front of him like a child playing blind man's buff. The dense oak resisted and he had to lean forward to push himself through. Once again his clothing passed ticklishly through him. Then he was inside Heather's home.

He padded through an archway into the living room, his bare feet moving from the cool of polished floorboards to the tickle of deep-pile white carpeting. The light of a dim rose lamp bathed couches upholstered in zebra skin. An immense system of shelves displayed a sixty-inch TV, a quadra-phonic sound system with speakers the size of coffins, and all sorts of elegant doodads—figurines, china birds, Japanese dolls. The apartment was the most gorgeous place Josh had ever seen.

"Wowwwww," he murmured. "It's like Fuckingham Palace."

He passed into a bathroom with lavender tiles and little gold stars painted on a cobalt-blue ceiling and warm, moist air still fragrant with Heather's last shower. The curtain featured blue and pink bunnies humping one another. Josh tipped a bottle of bath oil into the palm of his hand and sniffed it greedily. Then, like a worshipper entering the holy of holies, he stepped into her bedroom.

A white armoire with gold unicorns for door handles. A bookcase filled with the Great Books. A king-sized bed with flounces and ruffles and a white Persian cat lying on a silk pillow, eyes wide, poised for flight. Josh spoke to the animal, then realized that it was a mechanical cat, the kind that walks and purrs and requires no litterbox. Glancing up, he was startled to see the bed, the cat and himself repeated in the depths of a mirrored ceiling.

He opened a closet door, touched a light switch, and gazed in wonder at rainbow-hued clothing and shoes enough to sate Imelda Marcos. He pulled out a slender drawer in a tall white cabinet and blushed to discover a treasury of lingerie. He touched the garments, not even knowing the names of most of them, and they slipped between his rough red fingers with the silken ease of garter snakes.

He was still fondling these strange and elegant garments when a lock clicked and he heard the front door open.

"The action quickens," I murmured.

The Beatles were singing "Lucy in the Sky with Diamonds". Darkly the amber beer swirled into my glass. I felt like Voltaire's man of Jupiter striding among the planets; like Poe's Dr. Hans Pfaal, or Wells's Mr. Cavor visiting the Moon. It was a science-frictional evening.

Sighed Josh, "I'd never a guessed she'd be back so soon, not in a billion years. Even a million. She musta made a date with Kong ahead of time."

"So what was your lookout up to? Why didn't Doss spot them coming and knock on the door?"

"Well, I kind of wondered about that. But later on he splained. He said—"

All this while, Doss was waiting in the van. He'd collected his friend's clothes and dumped them in the back among his grimy tools, and now sat behind the wheel, chewing a fresh stick of gum. The car radio had died long ago, so he amused himself by trying to chew gum and whistle at the same time.

Then Heather hove into view. Briefly the corner streetlamp illuminated her and her companion. Doss stared.

My Jesus, he thought, *this guy is two linebackers wearing one suit. If he finds Josh hiding he'll turn him inside out through his own asshole.*

His hand was on the door of the van—there was no latch any longer; he opened the door by hitting it with his shoulder—and he was tensed to sprint to the house before Heather and Kong arrived, when something roared and sputtered and a light flashed in his eyes. It was a cop on a motorcycle.

Doss blinked and gave the cop a big false smile.

"Good evening, officer."

"License 'n' registration."

Fumbling desperately, he found the two forms. The cop viewed the papers under his flashlight, then returned them with his judgment.

"You cain't park by this here hydrant," he said.

"I'm not parked," Doss protested. "I'm just waiting for a friend."

"You wanna argue, I can give you a poisonal tour of Central Lockup."

"Officer, I'm on my way."

"Say, you ain't one a them fuckin' college students, are you?" the cop demanded with a sudden excess of belligerence.

"No, sir. I'm a working man."

"Shitty way to live, ain't it?" said the cop and roared away.

By now Heather and her friend had disappeared into her dwelling. Doss started up his motor and began the slow process of circling the block. Everywhere except on Talleyrand Street itself, the traffic was impacted as a mouthful of wisdom teeth, and his progress was slow.

"And meanwhile, Josh, you were—"

"Well, Uncle Bert, like I say, I heard 'em come in the front door. But they didn't stop there. Heather headed straight down the hall to her bedroom, while Kong, he come by way of the bathroom where he started to pee. My Lord, you shoulda heard him pee! He sounded like Viagra Falls.

"I hid in the closet, but guess where Heather headed for first? So there I was, caught, and just as she come in the closet door I jumped through the wall at the end without no idea of where it might lead to."

—.—

Under the sheetrock the thick wall of nineteenth-century bonded masonry felt gritty and resistant. For a moment Josh was terrified by the thought that he might get trapped in it and suffocate. He gave a frenzied kick and suddenly stumbled into a scene from a madhouse.

People with horse's heads, with hoop skirts, with suits of armor, with nets and tridents; men and women painted gold or silver, many wearing only a tad more than Josh himself. Lights flashing in many colors, and deafening rock.

A tall bony woman impersonating Morticia sidled up and took Josh's arm. Under a slim mask she had a wide raspberry-colored mouth and teeth like sugar cubes. Her breath was distilled Southern Comfort.

"Hey, that *is* a costume," she said admiringly. "But the invitation said Masks Required. Come on."

She led him—feeling he had entered a dream; strolling naked among a crowd of strangers, none of whom spared him more than a glance—into a small room where a pile of masks reposed on a table.

"Some people forget," she said, fitting a mask onto his face. Then she pushed him back into the party.

"Hey, Sybil, this yours?" she asked a woman in a Hillary Clinton head-mask.

Through the eyeholes, two critical orbs swept Josh from head to toe.

"Nuh uh. Must be Cherie's—she likes pipsqueaks. Kid, you oughta work on those pecs. And that pecker."

"Be nice," said the hostess. "Not everybody has the balls to come to a party naked."

"Ball bearings, you mean," said Sybil.

"Pay no attention, honey," said the hostess. "I like a man who's at ease with his own inadequacy. Wanna dance?"

Josh mumbled that he couldn't dance.

"Then let's go where it's private and suck some face," she said, leading him back into the dressing room with the pile of masks. It was while she was closing and bolting the door that Josh leaped into the wall.

Again the bricks and mortar were resistant. He felt the mask pass through his brain like a nagging headache and vanish. He was standing in near-darkness, amid a crowd of strangers in sinuous, somehow coordinated motion. The rock was, if possible, louder than before.

Somebody embraced him and drew him into the surging mass. Belatedly, Josh realized that he needn't feel out of place here: everybody was naked, and everybody was male.

"W-what's going on?" he managed to gasp.

"The orgy, Sweetheart, the orgy," said somebody behind him. "Can you spread a little?"

The smells of sweat and incense were thick. Everyone was heavily greased, so Josh was able to squeegee through the crowd and find another wall into which he plunged, head first. But when he was half through, strong arms caught him around the waist.

For a long moment he floundered, arms and legs waving ineffectually on opposite sides of the wall, while unseen fingers began to do the spreading for him. A desperate kick sent him head over heels into a flagstoned patio, where for a moment he rested, gasping for breath.

Far above, coolly ironic stars were shining, and down below Josh was just reaching the point where he could rationally evaluate his situation when a dense form detached itself from the shadows and a low growl informed him that his night's adventures were not yet over.

There was a Rottweiler in the patio.

"Well, go on!" I urged Josh.

"Uncle Bert?"

"What?"

"I was just wondering if you really, really believe me. Because for once in my life I ain't been telling you nothing except the honest truth."

I clapped my right palm against my sternum.

"I believe you, Josh, because I believe in the profound truth of fiction. The underlying, the submarine, the subterranean truth. The truth that doesn't lie on the surface, but surges beneath like an alligator making ripples in a carpet of duckweed. Allow me to buy you another beer," I added, waving at Jimmy.

Josh stared at me in utter bafflement. I think he relished my good will, without in any way comprehending what the good will was based upon.

"Now," I said firmly. "Back to you and the Rottweiler."

The dog looked in the dim light like a fuzzy battering ram with teeth. Josh had a distinct feeling that saying Nice Doggy wouldn't work.

Instead he gathered his weary legs under him and suddenly leaped up and sprinted for the nearest wall. He heard a furious scrabble of claws behind him and dove headlong.

Once again he did a somersault, only this time he wound up resting on his shoulders with his feet high above his head. A quivering banana tree had stopped him in mid-revolution. Looking up, he saw his toes outlined against the sky.

Cautiously he lowered his legs and righted himself. After orgies and Rotts, he seemed to have gone up a notch on the social scale. The patio was large and hidden globes backlit masses of white azaleas. Ten or twelve couples were seated at little tables on which candle flames quavered.

Polite, muted conversations were underway. A string quartet played something classical. Josh began to sidle along the wall behind the screen of trees. Then froze; an elderly man and woman were staring at him.

"I saw it move."

"What the hell do you mean, you saw it move?"

"That statue of David or somebody. I'm sure I saw it move."

"Either you've had too much champagne or not enough. Let's assume not enough. Waiter!"

The woman continued to stare.

"It's an absolutely rotten copy," she opined. "With all her money you'd think Dallas could get something better."

The waiter appeared with a fresh bottle and began the ritual of uncorking. Josh was wondering if it was safe for him to move on when the cork blew off and smacked him above the left eye.

"Ow!" he said, but the quartet just then began to saw away again and his cry of pain went unnoticed.

Since everybody seemed oblivious to everything except talk and booze and, possibly, the music, Josh began to hope that he could find some way to end his night's adventure.

Then the answer came to him. While everybody was here in the patio, he would enter the house through the nearest wall and begin a search for male attire, any male attire that would let him walk out into the street and find Doss's van.

Having a plan felt so good that he almost laughed aloud. The quartet was working itself into a frenzy and all the guests were deep in talk and the waiters were occupied waiting. Josh slid along the wall, freezing whenever somebody turned in his direction.

A tuxedoed bartender lounging near an array of bottles blocked access to the main house. But an ell projected—slave quarters or kitchens in times past—and Josh took a breath and pushed through still another thick Quarter wall into a narrow, dark space.

Something promptly whacked him on the shins, and when he moved something else jabbed his ribs.

"Ow!" he said again.

He was in a storeroom of abandoned furniture. Chairs were heaped on chairs, tables on tables. Slowly he worked himself through the maze, things passing through him that he never saw, nudging internal organs, shedding dust into his lungs and making him cough. He found a narrow stair, climbed to the top, slipped through a locked door, and emerged into a hallway of creamy plaster.

He was in the main house now, a Persian runner caressing his feet, oil portraits of sour-looking gents gazing down in disapproval at the little bony naked nobody in their midst. Feeling that his troubles were almost over, Josh sprang like a gazelle through a wall into a plushy boudoir, where an old lady sat, reading a copy of *Vogue* and smoking a joint.

She turned toward him a smooth, immobile face with a nose shaped like the business end of a cottonmouth moccasin and nostrils that ran up instead of out. Josh had never seen such a face and he stopped dead, gawking.

—.—

"Many lace fits," I explained.

"What?"

"Many face lifts," I corrected myself, realizing that I had, after all, had a lot of beer by this time. "Somebody gets too many, that's how their face looks."

"Oh," he said. "It was kind of scary."

"So what did the snake lady do when she saw you?"

"Well, she's like, 'Where the hell you come from, Sonny?' And I'm like, 'From the party downstairs.' And she's l—"

But I can't bring myself to reproduce any more of Josh's narrative style.

She said, "Yeah, right. I can just see you down there with that bunch of bores, sitting around in your bare ass listening to Mozart."

She added, "They probably think Moe's his first name."

Josh had assumed the traditional posture of a man exposed, crossing his small hands over his smaller private parts.

"Me, I'm Dallas Doolittle," the woman continued. "I entertain this bunch of prominent assholes because I'm a civic leader. But from time to time I just gotta take me a dope break. Sit down, for Christ sakes."

She patted a cushion beside her on a glossy divan with a hundred silken buttons. Josh sat down uneasily, as far away from her as possible.

"Don't think because you got no clothes on and this is my bood-wah, you can do whatever you like," Dallas warned him. "I don't rape easy. You wanna blow some pot?"

"Uhhhhh . . . yes, ma'am," said Josh. He had heard the phrase once before, in a Cheech and Chong movie.

She passed him the joint and he inhaled deeply. It was superb, a product of cannabis buds developed under grow-light in a secret attic by some anonymous genius of intoxication.

"Wowwwwww," he murmured. Dallas took the joint back and puffed reflectively.

"Now," she said. "Cut the crap, Sonny, and tell me how you lost your clothes and how you got in here."

"I come through the wall."

"You what?"

"Like this," he said and, half-turning, thrust his arm into the wall behind him. He pulled it out covered with whitish plaster dust, and brushed it off with slow, casual strokes.

"Oh, my God," gaped Dallas. "Oh, my God. This old brain's going. I've smoked too much of this fucking dope."

"No," said Josh. "It's my talent. I walk through walls. Can I have that joint back?"

Dallas passed it to him, saying, "You finish it. I'm off this shit till Tuesday. Maybe longer."

"This is *summmmm* powerful," he muttered, inhaling deeply. "See, I was in a house somewheres around here. It belongs to this lady name of Heather. I wanna get next to her but she's like, 'Whoa—who needs it?' and I'm like, 'Hey. I do.' And she's like ... and she's like. . . . "

Josh lost the thread of his discourse. Dallas came to his aid.

"Heather Crome? She lives next door."

Dallas pointed at the wall opposite.

"I've tried to talk to that girl. I tell her, 'Honey, it's okay to be a whore, if it worked for Pamela Harriman it can work for you, but you keep hanging out with wiseguys, you gonna regret it.'"

With no joint to hold, her long thin right hand was free and she ran it down the rack of bones he called a chest. Sweat broke out on his brow.

"Uh, ma'am?" he said. "I don't—I don't think—I—"

"Whassamatta, honey? Lemme check this out," said Dallas, checking. "Christ, how do you get it out to pee? Go fishing with a buttonhook? Oh, well, it's kind of cute, actually. Makes me think of diapering my grandson."

"Whoa!" cried Josh, shaking off her hand and jumping to his feet.

His head swimming from the superpot, he stared wildly around the room, at silken overstuffed furniture, at Dallas's ophidian face.

Then in three wildly uncoordinated leaps he reached the far wall and plunged into it head first.

—.—

"You know what, Josh?"

"What?"

"Tonight, for the first time, I truly feel that we are kin. You have devised a veritable Thousand-and-Second Tale of Sheherazade. Such richness of invention, supported by such a plethora of almost convincing detail!"

The Platters were singing "The Great Pretender", and for a few minutes I sang along with them, to Josh's evident embarrassment. To stop my impromptu karaoke, he said hurriedly: "It's great having you believe me, Uncle Bert. Lotsa people wooden."

I smiled upon him like a Happy Face come to life.

"Please continue, nephew of mine. You plunged into the wall, and—"

Josh saw the apartment above Heather's only as a brief, incoherent jumble of lights before falling head first through its polished floor.

Then he was hanging halfway out of the mirrored ceiling of Heather's bedroom over the immense white bed. Large and white too was Heather's upturned backside and, as Josh looked on in horror, Kong, stripped to his fur, deliberately swung a broad black belt and smacked her quivering flesh.

Heather twisted in pain and a kind of despairing moo escaped her lips, but no more, because she had been gagged with some of her own underthings and her hands and feet had been tied with similar silken bonds.

"CUT THAT OUT!" roared Josh in a voice he didn't know he owned.

Her tormentor looked up and saw Josh dangling from the mirror, bizarrely centered amid octopuslike images of his head and arms. Kong's mouth fell so far open that Josh could see two gold molars in back. Then Josh slipped the rest of the way through the ceiling and plunged downward, holding both arms stiff and fists knotted. Kong's nose crunched and splattered under the impact.

Together they crashed to the floor. Josh was up first, seized the belt and began to use it on Kong, who, blinded by his own blood and holding his dripping face in both hands, stumbled about the room, shattering bric-a-brac and crushing the mechanical cat, which perished with one despairing cry.

Then he lurched into the hallway and thundered to the front door, threw it open and ran into Talleyrand Street, where by one of those coincidences so common in life, though forbidden in all respectable fiction, Doss's van flattened him like an armadillo on a Texas highway.

Josh slammed the front door and bolted it firmly. He dropped the belt, returned to Heather's bedroom, and gently untied her. When he took out the gag she spoke to him in a voice as dulcet as the melodies of Moe Zart.

"Christ, Honey," she murmured, awestruck, "how'd a shrimp like you run that big motherfucker off?"

Later on, when a blushing Josh had applied Benzocaine to her injured hiney, and she'd fixed them both scotches from a wet bar concealed behind the Great Books, and they were resting together on her bed—Josh sitting up, Heather on her tummy—she had other questions.

"Where was you hiding at?" she wanted to know. "And where's your clothes? Say, ain't you that little jerk been after me to go out with him?"

He admitted as much.

"And if you'd a been with me," he pointed out, "you'd a been better off than with K—with that other guy."

"I know," she sighed. "It's the only thing I don't like about being a whore. You meet such lowlifes sometimes."

Wincing, she sat up. Josh was fascinated by the hooters Doss had earlier commented on. One of them seemed to gaze straight at him with a moist brown/pink eye, while the other, sagging to one side, appeared pensive, dreamy.

"So what'd you do?" she resumed. "Sneak in here and hide?"

"Sort of," he mumbled.

"Why? Joo wanna watch me git nekkid?"

Staring deep into the amber depths of the scotch that was now numbing his brain, which was still imperfectly denumbed from the effects of Dallas's pot, Josh mumbled the truth.

"Nuh uh. I wanted to see what you was doing with those other guys. I got jealous because I love you."

"Love?" she asked, as if the word denoted some exotic mineral available only on the Planet Krypton.

"Yes, ma'am."

"Well, Honey"—her voice was like wind chimes on a fern-and-flower-burdened Quarter balcony—"I'm not into that exactly, but you just lay back and relax. I guarantee to give you a real serious fuck."

So he did, and she did.

"Really?" I asked. "You're not putting me on?"

"Nuh uh," Josh replied, modestly proud. "It only lasted about a minute. But it was real great, anyway."

"First rate," I murmured. "Absolutely first rate. The fantasy climaxes in sexual . . . sexual . . . whatever. Fulfillment. *Ah! m'extase et mon amour!* The narrative arch is now complete. Son, I'm deeply impressed," I told him. To my surprise, he started to cry. Of course, beer has that effect on some people.

"What's the matter now?"

"Getting some ass made me want more," he sobbed. "So after she went to the French Market flea market that morning and brung me back some clothes, I asked her could we do it again."

"And she said—"

"She said she was my friend for life, and she'd never, never forget what I done for her. Also, she don't mind me being kind of small, because big guys hurt and she likes a good tickle. But when it comes to sex, she's got rigid principles: any guys want to do it with her got to give her either money or nice things. And I just don't qualify."

He wiped his eyes with a bar napkin.

"Then, when I got home, Doss was packing. The cops didn't charge him with Van Slaughter because they were glad to see Kong out of circulation. But they warned him that Kong has mean friends and Doss might want to leave town for a short while, like the rest of his life.

"So I lost my roomie, too, and my job's gone, and I can't afford to keep the Squat and I want to move into that great place of Heather's and keep on tickling her, only she won't let me because I ain't got no money to get her nice things."

"What about stealing the pearls?" I asked. Yes, I admit it: by now I was sufficiently potted to be sharing the fantasy.

"I tried that with Doss last night, just before he left town," he said bitterly. "And I almost got my butt in the slammer. The store's got security cameras and gadgets with little red lights that blink when they see you and a silent alarm went off and cops come running, and I grabbed the pearls and pushed them out through the mail slot only the cops was there so I couldn't get them, and I had to jump through a wall to get away and Doss was supposed to be waiting for me but he drove off when he heard the sirens, and I had to run four miles to home with no clothes on, and the whole thing was like a total fucking mess, and now, Uncle Bert, the cops've got my picture and my fingerprints from the store because I couldn't wear gloves or a mask when I went in through the wall, and when I seen myself on TV tonight I called you up quick 'cause you're the only relative I got ever liked me, and what I want to know is this: can you loan me about four or five thousand dollars to run away and start a new life on?"

Do I blame myself for what followed? Yes. But drunk as I was, how was I to think, how was I to know? Indeed, I believed I was being kind.

"Josh," I said, "the state of my bank account, combined with the ferocity of my wife, won't allow me to loan you a dime. But I'm prepared to make you an offer I've never made to another human being."

He stared at me, blearily—he'd also taken a lot of beer aboard, and into a much smaller body—hardly daring to hope.

"Of late," I confessed, "my imagination has not been as lush, as purpureal, as it once was. Nor do I write as well. My demons don't terrify, my aliens don't alienate, my invented worlds look more and more like Houston on a bad smog day. Do you understand?"

"No."

"What I'm proposing, my boy, is that you continue to devise magnificent fantasies, that I turn them into saleable fiction, and that we split the profits. I could guarantee you—oh, say for the first year—"

Josh was staring at me in horror.

"Uncle Bert," he whispered in the most betrayed-sounding voice I ever heard, *"you don't believe me!!"*

"Ah, but I do," I assured him. "I have always believed in the extra-dimensional truth of fiction. You, Joshua, having been in a sense walled out of human life, imagine that you've found a way of passing through the barriers that surround you. Is this truth? Yes, a thousand times yes!" I exclaimed, slamming the bar with my fist. "Your imagination's truer than the ordinary—truer than the commonplace—*truer than true!!*"

But Josh continued to stare. His eyes made me uneasy; they were grayish-green, like sick clams, and like clams they gave one a terrible sense of complete discovery: once the shell opened, you saw the whole inside.

"Oh, no," he said, clambering down from the revolving barstool and almost falling in the process. "Oh, no. Oh, no. Oh, no. Uncle Bert, this is for real. This is the only real thing ever happened to me. I'ma show you. Watch."

"Josh—" I began. But Josh, lowering his head and extending his arms, charged the painted circus riders on the wall.

"No!" I shouted, and Jimmy yelled something too, I never knew what.

As I watched, Josh plunged—there is no other word—into the wall like a diver into a vertical river.

No quicksand ever swallowed a careless traveler more quickly; no tsunami ever gulped down a seaside resort more completely. A split second, and the circus riders and acrobats were all that remained to be seen, except for a little pile of grungy clothing settling into a heap against the solid wall of the Circus Lounge.

I dismounted from the barstool, staggered, fell, was helped up by Jimmy, and the two of us stood staring down at all that remained of my nephew—a T-shirt labeled CONFEDERATE COTTON COMPANY; a torn pair of jeans; loafers without heels; the dirtiest white socks I ever saw; a thin eelskin wallet; thirty-six cents in change; and a brass key that probably gave entry to the Squat.

"Where the fuck'dee go?" Jimmy demanded, staring wildly here and there.

But I was thinking of the French Quarter twenty-three floors below us, choked with hysterical traffic. I turned away and lurched toward the nearest elevator.

—.—

47

As I fumbled my way into bed later that night, Alice stirred in her sleep and halfway woke.

"You get rid of your idiot nephew?" she asked.

"Alas, yes."

"Good riddance."

"Don't say that. He's dead."

She woke up entirely. "*Dead*? At his age? Of what?"

"Of lack of imagination. Of rank literalism. Of clinging to mere experience when he might have progressed to the higher truth of fiction. On a less astral plane, he died by falling twenty-three stories, passing completely through an RTA bus—several hysterical riders were telling a cop about it when I arrived on the scene—and plunging God knows how deep into the mucky subsoil beneath Decatur Street.

"He lies there now," I mourned, "embedded deep in the Pleistocene sediments, among the bones of extinct sea-creatures. It's a science-frictional ending."

"A what? Are you drunk?" She sniffed audibly. "You *are* drunk. Go to sleep. We'll sort this out in the morning."

Instead, I got up again.

"Where are you going now?"

"To write a story," I answered.

"At two in the morning? What are you really going to do?"

"Write a story," I answered with dignity, "because at last I have a story to write."

Here's a haunting tale sure to resonate with anybody who's ever found that a new dwelling contains surprises—sometimes nasty surprises.

THE HOUSEWARMING

"NOW, PHIL," said Nancy Forêt, "I know you believe in souls and all that crap—"

"No more," he said flatly. She was still thinking of him as the priest he'd almost become. Years ago, during their brief intense relationship, she used to call him Altar Boy.

"Well, of course you were defrocked—"

"I was not," he said with dignity. "I found out I didn't believe the stuff they were handing out at the seminary. Besides, not being a pedophile, I felt out of place. So I left. But what's all this got to do with real estate?"

"See over there? That old stable against the wall? Well, it's haunted."

Phil Santos threw back his head and laughed and his bray bounced around the courtyard and echoed back. The ghost put the cap on an odd morning.

One-eleven Rêve Street, an hour ago when Phil first saw it, seemed to consist of a big door—two tall, thick nineteenth-century oak panels—set in a high brick wall. Cat's-claw vines topped the wall and provided nesting sites for noisy but unseen birds. Nothing else. Sprayed-on gang graffiti and recumbent gutter punks completed the local scene.

"Damn," he'd muttered, recalling the phone call that had brought him here. Nancy was trying to sell him *this*?

Then she pulled up to the curb in the big gray Jag she drove to impress her clients—*Hey, this lady must handle upscale property, right?*—and got out.

As usual, she looked businesslike in basic black, with a single gold pin in the shape of a dollar sign on her large firm bosom. At a few years short of forty, her face was twenty-something smooth, her hair glossy and fragrant.

With embarrassment, Phil had felt his heart speed up a couple of syncopated beats. Was it possible for even an altar boy to cling so long to the image of his first love? Apparently so.

Nancy let him peck her cheek, but that was all. Sometimes the way she held him at arm's length made him wonder if she still felt something for him, too. If so, she concealed it well.

"Now Phil," she began, "I know this property doesn't look too great from the outside."

"Honey, you got a real gift for understatement."

He helped her turn an old brass key in the lock and drag open the door. A hot late-summer breeze tossed random bits of litter like confetti on the paving stones of a vaulted carriageway.

"I guess there's a house in here?" he asked.

"Wait. It's really a secret kind of place."

Their voices raised echoes. They entered a courtyard enclosed by high walls where ferns had taken root in cracks and crannies. And yes, there was a house after all, and it was old and handsome.

Galleries overlooked the patio; rough tawny stucco walls glowed in a shaft of sunlight. A two-story wooden ell once had provided housing for servants. Doves fluttered about the eaves, cooing obsessively. Above the slate roof and Dickensian chimney pots hung the worn silver coin of a daytime moon.

"It's totally unspoiled," she pointed out, and he had to agree.

Producing more keys, Nancy led him through high-ceilinged rooms that would need minimum work to be made liveable and saleable. Phil found himself planning the renovation: over here, a new master bath with retro fittings—quadruped tub and marble lav; over there, a new kitchen with granite countertops and enormous costly range.

Sure, the neighborhood stank. But move in a pair of yuppies and a brace of Rottweilers, and hey—another victory for urban homesteading!

"You can't help but make money," Nancy said, seductively. "The owner only wants six-fifty for it."

"I truly admire your ability to say that with a straight face."

"It belongs to a real estate investment trust. The REIT's getting rid of a bunch of less desirable properties, so they're open to offers."

Outside again, Phil stood for several minutes absorbing the feel of the patio. Haunted by little pale geckos, it was like the bottom of a well; not a single neighbor's window looked into it. Suddenly he understood—111 Rêve Street had been built for stealthy pleasures.

"Who was the original owner?" he grinned. "A prominent madam? A disciple of the Mad Marquis?"

Nancy raised well-plucked eyebrows. "That's really clever of you, Phil. His name was Alfonso Villarubia. He was a cotton factor in the 1840s, and he died at his own housewarming from an overdose of Spanish Fly. In his obit the *Picayune* commented on his 'singular propensities' without, dammit, revealing exactly what they were."

She hesitated as if about to take a plunge. Hesitation was so unlike her that he stared. "Now Phil," she began, "I know you believe in souls…."

Then followed the ghost stuff that left him laughing out loud. Trust Nancy to come up with a hook nobody else would ever have thought of! *A unique feature of this desirable, fully reconditioned early-Victorian gem is the ghost in the stable.*

"Just don't go in there after dark," she went on, "unless you want a really bad case of the willies. A rent-a-cop from the REIT checked the place out one night, and he wound up on Thorazine."

She led him across the mossy flagstones to the one-story building. Inside, the walls were bare bricks and beams, the floor wide pine boards with gaps between for easier mucking out. A skylight suggested that at some point Dobbin's dwelling had been turned to other purposes. Shelves of cloudy bottles, a stained work table and a rusty sink hinted at a taste for chemistry. In the corner stood an iron cot with a thin, stained mattress.

"Who was the mad scientist?" he asked.

"No idea. Some old woman lived here for about a million years. Well, that's one-eleven," she finished abruptly. "So, Phil, would you like to make me an offer?"

"Oh . . . why the hell not?"

He followed the Jag to her office, where she wrote up his offer for something called Deep Delta Real Estate Investment Trust to consider. Within sixty days Phil Santos became owner of 111 Rêve Street and all that lay within it.

Whatever that might be.

Everything went fine at first. A month after the act of sale, New Orleans got a new and serious police chief and a federal grant that enabled him to flood murder-prone areas with cops.

Rêve Street was one of the first to benefit, and soon the neighbors started crawling out of their dens like lizards, blinking in the sunlight—and even in the moonlight, which many of them hadn't seen for years, except through barred windows. Property values started to rise and developers began nosing around. Meantime Phil's contractor had set to work, rewiring and replumbing, sanding floors and polishing and painting and papering, bringing in three phone lines and cable TV. The stable served for storage; the workmen left at five P.M., and the spare sheetrock and the paint cans and other detritus they left overnight did not seem to disturb the ghost.

For Phil, redoing the place was fun. It was so odd—unique, really. Nothing like it in the Quarter, where every house looked outward to the street as well as inward to the patio. One-eleven was a mystic, all its attention turned within. He tracked bargains, getting a deal from the Stone Company on granite countertops for the kitchen, buying fittings from a bankrupt plumbing supply company for the baths.

He took to coming by after the workmen had gone—parking his Honda beside the stable, climbing out with a bottle of wine, sprawling on one of the old-looking new iron benches. Drinking slowly from a plastic cup while the sky turned red, then purple, and finally blue-black. Watching the evening star emerge, the sole eye privileged to look into his kingdom.

The ghost stayed in the dark stable. Phil sensed nothing in the patio but vagrant winds and the scent of flowers, delicate or cloying. From somewhere came echoes of music—the expected snatches of rap and rock, but also something older, a bit offkey as if tuned to an unfamiliar scale. Maybe a bunch of medieval-music freaks, sitting around a slum apartment nearby, tootling recorders and sawing rebecs. The Rêve Street Consort.

That made him smile. *You can take the boy out of the seminary*, he thought wryly, *but you can't take the seminary out of the boy.* Long years after quitting St. Jude's, he still longed for a place of refuge, with high walls shutting the world out and distant notes of ancient music.

He drank his last cupful of wine to one-eleven's previous owners—to Alfonso Villarubia, the old woman, all the others whose names he'd never know. To live in this place, surely they must have wanted something out of the ordinary, too.

When he was ready to leave, he turned on the patio lights and checked the locks on the house and the carriageway doors before heading home. He saw no reason to lock the stable. In time, this had tragic consequences.

Among the gutter punks littering the neighborhood was a seventeen-year-old runaway from North Dakota named Steve. No last name; Steve Nobody.

Steve was schizophrenic, HIV-positive, and when conscious spent a lot of time arguing metaphysical questions with the phantasms that populated his head. At any rate, that was what other members of his tribe told the cops when they came inquiring.

With the workmen gone, Phil's gardener was creating a new look for the patio with bedded oleanders and flowering shrubs in yellow-glazed Spanish ollas. Maybe he left the doors to the carriageway unlocked when he went to lunch, and that was when Steve slipped inside, carrying his stash of pills, and hid in the stable behind the sheetrock panels.

Maybe he was thinking he'd be safer spending the night there than on the street or in a shelter. If so, he was wrong.

Next morning, while Phil was sipping his second cup of coffee in his condo uptown, he got a call from the gardener, considerably shaken. Coming to work, he'd found a body lying in the carriageway and called the cops.

Phil drove downtown to check the situation out. A big black detective let him slip under slick yellow tape being strung by a uniformed cop. Just inside the heavy oak panels of the carriageway door, the still nameless corpse was lying in a hunched-forward position with arms folded underneath. Despite a pool of blood around the head, it didn't look particularly damaged, except that it had no neck.

"He run head-on into the door," said the detective. "Hard, too. Look to me like some of his backbone is down inside his chest."

"Going about forty m.p.h.," volunteered the cop, whom the detective ignored.

"We found his pills in that building over there," said the detective, pointing. "He prolly saw snakes or something coming out the walls, and took off."

"I'm sure you're right," said Phil, looking away.

"You know, it's funny," said the uniformed cop, a meaty young guy with a broad, puzzled face. As before, the detective ignored him.

"What is?" Phil asked.

"I was here once before. Six, seven months ago. The big door was standing half-open, and a neighbor seen this old lady laying here dead."

"What, right here?"

"Yeah. In just about the same place as this one. Funny, huh?"

Back in his car, Phil searched through a pack of business cards fattening his wallet, picked one and punched a beeper number into his cell phone.

"Nancy," he barked when she rang him back.

"What?"

"Did you know the old woman was found dead right inside the door of one-eleven?"

"As a matter of fact, yes. So what? People have to die someplace."

"I'll tell you so what. Now I got a kid dead too, lying right where she was. What do you say to that?"

"What am I supposed to say? I didn't know her."

"You don't remember her name?"

"W, I think. Something like that."

"Like the president?"

"No, some name that sounded like W. She was about a hundred years old. Look, exactly what's the problem, Phil? Who was the dead kid?"

"Well, he was a street punk. A druggie."

"Oh, for heaven sakes. An old, ancient woman and a druggie. People like that die all the time. I know it's kind of weird, finding both of them in the same place, but coincidences do look weird. You think there must be a pattern, only there isn't."

Exactly what *was* Phil bothered about? A dead boy, a patternless pattern? He didn't protest when Nancy switched the subject.

"Look, I want to talk to you about one-eleven," she said. "If you're not tied up, let's do lunch at La Chaumière."

This was the newest hottest place in the French Quarter, where common mortals famously waited six months for a reservation. Nancy now revealed that she owned it, had a permanently reserved table, and went whenever she pleased.

"How could you afford to buy a place like that?" Phil asked, astonished.

"My divorce was more profitable than I expected," she told him. "One o'clock okay?"

It was. Sitting across from her, sipping an iconic martini, Phil looked around La Chaumière and noted how—with exposed beams, prints from old French garden books and bestiaries, rusty scythes and oaken ox-yokes, handwoven baskets of fresh flowers and bright, slightly lopsided Provençal pottery—somebody had given a country-inn feeling to a feed trough of well-to-do urbanites.

Considering her ability to manipulate reality, he wondered if Nancy might have chosen the decor. What an odd pair they'd made, after all—the Altar Boy and the Artful Dodger. No wonder it didn't last.

The food arrived, and it was fancy but filling and the waiters groveled nicely. Phil sprang for a grossly overpriced bottle of Vouvray and was floating in a mild alcoholic buzz when Nancy asked him about his plans for 111 Rêve Street.

He sighed. "Sell quick and get out, I'm afraid."

"Oh, Phil, that's so dumb. Take my advice and hold onto it for a while. I've got a dozen new listings for that neighborhood. There's a paradigm shift underway. Values will double or triple in the next few years."

"I've got a load of short-term notes to cover. The interest's eating me up."

"Then let me sell your condo for you. It's at peak anyway, and it's got no place to go but down. On the other hand, one-eleven's got no place to go but up. Clear your debts, live there for a while, enjoy it. Let it soar."

Sell my apartment?" Her sheer brass still had the power to amaze him.

"Why not? With one-eleven as your principal residence, you won't have to pay capital gains on the first quarter mil of profit. With that and the twenty percent renovation tax credit, you'll make a real killing when you sell."

"Forget it. No way."

"Oh, Phil. You're afraid of the ghost."

"Bullcrap," he said, thinking of his long private sessions in the dark patio.

She held out her glass for a refill. "Just think it over, okay? In time you'll come to see it the way I do."

"No. Absolutely not. Never."

When Phil put his condo on the market, Nancy took all of a week to sell it for top dollar.

The buyer was a young Texan who was blissfully unaware of the fact that in a year or two—besides the mortgage, fees and taxes—he'd also face an assessment in the twenty K range when the building's deteriorating roof had to be replaced.

Nancy managed the closing with all her customary expertise, and Phil signed the papers while smiling at the Texan and thinking, "Tough on you, pal."

It was exhilarating, doing business Nancy's way for once, instead of with his usual scrupulous fairness. And no doubt about it: she'd read his mind.

He was doing what he really wanted to do—take over one-eleven, and live for a while behind its walls.

He moved in on a warm autumn afternoon. Rêve Street was peaceful. Kids were playing stickball and gossiping grannies sat on stoops from which developers would soon evict them. Guys with strong backs carried in his furniture, because the big van couldn't fit through the carriageway. When the movers suggested piling some of the crates and boxes in the stable, Phil told them, "Nuh uh. It's full of rats."

He waited until they were gone to check the stable out. He had to unlock it to do so, because after Steve's death he'd personally fitted the door with a hasp and a blue-steel padlock. Inside the little building, with its vague smell of disuse, everything looked normal. The sheetrock had been removed, the cot and the bottles thrown away, the cabinet turned into a paint locker. The skylight illuminated every corner; there was no place for anything to hide, even a ghost.

Phil slept that night on a mattress on the floor of his new bedroom. The next week was devoted to sorting out boxes, shoving furniture around, putting books on shelves in his study, hanging his pictures. A Sunday painter, he did abstracts that Nancy had compared unkindly to an explosion in a stained-glass studio. But they brightened the walls.

He was a little embarrassed to discover how many devotional books he still kept: an old Latin missal, *The Imitation of Christ,* St. Thomas's *Summa,* St. Augustine's *City of God.*

"Look, all I do these days is fix up old houses," he told the books. But he put them on his new shelves anyway.

Like Nancy, the books reminded him of an enduring passion. In this case, a yearning to know what the universe really was about. Beside the religious books he put a few tomes on science—Darwin's *Origin,* Stephen Jay Gould's essays, a life of Einstein. He'd found them disappointing, too. Religion meant something, but had all the facts wrong; science had the facts right, but meant nothing to him.

On the lowest shelf went art books, and the same theme reappeared. A volume of El Greco's mystical Spaniards—their thin faces, licorice-drop eyes and blue chins much like Phil's own—stretching their bodies, yearning skyward. Bosch's nightmares of toads and tiny monsters and little black devils. *Oh yeah*, thought Phil with wry self-knowledge. What he read in his library were the secrets of his own unfulfilled heart.

When everything was in order at last, like Jehovah he took a day off to admire his own handiwork. The house glowed; the new plantings had already managed to produce a few autumnal flowers: scarlet camellias, other blossoms nameless in pink, cupped and hollow like small breasts seen from inside. Phil felt his lungs expand; even his shoes seemed looser. Home at last!

Now that one-eleven was really his, he wanted to show it off. That evening he drank his usual toast to the previous owners and put in a call to the black lady who did parties for him. He e-mailed invitations to his few friends and many business contacts, hired a zydeco band, and gave a big order to Martin's Wine Cellar.

The night of the party, Nancy arrived with a fat, spade-bearded guy as her escort. She seemed genuinely stunned by the transformation he'd wrought in one-eleven.

"Oh, Phil, it's *gorgeous*," she said. He merely nodded. She was right; it was.

The November night was warm and the guests flowed from house to patio and back again. Everybody loved the up-to-date retro reworking of one-eleven's interior. Everybody was fascinated by the story of the ghost in the stable. Everybody danced to Cajun music and soaked up booze. Nobody died taking Spanish Fly, but a lot of dick-stiffeners got consumed; even young guys were taking the drugs as enhancers.

A tad past midnight, Phil was doing a snuggle with Nancy on the upper gallery of the servants' wing. He was trying to get her to help him warm his bed, as well as his house.

When he came out of the seminary as a twenty-two-year-old virgin, he'd gone through agonies of long-delayed first love with her. Six years older than he and infinitely more experienced, she'd been fascinated by his naïveté, then lost interest when that faded. Still, he thought hopefully: revivals don't happen only in church.

Underneath the airy scent she wore, the indefinable smell of her body made his juices run embarrassingly; he'd taken no pills, but felt hidden stirrings anyway. When you lived an essentially celibate life—as he still did, more so than many of the clergy he'd known—passion assailed you suddenly, like a mugger.

Phil breathed damply into her left ear and murmured, "Why don't you stay over? We could add a whole new chapter to our meaningless relationship."

"Oh Phil, I can't."

"Sure you can. Come on, Honey. Let your date find his own way home."

"He's not my date, he's my husband."

"Your what?"

"Husband. We've been married for two years. His name's Felix Grossman. He's a lawyer specializing in real estate. We have so many interests in common, it just seemed natural to—"

She fell silent, her head turned and lowered.

"What's the matter?"

"I thought you weren't letting anybody into the stable after that kid died."

"I'm not."

"Then why's the light on?"

"There's no electricity in—"

He took that long to focus on the skylight of the stable down below. Not only was it dimly illuminated, but a shadow was moving around inside.

"Some idiot broke the lock," he muttered, and turned to head for the stairs.

"Phil," she said, grabbing his arm, "don't go down there. Please."

"Why not?"

"Don't. Please don't. It's a trap. It's meant to lure you in."

"Are you nuts?"

"Please."

They stood in the half-dark with the sounds of life all around them. The band was taking a break and chatting with the guests; a CD was playing an Ella Fitzgerald scat song; laughter was chiming up from the patio, where friends or lovers wandered two by two among the fresh plantings.

Meanwhile the skylight of the stable glowed with a dull greenish light like a gibbous moon and the shadow played the game of shadows—changing shape, growing squatter, longer, shorter, as whatever was casting it moved around. Then the light expired in a slow, cinematic fadeout. Nancy drew a deep breath.

"Just stay out of there at night!" she whispered, and suddenly hugged him with a kind of desperation.

Phil was so surprised that he hardly registered the complete disconnect between her action and her face, which showed no emotion at all.

He took the next day off from work to tend his headache and think about his situation.

At ten-oh-five he was lying in a tall Victorian bed in the master suite, a clean linen tester drooping over his head, morning sunlight pouring in through French doors opening on the courtyard.

The automatic coffee maker in his dressing room started to perk, and the deep black smell of Arabian beans filtered in. He poured a cup, returned to bed and sipped and thought about the light in the stable. What was most scary about it, he recognized, was the fact that Nancy had been scared. But of what, exactly?

He lay back on the pillows, mouthing coffee and thinking—for the first time seriously—about the rent-a-cop who'd had to go on Thorazine. About Steve Nobody. About the old woman named W. He put down the cup, reached for the phone book and spent a minute or two leafing through the blue pages. A cordless phone rested in its cradle by the bed, gazing at him with one red eye; he picked it up and tapped in the number of the coroner's office.

A bored city-employee-type voice answered. Phil explained that he owned the property where a young man had been found dead of head trauma, and could somebody give him more information about the case?

"We don't give out stuff like that."

"I'm concerned about, uh, possible legal liability. I can have my lawyer call you instead."

"Uhhh. I'll connect you with the lab."

"Thanks for your help."

"Uhhh."

A concert of elevator music followed. Then another and brisker voice answered, agreed to check, and informed him that the decedent had been identified as Steven B. Olafson of Minot, N.D.

"Sad case. Kid had a history of mental problems and drug use. But the blood tests indicated he was clean the night he died."

"He was what?"

"Clean. The cops had busted a couple of the main suppliers for that area, and there was a drought. Then this kid found a new supplier and a private place to take the stuff—but looks like he never got around to doing it."

Phil hung up, feeling a distinct chill. Whatever had driven Steve wild, it wasn't pills.

He got out of bed again, poured himself more coffee, and padded barefoot into his study. On his desk lay a fat file bulging with documents relating to one-eleven. Leafing through the wad of slick legal paper, he discovered in the title insurance documents that Deep Delta had bought the property from the estate of Henriette DuBlieux.

Then paused, baffled. He knew a little more, yet he really knew nothing. Nancy, the most fearless woman he'd ever known, had been scared last night. She knew something that she wasn't telling him, but what?

Trouble was, when you spent a while between the sheets with somebody, you thought you knew them. Dumb idea. He really knew very little about Nancy.

When they were together, she'd been a young businesswoman trying to make a buck in the devastated New Orleans real estate market during the oil bust. Her husband of the time, Jimmy Forêt—she still used his name in business, including the little hat over the e—had been an amiable Garden District drunk, accustomed to his wife's infidelities. His favorite joke when he met one of her lovers was a line of Rodney Dangerfield's: "What? You too?"

Phil remembered her moaning about Jimmy's fecklessness. Saying that his forte was spending money, not making it. "I think he wrote Chapter Thirteen," she said, meaning the personal bankruptcy law. Yet during that lunch at La Chaumière she'd told Phil that her divorce had been more profitable than she expected. How could it have been?

When you started thinking critically about Nancy, there were so many things that just didn't add up.

Well, she was going to give him the truth about this goddamn ghost, or else. He found his wallet in last night's trousers and started shuffling through the business cards, looking again for her beeper number.

And yeah, here was her card, announcing in embossed letters that she was Annette (Nancy) DuB. Forêt, Business and Domestic Properties, plus a string of letters for professional societies she belonged to.

"Oh, you lying bitch," he muttered.

What were the odds that her maiden name was DuBlieux? What were the odds that when Deep Delta bought one-eleven from Henriette DuBlieux's estate—no doubt for top dollar—it was really buying from the old woman's heir, and the heir was Nancy? How many ways had she contrived to make money out of this unpromising property?

Phil returned to the Hewlett Packard and checked out the directors-of-record for Deep Delta REIT. There were only two: Annette and Felix Grossman.

He threw back his head and laughed. Had to—either that, or grab a gun and go kill the damned woman.

"Henriette Dublieux was my French grandfather's sister," a much subdued Nancy explained.

They were lunching at La Chaumière again. This time Nancy was bearing the entire expense, including the wine.

"I *suppose* I should've told you all this," she added, as if there was some doubt about it.

According to her, the story went all the way back to Alfonso Villarubia. "Some great-great-great-great of mine inherited everything he had—house, slaves, cotton business, brothel property, you name it. And one-eleven stayed in the family."

The DuBlieux family tree produced two kinds of shoots, people who made money and people who threw it away. Clear enough which tradition Nancy belonged to. As a girl she'd been fascinated by her great-aunt, who was just such another.

"I called her Tia," she explained, while the waiter was supplying them with platters of excellent grillades, stone-ground grits and mushroom flan. The wine was a Chianti.

"She was the smartest person I ever knew. She had a regular seat downtown at Broussard Frères, so she could watch the ticker tape come in. That was how she made her money, buying and selling stocks with absolutely uncanny foresight. I asked her once how she knew which stocks would go up. She said from her Tarot cards, and I never knew whether she was telling the truth or laughing at me.

"She had some kind of scientific degree from the Sorbonne, and she was always brewing things out in that stable she'd fixed up as a laboratory—creating her own cosmetics and making teas and infusions I had to drink when I was sick, because she said they worked better than antibiotics. I don't think she made love potions. She claimed she could make any man want her, but she did that by another kind of chemistry.

"She must have been spectacular looking once—not a beauty, her face was like a cleaver, but rather stunning in a way, and up to the very end she had great clothes sense. You know the portrait by John Singer Sargent called *Madame X*? This very cold, very sexy-looking female with a bosom the color and probably the temperature of a snowbank? Madame X was a New Orleans woman too, one of the Gautreaux women, and I think Tia must have been the same type when she was young.

"Not that she was frigid! I saw technicolor photos of her from the Forties, wearing bizarre hats and sleek nylons and padded shoulders—her skirt up above her kneecaps, lipstick you could see a block away, and this insolent sort of try-me-if-you-dare expression on her face. She told me I should practice walking the way she did, very deliberately and slowly, at kind of a regal pace, because then every eye would be on me—women as well as men. I asked her which she enjoyed provoking more, lust or envy. She said both were *très agréable*.

"She gave me wonderful gifts, jewels and little gold music boxes that played strange tunes I've never heard anywhere else. Sarabands, tarantellas—I don't remember all the names she called them. I'd go to sleep with the sounds tinkling in my ear and dream about funny little animals dancing.

Two-legged dogs with the heads of birds—and marabou storks that hopped around, looking so awkward and solemn—and a ridiculous little bundle of feathers with long skinny legs, and the head of a very old man.

"She told me my dreams were of the *Sabat*. She said she held *Sabats* in her courtyard, and strange things came to them, down from the sky and up out of the earth. She promised to invite me to one of her parties when I grew up. But she never did."

"You're describing a witch," Phil pointed out. "Are you serious?"

"Phil, I don't know what she was. She had a lot of occult beliefs, only not the banal, boring stuff you're always hearing from psychics. She never mentioned souls or auras or any of that crap. She thought outer space is full of wandering—well, I don't know what exactly. Little sentient whirlpools that form in the dark matter. She called them *les vagabonds*, or if she was talking English she called them drifters.

"She claimed that our kind of life starts when the chemistry's right on a planet; then these things come down and enter the molecules and organize them and they begin to live. That's where we all came from originally. And she thought that when you die, unless you can find another body, you have to go back out there."

"And you believed all this stuff?" asked Phil, baffled. Of all the people on Earth he'd never have suspected of occultism, Nancy headed the list.

"I wouldn't, except for one thing," she said, lowering her voice so that Phil could hardly hear her. "I never told anybody this before. Tia got old, and all her brains didn't help her with love. Maybe the reverse. She had dozens of lovers but never kept any of them. You know, I'm the same way.

"She lived all alone while Rêve Street was turning into a free-fire zone, and she got crazier than she'd ever been—trying to brew some elixir of immortality, and I guess she had as much success as anybody else who's tried that. Meaning none at all. The last few months of her life she virtually lived in the stable, with a gasoline lantern for light and a cell phone for emergencies.

"Well, I got a call in the middle of the night. Tia was having a heart attack. She kept gasping, 'I don't want to die, *mon Dieu*, I don't want to go back out there, it's so dark and cold and I'm so afraid!'

"I threw on some clothes and drove down alone to that horrible neighborhood. I was sure I was going to be mugged or raped or something, but I had a key to the door, and while I was trying to get the lock to turn I heard something scratching on the inside. I dragged it open. The light of a street-lamp came in and a dagger of light fell on the stones, and there she was on her hands and knees, gasping and choking.

"Now I know you won't believe this, but it's true anyway.

"She looked up at me and I began having this dreadful experience, as if I was a reflection in a mirror looking back at myself. Then her face turned blue, her strength seemed to fade out, and suddenly I was me again. It wasn't until later that I realized all her efforts to save her own body had failed, so she was trying to steal mine.

"I was terribly scared, more scared than I'd ever been, but I dragged Tia into the street and slammed the door behind me. She vomited on the side-walk and seemed to recover a little, and I was able to get her into my car. Christ, she smelled awful! I drove her to Charity's ER, and they saved her life, and out of gratitude she made me her heir."

"Hence La Chaumière," murmured Phil.

"Yes. She was worth millions and millions. One day a neighbor found her lying dead—she'd had a second heart attack—and as soon as I heard about it, I went right out and bought my first Jag."

"Lucky you. Now tell me what I've got in the stable."

"Phil, I honestly before Christ and Mary don't know how much of her is left. That shadow last night scared hell out of me. I used to think, well, if there's a drifter clinging to the stable as its last refuge, well, who cares. It'll fade out and vanish in time. Then we saw that thing moving around, and I was like—oh my God, what have I done, conning my poor little altar boy into living in Tia's house, in a witch's house, just for money, just for some dirty money I don't even need anymore."

Her voice sounded strained, anxious, even terrified, but her face never moved. That was when Phil realized that it was botox, that he was looking at a botox mask and not a face at all. What was really going on behind it, he didn't know—would never know.

When they were leaving La Chaumière, Nancy accepted the groveling of the waiters and the maître d' as her due. An attendant brought her car, and she climbed in and sat there checking herself in the mirror and touching her seams and the gold pin on her bosom, as if afraid something might have gotten disarranged.

Just before the window closed, she said, "That lunch is one of the best things they do, and I don't think either one of us really enjoyed it. I know I didn't."

Back home, Phil reverted to form: he decided on exorcism.

Though deeply embarrassed, he dug out his Latin missal, opened to the ritual, and spent a quarter of an hour mumbling all the traditional maledictions, cursing the *daemonium nocturnum*, the *creatura ligni*. Then added one of his own: "Out, drifter! Get the hell out! Back into the dark!"

Those words he shouted, and the echoes bounced around the courtyard and came back at him. Then, like a sensible man, he called his contractor and told him to bring a crew to demolish the stable and carry away the pieces.

Next day Phil took a few hours off from work—he had a new project going, downriver in the Bywater—to watch the process. Feeling somewhat edgy the whole time, wondering what the workmen would find.

They found nothing much. The old brick walls were solid. Under the wide pine boards of the floor were the same sort of flagstones that covered the rest of the patio, set solidly down in ancient mortar and immovable unless he wanted to bring in a jackhammer. Plus the dusty brown manure of long-vanished horses, and one rusted iron shoe with the nails still in it.

When the little building was gone, Phil relaxed. Whistling, he locked up and set out to work. That evening he had a drink at The Columns, ate dinner with a prospective client at Mr. B's Bistro, and headed home after dark.

The carriageway door, now fitted with an automatic opener, swung out to receive him. He collected his mail from an iron basket. As he drove into the patio, sensors turned lights on both there and in the house. Standing beside his Honda, Phil viewed backlit greenery and the warm crescents cast by doorway lanterns. Over the chimney pots a vast moon was rising, shedding its gold vestment, donning silver.

He relaxed, feeling more than ever at home. In the new kitchen he poured himself a glass of Syrah, sat down at a fashionable island topped with red granite slabs, and began to leaf through his mail.

A phone was blinking on the wall and he leaned over and pushed the button, half-listening to the usual farrago of messages from people wanting to lend him money, clean his chimney, sheathe his house in vinyl siding, sell him retirement property, obtain his vote at the next election, and share a business opportunity too good to pass up. The phone's robot voice announced, "End of messages."

Then a throaty, almost hoarse contralto spoke up. "My poor little man," it said, "now you'll have to share your house with me."

The mail slipped from Phil's hands, the wineglass fell and shivered on the quarry-tile floor.

In the silence that followed he heard a gentle sound he couldn't identify at first: he thought of silk rubbing silk, or a snake sliding over smooth boards.

He rose trembling and followed the sound into his study. A tall figure stood running its fingers over the spines of his books with a gentle, slippery sound. The titles were dimly legible through its hand. Through her hand.

Tia turned and smiled. She had a wide mouth and a slash of red that might once have been lip gloss made it seem fuller than it was. Actually her lips were quite thin, intersecting the plane of her sharp face like two blades. She wore the memory of a red dress that had faded to rust.

"You're more interesting than I thought," she murmured, her voice descending another half-octave into her throat. "Your love of the sacred sciences is quite unexpected."

Did the words pass through his ears or distill themselves inside his mind? The sound echoed faintly. She was approaching him now, moving at a slow regal pace like a dancer setting her feet on chalk marks. Her eyes were black. When she passed before the desk lamp its glow turned bronze.

She put out a long hand and touched his face. Like dry ice, her touch burned coldly.

"I see why she liked you," she murmured. "All roués are drawn to innocents. A fascination with virginity is the great weakness of the corrupt. Now call Nancy, and tell her to come here."

"No," he whispered. "No."

"Let me tell you how I died. One night I felt that crushing pain again. I called her. The pain got worse. I tried to reach the outside door. I was on my hands and knees when it opened, and she was standing there. Since my own body was dying I tried again to take hers. But I was weak, and she'd grown stronger, much stronger than before. She watched me die, then went away leaving the door open, so that someone else would find me.

"You'll call her now. Tell her... tell her you found my diary hidden behind the cabinet in the stable. That ought to bring her. Say it's in French, ask her to come over and help you understand it. You love her, don't you, Altar Boy?"

"Yes." Was that his own voice, coming from so far away?

"Together we'll take her unaware. Your reward will be to enjoy her body again, only this time occupied by an older and wiser *vagabond*. Oh, what things I can show you! You always wanted to know what the universe is really like, eh, eh? Well, you'll learn many things that will surprise you.

"Now make the call. Listen, I've invited some friends and they're gathering."

She clapped her hands. Distantly the Rêve Street Consort began tuning up. Feet shuffled on the floor above, and in his bedroom Phil heard tiny shrieks and cries and muted laughter. A hairless something like a fetal monkey popped into the doorway, gazed at him with startled pink eyes, then swarmed up the doorframe and hung upside-down from the lintel, still staring.

Tia laughed. "How long it is since I've danced naked in the moonlight! When Nancy comes, it will be time *pendre la crèmaillére*."

"What does that mean?" asked Phil's remote voice.

"To have the housewarming," said Tia, and pointed commandingly at the phone.

A fine example of alternate history that looks with an unflinching eye at the horrors of World War II—those that happened and the even worse ones that might have.

POISON VICTORY

2 **SEPTEMBER 1949.** Ordered to appear at the prison in Kalach this morning. The Gestapo's nabbed a serf named Nevsky who claims to be one of mine. The charge: terrorism.

Poor devil was already a mass of blood and bruises. Oberstürmführer Müller—an insufferable little beast dressed up in a new black uniform with the silver skull insignia—wanted me to identify him. I wouldn't have known him even before they worked him over.

"You're aware that I have over a thousand serfs?"

"Yes, the biggest landholder in the Great Bend of the Don," said Müller, voice dripping with envy. "Perhaps you have too many for proper control."

"What exactly is the charge against this man?"

Well, he'd been spotted carrying a rook rifle.

"Is it conceivable that he may have been shooting rooks? The peasants hate them because they steal grain."

"It is absolutely forbidden for a serf to have a weapon of any type whatever. As you may be aware, we live in uneasy times."

"I suppose you mean the guerrillas. Perhaps dealing with them is too big a job for the SS, and that's why you're unable to exert proper control."

Rather a neat riposte, I thought. They can't catch this guerrilla chieftain who calls himself the Ataman, so in order to look busy they arrest a peasant with a pellet gun. I can see the report they'll send to that Eichmann fellow who struts around as Reich Protector of the East: *An armed Russian was arrested and under severe interrogation confessed to—*

Whatever they please. And I can do nothing. Eichmann would automatically reject any appeal on Nevsky's behalf, and I'd merely get myself even deeper into his black book. *Scheissdreck!*

Took the Porsche for a drive up the new Volga parkway, hoping to recover my equanimity and clear the smell of the prison out of my head.

A few kilometers were enough to heal my spirit. What a glorious country this is! The rolling, wheat-heavy steppe, birds wheeling and crying, sunlight the color of pollen. Some of my serfs were helping to landscape the parkway, and they paused in their work to take off their caps, the honest fellows! I gave them that stiff half-salute that makes Marya tell me I must think I'm waving a scepter.

Near Führerburg I turned onto a side road, parked in a peaceful spot, and lit up a cigarette. The city lay before me—the Krupp-Ost factory, the new worker housing under construction, pillars of steam and smoke staining the clear air. At that distance the Victory Monument on the old Tartar burial mound of the Mamayev Kurgan seemed only an enigmatic shape, and the sun slanting through veils of smoke gave it a grandeur it entirely lacks when clearly seen.

God, what a hell this place was once! How many beloved comrades died for it! How many brave Slavs were entombed here beside them! They say you can't dig a cellar without finding bones. I accept the view endorsed by so many experts—English and American as well as German—that we Aryans form a superior race. And yet in death, when the brain is gone and nothing lingers but the bones and the soul, how hard it is to tell Russian from German, serf from master!

Shaking off these grim thoughts, I started the engine and drove to my fine new townhouse overlooking the Tsaritsa Gorges. A kiss from Marya. Dinner, then my daily task of filling a few pages in this journal. I visualize the text in English, which all Germans of my generation had to learn, then transpose it into my personal cipher. Rather a simple one, as anyone managing to read this must know! But it will have to do—I don't have an Enigma machine, and if I did I'd be afraid to use it, after all we've learned recently about the work of English code-breakers.

Marya is preparing for bed, humming an old Cossack folk song as she shrugs into a nightgown embroidered with little roses. A faint smile lights her round face, like the face of a *matryushka* doll, and her slanted eyes touch me lightly with a certain glance. She says, "Are you going to scribble in that silly notebook all night?"

Nein, meine Liebe, nein! A moment only, and I'll put it away inside my big, ornate presentation copy of *The Complete Writings and Speeches of Adolf Hitler*—in the space I've hollowed out with a razor (as if the original contents weren't hollow enough!). Then back into the safe my silent friend and father confessor will go, for the time has come to live my life, not write about it.

3 September 1949. Waked at 0530 by a call from Müller's adjutant. Nevsky has been beheaded by guillotine.

Very curious, this fondness of the Gestapo for the chief implement of the French Reign of Terror. At least it's painless, unlike their other methods involving piano wire and meat hooks.

I was ordered to drive Nevsky's family out onto the road to starve, as a warning to others. Well, one advantage of being a big landowner is that I can move them to another of my villages, where they'll lie hidden until the whole episode is forgotten. Sent Marya to the estate to take charge of this duty, which I'm sure she will discharge with her usual cleverness and womanly compassion.

Meanwhile, I sat down to deal with a vast pile of paperwork generated by the bureaucrats at the *Ostministerium*. I'd barely started on this unpleasant duty when the telephone rang again. I picked it up with foreboding, only to hear—with astonishment—a friendly voice!

My wartime comrade Dietrich Wallenstein had arrived, all the way from Berlin. At once I abandoned my task and drove, a happy man, to the Veteran Officers Club where Dietrich was staying. And there he sat at the bar, clutching an elegant new attaché case and looking as much like his old self as anybody can after gaining thirty kilos. Well, he's a big cheese now, a troubleshooter for the General Staff, so I suppose he comes by his big gut honestly.

Soon he and I were seated at a quiet table, a schnapps bottle and two glasses between us. When I asked for news, he passed one fat hand over the pepper-and-salt bristles on his head and responded, "*Na*, can you guess who's become a nobleman?"

I groaned. "Not you!"

"*Jawohl!* I am now Graf von und zu Rostock."

"Another Nazi nobleman," I said, when we'd toasted his new distinction. "And to think how Hitler hated the aristocracy!"

He leaned toward me, small pouchy eyes gleaming. "It grieves me deeply to tell you this," he whispered, "but our beloved Führer is dying."

No surprise there. On 20 April of this year—his sixtieth birthday—Hitler visited the Volga frontier to see the War Memorial dedicated. I was granted the honor of being seated close enough to smell his farts, which were frequent. He looked dreadful—gray-faced, trembling. Astounding contrast with the heroic figure on the monument. I'm surprised he's lasted this long.

I nodded, and Dietrich went on, his voice sinking even lower:"Last week there was a funeral rehearsal at the Great Hall of the Reich. Pal of mine's a theatrical director, did some work with Riefenstahl, and he was in on it. The whole thing's to be broadcast on television—first time ever—so Goebbels had actors play the leading Nazis to get the lighting perfect. They got hold of a 300-kilo freak from the circus to stand in for Göring. Since he was too fat to walk, a couple of Polish serfs wheeled him in. Everybody had to keep a straight face, but I understand there was a lot of giggling in the wings.

"By the way," he added casually, "you've been invited to the funeral. I made sure of that."

"I won't go."

"Oh, yes you will. I'll tell you frankly, rumors have reached Reich Security that you're no longer politically reliable. High time for you to do some fence-mending, old boy! Attend the ceremony, look solemn, wipe away a tear, salute like an automaton, and prepare to enjoy the spectacle when the long knives start flashing. Things are going to get nasty as the satraps fight for the succession. With luck, they'll kill one another off, and the Nazi business will be over for good. Here—take this."

He handed me the attaché case, a capacious one covered in crocodile skin. Inside were some welcome gifts and one unwelcome one. A framed enlargement of an old photograph—God knows how it survived—of Dietrich and me during that other life we lived during the war. Also a bottle of good Scotch whiskey; and six cartons of real Virginia cigarettes. All most welcome and deeply appreciated. But also a large envelope of heavy cream-laid paper, with black borders and an embossed swastika, which was *not* appreciated.

"I don't see why I've got to go at all," I complained. "I'm no politician, not even a soldier anymore."

"My friend, you're a hero. That's your burden, so don't try to escape it now. Without you we'd have lost Stalingrad—pardon me, Führerburg—and then the whole war would've been in the toilet."

He leaned forward and gently struck my shoulder with his closed fist. "I've always regarded you as Germany's savior. The monument on the Mamayev Kurgan should be to you."

I had to turn away for a moment to hide my emotions, which as usual were contradictory and troubling. Dietrich has a heavy thumb, and he'd put it down on my greatest shame and my sole claim to historical importance— that to save my life and the lives of my comrades, I made it possible for Hitler and his cronies to dominate the world.

When I regained my composure, our talk turned to practical matters. Dietrich warned me that the guerrillas are growing bolder. I should watch out for the Ataman. He's supported by the Russian government in Siberia, and Khrushchev—that crude, tough Ukrainian peasant who overthrew and executed Stalin—is receiving aid from the British and Americans.

"So don't," said Dietrich, "be surprised if some very sophisticated weapons start showing up in guerrilla hands. We're *die Übermacht*, the superpower. Naturally, everybody hates us."

Then it was time for him to go about his business—something secret, he didn't discuss it with me. I tried to return his attaché case, but he absolutely refused. The container, he said, was part of the gift. We gripped each other's hands and he exclaimed, *"Auf wiedersehen, mein alter Freund und Kriegskamerad!"*

Farewell, my old friend and wartime comrade—words that sounded to me like the end of a funeral oration.

Marya was waiting for me on my return home. I asked how the widow was holding up, and she shrugged, "Pretty well."

"It must be hard for her."

"Sure it is. But we all have to bear what we have to bear. Life's not just a walk across a field, you know."

That's a peasant saying. One hears it everywhere.

She tells me she hid the family in Gorodok village, where hatred of the Gestapo is so intense that betrayal is unlikely. Last year the Orthodox priest there turned out to be an SS informer. On a winter's night, in thirty degrees of frost, his house caught fire and he and his family were roasted alive. Later, Marya told me she'd heard that the door and the window shutters had been nailed shut. Yes, I think Nevsky's survivors will be safe enough there.

4 September 1949. This evening I'm all alone in my country house on the banks of the "quiet flowing" Don. Here on my 5000-hectare estate I truly feel like the great feudal lord I'm supposed to be. But also, in Marya's absence, quite lonely.

The wheat harvest's beginning, and like old Tolstoy I'd hoped to join the peasants in some good, honest toil. Alas, it was not to be. I spent the whole day on the damned phone, trying to find the new tractors I'd ordered. Meanwhile the serfs began reaping with scythes, and I crossed my fingers, hoping the Gestapo wouldn't decide those are weapons too, and arrest my whole workforce.

Tonight all's peaceful. Outside the circle of light cast by my lamp the shadows press close. In the country darkness crickets are shrilling, no idea in their little heads how soon the first frost will arrive. Seemed like a perfect time to open my new attaché case and take out the photograph, the whiskey, a few packs of cigarettes I brought with me, and of course the *Writings and Speeches*. The fact that I choose to hide my treasonable journal inside Hitler's book is, I suppose, an example of heavy Teutonic irony. But then, as Marya sometimes hints, I am a rather heavily ironic Teuton, in my own way!

This month is a dark anniversary for me. Just seven years ago, I arrived on the Eastern Front for the very first time. A lifetime, no an age ago.

I'm staring at the picture now, hardly able to recognize the skinny young fellow in the wire-rim glasses who stands beside grinning Dietrich. Twenty-nine I was then, old enough to have missed the Hitler Youth and all that Nazi rubbish. Something of a child despite my age, the product of a loving home and years of quiet work in schools and laboratories. A frightened child too, for in those days we Germans dreaded an assignment to Russia as Christians feared an assignment to Hell.

Never will I forget my first sight of Stalingrad from the rattletrap old Messerschmidt that brought me. First, brown streamers of smoke rising and dirtying the pure late-summer air. Then the city itself, its broken buildings like headstones in a desecrated graveyard. We bumped and shuddered down on the pockmarked runway, and I climbed stiffly off the plane like a damned soul disembarking on the wrong side of the River Styx. It didn't help that two dusty, disheveled veterans unloading my spotless new luggage grinned and asked sardonically, "How's the weather in Berlin, sir?"

At HQ I met Dietrich for the first time. He was an adjutant and took me in charge, finding me a place to sleep, then arranging a five-minute meeting with General Friedrich Von Paulus. My new commander wasn't at all what I'd expected—a pale, cool, fastidious man who spoke courteously even to a *Grünschnabel* like me. Later on, Dietrich confided that the general always wore clean underwear, even on the battlefield.

"He's what the Tommies call a *gentleman*," he explained, using the English word. "More scientist than soldier, I'd say. You two ought to get on well, though why in the world we need a chemical officer I'm sure I don't know."

Yes, that was my title. I was straight out of the I.G. Farben laboratories in Frankfurt-am-Main, where I'd hoped to evade military service by doing research for the war effort. Instead, by 1942 we'd lost so many men in the East that the army was ready to grab anybody—even me!

Dietrich and I soon became pals, and began calling each other *du* instead of the formal *Sie*—in fact, the photo records the day we sealed our friendship by drinking a small glass of schnapps with linked arms. A good fellow to know. He'd already developed his remarkable talent for getting his superiors to do whatever he wanted them to, and within a month, at his suggestion, Von Paulus relieved me of my useless task as chemical officer and made me his personal aide.

As a result, I was soon learning things about the war that I'd rather not have known. Our atrocities, for example. The full history of our treatment of the Jews has never been written and now, I suppose, never will be. At home one was aware of the vulgar Nazi attacks on them, which began with insults and ended with mob assaults. Nonpolitical people like my family thought the whole business a *Kulturschande*, a blot on civilization, and we averted our eyes as I suppose civilized Americans avert theirs from the lynchers who murder their blacks.

Russia made such evasion impossible. In our own army area, seventy-five Jewish orphans were imprisoned by the SS under vile conditions, then ordered to be shot. When Colonel Mannstein, our chief of staff, tried to save them, the SS sent in a party of Ukrainian militiamen who murdered all the children right under our noses. I was present when Mannstein stormed into HQ and shouted at Von Paulus, "We can't and shouldn't be allowed to win this war!"

Some commanders would have backed him up—others would have arrested him. Typically, Von Paulus did neither. He merely listened, shook his head, said nothing. I thought this cowardly of him, little guessing the role I myself would play in the war. Today he's Chief of Staff in Berlin and I'm a great feudal lord in the East, while Mannstein's broken bones lie in some Gestapo killing ground, buried in quicklime. In 1944 he joined a group that tried to assassinate Hitler; he was betrayed, arrested, tortured in a disgusting manner, and strangled in six stages with a piano-wire noose.

Is this always the fate of the decent and the brave? Will Von Paulus now take vengeance for him and all other victims of the regime by staging a military coup? Surely his chance will come after the Nazis have finished bloodying one another. Looking back on the cautious general I first got to know in the autumn of '42, I have deep doubts whether he possesses the nerve for desperate deeds. Yet at Stalingrad he did one thing that was totally out of character, and by doing it saved all of us—yes, and the Führer too.

5 September 1949. All day hard at work outside. Glorious weather!

The new tractors finally arrived, but with them came a human pimple from the *Ostministerium*, who informed me that only Germans can drive them! He spouted the usual rubbish that only Aryans can handle complex machinery, when the real purpose of the SS is to prevent Russians from learning to do anything but the crudest hand labor. They are to become a people without skills, without knowledge, even without songs.

Well, we didn't have any Aryans available, so I sent the pimple away, put my men and women into the drivers' seats, and off they went to do the job. Many had been trained as tractor drivers on the collective farms that still existed a mere nine years ago, so why not make use of them? Another black mark against my name in Herr Müller's book, damn him, and another tidbit he can pass on to Eichmann.

I returned to the country house about sixteen o'clock, greatly in need of a bath and a nap, both of which I took. Waking refreshed, I found that Marya had arrived to help with the harvest. So we made love, a fine ending to a fine day. I need her to remind me that I'm still a young man in years, even though old in spirit.

And now I sit here once again, pen in hand, ready to encode my memories. My lethal memories. Oh yes, they are deadly. For I am one of the few still living who know how we really won the war. Now perhaps the time has come to set it down, even if only in cipher.

The battle had been raging for a month when I arrived in Stalingrad. Much of the city had been ground and pummeled to a coarse dust, and the first chill wind of the approaching fall swept up the grit and scoured my face like a sandstorm.

The ruins stank of cordite, feces, rotting corpses. Everywhere were hidden ditches and sewers and storm drains, from which Ivans would suddenly emerge with tommyguns blazing. Shrapnel-battered steel and concrete buildings had to be cleared of their defenders floor by floor—one such fortress held out against fifty-eight days of continuous assault. We paid a heavier toll of men to win a single block of Stalingrad than to conquer whole western nations.

We'd already lost so many that our flanks were held by our Axis allies, all of them ill-equipped and unhappy to be fighting so far from home. Von Paulus was too intelligent not to see the danger in this situation. And he was getting disturbing reports from patrols and from the Luftwaffe about vast enemy movements to the north and south of the city.

A terrible scenario formed in his mind, and began to invade his dreams.

I slept in the same bunker as he, and one night heard him cry out. I ran into his quarters and found him awake, sitting up on his cot, shivering and rubbing his eyes. In a whisper, he told me that in a nightmare he'd seen the Russians assail both our flanks at once, trapping the whole Sixth Army in a vast encirclement. Next day I whispered the story of the general's dream to Dietrich, and he expressed deep concern.

"Still, what can be done?" he shrugged, with true Teutonic fatalism. "If it happens, it's *unsere Schicksal*, our destiny. That's all."

Well, I thought something could be done. That evening when the general and I were alone for a few moments, I presumed to tell him a secret known to very few. The laboratory where I'd worked in Frankfurt had invented a war gas that could defeat the Russians, if only we dared to use it.

"Poison gas?" he asked skeptically. "Everybody used it in the last war. A cruel and stupid weapon that made war uncomfortable, to no purpose.

Anyway, Hitler's forbidden its use, maybe for personal reasons. You know he was temporarily blinded by gas in 1918. Or maybe he's simply afraid of Allied retaliation."

"*Herr Generaloberst*, this is not your ordinary war gas."

I told him how, back in the thirties, one of our chemists began to fear that he was going blind. A microscopic amount of a new organic insecticide had caused the pupils of his eyes to close partway, shutting out the light. In time we learned that the chemical was a cholinesterase inhibitor. The precise formula was a closely held secret, but everyone could see how it worked—it affected the motor nerves so that the muscles could contract, but could not relax.

It was given the name Tabun. In larger quantities it caused violent cramps, followed by convulsions of the whole body and paralysis of the muscles that control breathing. Conventional gas masks were useless, and even rubber suits couldn't protect fully against it. We now had three types of the gas: Sarin was twice as toxic as Tabun, Soman three times as toxic as Sarin.

"Well then," said the General, who had been listening with obvious distaste, "we can't use it. Our lines are often only a few meters from the Ivans. We'd be poisoning our own men."

"Then don't use it in the city," I replied eagerly, quite forgetting my inferior rank. "With Luftwaffe cooperation you can use heavy bombers to break up the enemy concentrations to the north and south of us, and also on the east bank of the Volga. When the enemy forces in the city have no support and receive no reinforcements, we can destroy them."

He shook his head wearily.

"A pretty theory! And how long would it take to manufacture the quantities we'd need and load it into bombs?"

"It's already there. Slave labor from three concentration camps has been at it for years, suffering great losses in the process. Himmler himself gave the green light to make the bombs and stockpile them in underground arsenals, in case Hitler ever gives permission to use them."

"And you expect some bureaucrat in Munitions to defy Hitler's orders and ship this stuff to us?"

"Not a bureaucrat. The new Munitions Minister. I met him years ago at the Berlin Institute of Technology. His name's Albert Speer. He's the Führer's fair-haired boy, and because of that he can take risks that nobody else would dare even to think about."

At first Von Paulus wouldn't hear of my idea—indeed, he ordered me not to bring it up again. But reports of the Russian buildup continued to filter in, and the messages we got from higher headquarters diverged farther and farther from reality. One day in mid-October, he brought up the forbidden subject himself.

"I think you need to take leave," he told me abruptly. "Your mother's dying of cancer—didn't know that, did you? She doesn't know it either, the lucky woman. Compassionate leaves are routinely denied, but I'm the commander, and herewith I'm giving you ten days and putting you on the first flight out.

"See your old school chum in Munitions if you can, and if he agrees to supply us the stuff, head for Luftwaffe HQ. I'll give you a letter to a friend of mine, a general in Transport Command. The weapons will have to be delivered by air, and quickly. I believe the Ivans will attack us at the first snowfall, or shortly after."

So that was how it all began. Once in 1947, when I was drunk at the Veteran Officer's Club, I called our triumph *das Giftsieg*. The poison victory. Thank God, everybody else was as drunk as I was and the remark passed unnoticed! There are things that a man who wears two Iron Crosses and the Knight's Cross can say with impunity, and others he cannot.

Yet I spoke the truth, and though I have no religion I can't help but believe that one day I will be called to account by a higher and juster power than the Gestapo. Mannstein was right, after all—we shouldn't have been allowed to win the war.

I know that now. But in 1942 I was twenty-nine and wanted to live, no matter what.

6 September 1949. Another day of splendid weather. Hard work—how beautiful hard work is! The muscles ache, but the spirit knows peace. Then home for a hot bath, a nap, love in the afternoon, and dinner.

And now, late at night, I get back to my self-appointed task as stenographer to Clio, the Muse of History. Speaking of fate, I now realize that this is mine. Like the tyrant in Shakespeare's *Coriolanus*, the Nazis cut out the goddess's tongue so that the crimes of the past cannot be told. But through me she speaks—even though no one may ever listen!

I saw Speer. Handsome as ever, superbly intelligent, yet devoted heart and soul to the Austrian necromancer. So devoted that he would even disobey him in order to save him. Who can explain it? With his promise in my pocket, I hastened to Luftwaffe HQ, where the necessary cargo planes were made available to move the weapons to the Stalingrad Front.

Meantime the Russians too were hard at work. In late October they seized a number of strategic hills inside our lines. As if to aid their attack, winter arrived early with twenty degrees of frost. Intense cold already gripped the northern reaches of the Volga and ice floes drifted past Stalingrad, grinding against each other so loudly that our men in advanced positions could hear them groaning all night, like the souls of the lost.

By then I'd returned from Germany. With Von Paulus's permission I let Dietrich in on the secret, and it became his task to track the movement of the weapons. The nerve-gas bombs were in crates stamped "oxyacetylene cylinders, extra large size," so that he could follow them through routine supply messages. On 10 November 1942 an encrypted signal brought word that planes carrying the weapons were even then droning over the snow-powdered fields of western Russia.

At this supreme moment, I found Von Paulus drawn and white. If he failed to use nerve gas, the Russians would destroy him; if he did use it against Hitler's explicit orders, he might be arrested and shot. And I might be shot too, though I could always plead that I was only following orders, something the commander could not do.

I don't think either of us slept more than a few hours during the next five days. Nor did Dietrich, who for the first time in our friendship lost his bouncy good spirits. The usual glitches developed in the rear areas. At an airfield near Rostov where the weapons were to be transferred from the transport planes to the bombers, they were almost lost through a paperwork error. After a frantic search of ninety minutes during which we all aged a year or two, they were discovered in a warehouse, stored among ordinary oxygen and acetylene tanks. If welders had actually used them, the results would indeed have been interesting!

At last came the night of 15 November. I'll never forget it. The weather was still and bitter cold—one of those Russian nights when the Kalmuk steppe seems to hold its breath and even the dead grasses cease to tremble. A thick crust of ice had formed over the autumn snow and lay hard and white as bone under a carborundum sky.

The bomber pilots knew only that they would be dropping some sort of experimental device, and since Hitler was always ranting about secret weapons, they accepted this story without question. Leaving Dietrich behind, I accompanied the General in his staff car to the Italian sector of the line. We were a few kilometers west of the city, a place of acute danger where the Russians held bridgeheads over both the Volga and the Don, and so could attack at will.

We stepped out into the terrible cold, and walked slowly toward the north. The car waited with its blue-shielded headlights off, the motor grunting and a plume of white smoke jetting from the tailpipe. And then we heard overhead the Focke-Wulf-190s droning toward the enemy positions!

White fingers of searchlights began to spring up and the *put-put-put* of distant antiaircraft guns began. The lights would find a plane and lose it again. Tiny objects tumbled through the beams, but we didn't hear the usual deep grumble of exploding bombs, for the weapons carried only small charges designed to rupture the casings and disperse the gas. I tried to imagine what it must be like for the Ivans, meeting a silent and incomprehensible death. Then I decided not to think about such things, remembering how back in Frankfurt I'd disgraced myself by passing out during a movie that showed the effects of Tabun on a flock of sheep.

Von Paulus was smoking a cigarette, which of course was strictly against the blackout regulations. He offered one to me, and though I'd never smoked up to that time I felt obliged to take it with a *"Danke, Herr Generaloberst."* He struck a match, I inhaled and promptly went into a coughing fit.

He laughed and slapped me on the back. "That's right, *mein Junge*," he said. "Stay away from tobacco. It's not healthy."

Next day brought unmistakable evidence of great disorder in the enemy's buildup areas, plus hysterical accusations from Radio Moscow that we had opened gas warfare. Ignoring all of this, plus a barrage of queries from Army Group South trying to find out what was going on, Von Paulus imposed radio silence and ordered a full-scale assault against the Russian positions in Stalingrad.

The time was well chosen. Our troops split the center of the enemy's line and began rolling up the pockets that still held out. After three months of desperate fighting in the greatest urban battle known to history, our sorely tried and war-weary soldiers stood at last upon the riverbank, gazing at the famous Volga—a wide, bleak, turbulent stream surging with brown water and dirty white ice. A sight for which their comrades had already paid a hundred thousand lives!

Now Von Paulus had to face Hitler and tell him what he had done. Cleverly, he sent first a radio message: *Mein Führer! I am pleased to lay at your feet the conquered city of Stalingrad. Your genius in directing this assault now stands clear for all the world to see. Heil Hitler!*

Then he flew off to the Wolfschanze, the Wolf's Lair as Hitler called his headquarters. Whether he would be shot remained in doubt for at least a week, until it became clear that the Western Allies possessed no nerve gas and could not use conventional poison gas to retaliate without running the risk of seeing London and other English cities submerged in clouds of Tabun, Sarin, and Soman.

Shortly afterward Von Paulus returned, much older in appearance but with the jeweled baton of a Field Marshal clutched in his hand. As so often happens in war, bold action by a local commander achieved what the bigwigs at higher headquarters had failed to do. Of course it was death for anyone to say so—Hitler as usual claimed all the credit for himself, and a falling blade, a bullet, or a wire noose awaited anybody who told the truth.

But truth, like the bones of the dead, has a way of reappearing over time.

7 September 1949. Disturbing news this morning. Müller, the prison commandant, has been found lying in his comfortable country house with his throat cut.

I heard the news from Marya, who got it from a peasant. She whispered that an order went out from the Ataman last week condemning Müller to death for his many cruelties. Of course everybody on the lower Volga knew about it, except us Germans!

I asked her if she had any idea who'd done the deed. She said no, gazing at me with the special limpid innocence in her round face that means she's lying.

"Come now, my girl," said I, "don't try to deceive your old soldier! It wasn't one of our people, was it?"

She hesitated, then after a moment said softly, "*Vdova* Nevskaya was missing from her new home this morning. Her children are crying."

Good God! Nevsky's widow! If this leads to the discovery that I've been sheltering the family, then it's good-bye to my feudal estate on the Volga! In this world, can one perform any decent act without regretting it?

Noon. This is turning into a busy day. The radio brings news that Hitler is dead at last. If only some Austrian nursemaid gifted with prophecy had strangled him in his crib, how much the whole world would have been spared!

He's being embalmed and his funeral is set for a week hence. So I'll have to go to Berlin. Dietrich was right—I can't afford not to, especially with this Müller business hanging over me. On the other hand, that will leave my people here with no defender when the SS descends on them like the Biblical iron besom of destruction.

One can only hope that the bloodletting in Berlin will begin very soon and distract the butchers from what is, after all, only a local crime.

Later still. Marya reports that Müller's serfs have been arrested and are undergoing interrogation. Trying to distract their tormentors, they'll begin to accuse anybody and everybody. Those they name will be arrested and tortured, and so on and so on, until the entire district is depopulated. What will happen to the harvest now, God only knows.

Marya is helping me plan my trip. Lufthansa is putting on extra flights to Berlin, and a single phone call got me a first-class seat. I have four days before my flight takes off. I can only hope the Gestapo mars its hitherto perfect record of incompetence by finding the real murderer quickly—and that the killer's not one of my people!

With that off my mind, I could almost enjoy seeing Hitler off to Valhalla, or to Hell, whichever it may be.

8 September 1949. No fresh news about the murder, but arrests have begun in the serf-warrens outside the city. Everywhere the fear is palpable. I feel it too, although the danger's far greater for the Russians.

I rely on Marya more than ever to keep me informed. She tells me that the Nevsky children have been taken into other houses of the village. The prison at Kalach has been sealed off, and nobody knows what's happening inside, although one can easily guess.

The harvest is almost done. I was in the west field watching the mechanical reapers at work this morning when I was summoned back to the house to take a long-distance call from Dietrich. A special hundred-man Heroes' Farewell to our beloved leader is being planned for the small Memorial Chapel on the morning of the funeral. No doubt a Goebbels inspiration—a kind of Viking farewell to the supreme warlord. Through Dietrich's intervention, I'm to be one of the Heroes. The whole Nazi gang will be there to honor us—Bormann, Himmler, the younger generation like Eichmann.

I know Dietrich set this up because he's trying to save my neck, but sometimes I wish he wouldn't work so hard at it!

After the service, we'll leave the chapel and march at the head of the funeral cortege down the whole length of Adolf-Hitler-Allee to the Great Hall of the Reich, while the Berlin Philharmonic plays the slow movement from Beethoven's *Eroica*. Good thing the composer, who hated tyrants, won't be around to hear it!

9 September 1949. Back in the townhouse. Let me try to be calm.

Eichmann is here in Führerburg. Local landowners were ordered to assemble today on one hour's warning at the Veteran Officers' Club.

There we were harangued by the Reich Protector—tall, sallow, cleanshaven, arrayed in black and silver like a pall draping a coffin. Unless rumor lies (and in these matters it seldom does) he was a key figure in butchering the Jews—nobody even tries to guess how many died in that *Aktion*—and is now engaged in liquidating some forty percent of the population of White Russia who have been judged to be "racially unworthy of existence."

His talk was brief and to the point. Himmler has ordered a drastic security clampdown throughout the Eastern Territories. Spots of rebellion are to be stamped out with utter ruthlessness. Obviously he fears that the news of Hitler's death will lead to violent outbreaks, perhaps even a Russian invasion, just at the time when Berlin is in turmoil over the succession.

"Particularly important [said Eichmann] in the Volga District is the liquidation and annihilation of the band led by the terrorist kingpin who calls himself the Ataman. Müller's murder has been traced to a peasant woman, but of course she did not gain access to this officer's guarded home all by herself! She is now undergoing rigorous interrogation. No doubt the Ataman thought to deceive us into believing the murder was merely a case of private vengeance. We're not as innocent as that!

"No, this was the opening of a campaign to destabilize German authority throughout the East. We National Socialists know how to deal with such threats! I remind you gentlemen of your duties in this regard. Every whisper of information is to be passed on to Gestapo headquarters at once. No shielding of pet serfs will be tolerated."

Fixing me with a raptor's eye as he said it. Nazi bluster but, as usual, real ferocity behind it. I was more shaken than I like to admit. The Nevskaya woman may not know that I ordered her and her brats to be hidden, but she certainly knows that Marya arranged it all, and if she talks—

And of course she'll talk.

Back in 1944, after the conspiracy against Hitler failed, Mannstein was so unfortunate as to be taken alive. Foolish of him, but I think he had religious qualms about committing suicide.

At the Club, years after the event, I heard an SS man describe what happened to him. They worked him over for a whole day and in the evening, when he was weak and in great pain, they brought him a bucket with his daughter's head in it. At that he broke down completely and confessed to everything, for he had no more desire to live.

The creature who told this tale—loudly and drunkenly, while standing at the bar—gave a laugh at the end and said, like some burlesque Nazi in a BBC comedy skit, "We have ways, you see. We have ways."

Later. I drove to the estate, hoping to calm my spirit by watching the harvesters finish up their work. I was in the fields when a serf ran up and told me that in my absence a Gestapo car arrived in Führerburg and took my Marya away.

Later still. Drove like a madman to the serf-prison, but could not see her. Eichmann was there, I saw his big black Mercedes with his flag and his motorcycle escort lounging around. He wouldn't meet me, being—as a little *Unterstürmführer* said with an undisguised sneer—"busy."

Busy! I know how these people keep busy.

Midnight. Back at the townhouse. No word yet. I have the bottle of Scotch and my Luger lying on the table in front of me. I will not repeat Mannstein's mistake when they come for me. But *what is happening to Marya*?

I can only hope that she gave them everything and everyone to save herself pain. Tell them whatever they want to hear, my love, tell them I'm a Russian agent, tell them I'm Khrushchev in disguise, it doesn't matter. They will take nothing but my corpse, and to that they are welcome.

What is happening to her now?

10 September 1949. The call came at 0520. The ungodly like ungodly hours.

A gelid voice announced her death "in process of judicial interrogation." So that's what they call it now.

"You will be responsible for funeral arrangements," the voice continued. "The body must be collected today. Otherwise it will be cremated."

Somehow I spoke coherently, though without feeling, the way one walks on frostbitten feet. "You're releasing her body, then?"

"The juridical process failed to reveal that she was involved in illegal activities or had knowledge of such activities."

His voice betrayed his disappointment. They were gunning for me, but I'm a pal of Dietrich Wallenstein, a big landowner, an official Hero of the Reich with two iron crosses and a knight's cross. To catch me, they needed evidence.

And Marya didn't talk. In spite of all their little ways, she didn't betray me. *Later.* I have seen her body. That's why they returned it to me. They wanted me to see what they'd done to her.

Stupid of them. Do they think only they know how to kill?

Took the Porsche, drove to Gorodok. Typical run-down Russian village. The ruins of the priest's house haven't been cleaned up yet. I called the village elders together. They were out in the fields and took some time to arrive.

I waited, smoking American cigarettes. Hands quite steady. Now all compromises are over. I know what I'll do, provided I can get help to do it.

I'm leaving for Berlin tomorrow, so things will have to move fast. That worries me a bit. Things don't usually move fast in Russia.

Finally the elders showed up, two graybeards wearing boots and embroidered peasant smocks. Both looking like Rasputin. I explained what I needed. Obviously they knew all about Marya, and nodded silently when I promised to attend the proposed meeting anywhere, to come alone, and to carry no weapon.

They sent for vodka. However poor they are, they always have vodka. We drank, and I got it down without choking, though it was dreadful stuff. Home brew.

Then back to this house. Hand steady, I wrote out the key to my code, folded it into my journal. Think I'll sit up tonight, don't feel like sleeping. No tears, no prayers. Reread Tolstoy's *Death of Ivan Ilyich*, which has always moved me greatly. It tells about the redemption, not of a hero, but of an ordinary mediocre man, when at last his evasions and pretenses come to an end.

11 September 1949. A peasant lad guided me to a small patch of woods near Gorodok. I began to comprehend that this village must be the command center of the guerillas. No wonder the priest was burned!

Two rough-looking fellows confiscated the attaché case I was carrying, stared blankly at the manuscript inside it, then patted me down and led me deeper into the stands of birch and larch trees. The man I'd come to meet was sitting on a log, smoking. I noted that he too favors American cigarettes. Nice of Khrushchev to keep him supplied.

The Ataman is a small man but wiry and strong. Round head and black, thinning hair. Asiatic eyes.

"I asked Marya about you a couple of years ago," he began. "We're both Cossacks, you know. That's why I call myself Ataman, meaning head man. Once I asked her, 'What's this "good German" of yours really like?' She answered, 'He means well, but he's a man from whom truth is hidden.'"

"What truth?" I asked, feeling like Pontius Pilate.

"That you can't rid yourself of the guilt of your crimes as long as you continue to profit from them. That was what she told me, anyhow."

"My profiting is over. You have the sort of device I asked for?"

"Maybe. Anyway, I know what you're talking about. Things like that have been arriving lately. All the way from America, just like Mickey Mouse. Tell me how you plan to use it."

I explained about the Heroes' Farewell. "I'll be in a small chapel with them, the whole bunch of them. The Nazis who corrupted my people and butchered yours. It's a confined space and it'll make a fine gas chamber. When they realize what's happening, they'll rush the door, but it's narrow, so they'll get jammed in the opening. Some may get out, but not many."

He grunted. "At first I wasn't inclined to help you. We're not supposed to use the stuff for personal vengeance, only for political and military advantage. But if you can wipe out the whole leadership…well, that's about as political as you can get. This stuff is stronger than the old nerve gases, or so I'm told. About thirty times stronger. It's an American improvement. Americans are always making things better, aren't they? It's compressed into small containers. Open one and it rushes out, howling like one of those new jet planes coming right at you. You know how it kills?"

"Yes."

"It's not a pleasant death."

"No."

"Why are you doing it? I suppose it's Marya, what they did to her."

"Yes."

"All those millions of dead, and the torture of one Cossack woman drives you to this."

"Yes. You know, she never betrayed me."

"In *The House of the Dead* Dostoevsky said, 'The people know how to suffer.' *She* knew how to suffer."

"Yes. Give me the stuff and let me go."

He stood up then and kissed me. I've never gotten used to this Russian custom. "May God receive you. I'm a Communist, and I shouldn't say things like that. But what the hell, when you find somebody who's decent, you have to treat him decently. Life isn't a walk across a field for any of us."

"No. *Pozhal'sta*, give me the stuff and let me go."

And so he did—a yellow cylinder about forty centimeters long, easily concealed. Obviously designed for use by terrorists. I have a thermos bottle that'll hold it nicely, if I remove the glass lining. I tried it in my new attaché case, and it fits.

To make room for it I had to take out this journal. "What's that?" the Ataman asked.

"Secrets the world may want to know. Or may not, I don't care. I want to make a last entry, about this meeting. It'll take me only a few minutes."

He nodded, and I sat down on the log beside him and began to write. Once I looked up and he was eyeing me oddly.

"What's wrong?"

"Just wondering what you've got to smile about."

I tried to tell him, but couldn't. To understand, he'd have to be here in this place where my soul stands at last. So close to the end, so close to the beginning.

A finely crafted tale of brotherly love and hate. What does it really mean to be undead? The answer comes with a bloody sword and disturbing psychological insight.

TWILIGHT STATES

ADUSTY SHOP WINDOW, a darkening street outside. Streetlights winking on at three o'clock. A summer storm brewing. Milton's reflection—dim, bent, somehow older than his fifty-two years— stared at him through backward lettering that said *Sun & Moon Metaphysical Books*.

He sighed and flipped the pages of his desk calendar. June 1979 was drawing to an end. Could he afford to close for the day? A customer might yet be driven in by the threat of rain. . . .

As if summoned, the doorbell jangled and a fat old man carrying a furled umbrella erupted into the shop. He strode to a bookcase, browsed for a moment, then snatched down a faded red volume.

"Why d'you stock a fool like Montague Summers?" he boomed.

"Because he s-sells," Milton answered.

Why the stutter? He hadn't stuttered for years. Decades, maybe. Then he knew why: he'd heard that voice before.

"A superstitious Jesuit who thought vampires were real," the intruder was grumbling. "I'm a scientist myself.... Somebody told me you stock old science fiction."

Milton took a deep breath. "Like *Weird Tales, Astounding, Arcana?*"

"That's it. *Arcana.*"

He drew out a ring of keys and unlocked a cabinet. "You're a collector?"

"No. I read for pleasure. And professional interest."

Milton explained that *Arcana* lasted only twenty issues, from mid-1941 until wartime scarcities of paper and ink shut it down. Yet in its brief lifespan it published everybody—big names, promising unknowns.

"Do you have the January '42 issue?"

Milton took another deep breath and offered a flawless copy in its plastic jacket.

"Of course it's pricey. But very rare."

"I'll take it," said the fat man, paying two hundred dollars for a pulp magazine thirty-seven years old. The check he wrote identified him as Erasmus Bloch, M.D., and gave his address and phone number.

The name too rang a bell. An alarm bell, maybe? Yet this was a customer Milton wanted to keep.

"This issue's got a bit of history attached to it," he said, wrapping the package. "My brother Ned was a World War Two hero—Navy Cross—and he got this *Arcana* just about the time of Pearl Harbor. He volunteered so quickly that he never had a chance to read it."

Actually, Milton had bought the copy (and a dozen others) at a newsstand on Royal Street. But people liked pricey purchases to come with a legend.

"Your brother," came that loud, abrupt voice. "Is he still alive?"

Instantly Milton's stutter resurfaced. "No. He was m-murdered. After the war. T-terribly."

Even Bloch seemed to realize he'd put a heavy thumb on an old wound. He touched Milton's bony shoulder with a hand like a flipper.

"This copy will be treasured," he said.

An instant later, the bell jangled, his umbrella deployed with a snap, and the door clicked shut behind him.

Milton folded his arms tight against his concave chest. How could you?

he silently berated himself. How could you say so much to a stranger? Worse yet, to somebody who may not be a stranger at all?

By now the French Quarter was adrift in rain. Gutters spouted like whales and ankle-deep water washed the streets clean of tourists. No more customers today.

Milton locked the shop and climbed a circular staircase to his living quarters on the second floor. At the top he paused, wheezing. The hall was deep in shadow and rain streamed down the only window. Four closed doors stood in a row: his parents' bedroom, Ned's, his own, and the bath. Something scratched at Ned's door with a sound like a wire brush.

"It's all right," said Milton. "Don't you be worried. I'm not."

In his room he took off his shoes, stretched out on the bed, and flicked on an old brass lamp. Erasmus, Erasmus. Odd name. Now where—?

In search of an elusive memory, his eyes traveled over the yellow walls, the scarred plaster, the heavy purple furniture, the wall clock missing its pendulum. But no memory came.

Rain drummed on the balcony and rattled the wooden shutters. Gradually Milton's breathing became regular, and sleep fell on him like a coverlet.

He began to dream. Ralph O'Meagan, aged ten, lay in bed listening to his mother curse his father. She was out of the hospital again, and as usual the drying-out treatment hadn't worked for long. She was drinking, and the drunker she got the more she tried to fight with her silent husband, and the more he ignored her the sorrier she felt for herself and the more she drank.

Ralph suffered from nightmares and his parents allowed him to keep a nightlight burning. He lay on his side staring at the wall, at the scars and bumps in the old yellow plaster. *"Why don't you SAY something?"* He concentrated, doing magic, knowing that when his eyes grew tired the wall would seem to move. *"You miserable BASTARD!"*

It was stirring now. Wavering, rippling like a broad flag stirred by a light wind. Then it bellied out like a sail.

Startled, he closed his eyes. Looked again through his lashes. The wall was swollen and straining. When he tried to will it back, it burst in a soundless explosion, flinging sparks in every direction.

The dazzle faded. Ralph was lying on a wet field of grass and reeds. He felt the damp and the cold through his PJs. His breath came quickly and he could hear the beating of his heart.

Bewildered, he sat up, shivering in a raw wind. The sky was blue dusk except for one smear of red in the west and a dim moon rising in the east. Far away, he saw a roller coaster's snaky form outlined in lights. A calliope hooted a popular tune of 1948, "The Anniversary Waltz."

Something scratched and snorted and he turned his head. No more than ten yards away, a giant wild boar was digging at the grass. Its flat bristly nostrils blew puffs of smoke; it braced its thick legs, pulled with orange tusks, and a human arm lifted into view. The fingers moved feebly—

Milton sat up, sweating.

He was safe in his own bed, in his own room where he'd slept all his life. Rain pattered against the shutters. And Ralph O'Meagan was back where and when he belonged, in the January '42 issue of *Arcana*, his name forever attached to an intense and disturbing transdimensional story called "Border-land."

The wire-brush sound came again from Ned's room next door, and Milton muttered, "I told you it's all right."

He got up stiffly, put his shoes on and shuffled downstairs. In a small kitchen behind the bookshop he made green tea on a hot plate and inserted a frozen dinner into a dirty microwave oven.

He sat down at a metal-topped table, sipping the tea, and listened to the fan droning in the microwave. He had no way to avoid thinking about Ned, and about himself.

They'd shared Mama's fair coloring, sharp nose, and prominent chin, but not much else.

The product of an earlier marriage, Ned was a bully and a braggart, a fanatic athlete with an appetite for contact sports. Feared in grade school, worshipped in high school. Milton lived in terror of him, never knowing from day to day whether Ned would use him as a playmate or a punching bag.

Early on, Ned demanded and got a separate room so he wouldn't have to live with The Drip. He warned Milton not to talk to him at school, because he didn't want anybody to know they were related. Ned's door sported a poster of a soldier in a tin helmet and a gas mask. A hand-lettered sign said *POISON! KEEP OUT!*

"I ever catch you in my stuff," Ned warned him, "I'll fix you a knuckle sandwich. You hear that, Drip?"

What was Ned hiding? On December 1, 1941—Milton was an obscure freshman in Jesuit High School, Ned a prominent senior—thinking Ned was out, he fitted a skeleton key into the old-fashioned lock and went exploring.

The yellow walls were exactly like those in his own room, only stuck all over with movie posters of Humphrey Bogart and Edward G. Robinson looking tough. On Ned's desk, athletic trophies towered over a litter of papers and schoolbooks. Magazines—fantasy, sport, muscle, mystery—lay scattered over the rumpled bed.

Not knowing what he wanted to find, Milton began pawing through papers, opening desk drawers. He was still at work when the door crashed against the wall and Ned erupted into the room.

The memory lingered after almost forty years. Milton stopped sipping his tea and ran his fingertips over his ribs, touching the little lumps where cracked bones had healed. He shivered, reliving his terror as Ned's big hands pounded him.

"God damn you, you fucking punk," he bawled, "keep outta here! Keep outta here!"

The boy Milton had hunkered down, trying to shield his face—that was when his ribs took the pounding—and waited for death. But Ned was fighting himself, too. His face and whole body twisted as he tried to regain control.

Milton slipped under his arm and ran away and locked himself in his room, sobbing with rage and shame. Little by little the sparks of acute pain died out and a slow dull throbbing began in his chest, shoulders, arms, face. Blood soaked his undershirt and he tore it off and threw it away.

Later, when Daddy asked him what had happened to him—most of his injuries were hidden by his clothes, but Milton was walking stiffly and sporting a plum-sized black eye and a swollen jaw—he said he'd fallen downstairs at school.

"Clumsy goddamn kid," said Daddy.

By then Pearl Harbor had happened and Daddy was signing papers so that Ned could volunteer for the Navy. "One less mouth to feed," remarked Mr. Warmth.

Ned vanished into the alternate dimension that people called The Service, and Mama locked up his room, saying it must be kept just as he left it or he'd never return alive.

"Crazy bitch," said Daddy, whose comments were usually terse and always predictable.

Night after night for weeks afterward, Milton opened his window, slipped out onto the cold balcony that connected the three bedrooms, lifted the latch on Ned's shutters with a kitchen knife, and silently raised the sash.

One at a time he took Ned's trophies, wrapped them in old newspapers, and put them out with the trash. He threw away Ned's magazines, books, and posters.

He was hoping that Mama was right and Ned would never return. He hoped the Japs would capture him and torture him. He hoped Ned would fall into the ocean and be eaten by sharks. The depth of his loathing surprised even him, and he treasured it as a lover savors his love.

Then he received Ned's first letter. "Hi, Bro!" it started breezily.

Ned told about the weird people he was meeting in the Navy, about the icy wind blowing off the Great Lakes, about learning to operate a burp gun. Milton read the letter dozens, maybe hundreds of times.

More letters came on tissue-paper V-Mail, the APOs migrating westward to San Diego, then to Hawaii. Ned told about the great fleets gathering in Pearl Harbor for the counterpunch against Japan, about the deafening bombardment of Tarawa before the Marines went in. Gifts began arriving for Milton, handfuls of Japanese paper money, a rising-sun flag, a Samurai short sword.

Why had Ned turned from a domestic monster to a brother? Milton never knew. Maybe the war, maybe the presence of death. As the fighting darkened and lengthened, he could see something of the same spirit touching them all.

Mama went to work for the Red Cross and stayed sober until evening. Daddy took the Samurai short sword and hung it over the fireplace in the living room, where everybody could see it. When Ned sent Mama the Navy Cross he'd won, Daddy sat beside her on the sofa, staring at the medal in its little leather box as if a star had fallen from heaven. That was when he stopped calling Ned "my wife's kid" and started calling him "my son."

In the summer of 1945 Ned himself arrived at the naval air station on Lake Pontchartrain. Broad-shouldered and burned mahogany, he burst upon their lives like a bomb blowing down a wall and letting sunlight pour in.

He ordered Mama to stop drinking, and she put her bottles out with the trash. He ordered Daddy to stop insulting her, and he obeyed. At the first sign of backsliding, Ned would fly into one of his patented rages and his parents would hurry back into line. He was still a bully—only now he controlled his chronic abiding fury and used it for good.

Did hatred really lie so close to love? Could God and the devil swap places so easily? Apparently so.

Now Milton loved him and wanted desperately to be like him. An impossible job, of course. But he tried. Out of sheer hero-worship he decided to volunteer for the peacetime Navy and began going to the Y, trying to get in shape for boot camp. The new Ned didn't laugh at his belated efforts to be athletic. Instead, he went running with him at six in the morning, down the Public Belt railroad tracks along the wharves, among the wild daisies, while a great incandescent sun rose and a rank, fresh wind blew off the Father of Waters.

Life seemed to be brightening for all of them. Who could have guessed it would all go so terribly wrong?

Next day Dr. Bloch dropped by the shop to tell Milton how much he'd enjoyed reading *Arcana*.

"I love pulp," he confessed. "I like the energy, the violence, the fact that there's always a resolution. The one thing in *The New Yorker* I never read is the fiction."

They chatted cautiously, like strange dogs sniffing each other. Bloch explained he'd retired from practice but still did a little consulting at St. Vincent's, the mental hospital where both of Milton's parents had been patients.

"You're a psychiatrist?" asked Milton, astonished. Bloch was so noisy and intrusive that he wondered how the man got anyone to confide in him.

"The technical term is shrink," Bloch boomed. "I suppose it's all right to say this now. Your brother was a patient of mine long ago. Somebody who knows I'm a fan of old sf told me about your shop, and as soon as I saw your face it all came back. You're very like him, you know."

Milton sat open-mouthed, while—like some cinematic effect—the lines of a younger face emerged from the old man's spots, creases and wattles. How could he have missed it? Dr. Erasmus Bloch was *Dr. Erasmus Bloch*.

"When did you treat Ned?" he asked, his voice unsteady.

"In forty-eight, I think. Gave him a checkup first, naturally. Well set-up young fellow. Athletic. No physical problems at all."

"Was he...ah...."

"Psychotic? No. But he was hallucinating, and of course he was scared. We ruled out a brain tumor, drug use, and alcoholism—I don't think he drank at all—"

"No. Because of our mother. I'm the same way. So what was wrong?"

"He was terribly unhappy. He'd grown up isolated, with a drunken mother and a rigid, cold, possibly schizoid father. He had violent impulses that he found hard to control. Frankly, he scared me a bit. These borderline cases can be much more dangerous than the certified screwballs. And he was *strong*, you know?"

"Yes," said Milton, "I remember.... You said he was hallucinating?"

"Yes. Quite an interesting case. He believed his frustration and rage had turned him into a god or demon that had created a world. He'd written a story about it, and he loaned me a copy of *Arcana* so I could read it. Matter of fact, I read it again just last night."

Milton nodded. "I've known for years that Ned wrote the story. But I never imagined he thought the—what did he call it? the Alternate Dimension—was real. I mean . . . it's hard to believe he was serious."

"Oh, he was serious, all right. I knew that when I saw the name he'd signed to his story."

"Ralph O'Meagan?"

"It's the closest Ned could come to Alpha Omega. You know, as in *Revelations*: 'I am the Alpha and Omega, the beginning and the end.' Yes, he actually believed he was a god and he'd made a world."

That was a riveting insight. Milton wondered why he'd never seen it himself. His breath came quicker; this was turning out to be the most involving conversation he'd had in decades.

"How do you treat something like that?"

"One technique for dissolving a delusional system is to move into it with the patient. It's such a private thing, it disintegrates when he finds another person inside it. So I told Ned, 'I want to hear more about this world of yours. Perhaps I can go there with you.'

"Something about that scared him. He skipped our next appointment. My nurse tried to call him, but it turned out he'd given her a wrong number. When she looked him up in the phone book, he claimed he'd never heard of me. Sounded as if he really hadn't. Might have been stress-induced amnesia—rather a radical form of denial."

"Yes," murmured Milton. "That does sound radical."

Bloch glanced at his watch, said he was due at the hospital and took his leave. Milton sat for a few minutes hugging his midsection, then got up and locked the door.

This wasn't his regular day to dust Ned's bedroom, but he went upstairs anyway, for the terrible past had taken him in its grip.

His key chain jangled and he sensed something beyond the door as the key turned silently in the well-oiled lock. But the shadowy room held only a faintly sour organic smell.

He opened the window, unbolted the shutters and flung them wide. Light flooded in. The room looked just as it had the week before Christmas 1945, when Ned had thrown his second-to-last tantrum and stormed out of the house.

Milton hadn't actually witnessed it, but he heard about it later. Ned went into a fury because Mama, possibly in honor of the season, had disobeyed his orders and started drinking again. After he walked out, of course, she drank more. Milton came home carrying an armful of presents to find her staggering, and Ned forever gone.

God, how he'd hated him that day. Tearing out the underpinnings of his life just when he'd begun to be happy.

On the dresser stood a mirror where Ned had combed his hair, and a tarnished silver frame with a faded picture of him as a young sailor wearing a jaunty white cap. Ned was smiling a fake photographic smile, but his eyes didn't smile. Neither did Milton's as he approached and stared at him.

His face hovered in the mirror, Ned's in the picture. Youth and decay: Dorian Gray in reverse. Suddenly feeling an intolerable upsurge of rage, he growled at the picture, "You were such a lousy stinking bastard."

That was only the beginning. Grinding his teeth, he cursed the picture with every word he'd ever learned from chief petty officers and drunks brawling on Bourbon Street and his own unforgiving heart.

Exhausted by the eruption, trembling, clutching his ribs, Milton staggered back and sat down suddenly on the bed. Little by little he calmed down. After ten minutes he stood up and carefully smoothed the bedspread.

"Time to open the shop again," he said in a quiet voice.

He closed Ned's room and locked it, knowing it would be here when he came again, exactly as it was, never changing, never to be changed. The love and hate of his life, shut up in one timeless capsule.

The afternoon brought few customers, the following morning fewer still.

Milton filled the empty hours as he always did, sitting at his desk with his hollow chest collapsed in upon itself, taking rare and slow and shallow breaths, like a hibernating bear. Musing, dreaming, rearranging the pieces of his life like a chessplayer with no opponent, pushing wood idly on the same old squares.

How much he wanted to put his family into a gothic novel. How often he'd tried to write it, but never could. He smiled ruefully, thinking: *Where are you, Ralph O'Meagan, when I need you?*

All around him, stacked shelf on shelf, stood haunted books full of demons and starships, the horrors of Dunwich and Poe's Conqueror Worm. But none held the story he longed to tell. He smiled wearily at a dusty print hanging on the wall—Dalí's "The Persistence of Memory," with its limp watches.

He knew now why people talked to noisy Dr. Bloch. It was quite simple: they needed to talk, and he was willing to listen. Shortly after eleven o'clock, Milton dug out his customer file and called Bloch's number. It turned out to belong to a posh retirement home called Serena House.

"This is God's waiting room," the loud voice explained, and Milton moved the phone an inch away from his ear. "God's *first-class* waiting room. Want to join me for lunch?"

Milton found himself stuttering again as he accepted. He locked up, fetched his old Toyota from a garage he rented and drove up St. Charles Avenue to Marengo Street. The block turned out to be one of those odd corners of the city where time had stopped around 1890. The houses were old paintless wooden barns, most wearing thick mats of cat's-claw vine like dusty habits.

But in their midst sat a new and massive square structure of faux stone with narrow lancet windows. Serena House was a thoroughly up-to-date antechamber to the tomb. After speaking to the concierge—a cool young blonde—Milton waited in a patio that was pure Motel Modern: cobalt pool, palms in large plastic pots, metal lawn furniture, concrete frogs and bunnies and a nymph eternally emptying water from an urn.

"You see what you have to look forward to," boomed Bloch, and they shook hands.

"I can't afford Serena House. Don't you think my shop's a nice place for an old guy to dream away his days?"

"Yes, provided a wall doesn't blow in on you!"

Bloch, that impressively tactless man, laughed loudly at his own wit while leading the way to the dining room. The chairs were ivory-enameled with rose upholstery and the walls were festive with French paper. By tacit agreement, they said nothing about Ned until the crème brûlée had been polished off.

Instead they talked sci-fi and fantasy. Milton found Bloch a man of wide reading. He knew the classics by Cyrano and Voltaire, Poe and Carroll and Stoker and Wells. He'd read Huxley's and Forster's ventures into the field. He declared that *Faust* and the *Divine Comedy* were also fantasy masterpieces—epic attempts to make ideas real.

"Because that's what fantasy is, isn't it?" he demanded. "Not just making things up, but taking ideas and giving them hands and feet and claws and teeth!"

After lunch they moved to poolside. Bloch lit a cigar that smelled expensive and resumed grilling Milton. "Your brother—did he die in the room where the story was set?"

He had a gift for asking unexpected questions. Milton cleared his throat, hesitated, then evaded—neatly, he thought—saying where Ned actually did die.

"No. He was found in the marshland out near the lake, about a quarter of a mile from that old amusement park on the shore."

"Any idea what he was doing there?"

"The police thought he'd been killed elsewhere and dumped. I wasn't much help to them—hadn't seen Ned in years. Actually, we'd been on bad terms, and that was sad."

"And your parents…what happened to them?"

"Mama drank herself to death. Daddy went senile. Alzheimer's, they'd call it today. He died in St. Vincent's. I got a call one night, and this very firm Negro voice said, 'Your Dad, he ain't got no life signs.' I said, 'You mean he's dead?' 'We ain't 'lowed to use that word,' said the voice. 'He ain't got no life signs is all.'

"'That's okay,' I said. 'He never did.'"

Bloch smiled a bit grimly, exhaled a puff of blue smoke. "Tell me…exactly what killed Ned?"

Milton took a deep breath. He'd left himself open to such probing, and now had no way to evade an answer.

"Hard to say. He was such a mess by the time they found him. It was November, nineteen-forty-eight. The—the damage to his face and body was devastating. There was a nick in one thoracic vertebra that possibly indicated a knife thrust through the chest. But the coroner couldn't be sure—so much of him had been eaten—there were toothmarks on a lot of the bones…."

"Eaten by what?"

Milton squinted at the cobalt pool. Sunstarts on the ripples burned his eyes. He said, "The c-coroner said wild pigs. Razorbacks. The m-marshes were full of them."

Bloch's little pouchy eyes gleamed with interest.

"Amazing. The monster in his story was a wild boar. You're saying he wrote the story in nineteen-forty-one, and seven years later actual wild pigs mutilated his body?"

When Milton didn't answer, Bloch said soberly, "You seem to have lived a Gothic novel, my friend."

"I was thinking the same thing this morning," Milton said, getting up to go. "You know, you're filling your own prescription, Dr. Bloch. You're moving into the fantasy."

"Good Lord," said he, knocking the ash off his cigar as he rose. "I hope not."

By the time he reached the shop, Milton was finding his own behavior incredible. After decades of silence, he couldn't believe the things he'd been saying—to Bloch, of all people.

He was confused as well, angry and fearful yet not sure exactly what he was afraid of. Sitting slumped at his desk, he worked it out.

There was the practical danger, of course. But beyond that lay a meta-physical peril: that he might somehow lose his world. *It's such a private thing*, Bloch had said, *it disintegrates when another person moves into it.*

Rising, Milton unlocked his cabinet and took out a second copy of the January '42 *Arcana*. Six others reposed in the same place, awaiting buyers. He put on white cotton gloves to protect the old brittle pages, and began leafing through them. The words of Ralph O'Meagan were an echo of long ago.

For many long weeks I lived in trembling fear of the night, when I would have to go to my room and see the lamplight on that wall. For now I knew that the world called real is an illusion of lighted surfaces and the resonances of touch, while underneath surges immortal and impalpable Energy, ever ready to create or kill.

There was no possible way of explaining to my father why I should sleep anywhere else, and no way of explaining anything to my mother at all. I tried to sleep without the nightlight, only to find that I feared the demons of the dark even more than those of the light.

Yet I grew tired of waiting and watching for something that never happened, and as time went by I began to persuade myself that what I'd seen that one time was, after all, a mere nightmare, such as I often had.

I was sound asleep, some three or four weeks after my first visit to the Alternate Dimension, when something tickling my face caused me to awaken. At first I had absolutely no sense of fear or dread. Then I felt a prickling on my face and hands like the "pins and needles" sensation when a foot has been asleep— and a memory stirred.

Reluctantly I opened my eyes. I was lying as before in that field of dying grass. One coarse stem was rubbing against my nose; other stems probed my hands and bare feet.

I raised my head and saw the great beast once again. This time I waited until it had finished its horrible meal and had turned away, like an animal well satisfied and ready for sleep.

Trembling, I stood up. I was soaked and shivering and felt as cold and empty as the boar was warm and full. I approached the body it had been mutilating, and it was that of a grown man, with something intolerably familiar about its face—for the face remained: remained, frozen into its last rictus of agony: and I knew that the face one day would be mine.

Milton closed the magazine. Poor Ralph O'Meagan. Poor Alpha Omega. Caught in an eddy of the time process, condemned to return again and again to the same place to undergo the same death and mutilation.

The Alternate Dimension was not the past and not the future. Ralph was encountering Forever.

How extraordinary, Milton thought, that a fourteen-year-old boy should have such ideas and write them so well and then live mute forever afterward. But fourteen, that's the age of discovery, isn't it? Of sexual awakening? Of sudden insights into your fate that you spend the rest of your life trying to understand?

And that rhetoric about immortal and impalpable Energy—was it mere adolescent rubbish? An early symptom of madness? Or a revelation of truth?

That night his sleep was restless. Bloch kept intruding into his dreams, with spotty face thrust forward and eyes staring. Their dialogue resumed, and soon the dream Bloch was breaking into areas the real one hadn't yet imagined.

—*That's what happened, isn't it?* accused the loud metallic voice. *You killed Ned, didn't you?*

—*Christ. Well, yes. I didn't mean to.*

—*No, of course not.*

—*I didn't!*

—*Oh, I think there was a lot of hatred there, plus a lot of rather unbrotherly love. And I don't think you're a forgiving type. . . . How'd you do it, anyway?*

—*With a samurai short sword he'd sent me from the Pacific. When he came at me I snatched it off the living room wall and ran it into his chest. Or he did. I mean, he was the one in motion. I was just holding the sword, trying to fend him off. Really.*

—*Why'd he attack you?*

—*He was in one of his rages. It was late at night. Mama was dead and Daddy was in the hospital. I was out of the Navy and living here alone when Ned came bursting into the house, roaring. He'd found out I'd been going to a shrink and using his name instead of my own.*

—*Why'd you do a thing like that?*

—*I was afraid. It was 1948 and people could be committed a lot more easily than they can today. I was afraid I was going crazy and you'd have me put away. It was a dumb trick, but I thought I could find out what was happening to me without running such a risk.*

—*Ah. Now we're getting at it. So you and Ned had your second big fight and—*

—*Just like the first time, he won.*

—*How could he, if you killed him?*

—He only died. I died but went on living. He became one of the dead but I became one of the undead.
—Oh, Lord. Not Montague Summers again.
—Yes. Montague Summers again.

Milton woke up. The clock said 4:20. He got up anyway, and made tea. Except for one light the shop was dark, the books in shadow, all their tales of horror and discovery in suspended animation, like a freeze-frame in a movie.

Milton drank green tea, and slowly two images, the dream Bloch and the real one, overlapped in his mind and fused together. What he'd discovered in the dream, the real fat noisy old Bloch would discover in time—the pushy devil.

So, Milton thought. *I'll have to get rid of him, too.*

He added *too* because over the last three decades there had been other people who seemed to threaten him. He no longer remembered just how many.

Bathed, breakfasted, his long strands of sparse hair neatly combed across his skull, Milton opened his shop as usual at ten. Just before noon Bloch came in, puffing, intruding with his big belly, shaking his veinous wattles.

"'Welcome to my house!'" Milton quoted, smiling. "'Enter freely, and of your own will!'"

Bloch chuckled appreciatively. "Thank you, Count."

"That was a fine lunch yesterday," Milton went on warmly, "and the talk was even better than the food."

As usual, they chatted about books. Bloch had been reading an old text from the early days of psychoanalysis, Schwarzwalder's *Somnambulismus und Dämmerzustände*—somnambulism and twilight states. To doctors of the Viennese school, he explained, somnambulism didn't mean literal sleep-walking but rather dissociated consciousness, a transient doubling of the personality.

"Those old boys had something to say," Bloch boomed. "They believed in the reality of the mind. Modern psychiatrists don't. Today it's all drugs, drugs, drugs."

So, thought Milton, Bloch had been analyzing him. He said, "As long as you're here, would you like to see Ned's room? I've kept it exactly as it was when he was alive."

Bloch was enthusiastic. "Indeed I would. I wasn't able to help him, and I seem to remember my failures more than my successes."

"Success always moves on to the next thing," Milton agreed, as Bloch trailed him up the circular stair. "But failure's timeless, isn't it? Failure is forever."

Upstairs the hall was clean and bright, with the sun reflecting through the patio window. There was no sound behind Ned's door.

Bloch stopped to catch his breath, then asked, "I'm invited in here too? Otherwise I wouldn't intrude, you know"—carrying on the Dracula bit in his heavy-handed way.

Smiling, Milton unlocked the door and bowed him in. He opened the window and the shutters, and suddenly the room was full of light. The young sailor's face grinned fixedly from the picture frame, and Bloch approached it, eager as a collector catching sight of a moth he'd missed the last time.

"Ah," he said. "Yes, I remember. He looked a lot like this thirty years ago, when I treated him. Or—"

He paused, confused. Milton had come up behind him and looked over his shoulder. Frowning, Bloch stared at the picture, then at the reflection, then at the picture again. It was the first time he'd seen the brothers together.

"You never really knew Ned, did you?" Milton asked.

"But the man I saw—the one who came for treatment—he was built like an athlete—"

"I spent more than two years in the Navy before they Section-Eighted me. It was the only time in my life I was ever in shape."

That was another bit of news for Bloch to absorb, and for the first time Milton heard him stutter a little.

"And the, ah, r-reason for your d-discharge—"

"Oh, the usual. 'Psychotic.' As far as I could see, the word meant only that they didn't know what they were dealing with. At that time, neither did I."

"The story... you wrote it?"

"Have you ever known an athlete who could write, or a bookworm who didn't want to?"

"And the things you told me about Ned—"

"Were true. But of course about me. Hasn't it occurred to you that Ned discharged his rage while I buried mine deep? That if there was a maniac in the family, it was far more likely to be me? What kind of a lousy doctor are you, anyway?"

Despite the harsh words his voice was eerily tranquil, and he smiled when Bloch turned his head to see how far he was from the door.

Then he turned back, staring at Milton's bent and narrow frame, and his thoughts might as well have been written on his face. *This bag of bones— what do I have to fear from him?*

Suddenly his voice boomed out. "Ralph O'Meagan, I'm delighted to make your acquaintance at last!"

He stretched out his fat hand and as he did the yellow wall bellied out and burst, blowing away the room and the whole illusion of the world called real.

Gaping, letting his hand drop nervelessly, Bloch stared now at the smudge of fire in the west, now at the rising moon in the east.

A raw wind blew; delighted shrieks echoed from the roller coaster; the calliope was hooting, and Milton hummed along: *Oh, how we danced on the night we were wed—*

"Welcome to my world," he said, standing back.

Swift trotters were drumming on the earth and splashing in the pools and Bloch whirled as the huge humpbacked beast came at him out of the sunset, smoke jetting from its nostrils, small red eyes glinting like sardonyx.

"What did I do?" Bloch cried, waving his fat hands. "I wanted to help! What did I do?"

The boar struck his fat belly with lethal impact and his lungs exploded like balloons. He lived for a few minutes, writhing, while it delved into his guts. Milton leaned forward, hugging himself, breathlessly watching.

The scene was elemental. Timeless. The beast rooting and grunting, the sunset light unchanging, cries of joy from the roller coaster, and the calliope hooting on: *Could we but relive that sweet moment divine/We'd find that our love is unaltered by time.*

"Now you're really part of the fantasy," he assured Dr. Bloch.

Not that Bloch heard him. Or anything else.

Life returned to normal in *Sun & Moon Metaphysical Books* where, of course, things were never totally normal.

Milton's days went by as before, opening the shop, chatting with the occasional customer, closing it again. Drowsy days spent amid the smell of old books, a smell whose color, if it had a color, would be brownish gray.

Serena House called to inquire about their lodger—Dr. Bloch had left Milton's number when he went out. Milton expressed astonishment over the disappearance, offered any help he could give. Next day a bored policewoman from Missing Persons arrived to take a statement. Milton described how Bloch had visited the shop, chatted, and left.

"He was one of my best customers," he said. "Any idea what might have happened to him?"

"Nothing yet," said the cop, closing her notebook. "It's kind of like Judge Crater."

More than you know, thought Milton. Where Bloch's bones lay it was always 1948, and whole neighborhoods had been built over the spot, a palimpsest of fill and tarmac and buildings raised, razed and raised again. Milton's voice was confident and strong and totally without a stutter as he chatted with the policewoman, and he could see she believed what he told her.

After she left, the afternoon was dull as usual. Around four Milton got up from his desk and took down his copy of Montague Summers's *The Vampire in Europe*. He hefted it, did not open it, put it back on the shelf and addressed its author aloud.

"Reverend Summers, you're a fool. Thinking the undead drink blood. No, we suck such life as we have from rage and memories. It must be a nourishing diet, because we live on. And on. And on. And on. I knew that when I wrote my story."

An hour later, after closing the shop, he entered Ned's room and for a time stood gazing into the mirror. The sun was going down. As the room darkened, he heard the unseen beast rubbing its nap of stiff hair against the wall and smelled the morning-breath odor of unfresh blood that always attended it.

Was it something or somebody? Was it his creature, or himself? Did he dream its world, or did it dream his? Milton brooded, asking himself unanswerable questions while his image faded slowly into the brown shadows, until the glass held nothing, nothing at all.

Stormy times on the Redneck Riviera rendered in a serious and moving tale where—at immense cost to itself—love triumphs over death.

GREY STAR

W HAT A DAY! Sarah thought as she passed through the gilded doors of the Win or Lose Casino into the buzz and flicker of a blazing neon marquee.

Waiting for Burke to bring the car, she paced back and forth on a concrete apron covered with crimson carpeting. The night had turned restless. Rain had fallen; the carpet was sopping and pools on the causeway were reflecting the frenzy of the lights.

Gusts of warm wind off the Gulf of Mexico fanned her short-cut blonde hair, and she brushed it back with one hand—capable, strong, no polish on the nails—a workman's hand, only smaller. Raising her head to emphasize her long smooth neck, thrusting her big bosom just a bit forward, she posed unconsciously, like a cat, not to make others look at her but to fulfill her own image of herself.

At the other end of the causeway, a thousand lighted windows outlined the Hotel Grandview, and her thoughts slipped back to the morning, the dim beige light of a room where she'd had some really, *really* good sex with Burke. How did Mae West put it—a hard man is good to find?

She had so many memories of him; when she was alone she fingered them like a miser counting coins.

Their first meeting in the ER of the New Orleans Hospital Center. It was the first day of her residency in emergency medicine and she was, let's face it, scared to death when a male patient, for no visible reason, started turning blue. Burke was passing by, and without a word grabbed a breathing tube and slid it down the guy's throat through the epiglottis into the trachea with one deft turn of the wrist. Then gave her a wink, and moved off about his duties.

And what profound thought had passed through Sarah's mind? *I've heard that forty percent of male nurses are gay. Does that mean that sixty percent of them aren't?* Even today, she felt rueful about that. Banality didn't go with her image of herself.

The Saab pulled up. Burke's broad freckled face grinned at her and she jumped in.

"Be raining like hell later on," he opined.

"Well, take I-10. It's the quickest."

"Uh-uh," he said. "Driving that goddamn road would put me to sleep fast."

True, the interstate was hypnotic, a concrete arrow flying through a tunnel of pines. But Sarah frowned. She liked to think she hated the hospital caste system, with docs issuing orders to RNs like Burke who knew more than they did. In fact, she issued orders even at home in their condo, and was always somewhat shocked when he ignored them.

What had her therapist warned her against—letting her free-floating anxiety turn her into a control freak? Believing nobody could do anything properly unless she told them how? With some effort, she took a deep breath, composed her cameo profile that she kept ivory-pale, even on the beach, with layers of sunblock.

Outward calm defends against inward impulse. Right.

A strong gust struck and the car shimmied, the tires squeaking a little. A tremor also ran through the causeway, as if the Las Vegas outfit that built the casino hadn't been up on the problems of construction on an oozy continental shelf. But Burke, driving as usual with two strong stubby fingers, seemed to control the car without effort.

At the end of the causeway a red light had gotten stuck. Creeping past was the impacted traffic of the Strip, a slow river of steel and lights. Burke flashed his grin at a startled driver in the eastbound lane, slipped between two SUVs, touched the brake to let an eighteen-wheeler thunder past, spun the wheel, slid into an opening only a bit longer than the car—and there they were, heading west.

"How do you *do* that?" Sarah demanded, but got only a wink in return.

God, the man lives by his reflexes, she thought. How odd of me to fall in love with an animal—I don't think he thinks at all. Even sitting still he radiated energy, and she relaxed, warming herself at the fire.

Ignoring garish lights, a patter of rain, Tom drifted through the empty halls and emptier rooms of the Grey Star Hotel. The Sun & Buns Motel existed in a perpetual glare of neon, and chains of reflected light from the swimming pool danced across shadowy walls and ceilings.

He made a conscious effort not to hate the squealing kids and their beefy parents, taking a final dip before bedtime. After all, he'd been a kid here too—though it was a long, long time ago.

Daddy owned the Star, and Tom couldn't remember a time when he hadn't played and worked here. When he was eight or nine years old, he'd been earning nickels running errands for seersucker-clad gents who sat in green rocking chairs on the downstairs gallery. They called him Short Stuff and wanted lemonades brought to them, or juleps, or cigarettes, or matches; their wives sat beside them, wearing wide straw hats and summer dresses of pale linen. The ladies wanted things too, only they called him Honey and usually didn't tip him at all.

In those days people swam in the Gulf, not in chlorinated pools, and the water wasn't polluted, or if it was it didn't seem to bother anybody. Summer began in May, and by June Tom's initial sunburn had peeled off. By July he was brown as a pecan shell and living like an amphibian—half-in, half-out of the water every day. Christ, he could still smell those days, half briny water, half piney woods. Pale heat haze gathered on the horizon, grasshoppers chirruped in the brown grass, mirages danced on the white roads.

At night when the Gulf was smooth as mercury under a summer moon, Daddy put him to work carrying pitchers of ice water up the long curving stairs. He remembered the hot little rooms, the black electric fans rattling and turning, men lolling in their BVDs and handing out more nickels that felt greasy, passing from one sweaty palm to another. And the women, in straining bras or filmy nighties, with no bras at all. . . .

Meals had been serious rituals—breakfasts with the sweet toasty smell of pancakes and bitter black steam from the big silver coffeepots, the waiters hefting trays with dishes under silver covers, the chink and rattle of metal and china competing with the hum of conversation and the muted roar of cyclone fans. Ample luncheons, spread out on long tables, and more ample dinners. The business of calling in Rotunda, the cook—yes, her name really was Rotunda, and she lived up to it—to take credit for the meal.

He remembered her standard joke, kept in reserve for the inevitable lady who would say, "Oh, Rotunda, what *do* you put in your gumbo to make it so good?"

"Black fingers!" Rotunda would snap, and the whole room would break up in laughter. . . .

The kids at the Sun & Buns were squealing loud tonight. Tom sighed; sometimes he felt he had very little to say anymore, except a sigh. He moved through another empty room, past the shimmer of a mirror (or the shimmer of a memory?) on the wall, out onto the upper gallery. In the far distance, mounted on the sands of what had been Pelican Island, the ziggurat of the Win or Lose Casino flashed and glittered across the black water, where once there had been only the little lights of spear fishermen, bobbing and winking.

Why hang around? he wondered for the nth time. The world he knew wasn't coming back, nor most of the people, not after the deadly year when Hurricane Dolores had finished them. What was he waiting for? Did he go on clinging to memories because so little else was left?

Sadly, he felt the waste of his energy, the way it drained away, a little every day. He looked out toward the dark Gulf but could see nothing, not even the shape of death, though he had seen that once coming ashore from its home in the deep sea, where shifting white sand polished forever the bones of the lost.

The Strip fell behind, with its parade of towering hotels, ice-cream-colored condos with sapphire pools, seafood restaurants with flashing neon crabs and flounders. The Saab gained speed, plunging after its headlights into the darkness of coastal suburbia.

Sarah snuggled against the leather of the bucket seat. It was nice along here, driving down an avenue of oaks. To the left, the Gulf's long creamy curves of breakers assaulting the sand. To the right, endless bungalows with lamps glowing in the windows, and just occasionally a small off-the-beaten-track motel that catered to families with more kids than money. Half-asleep, Sarah seemed to catch a glimpse of an old plantation-style building, and that surprised her—she'd thought Hurricane Dolores had destroyed all the old places.

"There's Dad's church," she murmured, pointing, and Burke said, "What?" and then dutifully, "Oh, yeah. The church. I'm glad you brought me there, Honey."

The cameo profile never changed, but she wondered briefly why she *had* brought him there. He'd wanted to go to Cozumel for their vacation, but no, the coast it had to be. Sarah had pitched it on the joys of gambling and seeing the Cirque du Soleil, knowing how he loved anything with color and movement.

Actually, she had reasons of her own. Deep reasons, hardly to be put into words—wanting him to understand her, to know who she was and how she came to be. Somehow, that part of the program hadn't worked too well.

Oh, Burke had said all the right things while they stood, hand in hand, in the ugly new church with the cheap stained glass and the varnished pine pews. He didn't believe in religion any more than she did, but he felt at home in a redneck cathedral. Gazing at the memorial plaque Mama had put up, the small white bas-relief copied from an old photograph, and the inevitable stupid motto, in this case *The Spirit Giveth Life*.

Sure it does.

Burke comforted her when she wept and listened patiently to the story of how Mama survived the hurricane, losing everything—absolutely *every-thing*—but her life in the process. How she'd found a job as a records clerk in the Hospital Center; how in time she'd somehow gotten together the money to put her daughter through LSU Medical School before trailing off, far too young, into the mist of Alzheimer's.

Burke had listened, had sympathized, had not really understood. She could almost hear him confronting Fate with his small store of functional commonplaces: Death and madness, that's really tough; still, everybody's got troubles; you help out when you can and otherwise forget it. Brooding drives you nuts, and what good does that do, anyway?

He was such a simple beast, really; not dumb, but simple. She clung to his simplicity as a rock in a troubled world. Yet at the same time it sent her up the wall, because there were things, important things, that he just *couldn't see*. Such as the fact that she had imbibed, almost literally with her mother's milk, the sense that life hangs by a hair—always.

Her therapist had chided Sarah for living always with "a sense of the presence of death". But Sarah didn't see that as an illusion; death *was* ever-present. If the therapist doubted it, she should spend Saturday night in an emergency room.

"Oh, shit," said Burke quietly.

Sarah believed that if a large asteroid plowed into the Earth—which wouldn't surprise her in the least—Burke would say the same thing. Not even with an exclamation point. Just, "Oh, shit."

"What is it?"

For answer he spun the steering wheel. The Saab cornered, not exactly on two wheels but squealing, and shot through a channel in the median that Sarah hadn't even known was there. Burke floored the accelerator and there they were, hauling ass back toward the casino.

"WHAT IN THE HELL?" she demanded, when she'd caught her breath.

In the reflected light of the dashboard he spared her a grin and said, "Sorry," in a tone that meant he wasn't sorry at all.

It was that porcelain serenity of hers—like a boy, he just had to make it crack. On the gift he'd given her last Christmas, the card had read, "For my FPMD, Love, Burke." That, he explained, meant Fucking Perfect Medical Doctor. The porcelain had cracked then, too.

Now he said, "I left my checkbook in the safe at the hotel. And don't tell me I'm dumb because I know it already."

"No, Honey, I wouldn't say you were dumb. Idiotic, maybe."

They roared back toward the fizz and sparkle of the Strip, while Sarah tried hard to return her face to its customary cool perfection.

Somehow the emptiness of the Grey Star's rooms was the hardest thing for Tom to take.

So much had been lost that night in August 1969, when Dolores came ashore. The acres of white linen, the scarred but still serviceable bedroom suites that Daddy had always called suits, thousands of pieces of cutlery, hundreds of burnished pots from the kitchen, a glittering wealth of glassware.

But that was only the superficial loss. More painful were the personal things—like the photo albums that recorded his parents' lives and his own. The mother he hardly remembered, drowned in a boating accident when he was six. Daddy posing as a fisherman, as a grinning host with long-forgotten guests, as a pillow-stomached Santa Claus. Pictures of Tom himself, in scout uniform with his troop, in swimming trunks with a hammerhead shark he'd landed when he was sixteen.

Pictures of girls, plenty of them. His whole love life had been bound up with the Grey Star. At fourteen he'd lost his cherry in Room 203—afterward, he seldom passed it in the hall without a quick grin—with a chambermaid named Betty Lou Something, of whom he remembered little but the feel of her heels in the small of his back and the fact that her mouth tasted of spearmint gum.

There'd been others. By his late teens he'd learned to identify at a glance those female guests for whom the phrase "room service" had a special meaning. From a brief stint in the army after Korea he'd returned to the hotel with broadened shoulders and perfected technique. He could see himself now, striding through the halls, eyes bright and dick half-hard, a few packs of Fuck-A-Duck rubbers in one pants pocket and a jar of cold cream in the other. Hotel, hell. When he was warm and twenty-something, the Grey Star had been a garden of delights.

Then responsibility fell on his shoulders. Daddy, taking an early-morning dip in the Gulf, trod on the spur of a stingray, went into toxic shock, and drowned a hundred yards from shore in water only three feet deep. Suddenly the all-day, almost all-night business of running the hotel was Tom's problem, and he began to look for a partner.

How surprising that he'd been sensible enough to pick a neighbor and high school friend, Madge Conroy, who was not taken in by his redneck ladykiller ploys. Even now, hovering on the upper gallery and gazing into empty rooms, Tom remembered ruefully just how deftly she could deflate him, and his own surprise at how little he resented it. Maybe he'd simply had enough randy twits by that time and at last wanted a real woman with common sense and strength and, yes, a bit of cunning.

For she did want him, she wanted to marry him and be the mistress of the Grey Star, the local version of the Grand Hotel. What a surprise to find out that was what he wanted, too—to find himself deciding at last to stop being a happy asshole and grow up.

Tom had actually been fetching up the ghost of a smile, remembering Madge, when the thought of how short a time they'd had together wiped it away and returned him to his customary dismal rut.

All roads lead to Rome. All paths, if you follow them long enough, to sorrow. Of that at least he felt sure.

The desk clerk at the Hotel Grandview demanded four pieces of ID, then returned Burke his checkbook and unbent sufficiently to warn him and Sarah that NOAA had put this part of the coast under a tornado watch.

"Maybe we should stay the night," Burke suggested.

"No, I'm on call tomorrow."

"Edwards can take it for you."

"He's not good enough."

Burke had his mouth open to say, "He's as good as you are, maybe better," but then closed it. There were limits to what even he could say to her.

There she stood, face as placid as a glass of cold buttermilk, and inside all those little devils warning her that unless she saw to *everything*, nothing would get done, or at least wouldn't get done right. Burke had never in his life known anxiety of this loose, unfocused, random kind—this fear that went in search of something to justify its own unease.

Well, that was Sarah for you. He'd laugh her out of it when he could, and otherwise put up with it. Some people had problems with their nerves, some didn't—that was all.

"Okay, then, let's go," he said. Do it or don't do it, shut up and get moving: Burke's mantra fit all circumstances.

So they repeated their earlier drive westward through the traffic of the Strip, this time with lightning starting to flicker and the sounds of heavy surf just audible over the hum of wheels.

Of course, the fact that Madge got pregnant had been crucial to their decision to marry. The early BC pills hadn't been all that reliable . . . or had she, just possibly, skipped the pill in hopes of jogging him to a decision?

They were starting the planning phase when a rather ordinary hurricane named Dolores wandered into the Gulf of Mexico. At first they paid no attention; he and Madge had both grown up on the coast and thought of hurricanes as one more annoying fact of nature, like humidity or sandflies.

They were still debating their wedding, hung up between the expense of a church ceremony and a quickie civil splicing—maybe with a flight to Vegas thrown in, only then who would run the Star in their absence?—when the storm, sucking energy from the gumbo-warm Gulf water, exploded into a monster.

It headed for New Orleans, and they both felt sorry for the city, still recovering from Hurricane Betsy four years earlier. But hurricanes were unpredictable beasts, and Tom urged Madge to visit her relatives in Natchez until it was over.

"Not unless you come too," she said.

Tom had no intention of going anywhere; the Grey Star needed him, and it was a strong old building that had shrugged off dozens of storms in the past. So, instead of running, they planned a hurricane party, inviting friends and laying in a good supply of bourbon and gin and candles and kerosene.

Tom and the waiters spent a day tacking plywood over the windows and testing the bolts on the long louvered shutters that opened on the galleries. Then he sent the whole staff to their homes, where they were also needed. He was glad that everyone had behaved so responsibly and worked so hard when Dolores veered suddenly and headed for the coast.

He and Madge awoke that morning to greenish filtered light, the rattle of sashes, the hoarse breathing of the wind. They went outside on the upstairs gallery and stared out to sea. The horizon had already vanished and the steam of August had blown away on burly gusts that pounded the shutters and made the plywood flex.

As the morning advanced their guests arrived, shedding wet slickers and talking extra loud to be heard over the howl and creaking of the storm. Tom and Madge took a last walk, leaning into the wind, their clothes plastered to their bodies in front and flying like pennons behind.

The Gulf was already topping the seawall, and rain and spray mixed together stung their faces and the taste of salt seeped between their lips. Royal palms lined the drive, fronds rattling, and they clung to a trunk and gazed enraptured at the gray waves tossing white manes like wild horses.

Back inside, two guests had to help them push the heavy door of the hotel shut. Tom bolted it top and bottom.

"This storm'll be a good one," he promised, and went off to the empty kitchen to dish up scrambled eggs on the long black range the staff called Old Smokey.

Rotunda's pots were swinging erratically from hooks, clanging and clashing randomly like wind chimes for the tone-deaf. Tom stopped and frowned; windows and shutters and plywood were all tight. He had no feeling of movement, and yet—could the building itself be quivering?

This time there was no bantering between Sarah and Burke.

Both were thinking of the things that had delayed them so long after they left the hotel this morning—visiting the church, taking that last fling at the casino, the way the slots paid off for a while before betraying them, Burke forgetting his checkbook...they should be home by now, resting up for tomorrow.

Instead, he was driving with two hands because the alternations of gust and lull made the car shudder. He was driving slower, too, because pools had gathered on the road, and he didn't want to hydroplane. Rain drummed on the roof with erratic fingers.

Sarah slid her left hand into the pocket of his crinkly summer jacket and leaned back, looking past his dark silhouette at the Gulf. Somehow the familiar white lines of foam were looking odd, flattened—as if a big helicopter were hovering overhead, blowing off the tops of the waves. Then a flicker of strange reddish lightning revealed something that made her suck in her breath.

"*What* is *that?*" she demanded.

Burke glanced, whistled, and turned onto a rain-slick ramp leading into a dumpy little motel called the Sun & Buns. Sarah leaned across him and they both stared at the apparition.

Out in the Gulf an immense dark something was migrating toward the east. Lightning flickered again and the thing seemed flat, a cutout, a demon in two dimensions.

Burke said, almost reverently, "That's the biggest damn spout I ever saw." A moment later he added, "It'll hit the casino."

Tom saw the headlights of the car that had pulled off the road and stopped, and he understood: they were spectators too. Then he stared as if he'd seen a ghost. It was—surely it couldn't be—

It was *her*, and another kind of storm was threatening, a tornado moving over the Gulf and sucking up water like an immense siphon, heading not for the land but for an easier target, a building that was huge but shoddy and weak, perched insecurely on a sandspit. . . .

He'd barely grasped the stunning coincidence when the casino vanished and emerged sparking and flickering like the world's biggest Roman candle. Then all the lights went out and the casino, or whatever was left of it, disappeared in the darkness that enfolded its destroyer.

A bizarre cluster of lightning in the shape of a crab flared in the clouds with long crooked bolts flickering out of it. Tom had a brief vision of a black column heading out to sea. Then a shattering crash of thunder flung him back, back into the haunted corridors of the Grey Star, overwhelmed by memory.

Sarah was the first to come out of the trance. She tapped Burke on the shoulder and he started as if waking from some profound dream.

"Honey," she said in a voice from which all tension was absent, "be careful going back, okay? There'll be power lines down all over."

He stared at her, thinking how many times he'd seen her in the ER, wearing a green cap and bending over a black man with two nine-millimeter slugs in him, saying quietly, "It's all right. You'll be all right," and making him believe it by the sheer power and authority of her stillness.

That was why she continued to work in the ER, wasn't it? Because external crisis gave her inner peace? Or was that only psychobabble?

"Right," he said, finding his usual refuge in action. He spun the wheel, and for the second time that night gunned the Saab back toward the Strip, now lightless except for a distant erratic spark.

Tom wanted to shout, to hold them back—her and her friend, whoever he was—to make them share the sudden inundation of terrible memories that for long moments held him in a kind of trance.

In the dark late afternoon on that day so long ago, the lightning had changed color, just like tonight. Even after thinking about it for so many years, he still didn't know why. Maybe ionization caused by the storm, turning the whole sky into some sort of fluorescing neon tube?

Whatever. The point was, on that August day in 1969 the storm's eyewall was nearing the shore with wind so strong that nobody would ever know exactly what the velocity was, because at 200-plus mph the anemometers all blew away.

Powerlines went down and the lights went out. Tom fought his way to the garage, where the gasoline generator stood beside the Volkswagen van with GREY STAR HOTEL—*Mississippi's Finest* painted on the side panels. A few pulls at the cord set the machine chugging and trembling, and he slipped out of the garage through a back door, because opening the big doors in the teeth of the wind would have been impossible.

Overhead the lightning flickered red and green and the wind was no longer howling but emitting a steady, numbing roar like the exhaust of a thousand jet planes. It was stripping the royal palms and Tom saw the broad fans whirling overhead like the wings of dismembered angels.

Back inside the hotel, lights flickered dim and unsteady, but that contributed to the party's flavor. As he shed his streaming rain gear and tried to catch his breath, he noted people playing the slots, talking, laughing. Couples were dancing in the dining room, others had gathered at long tables piled with cold food. Jack and Jim—Daniels and Beam, that is—were making their usual contribution to the evening's entertainment.

Was there also an undercurrent of fear, people raising their heads, staring uneasily at the wind-hammered shutters? Sure. No peril, no fun. Nothing to remember, to brag about later on, when the storm was over.

Some guests wanted to get a look at the action outside, and two or three burly guys unbolted and opened and held the big front door while their ladies crowded around to look. Then somebody screamed. It didn't sound to Tom like an I-am-thrilled type of scream and he hastened across the lobby and looked over the women's heads.

The bare trunks of the royal palms were vibrating like metronomes against the strobe lamp of the sky. But what mesmerized the onlookers was a huge branch that had torn loose from an oak tree. Christ! The thing must have been forty feet long and two feet thick at the butt. Caught in an eddy of the wind, the branch was whirling upright on the sodden lawn of the Grey Star, spinning and pirouetting like a toe dancer. Then a sudden uprush lofted it and flung it like a javelin at the door of the hotel.

The crowd scattered like rabbits, the door slammed back against the wall and the oak limb, corrugated black and streaming water with a few green leaves still attached, crashed through the opening and hit the front desk where Daddy had received guests and smashed it to matchwood.

Standing by the stairs, clinging to the balusters, Tom gaped at the sheer size of the thing. Good Christ, it must weigh half a ton, and if the wind could play with a thing like *that*—

Nobody had died or even been hurt and yet the party had definitely gone sour. They huddled together in the dining room like cattle under a storm. When some woman starting screaming again, Tom, fearing panic, grabbed her and covered her mouth with the palm of his hand—and it was Madge, who never screamed at anything—and she bit him, not meaning to, just a reflex of fear. When cold water surged up over his ankles, Tom realized what had scared her.

Again the lights went out. The garage must have blown away, taking the generator along.

In the sudden cold wet darkness Madge calmed down, perhaps because things were so bad she imagined they couldn't get any worse. She helped Tom find and light candles and a couple of storm lanterns, taking comfort from the glowing crescents of flame springing up on the wicks. When she saw that his hand was bleeding, she exclaimed something he couldn't hear and pulled his handkerchief from his hip pocket and started bandaging him.

She had just tied the knot when, one after another, the shutters and the French doors blew out, cracking like ordnance and scattering like lost kites.

Wind screamed through the room and tablecloths flew wildly and dishes scattered and smashed against the walls. Tom fought his way to one gaping doorway and clung to the frame with both hands. He was thinking with manic calmness, *Well, sometimes the wind does that—creates a partial vacuum and things blow out instead of in—*

And all the time he was watching a huge mound of black water rising beyond the oaks, crest etched by red lightning, foam sliding down its face. *So that's what death looks like*, he thought. *I've always wondered.*

The wave hit, and the Grey Star began to come apart.

There was a gap in time. How had Tom gotten out, with Madge in tow?

The wave itself must have carried them along, and maybe the wind and water blew out the back door or the barricaded rear windows or the wall itself, but for the life of him he couldn't remember. All he knew was that they were suddenly outside and alive, but helpless as driftwood on the rush of the water.

And where had the rope come from? The detail troubled him, because he knew every item, every roll of toilet paper, every scrap of string in the Grey Star, and he couldn't remember ever seeing the rope before. And yet suddenly there it was in his hand, wet and coarse and strong, and when they caught hold of the branchless trunk of a hundred-year-old oak that stood in back of the hotel, he was able to tie Madge on.

Things were flying through the air and splashing into the water and Tom clung to her, protecting her body with his own. In a momentary lull he turned his head to see what had happened to the Grey Star. *Is that my life?* he wondered, staring at the shifting heap that weltered on the black water.

A new gust hit and the remaining slates from the roof went spiraling up and vanished. He pressed his wet cold face against hers, searching for words of comfort, but all he could do was whisper over and over, "It's all right. We'll be all right."

Something struck him a tremendous blow on the back of the head. He had no actual memory of drowning.

When they reached the Strip, Burke and Sarah found it littered with downed signs and sputtering wires, the air still restless with a spastic wind jerking at flags and dangling streetlights.

"Could be worse," Burke opined, unruffled.

The buildings though dark, looked unhurt. Wide-eyed people gathered behind unbroken windows, like painted backdrops, and watched as Burke guided the Saab through the mess, twice climbing onto sidewalks to get through.

Sirens were howling and braying somewhere; the spout had only grazed the coast and the emergency services, the cops and firemen and EMTs, were alive and on the move.

In fact, state cops had already reached the causeway, where a massive redneck in yellow raingear halted Burke and Sarah.

"You all cain't go out there."

"We work in an ER," said Burke. "Doctor and nurse. You got a use for us?"

Naturally, the cop assumed that Burke was the MD.

"Well, thank you, Doc," he said. "The casino roof is fell in. We called the Trauma Center in Nawlins and they scramblin' some helicopters. We got ambalances comin' in from Biloxi and Gulfport, but I reckon we can use everybody. Just watch out. It's black as the inside of a well-digger's asshole out there—'scuse me, ma'am."

Burke and Sarah exchanged a quick grin and he turned onto the causeway.

A huge swell had submerged it to a depth of three inches or so, but now the surge began to withdraw, foaming around the stanchions of the guardrails, making deep grumbling sounds as it sucked tons of sand from around the piers beneath the roadway.

Ahead of them, on the concrete apron in front of the casino where Sarah had waited for the Saab, a blue light was revolving. At least one cop car was there already.

"They'll have to bring the survivors outside," said Sarah. "Building's been weakened, whatever's left of it—what *is* left of it? Can't see a damn thing. Civilian triage is easy, you go for the worst cases first. Military triage, that's different, you save the ones who're saveable and let the rest go. . . ."

"I know, Honey."

But she went on, speaking calmly, like a penitent reciting unimportant sins to an indifferent priest, arranging things in her mind. Burke's loafer-clad foot touched the gas and the car moved a little faster, now that the roadway was clear and shining black in the headlights.

That siege of memory had sucked the last bit of energy out of Tom; surely now he could fade finally into the night.

The image of the Grey Star he had inhabited for thirty years was going too, losing shape and luminosity, dimming with its master. The motel built on the plot of land where the hotel had stood was dark for once, its lights extinguished by the destruction of transformers further down the coast, and people crowded out of their rooms, talking in awed tones.

A little boy and a girl saw a strange silvery something reflected in the water of the swimming pool and tried to point it out. But nobody was paying attention to them, and in any case the image of columns and galleries was growing dim, like a cloud lit by a waning moon.

Just short of the nescience he now longed for, Tom looked a last time out to sea. A memory struggled, just managed to take form. She was there, she was there, and something else, too…the sand had been scoured out, down to the underlying clay, and something white gleamed—something too small and far and deep beneath the waves for any eye to see. But then Tom had not been seeing with his eyes for thirty years.

Only the mind, fading like an old thin moon but still faintly alight, only the mind could see it and pursue.

"Anyway, we can start the triage," said Sarah. "Oh, Christ!"

An injured man had popped up directly in front of them, frantically waving his arms—a skinny, soaked guy with a face fishbelly-white, and thin, somehow ancient-looking rags hanging black and pulpy from his arms.

Burke pumped the brake like a driver skidding on ice, but a skein of water was again washing over the roadway and denied them traction. The Saab spun gracefully to the left, passing sideways by the man, flinging a long curved wave aside and coming to rest facing back toward the land.

The water receded, drawing back into the Gulf, streaming off the causeway. And there he was again, facing them as before, pointing seaward with both long skinny arms—and they had to be skinny, Sarah now saw, for they were nothing but long beautiful white bones, radius and ulna, fish-picked and sand-scoured—and the face was not a face, it was a cratered moon.

For once Burke was helpless, confronting something that all his experience and common sense told him couldn't be. He simply didn't know what to do, except stare and forget to breathe. Then Sarah felt a shudder beneath them, tore her eyes from the apparition and, following its gesture, looked back.

The causeway was beginning to heel slowly over, twisting like a Möbius strip, the movement starting at the casino where some connection had torn loose and continuing down its length toward the shore. A dreadful noise rose from pilings buckling as the structure collapsed, and the tarmac of the roadway split with a sound of fireworks, throwing black chunks into the air.

"Burke," she said quietly.

He turned and stared at her. The cameo face had never been stiller, more concentrated, more commanding.

"Drive. Do it now."

He slipped his foot from brake to gas pedal and the Saab slid smoothly forward, passing by the man a second time. Only Sarah caught a glimpse of a human face revisiting the white scoured skull for just an instant, before the whole figure vanished behind them, following the collapsing roadway down into the night and the sea.

Standing at the brink, Burke and Sarah and the cop looked at the wreckage of the causeway twisting down into black water still agitated by scurrying cat's-paws. Sirens whooped and whistled, now close at hand, pausing intermittently to bray like a herd of superbeasts.

Sarah was weeping, her eyes half-blind, her nose red and clogged—porcelain shattered, perfection lost. She shivered in the circle of Burke's arm, feeling and sharing the tremors passing through his body.

The cop said, "Doctor, that was some smart drivin' you did there. You and your lady friend are some lucky. You all ought to thank your father in heaven."

"Oh, I do," whispered Sarah. "I do."

*A classic tale of a demon who (like Frankenstein's monster) is both
appalling and pathetic. A feast for fans of the supernatural.*

THE STALKER

"**G**OD, IT'S NICE to know you've been an asshole, too," said Terry in
his quiet, friendly way.

We were real comfortable, sitting in busted chairs in the office
behind my French Quarter antique shop and working on a nice California
Merlot. It was a rainy night, a night for talk, and I'd been telling him a sad
story from, oh, nineteen, maybe twenty years before, when I picked up and
brought home from Ched's Lounge a very small, fragile female named Willie.

My object had been the usual one, but it hadn't worked out as I expected.
Was it her fragility, her delicate china-cup beauty, the sense I had that she
might break in my hands if I wasn't careful? Anyway, instead of enjoying and
then forgetting a one-night stand, I became—well, I guess the word is
besotted with her.

For the first and last time in my prosy damn life, I took to writing sonnets.
I compared her shy beauty to the flower of the purple wood sorrel and her

pure voice to the song of the mockingbird. I must have been really disgusting for a while. Then my store was burgled—clearly an inside job—and Willie disappeared. Well, the burglar left his fingerprints all over everything, and the cops caught the big coarse dumb lout and recovered most of the loot.

Do I need to say that he was Willie's lover? He went to Angola and Willie just vanished, I never knew where.

"I went through something a bit like that," said Terry. "Only more... offbeat."

He sighed and slowly detached his feet from his Gucci loafers and wiggled his silk-socked toes and started to look a little less like a tax lawyer and more like a human being. I had hired him for combat with the IRS and we'd become friends mainly out of mutual loneliness—Terry was living with five dogs, and for the time being I was living with nobody.

I settled back comfortably. With wine gurgling in my gut and the rain coming down in nine-foot cubes, I felt ready to listen to Terry's tale of how he, too, was betrayed by love and beauty. But I was not expecting anything like what I heard.

You're not, Terry began, the only guy dumb enough to think you'd found love in a saloon. One night about five years ago I was in The Exile over on Toulouse Street, swilling and hunting love, when suddenly I spotted this absolutely breathtaking blond at the bar. Even then I wasn't exactly the young Richard Chamberlain, so I thought: Sure, dream on.

But then a friend of mine came by. I said, Who's that over there? And he said, Oh, that's Pat Something. He's nuts, you don't want to meet him. Oh, yes I do, I said.

So my friend introduced us, and at first Pat received me with the total lack of interest I'd anticipated. Until I happened to say I was a lawyer, and then he said, Oh really? Maybe you can help me. I asked him what kind of trouble he was in, and he said he was being stalked.

I said, Maybe I can help. I was thinking, Sex maniac, I can believe that; skinhead, I can believe that. Pat said, I'm being stalked by a demon, and I thought, I can't believe that.

But the guy was gorgeous, so I said, Why don't we go to my place? I live right down the street and we can talk this over. He gave me a despairing look and said, I can't have sex right now.

Hey, I said with a smile, I'm not one of those guys like John F. Kennedy have to have sex every night or they can't sleep. Pat asked, Is John a friend of yours? I thought he was kidding, so I gave him an encouraging smile.

We left The Exile and walked, mostly in silence, to my house and I let us in. In those days I only had two dogs, but they greeted us joyously and Pat seemed to relax a little, tussling with them while I got us fresh drinks. And hey, he was even more gorgeous with his hair tousled and dog spit all over his face than he had been when he was nice and neat.

So we relaxed a little and then I got professional and said, Now tell me, Pat, how did this stalking begin? Thinking that once I found out who was doing it I might do something, get a restraining order or something, endearing myself to Pat in the process. So very slowly, at times in a trembling voice, he began to tell me his story.

Pat had been living at home with his mother in some ungodly place down near the Projects. He was a slum flower, I guess you might say; he must have been kind of a steel magnolia, too, because he grew up a sissy in a neighborhood where sissies are killed routinely. His mother drew welfare and worked part-time as a barmaid and she lived with a succession of guys who were all given the honorary title of Pat's father. Pat was thinking about moving out anyway when his final father came along.

By then Pat's mother wasn't as young as she used to be. Time was when the guys called her Skinny Minny, but at thirty-nine she had a pot belly and other signs of hard use and advancing years. Her men were no longer like the John Travolta of *Saturday Night Fever*, they were more like the John Travolta of *Pulp Fiction*. So when Pat came home after a hard day's work as a busboy at Jour et Nuit and heard familiar sounds from the bedroom he figured he knew what to expect. Minnie was in the sack with her latest toad.

The house was a shotgun—one room behind the other—so he had to walk through her bedroom to get to his own. He knocked and yelled and then waltzed in.

They had pulled up a tufted pink bedspread, but even so Pat had to make an effort not to gawk at the freak Minny had connected with this time. He was bald and his skull had strange bumps like little horns over the temples. He had a lantern jaw and protruding eyes and his lower left canine tooth was permanently outside his mouth. It stuck up and kind of fitted into a notch it had worn in his upper lip. Incredibly, he had only three fingers and a thumb on each hand, and it wasn't because he'd been in some industrial accident or something, it was because he was born that way. He was the single ugliest man Pat had ever seen, and he couldn't imagine how she could let him touch her, much less anything else.

"I suppose," I suggested, "that he had hidden charms. Hidden under the bedspread, that is."

"You know it," said Terry. "The sounds from his mother's bedroom kept Pat awake all the first night of Bodeau's reign—that was his name, by the way; Pat figured he must be a Cajun roughneck from the oil rigs. The old rusty box spring squeaked, and Minny squealed, and Bodeau grunted, and this went on until the dawn's early light."

"More wine?" I asked, and Terry said, "Definitely."

On his way out, he went on, Pat had to walk through his mother's room again, and there was Minny sleeping the sleep of the exhausted beside Bodeau, who was snoring with his eyes open and only the whites showing. One of Bodeau's feet was sticking out from under the covers and it had only three toes on it, all with long sharp nails.

Pat was staring hypnotized at this spectacle when the snoring stopped and Bodeau's right hand shot out and grabbed his wrist. That was when Pat realized something else. Bodeau was the strongest man he had ever had grab him, and in his short life quite a few had grabbed him. The bedspread slipped a little as Bodeau rose to a sitting position and Pat became aware that the guy had shoulders like King Kong, including the fur. Bodeau pulled Pat close to him and grinned into his face. He had dragon's breath and his teeth were brownish and round like pegs, with spaces in between.

Bodeau said one word. He said *Later*.

Then he slumped back and started to snore again, and his eyes rolled up until only the whites showed. Pat stood there paralyzed for a while, and then crept out of the house and never went back.

Pat had had some experience with bisexual "fathers" who viewed his mother and himself as, shall we say, main course and dessert. Or sometimes as appetizer and main course. But none of them had been flat-out disgusting; one or two had actually had a touch of savoir-faire, as if life was after all a French farce, so why not enjoy it? But Bodeau did not seem to be into savoir-faire, or French farces, or anything except violent barnyard sex with anybody he could catch, male or female. No holes, you might say, barred.

So Pat ran.

For a while his friends took care of him. This guy loaned him a clean shirt, that guy let him sleep on the sofa. They all screwed him sooner or later because he was kind of a damsel in distress, and you know what generally happens to damsels in distress. Then Bodeau started tracking him. One day Pat looked out of the kitchen at Jour et Nuit and there he was, peering in through the window from the street. That night Pat woke up to a skreeking sound and there was Bodeau, standing outside the window and scratching on the glass with a sound like a nail on a blackboard. What took it out of the realm of the merely scary and into the hair-raising was the fact that that window happened to be three stories up with no balcony.

Pat yelled for his friend and his friend came, and of course there was nothing outside the window. That was when Pat started to get the reputation of being crazy.

Every time Bodeau appeared he came closer. Pat moved on to another friend's, and the very first morning he was getting ready to go to work, standing in front of a steamy bathroom mirror and combing his hair. As the steam cleared he saw Bodeau behind him. He staggered, turned and— nothing. Nothing was there. That night when Pat was under the covers with his new host, he woke up because his friend seemed to be breathing more noisily than usual. Pat reached out to touch him and he found, under the covers, a three-fingered hand.

Next thing he knew, Pat was running down Bourbon Street in his briefs in the rain while heavy feet smacked wetly on the pavement behind him. The barkers and the few people who were out obviously couldn't see what was chasing him, they just yelled and whistled. I guess they thought Pat was advertising a gay bar or something.

Eventually he got back to the house he was staying in, and his friend asked him what in the hell did he mean, jumping out of bed like that and running out into the rain?

"One more bottle," I suggested, fetching a decent Cabernet from a file drawer labeled INVOICES. Terry nodded thankfully.

"I have to admit your story is a lot more interesting than mine," I told him.

"Thank you," said Terry. He sniffed the wine and then went on:

Pat told me that the thought of ultimately having to screw Bodeau was making all sex revolting to him. He said he was ready to enter a convent and take vows of chastity if only he would never have to submit to this creature. The trouble was, he didn't think Bodeau cared anything about convents and would come and abduct him and maybe take the Mother Superior, too, while he was at it. And what could he do?

He started to cry, sitting on my couch with my two dogs looking at him anxiously and wondering what was wrong. I comforted him and got myself all hot and bothered in the process, but whether he was merely having a violent stress reaction (which I thought was about a ninety-nine percent possibility), or whether he had actually caught the eye of a three-toed, three-fingered Cajun demon (one percent possibility?), I couldn't offhand see anything to be done. Take him to a shrink? Look for an exorcist?

What I actually did was put him to bed, crawl in after him, and lie there quietly holding him with my five-fingered hands until he went to sleep. Which was quite a while. I stayed awake as long as I could and then I conked out, too. For a little over a week we lived together, and during that time I never laid a hand on him except to give comfort—I swear it. As for the pleasure of his company, well . . .

Pat was, I think, the most ignorant boy I ever met. You could sit him in front of the TV and he would watch either a cartoon show or wrestling (for the tight pants) or Geraldo. For music he liked heavy metal groups, especially Flesheater and Slash'n'Burn, which were big at the time. I bought him a Walkman and stuck the earphones in his ears, and he'd sit there glassy-eyed, getting his young eardrums punctured.

He was pathetically amazed by ordinary pieces of information. He'd never heard of income tax. He thought Europe was a northern state. He thought safe sex meant doing it with a guy who wouldn't beat hell out of you. The acme of grandeur he could imagine was taking a trip to Miami Beach. I told him he could go with me to Venice next summer on my regular holiday and stay at Daniele's, and he looked disappointed but said hopefully, Maybe Miami some other time? And I said, Yes, if you want to. Anywhere.

I'd never felt like this before. Here this beautiful nineteen-year-old was in my grasp, and I wasn't, in the usual sense, doing anything about it. I was caring for Pat, protecting him from demons either real or imaginary, and demanding nothing in return. This dumb kid from the Projects had opened a window of generosity in my acquisitive lawyer's heart and I loved him for it.

I would watch him sitting in the lamplight turning the pages of *Gentlemen's Attire*, and he would look so little and helpless that my heart turned to Silly Putty inside me. Say, I hope I'm not disgusting you, talking this way.

"No more than I've disgusted myself on many occasions," I said, refilling his glass. "It is a kind of madness, isn't it?"

"You know it. But at the time it was more like a dream. Here I'd done what I had hoped, I'd found love in a bar. Sooner or later I believed Pat would get over his dementia or whatever, and he would kind of fold himself up and deposit himself in my arms like a well-wrapped Christmas present. And wow, was I looking forward to the opening.

"Soon, I thought, we'll be lovers in every sense and I'll educate him, I'll show him the world, I'll dress him in every expensive overpleated garment in *Gentleman's Attire* if he wants, and we'll live and love and grow old together. God, I felt like I was living an E. M. Forster novel."

He sighed. I was about to ask him what had gone wrong, but then I saw he was going to tell me anyway. So I shut up and waited.

Eight nights after I had found Pat in The Exile (Terry continued) we were doing exactly what I've described, sitting in my house peacefully, and every once in a while he would raise his head and gaze at me as if to be sure I was really there, and every time he did I would get the Silly Putty sensation again. And suddenly the dogs began to bark.

They were named Punch and Judy, just dog dogs, you know, guys I found on the street panhandling for garbage and brought home partly out of compassion and partly for security. Well, they had always been good barkers, but right now they were outdoing themselves. They were standing just inside the front door and Punch was furious and Judy was hysterical. The only gun I had was a Ruger .22, so I went and got it. Pat was staring in horror at the door and the dogs never shut up a second. I tried to put on my most John Wayne type of voice and yelled, Awright! Who's there, goddamn it!

Then I got this funny feeling, this trembling in my breastbone. The sort of thing you feel when you're waiting for a Mardi Gras parade and when it's still a long way off your bones start to tremble to the reverberations of the bass drum. Then a sound began like an approaching jet that's lost its way and grew to a hysterical roar that set the dishes tinkling in the china cabinet. My chess set was standing out on a table and the pieces started to dance and the Black Queen fell over and then the White King. It was like living through the big one in Kobe. First Judy broke and ran and then Punch, both of them peeing on the floor as they went. The roar increased almost beyond bearing and then began to diminish as if an express train was roaring past. It passed through the rooms and faded and finally vanished.

I turned around slowly. A mirror on the wall was smashed. At first I thought it was because the sound had broken it, but later I realized that I had fired a .22 bullet into it without noticing what I was doing. The couch where Pat had been sitting was empty. I slowly walked through the rooms of my little house. Judy was hiding under the bed and Punch was backed into a corner, snarling and smelling like a glue pot. And aside from a couple pieces of broken glassware, that was all that was in the apartment.

Pat was gone. The back door was bolted on the inside and there were bars on all the windows. I can tell you this—he didn't get out in any way known to science or to common sense. Yet he was gone.

After a little silence I felt I had to say something, so I said, "That's quite a story."

Terry replied, "That's only the beginning."

The next day, he went on, I reported Pat as a missing person and got the kind of reception from the cops you'd expect. Fag's boyfriend deserts him— big deal.

So I went looking for Skinny Minnie. I put on old ratty clothes and figured I'd probably get bashed anyway in that neighborhood by the Projects, but nobody bothered me except a couple of panhandlers. I started going from bar to bar, ordering a beer in each, unless it was a black place in which case I backed out hurriedly. Pat had never said that Minny liked black guys anyway. In about the fourth or fifth joint I spotted this little female with a spare tire around her middle. It was midafternoon, the time of serious drinking you might say, and she was alone except for the bartender, who was clearly bored by her conversation and moved on as soon as I joined her.

I'll skip all the preliminaries. I verified that she had a son named Pat and I told her that I figured Bodeau had kidnapped him. She said, That prick. Turned out she meant Pat. She said, Why in hell don't he get his own guys instead of stealing mine?

She seemed really aggrieved. I asked if she knew where to find Bodeau. She made me buy her a Magnolia beer and a shot of Jack in the Black before she'd answer. Then she said Bodeau was gone, that was all she knew, but he used to talk about his family who lived on the northshore. *Family.* That was a new one. I had been thinking of Bodeau as an isolated monster. But now it turned out he had some kind of kinfolk living in the woods north of Lake

Pontchartrain. I had a vague but truly scary vision of a sort of backwoods commune of horned three-toed monsters, and shivered.

Minny was watching me curiously and asked why I cared. I said well, I was worried about Pat, what Bodeau might do to him. She lost interest at once. Don't worry about that little prick, she said, he's been taking care of himself a long time.

I left as she was downing the shot of Jack.

Next I went to my office and started checking a northshore telephone directory. And my God, the Bodeaus. I mean, St. Tammany isn't a Cajun parish but lots of Cajuns live there and I counted more Bodeaus than Landrys or Rabalais or Sheksnaydres. They went from Bodeau, Alonso, to Bodeau, Zite. They lived on arteries like Rte. 1019 and Gray Moss Road, and I could just imagine the little narrow blacktop roads meandering through the pines and swamps, far away from the bright lights and music of northshore urban centers like Mandeville and Slidell. Then I had a thought and checked Bodo, and hell, there were three of them, too. And there was a Beaudeau, and even a Beauxdeaux, though that really seemed a kind of disgusting excess, even for a Frenchman.

They were listed in exchanges at Pearl River and Honey Island and Folsom and Little Bougfalaya. They were all over the goddamn place, up this little back road and that little back road, and the thing was, I couldn't even be sure that the Bodeau I wanted was one of them.

Weapons. I was absolutely convinced of my inability to handle Bodeau in a fair fight, and the .22 was clearly insufficient, so I bought a snub nose .38 and a box of hollowpoints from a dealer I know. But I was still dissatisfied. Lawyers don't like to shoot people, it seems unprofessional. Talking them to death is more our style, but I felt somehow that Bodeau was unlikely to be a conversationalist. Besides, what if he really was a demon? So I did what any sane, rational man of the late 20th century would do—I went to see a witch.

"A witch," I said, with a certain skepticism in my voice. "You know a witch?"

"You know Mamalou?" Terry asked.

"Oh, the voodoo store," I said. "Yeah, yeah. She's a complete phony, you know. The only people she bewitches are tourists."

"Maybe. But I'd done some magic of my own with her taxes once, so I already had a connection. Are you sure you want to hear the rest of this? I'm drinking up all your wine."

"Never did I spill wine for a better purpose," I said, and Terry gave me a grateful smile and went on:

I went by her place one hot afternoon, and it hadn't changed a bit since the days when I taught her how to make her profits look like losses. The same New Orleans Saints T-shirts were displayed out front, and in the show window were the same disgusting postcards of naked fat people alongside fly-blown pralines and examples of what used to be called Jim Crow art and is now known as Black Heritage art. I headed to the back, and there sat yellow-skinned Mamalou behind her counter with her dirty bottles of leaves and powder, varnished alligator heads and a collection of crystals glinting in what little light there was.

We said Hi and I gave her the outline of my problem—said my lover had been kidnapped by a rival and the cops were no help.

She gave me a piercing look and said, Well I don't guess you be a narc, Terry. Then she went behind a dusty curtain and brought back a little bottle and gave it to me, saying, You find a way to slip him this and he be out for two days. It's bitter, she added, so put it in somethin' taste strong.

I looked at the bottle of fluid and said, What is this stuff? A preparation made from mystic roots gathered in the dark of the moon? Hell no, she said, it be good old fashion chloral hydrate and it will knock your enemy ass over teakettle, gare-on-teed.

So I bought that and then, after shuffling my feet, I told her the guy might be a demon, and what should I do if he was?

She said, First gimme a round one. (That must have done her heart good, after what I'd charged her for my advice on taxes.) So I gave her the hundred, and then she said, Burn him up, Terry. No other way. Knock him out and set fire to him. If he is what you say he will burn all up and nuttin' will be left behind.

Hell of a position for an officer of the court to be in—burning people up. Even demons.

Next morning I put my career on hold and set out and drove across the World's Longest Bridge, getting scareder and more depressed the further I went. I got off the interstate quick and spent that whole day driving up and down little tiny back roads and asking directions at service stations with hand-lettered signs that said Serve Yourself, Worms, and Gatorade.

I saw poor Bodeaus and comfortable Bodeaus, all kinds of Bodeaus. Their houses included everything from imitation Taras in the pines to dirty little shacks not much bigger than the Volkswagens disintegrating in the front yards. And every single person of that name, male and female, was an ordinary man, woman or child with four fingers and a thumb on each hand and no projecting tooth in the lower jaw.

To each one who would talk to me I said I was a lawyer looking for a guy named Bodeau in connection with a small legacy, and gave a brief description. And for three days every Bodeau, Bodo, Beaudeau and Beauxdeaux said they didn't know him. Guy like dat don't belong *mah* fambly, was the usual response. Or, No, Honey, I ain't never see nobody look like what you just said, *cher*.

By the fourth day I had crossed every bloody Bodeau off my list except for one. At the house of Bodeau, Zite, the lady was out but a little girl with a very grown-up manner opened the door and when I described the Bodeau I was looking for she said, Thass Cousin X-avier. We don't talk to him. Mama says he ain't no good and if I ever see him coming up the front walk I should take her old thirty-ought-six and let him have it.

Oh, I said, my balls freezing, he's kind of a black sheep, eh? And the little girl said, No, he ain't black, he's kind of brownish and got fur.

She closed the screen door and latched it and said, Ol' X-avier lives on Sam Boot Road and I don't know where it's at. As she disappeared inside the house I called out, Is he in the phone book? (Because my list didn't include a Bodeau, X.) She said, Why would he have a phone? Who would he talk to?

So I set out to find Sam Boot Road, which wasn't marked on the only large-scale map I'd been able to find. God, did I waste gas. Up and down and all around. And the loafers and the women who take your credit card in the gas stations—you know the ones I mean? The ones who know everything about their neighborhood, down to every local dog and the sex of its puppies? None of them would admit to knowing where Sam Boot Road was, though one did say, Yeah, there's a road by that name, just a tee-nine-sy li'l road, but where it's at exactly I don't know.

It was late afternoon and I had wasted a week in St. Tammany and found nothing. I was barreling along a blacktop highway past some pretty horse farms when suddenly I slammed on the brakes. I had seen a dirty sign that said Sam Boot Road. I backed and turned and pretty soon I was deeper in shade than I'd been all week.

I mean, the pines met over the road. It was like a tunnel. Not that there weren't signs of humanity around—garbage lying on the roadside, along with discarded plastic bottles and the remains of a butchered deer being munched by a skinny black wild dog. No horse farms on Sam Boot Road. No anything that I could see, except, nailed to a tree, a beat-up old sign that said PREPARE TO MEET. If it had once ended THY GOD, that part was gone.

Then the damn road dead-ended at another highway. However, I'd noticed one little track turning off a ways back, so I drove back and parked and got out. The track was too narrow for a car, grown up with fat weeds and it vanished into the pines and thickets of cedar and wild holly. And I followed it, scared as hell and glad to have the snub nose in my right pants pocket and wondering if I'd ever have a chance to use the knockout stuff in my left. All around me was an ordinary Southern woodland, with bugs fiddling and clicking and so on. A big russet shadow drifted through the trees—an owl, I guess. Why he was awake at that time of day I don't know. Then I saw a fallen-apart shed or chicken coop, and then a real log cabin beyond it—hand built, I mean, with a tin roof, not the kind you order precut in a kit from some outfit in California for $60,000 with optional hot tub. The cabin looked absolutely desolate just sitting there in the middle of a grassy clearing surrounded by old rusty iron things with spikes and cogs— agricultural implements, I guess—half-swallowed by wild blackberry vines and honeysuckle.

I was standing in the trees, hesitating, not sure what to do next, when the cabin door opened and a squat figure came out wearing jeans and a blue work shirt. The guy put something under a flowerpot beside the door and then scratched his ass, scratched his head, adjusted his crotch, did all that personal stuff. At last he slouched away into the woods on the other side of the clearing. If that was Bodeau, he didn't look very impressive from a distance. I gave him a few minutes to get deep in the woods and then, taking a deep breath, I walked into the open and headed for the cabin.

Close up it still looked grim, but there were odd touches. A hummingbird feeder, for instance, with hummingbirds helicoptering around it. Wild azaleas growing as if somebody had transplanted them from the woods. Didn't seem demonic, somehow. I checked under the flowerpot, and sure enough, there was the key. I unlocked the door and gave it a shove. Oiled hinges; no squeak.

I stepped inside and it was poor but neat, with rag rugs and furniture from Goodwill and a hand-made rustic table. There was a butane stove and a little fridge and a sink. There was a steep staircase with treads but no risers, leading up to a loft. I climbed it, listening to the treads creak. I could see an unmade bed shoved back under the eaves. All of a sudden somebody snored. Christ, I almost wet my pants.

I crept like a little damn mouse up the last steps and looked over the edge of the bed. And just then Pat rolled over and opened his eyes. His blond hair was spiky from sleep and his eyes kind of gummy but his skin looked rosy and he seemed to be well. He had trouble focussing at first; he peered the way people do when they've just waked up, and then he recognized me and gave me a big smile of welcome. He kind of jingled when he moved and I sat down on the bed and hugged him. Without saying anything he pulled the sheet aside and showed me that he was chained to a big iron staple that was driven into the log wall.

I whispered, You okay, Pat? And he said, Sure. I said, He hasn't hurt you? No, he said, Bodeau loves me, he wouldn't hurt me, and the sex has been terrific. I said kind of stupidly, You been eating okay? And he said, Yeah, Bodeau makes great *sauce piquante*, too.

I was beginning to wonder what the hell I was doing there if things were so great when Pat burst into tears and said, Oh Terry, I'm so glad to see you.

I'm sure sick of being penned up in this dump. I begun to think I never would get to Miami Beach at all.

So we fixed up what to do. I guess the proper move was for me to see the Sheriff of St. Tammany and tell him that a kidnapper was holding his victim on Sam Boot Road. Or just to shoot off the chain and find Pat a pair of pants to wear and clear out. But I gave up both those ideas, listening to Pat tell about the night he disappeared from my house.

He said he was sitting there terrified, with the magazine still on his lap, when what felt like a tornado swept him up and flung him *through* the back wall so for an instant he saw the inside of the lathwork and roaches running in every direction. Then he was flying over Lake Pontchartrain in Bodeau's arms, and down below he could see the lights glimmering along the causeway and the little winking lanterns of the fishing boats. And then down through the pines, the rough branches and the needles whipping him and then through the tin roof into the cabin. He felt strange, as if he was full of bubbles, like champagne, and then he seemed to solidify and Bodeau had him in his grasp and carried him up the steps to the loft for their first night together.

If there was anything to this account at all—and frankly, I didn't think Pat was smart enough to make it up—then sheriffs and simple escape were both out. Bodeau couldn't be captured, couldn't be jailed, couldn't be evaded.

Leaving Pat where he was, I climbed downstairs again and went to the fridge. Inside were a number of bowls neatly covered with plastic wrap. I found the sauce piquante (which *did* smell great) and emptied the chloral hydrate into it, stretched the plastic over it again, and put it back as exactly as I could. Then upstairs to commune with Pat again.

I asked him, Is Bodeau smart?

Pat said, Not as smart as me.

That was the best news I'd heard in a while. So I said, Well, when he gets back and starts fixing supper, you tell him you got an upset stomach tonight and can you have just something cool, like fruit or something. *Don't* eat the *sauce piquante.*

Then I got the hell out. I went back to my car and drove it back to the highway with the horse farms, parked under a raintree, and went to sleep. Would knockout drops work on a demon? Was the stuff Mamalou had sold me even what she said it was, or had she palmed off some tapwater on me? I didn't know, and in a way I didn't care. If this plan was a washout I'd try something else. I was by God determined that Bodeau wouldn't get to keep his prisoner, even if he did love him and (this was kind of galling) the sex was terrific.

Seeing Pat chained to the wall had pissed me off, you know? That was really uncouth. Even a demon ought to have a sense of, I don't know, common decency.

So about dark I drove back down Sam Boot Road and God, it was scary. That damn tunnel of trees. I mean, trees are all right in their place, but there's some kind of atavistic fear connected with deep, dark woods at night and I was feeling it. I got out and started to walk, and luckily I was wearing Reeboks, but that didn't stop me from falling over stumps and clumps of invisible things that usually had thorns. I walked into trees. The last thing I walked into was the abandoned chicken coop, opening a cut on my forehead. And then I saw a light, and pretty soon I was standing on the edge of the woods looking at the cabin, with a steady white light that I figured was from a gasoline lantern streaming out of one window.

Okay. Time for Leatherstocking. I creep forward very, very slowly. Left foot, right foot, pause, inhale a couple of bugs, left foot, right foot. I creep around the mounds of decaying harrows and things. Something scuffles across my feet, I die a little, I decide it's a possum. Find I actually *have* wet my pants. Tense.

Finally I reach the cabin. Light's pouring out of the one window by the door. I'm standing there, not quite tall enough to see in, when the door opens and Pat yells, Terry! Where the hell are you?

Right here! I say, and he almost goes through the roof.

I slip inside. Bodeau's lying sprawled half-across the rustic table, sleeping noisily. I come up on him, trembling, and by God, he's got three-fingered hands, just like Pat said. The love of my life was not smart enough to think up such an exotic lie. And one brown tooth really did stick up outside Bodeau's mouth. Calling Phyllis Diller! I must have spent a full minute just staring at this bizarre mutation and feeling, maybe for the first time since I realized I was gay, that I belong to the majority after all.

Then Pat touched my shoulder and I came out of my trance. He was decently attired in jeans, T-shirt, and loafers. Obviously Bodeau only kept him chained and naked when he went out. Looking at my beauty I felt the first quiver of sympathy for Bodeau, obsessed with love or at any rate desire for this kid from the Projects. And look where it had gotten him!

Well, I didn't have any more time for introspection, so I said, Where's the gasoline he uses for this lamp? Pat brought it for me, the usual red can with a gooseneck, and I poured it all over Bodeau and the table. Pushing Pat ahead of me, I retreated to the door, holding the lantern, and then, swinging it over my head I smashed it down in the floor next to Bodeau. The flame hesitated for an instant—we were outside by now—and then it went *whump* and a blast of hot wind struck us from behind and pushed us onward. An instant later, as we were running across the clearing by the fire's growing light, the window burst and the glass tinkled.

We stopped at the edge of the woods. It was a great bonfire, shooting up, engulfing the old dry wood of the cabin and lighting up the trees. The roar sounded like Bodeau coming for Pat. I caught sight of the same old owl, or another one, blundering away from the light. The cabin was gone in ten minutes and as it collapsed I could see that something at the heart of the fire was burning not red or yellow but white. Bodeau was burning, burning I hoped to nothing. Even twenty yards away the heat was intense. I saw the grass catch fire. The hummingbird feeder was gone and the wild azaleas looked like big burnt matchsticks. Nearby trees were beginning to catch in a crown fire.

I hustled Pat back along the track, found Sam Boot Road, and bundled him into my car. Neither one of us stopped shaking until we had passed the tollgate plaza and were back on the World's Longest Bridge, with New Orleans glowing ahead, just over the horizon.

The wine was all gone. The rain had decreased to a mere sullen pitpat outside. I was drunk but still coherent, enthralled by the tale but, well, a mite dubious. There were a couple of points I definitely wanted to clear up before Terry left.

"First," I said, enumerating on my fingers, "was anything left of Bodeau when the fire was investigated, as I assume it was?"

"Nothing. Not a bone, not a tooth. Whatever he was made of, it burned real hot and nothing was left, just like Mamalou had said. In fact, a fugitive warrant was issued for Bodeau on a charge of arson, for causing a minor forest fire. For all I know, they may still be hunting him."

"Okay," I said, going to the next finger, "second. Tell me this. What happened to Pat? Why aren't you living with him at this minute? Why five dogs instead of one guy?"

"I took him to Miami Beach," Terry sighed. "There was a rock concert there by Slash'n'Burn that he just had to attend, so I gave him the money to go while I stayed in the hotel room and watched an old Ingrid Bergman movie. Pat never came back. Later on I heard that he had joined the harem of the band's drummer and was traveling the world as a groupie. Still later I heard that he had disappeared into the sexual underworld of Bangkok, where I'm sure he's surviving, as usual. At any rate, he's finally seeing the world."

"Third," I said, and hesitated. "The girl I was telling you about, Willie. Her name was Wilhelmina, which could also be rendered as Minnie. And her lover, the burglar, he was so dumb and dumbness is sometimes hereditary, whatever Forrest Gump may say, and well—you don't think—"

"No," said Terry, drunkenly positive. "Too much of a coincidence."

"You're right. It's ridiculous."

"Absurd. Look, I didn't mean to get this deep into my sex life and I hope it won't make you lock your door when you see me approach or anything. See you again?"

"You know it. You're the only real friend I have."

Wine talking, of course. Not the sort of truth I'd ever tell while sober, that's for sure. Terry hugged me and I hugged back, awkwardly.

Then Terry was outside, opening a big umbrella like a batwing. The whole Quarter was running water, torrents in the gutters, waterfalls spouting off the rooftops. He hesitated an instant before starting for home.

"You know, I still think about Bodeau sometimes," he said.

"Oh, yeah?"

"Yeah, the poor devil," said Terry, and lurched into the night.

Nowadays, it seems, the dead just don't want to stay dead. Too bad for famous author Ted Dance—this revenant is no mere ghost. He may be rotten, but he's still very, very mean.

MR. SWEETPANTS
AND THE LIVING DEAD

WHEN **TED DANCE CALLED** Five Star Protective Services with a plea for help, we were already up to our ears in work. I'd signed a contract to provide guards for a big society ball; and just as we were gearing up for that job, a dog wrangler at our K-9 affiliate coked himself up and neglected to feed his charges. So they ate him. Worse yet, our alpha dog died of an overdose, and I'd always been fond of Bruno.

With all that going on, normally I wouldn't have accepted a new client, but Ted and me go back a long way. And besides, there was all that wild stuff I'd seen on the morning news—famous author, rumored lover shot to death, etc.

So half an hour later I was in Copacabana Beach, parking at the curb in front of his Biscayne Boulevard mansion. I couldn't pull into the drive because the security gate had been knocked off its hinges, so I climbed over the wreckage and under a yellow strip of crime-scene tape and rang the doorbell. An eye looked at me through the peephole, a Latina voice yelled, somebody yelled back, and finally Marialena or whoever opened the door, led me upstairs and seated me in a window alcove. There in about ten minutes Ted joined me.

Basically he hadn't changed much since the old days at Walt Whitman Consolidated High—nice-looking guy, with sort of an anxious-to-please air about him, like a really good waiter. But now his face had a hunted look, forehead puckered, wrinkles around the eyes. Lots of my clients look like that.

We shook hands and he sat down at the other end of the tufted window seat, licked his lips, and folded his arms. Lots of my clients do that, too.

"Manny," he said. "Good to see you again. Only been about twenty years, right?"

"Don't seem that long, Ted. From all I hear, life's been good to you."

"It was—until this idiot decided to kill me. Crocodile was doing okay, but...."

"They're a competent bunch over at Croc."

The best way to run down the competition is to describe them as "competent." Makes people wonder if they can't afford something a bit better.

"Competent," he said, "isn't good enough for what I'm up against. I need a friend."

"What are you up against, exactly?"

Ted turned pink, like an embarrassed schoolboy. He looked at the floor and scuffed his Nordstrom loafers. "See... Manny... last year, something *really, really* rotten happened to me. I fell in love."

"Tell me about it," I said in my warm Father Flanagan voice. "In my business, I've heard it all."

"You've never," he assured me, "heard anything like this."

America's hottest, gayest novelist put on a rueful grin and unfolded his arms. "Thing was, I had my life all arranged. And then at a raunchy party in West Palm, I met a guy named Zane Cord."

Ted explained that in recent years his lifestyle had veered toward the humdrum. He practiced safe sex invariably instead of just usually. Had only one lover at a time. Lectured to women's clubs on titillating topics like "Fiction Gay and Straight." Contributed to good causes like fighting AIDS and feeding Africa. Served as chairman of the Copacabana Beach Community Fund. In short, he became a model citizen.

He also became nearly dead of boredom. Worse, he was running out of plot ideas shocking enough to grab his increasingly unshockable public. What the heck could he base his next book on—his volunteer work for UNICEF? Maybe, without knowing it, he was ready to meet Zane Cord.

"Not a nice guy, huh?" I hazarded.

"Only," he said grimly, "the slimiest creature to crawl the Earth since the Age of Salamanders. In spite of that, or maybe because of it, I was obsessed with him."

"Why'd he decide to kill you? I mean, I saw the piece about yesterday's excitement on the news, but—"

"There's only one good thing about sexual obsession, Manny. It doesn't last. One day I woke up and looked at Zane lying in bed and even his *toes* disgusted me. I told him it was over and offered him a nice parting gift. He said he wanted a million dollars, and when I laughed at him, he threatened to kill me. I called in my yard man and together we threw Zane— along with his clothes, most of which I'd given him—into the middle of Biscayne Boulevard. I changed the locks and the PIN for my alarm system, hired Croc to guard the place, and figured the episode was over. Yeah, right.

"Yesterday Zane cooked his tiny brain on something—probably meth, an old favorite of his—rammed a new Porsche I'd also given him through the gate, and came charging out, gun in hand. I was writing when I heard the crash, followed by two shots. I ran to my bedroom window, and down in the patio—well, it was quite a tableau. Zane was lying half-in and half-out of the Porsche with an automatic still in his hand. The guy from Croc was standing there with this huge kind of *Magnum Force* pistol in a two-handed grip. He'd just put a bullet through Zane's head."

A little silence ensued. "So if the guy's dead, what's the problem?" I queried.

"The problem is, dying hasn't stopped him. Last night I looked out of my bedroom window and there he was, standing at the corner of Seventeenth Street and Biscayne, watching the house. He's still after me."

"Well, Ted . . . I have to say, that *is* a new one."

I was headed back to my office in Boca Raton when a squall line blew in off the Atlantic Ocean. Creeping along at twenty m.p.h., with the car ahead of me fading to a shadow and the windshield wipers beating like metronomes, I had plenty of time to think about Ted sane and Ted wacko.

We met in high school. When he decided to come out—which surprised nobody—one of our muscular Christians threatened to beat him to death, as a warning to others not to get born queer. I was head of the Walt Whitman Karate Klub, so Ted hired me as his bodyguard. I offered to break a few of the Christian's legs and arms, and he backed off. Ted was grateful, and when he found out my grades were tanking, he became my tutor, piloting me between the reefs of Shakespeare and the shoals of Advanced Algebra all the way to graduation—which I wouldn't have attended that year, except for him.

And now, two decades later, here we were again. Just like before, except that in the meantime he'd gone crazy. Well, sex has that effect on some people. And it wasn't all bad. Five Star Protective Services (Manfred Riordan, President) now had the easiest job on Earth—protecting a client from a dead guy. I mean, talk about an easy gig!

All I had to do was make sure this Zane bozo really was dead. An amateur will look at a sprawling body with a lavishly bleeding head wound and think, *Wow, that's the end of him.* In reality, the vic's scalp has only been creased and in due course he wakes up with ten stitches, a terrific headache, and a lust for revenge. I made a mental note to check out the alleged death, then dismissed Ted from my thoughts.

The big issue of the moment for Five Star was a Halloween charity costume ball the financier Jonas Whelk was throwing to open his Museum of Oriental Art. A long-term security contract was on the line, so that was bread and butter, while Ted's little problem was merely pickles and olives. I decided to check things out at the museum, floated down an exit ramp, surged through flooded streets and parked by the ornate double doors with the big bronze Ws. A wet banner strung across the façade announced the party's theme, *Florida at Five Hundred Minus Five*. Meaning that those VIPs invited to the shindig should dress to celebrate the 495 years since Ponce de León waded ashore at Daytona. Smaller letters promised *All Proceeds Will Be Donated to Charity through FBCCA*. At the time I had no idea what the letters meant, except that if Whelk was involved, it must be a scam.

I was admitted by one of my own employees, who gave me a fishy look, as if unsure whether I was his real boss or merely a clever counterfeit. I spent a few minutes viewing the atrium, where workmen were unrolling a red carpet across a floor of gleaming fake-marble tiles. Then I took a stroll through the whole museum. The last time I'd seen it, it had been just an empty shell, but now the halls and galleries were crammed with Japanese screens and prints, antique Chinese dishware, big ugly vases, and statues of Hindu gods and demons.

My last stop was the nerve center of the security system, a basement office with a dozen flickering monitors and a drowsy rent-a-cop who dropped his comic book and came to attention when I walked in. I decided to post a response team of two guys here, while I put on a costume and circulated among the guests. I also planned to station one guy in uniform in each gallery, plus two more with dogs in the parking lot. Your average thug isn't much interested in Sung pottery, but cars are catnip and prosperous-looking people are always fair game for a mugging.

On the way out, I ran into Jonas Whelk himself. My wife Shelley once accused me of not liking the man, which was true but insufficient. In fact, I hated the bastard—his long skinny neck, his ball-bearing eyes, his handshake that felt like a deceased moray eel. He'd made his money as a hedge-fund manager, finding that safer than piracy off the Horn of Africa, and after the fund collapsed and ruined lots of people but not him, he moved to Florida's Gold Coast and began to reinvent himself as a cultural leader. Someplace along the twisting road of life he'd begun buying Oriental art, believing it would hold its value when the world economy collapsed, as he rightly expected it to. And so the Whelk Museum was born. He promptly button-holed me and started bragging about the famous people he'd invited to his grand opening ball.

"We'll have the Governor and the editor of *Art News* and the famous religious guy Dolly Lama and Chelsea Varoom the famous pop star, assuming she's outta rehab by then. The famous novelist Ted Dance is gonna make a pitch for the FBCCA—that's my outfit, the Fund for Blind Crippled Children with AIDS. He thinks it's a charity instead of a tax write-off! How about that? How can he be so smart and at the same time so dumb? I think the AIDS bit musta got to him. He's doing it because he's a fag."

I escaped outside. The squall line had passed, the Florida sun had come out, the temp was several hundred degrees, and the air smelled like glue. I skipped breathing until I was in my car with the A/C on. I decided to clear Ted's problem off my plate first, so back at the office I assigned a new employee named Bliss to guard his house overnight.

Then I contacted a mole I employ at Crocodile Security Services, a guy named Tony Dantoni, and told him I'd like a private word with whichever of Croc's operatives had shot Zane Cord. In the musical accents of Bayonne, NJ, he replied, "So whatchoo wanna know?"

"You did it, Tony? Great. Tell me about it."

"Subject fired once at me. Then I got him right between the eyes. *Bang.* Or rather, since I was using my old three-fifty-seven, *kaboom.*"

"You sure he was dead?"

"Well, he had a hole in his forehead the size of a Susan B. Anthony dollar kern. Also, I was using hollowpernts, so I assume he had bits of Teflon bouncing around inside his skull. Yeah, I'd say he was dead."

So that was that. Tony's pushing sixty, been in the game a long time, and knows a corpse when he meets one. I was just about to sign off when he added, "Oh, one other thing about that Cord business, Mr. Riordan."

"What?"

"Last night somebody stole his body out the morgue. I oughta get a bonus next month, telling you alla this."

At two the next morning, I got tired of lying in bed with my eyes open and lurched into the kitchen and got myself a glass of warm milk.

Sam Spade would've had a shot of whiskey, but Sam had a copper-coated gut and I don't. I was sitting at the table licking milk off my mustache when my wife Shelley shuffled in, wearing her pink robe and bunny slippers, and asked what was the matter.

"And don't say insomnia," she added. "I can see that. I mean, what's the *matter?*"

"You remember Ted Dance from high school?"

"Do I. Great guy, I loved him. He took me to the senior formal."

"Why'd you go with him?"

"Well, for one thing, you were hung up on Sonata Diaz and didn't know I existed. For another thing, Ted's well named—he's a great dancer. For a third thing, I didn't have to keep peeling his hands off my buns, like with certain other guys I could mention. For a fourth thing—"

"Okay, okay. Maybe you should have married him. He's got a ton of money now."

"Uh-uh. I can't sleep in a crowd, especially a crowd of strange men. Now, getting back to the original question, why can't you sleep?"

"Ted's a client now. Also he's gone nuts. At least I hope he has."

Naturally I had to explain about the zombie lover, the vanishing corpse, etc. Shelley agreed that the coincidence was sort of twitchy. But, she pointed out, corpses do not walk, period.

"Probably the body-snatching was something fairly ordinary. Like a crooked doctor wants to harvest the organs, or a necrophiliac likes the guy's looks."

"Where do you get your ideas of what's ordinary?"

"Watching Jerry Springer."

"On that note, I think I'll go back to bed."

When we were again side by side and horizontal in the dark, she murmured, "Try counting backward from a thousand."

"Why backward?"

"It's more boring that way. Nighty-night. Don't let the bedbugs bite."

I reached, I think, 987 before my eyes opened on a bright sunlit day. *Warm milk and counting backward from a thousand,* I thought while showering. *Got to remember the formula.*

Had a good breakfast. Kissed the nice lady who fried the eggs and went to work, while she set off for the University of Miami, where she was going for her M.A. in Literature, don't ask me why.

The phone was ringing when I got to my desk, and it was Bliss, the guy guarding Ted's place. He explained that when he went on duty the night before, he put a fresh tape in a security camera that sweeps Biscayne Boulevard, then watched the old one on a monitor. Turned out that early yesterday morning, there *had* been somebody watching the house. So Ted might be crazy, but he hadn't fantasized that.

"Guy showed up at 1:45. It's a real grainy tape, the image is lousy, but it's kind of strange the way he just stands there, staring."

"What's he look like?"

"He's wearing a white suit that's about six sizes too big for him, and he's got a birthmark or something right in the middle of his forehead. You wanna take a look?"

"I'll be down in twenty minutes. Anything else?"

"This morning about 2:30 we had a prowler. Somebody climbed up on the southside wall, where it runs along the service alley between Mr. Dance's place and the house next door. Musta got into the alley from the beach."

"What happened?"

"Well, I had Suzette with me. You know Suzette? Eyetalian mastiff, kind of a brindle coat?"

"Yeah. Sweet dog if she likes you. Otherwise you're Alpo."

"Right. Well, it was raining like hell when all of a sudden Suzette jumped up and went berserk. I switched on the floodlights and grabbed my Glock and ran outside. I could hear somebody walking on top the wall, because there's broken glass set in the concrete and he was crunching it. Suzette was kind of ravening, I guess the word is, and he musta got scared, because he jumped back into the alley and took off. I put on her leash and went out the back gate onto the beach, but nothing was there except footprints in the sand. The rain was washing them out fast, but I could see they was running prints—deep toes, no heels. And the guy was barefoot. Can you imagine a barefoot guy walking on broken glass?"

"He leave any blood on the wall?"

"Well, it took me a while to find a ladder, and if there was any blood the rain had washed it off by then."

So back to Ted's I went. I was starting to wear a groove in that highway. I viewed the old tape and saw the guy in white leaning on a building across Biscayne and staring at Ted's house with three dark spots, two of which were probably eyes. I told Bliss when he went off-duty to drop the tape at a photo lab called Image/Inc and ask them to sharpen up the face if possible, and also give me an estimate of the guy's height.

Then I tracked Ted to the windowless office where he writes his novels on a flat-screen HP and emails them to some lady in Portland, Oregon, who checks facts and copyedits. I asked him for a picture of Zane Cord, and he brought me a color shot. At first glance, Zane looked like just one more male prostie, slim and dark with plucked brows and greenish eye shadow. But he had a Hitler-type hypnotic stare and one of those smiles that stops where it starts and never spreads around. The eyes and the mouth looked totally disconnected, as if he'd borrowed them from different faces.

"So what do you think?" Ted asked.

"If he was a dog, I'd put him down."

He sighed. "Here I asked Dear Abby for advice on my love life, when I should've asked you."

"If you don't mind the extra expense, Ted, I think we'll go to two guards instead of one, and do twenty-four/seven for the time being. You have a nice day."

Back at the office, I dispatched Bliss's daytime replacement, instructing the guy to stick to Ted like duct tape whenever he went out. When they were at home, he was to prowl the house and keep an eye not only on the servants—Ted had three, plus the gardener—but also on tradesmen, meter readers, and mailpersons. Of course, if Zane Cord actually was walking around with a big hole in the middle of his forehead, he'd be pretty easy to spot even wearing cable-guy coveralls. But I wasn't ready to admit that was a real possibility.

I also had my secretary run copies of the picture, give one to the guard, and fax a copy to a morgue tech who was on my payroll. Five minutes later the picture came back, and scrawled across it were the words, "Checked him in night before last." So I phoned the tech, and we had an interesting if creepy chat. He's the only guy I ever listened to besides Peter Lorre whose voice sounds wet.

He said the M.E. had been clearing a backlog that night and they all worked late. Toward nine o'clock, he removed Cord from the fridge and prepped the stiff for autopsy, leaving it on a gurney covered by a plastic sheet. Meanwhile the doc was doing another body, using his branch lopper and oscillating saw and other delicate instruments of his craft to split the wishbone, take off the top of the cranium, etc. With everyone crowded around the table, Cord was forgotten until the M.E. finished and sent the tech to fetch the next customer. The gurney was there, but Cord was gone—sheet and all.

"Was the door locked?"

"Yeah, but not from the inside. You want to go to the john or something, you punch a button and the door opens."

So, I thought, somebody opened the door and an accomplice snatched the body. I promised the tech his usual bribe, then spent the rest of the day interviewing people we needed to beef up the staff at the museum. I selected four with plausible resumés and was just beginning to think about going home, when a lady from Image/Inc. called about the security tape.

Her basic message was wow, what a crappy picture to try to work with, so typical of security cameras. Just as a matter of curiosity, she added, what was the guy doing, anyway—going to a toga party?

"Toga party?"

"Yeah. I mean, he's wearing a sheet, right?"

I was still absorbing that when she explained that the image of the building he was leaning on had sharpened up enough so she could count the tiers of brick. That gave a fairly exact measure of the figure's height, about 1.8 meters.

"What's that in American numbers?"

She said about six feet. I thanked her, called Ted and asked him how tall Zane Cord used to be. He said oh, maybe six feet.

After that I left the office, went to my favorite watering hole, sat down at the bar and had a number of double scotches in quick succession. Maybe Sam Spade had the right idea after all.

Shelley was home when I got there, and she wanted to know the latest on Ted's problem. I told her that whether or not his ex-boyfriend was walking, he sure was getting around. I also admitted frankly that I was fresh out of ideas on the case, except maybe to hire a witch doctor.

She suggested trying instead to get a more rounded picture of Zane. "Find out what he was like, what kind of friends he had, what he was involved in. Try the Internet. Maybe you'll get a lead."

So next morning I started tracking the real Zane Cord. My Internet expert is a second-generation Haitian immigrant named Helène Duvalier, who can break into anything, including medical and juvenile-court records I used to think were secret. Just before lunch, she breezed through my office on a gust of flowery scent and dropped a wad of printout on my desk. I set aside the museum stuff I'd been working on, and proceeded to learn everything I never wanted to know about Zane Cord.

Most of his story was depressingly familiar. Abandoned by his father, Zane was arrested at age nine for trying to burn down his school. Arrested again at thirteen for attempting to murder his mother, he got sent to a snake pit called the Florida Training Facility for Boys, where he probably started as a rapee and ended as a rapist. Released back into the community at eighteen—lucky community—he got on with a gay escort service and made his living as rough trade plowing the rich soil of the Gold Coast, while also pursuing other interests, such as narcotics trafficking and possible involvement in a contract killing.

He described his profession as actor, had some small parts in *Miami After Dark*, and made a sixty-minute porno film entitled *Crazy Cock*. A drug over-dose took him into a psychiatric facility where he was detoxed and diagnosed with sociopathic personality disorder. Turned loose again, he was jailed on a weapons charge but ROR'd—released on his own recognizance—within hours, and later put on unsupervised probation. The charmed life he led despite his many brushes with the law indicated that he knew some important guys willing to go to bat for him. In return they probably took payment in trade, in the most literal sense of the term trade.

Shelley was shocked when I told her what I'd found out. She still thought of Ted as the boy who took her to the formal, who was handsome and polite and fun and sexy too, in his own way, yet so fastidious that people called him Mr. Sweetpants, because he used scented deodorant and never even said shit if he could help it. Somebody like that shouldn't have touched Zane Cord with oven mitts—unless he had a self-destructive streak like Oscar Wilde, who also got a thrill from associating with young thugs. "Feasting with panthers," he called it.

"Better check out his other lovers," she advised. "There may be another panther out there. Somebody who stole the body and now is setting Ted up for some kind of an extortion scheme. Or maybe just tormenting him for the fun of it."

Frankly, at this point I was running out of natural explanations for what was going on. But as an obedient spouse, who also had no useful ideas of my own, in the morning I drove back through the latest batch of rain to old Biscayne Boulevard, where the storm drains were spouting like whales. The guard I'd sent for the daytime shift admitted me through a brand new security gate that looked strong enough to stop a Russian tank.

I found Ted upstairs in his office, doing research on an Internet site called Occultworld.com. I asked if he could think of anybody in his past who might be exploiting his problem with Zane Cord for fun or profit. He shook his head.

"I have good relations with my exes, exchange Christmas cards, send wedding presents when they marry, especially when they marry each other. Until I met Zane, *keep it civilized* was my motto."

"Just for my own peace of mind, Ted, send me a list of your exes' names and current addresses. Let me run them against a couple of databases I have illegal access to. If anything turns up, I'll bring you the information and let you decide whether I check them out any further."

He didn't like that. Said he hated to kiss and tell. But as I pointed out, unusual times require unusual measures, so in the end he agreed to give me what I wanted. I headed out into the hall, only to meet my man Bliss wearing clothes that seemed a bit rich for a guy making 28K a year.

"I wasn't feeling too good when I got off-duty this morning," he explained, "so Mr. Dance let me sack out in one of his guest rooms."

I gave Bliss a really hard look, maybe for the first time—big guy, blond, almost a baby face. Good record with the MPs in Iraq, which was why I'd hired him. What was he up to, anyway? I don't give a damn about my employees' private lives, but I don't like them hustling the clients.

"He loan you some of his clothes, too?"

"Well, the maid's getting mine cleaned and pressed."

"Don't forget you go back on duty at eight P.M."

"Don't worry, Mr. Riordan. I'll be right here."

In the foyer I stopped to say hello to the daytime guard, who was sitting at a gilded table sloppily eating a meatball sandwich.

"I guess Bliss will be on time tonight?" he asked through a mouthful. "I got me a date with a hottie."

"Should be. He doesn't have far to travel."

That afternoon Ted's list of exes arrived by fax and I passed it on to Helène. She researched it and deposited a pile of hardcopy on my desk that could have choked a Budweiser horse. Included were guys from the worlds of art and publishing, half a dozen military types, the mayor of a small town in New England, two ordained ministers, and three men I knew personally, all now husbands and fathers. No criminals, nobody with a record of violence. At home I told Shelley she was wrong about Ted having other panthers in his zoo. Zane really *had* been an aberration.

"And," I added firmly, "that's all the time I waste today on our favorite fag's goddamn love life. Tomorrow night's the ball, but tonight you and me are eating out, just the two of us, candlelight, wine, the works. And when we get home, we're gonna have some love life of our own."

"Good plan, Manfred," she replied.

We went to Alciatore's, had cocktails, ate stone crabs, drank a bottle of Pouilly, returned home pleasantly buzzed, went straight to bed and carried out the rest of my plan. Several times, in fact—not that I'm bragging. So the night started real well, but it didn't last. Phone rang at 4:21, and it was Bliss reporting a new incident.

"Bastard bent the security gate," he said, sounding rattled.

"Bent it? Those bars are three-quarter-inch rolled steel. He hit the gate with a tank, or what?"

"He didn't hit it with nothing," said Bliss. "The bars are bent out, not in. He used his hands, that's all."

"He used his hands?"

"Yes, sir. And you ought to smell where he had a grip on the bars. There's some black juice smeared on the steel that come off him, and *yuck*. It smells like my Aunt Bea's freezer that I had to clean out after the last hurricane shut off her power for five days. I got Suzette chained up. You know how dogs go for anything that stinks."

"I'll be right down."

It was still dark when I got there, but floodlights blazing up under the eaves turned Ted's patio into a movie set. Bliss had made an accurate report, impossible as it sounded. The bars of the gate had been bent out more than an inch, just as if somebody had hitched a chain around them and yanked hard with a big truck. But I checked carefully and there was no mark of a chain, no scraping of the metal, nothing. The gunk on the steel smelled just as bad as Bliss had said.

I'd brought a kit and checked for finger- or handprints, amateurishly I'm sure, but no dice. Plenty smudges, but that was all. It would've been nice to have a professional CSI job done by the cops, but fat chance that we could get them interested, the kind of story we had to tell.

Bliss and I were just finishing when Ted came out of the house fully dressed, not a hair out of place. He looked more like a top-notch waiter than ever, for he was carrying a silver tray with three tall Bloody Marys and a quart of good gin and a bowl of ice. He even had a bag of dog munchies that he gave Suzette, thereby gaining still another female admirer. Meanwhile, us humans sat down at a cast-iron patio table and swilled and talked the situation over. It was a little early for serious drinking, but as I had told Ted, unusual times require unusual measures.

"Zane's not just a zombie anymore," he said after downing his drink. "I've been reading up on this occult stuff, and nobody dead or alive has that kind of strength. His hatred is so intense he's become demonic. And that's the bad news."

"Any good news?"

"He's starting to decay. He needs his body to carry out his revenge, but it's starting to fall apart. Thank God for the Florida climate. If we were in Michigan, he might be around for months."

"I can have the stuff on the gate tested for DNA—"

"Manny, will you for Christ's sake cut out this fatuosity about gathering evidence? We know who's doing this. More information is exactly what we *don't* need."

"And another drink is exactly what we do need," I suggested, not knowing what fatuosity meant anyhow.

After that we drank gin on the rocks while the stars faded out and the sun rose in a burst of rose and lemon and other colors Shelley could name but I can't. A cool salty breeze came off the ocean, a mockingbird started to sing in a white oleander, and the sky was blue with little pink clouds like the cotton balls she uses to take off nail polish. About the time we finished the bottle, a small plane buzzed overhead towing a sign that said GO, GATORS!

It was the kind of day that makes Florida worthwhile, especially when you're drunk at dawn. Ted and Bliss seemed to agree, because they were holding hands and giving each other melting glances. It was time for me to say *ciao*, go back to work, and make final preps for the ball.

"See you guys tomorrow," I said, unsteadily rising.

"No," said Ted, surprising me. "We'll see you tonight, at the museum."

"You're going *out*? After *this*?" I pointed at the bent gate.

"Yes by God, I am. I said I'd make a pitch for those crippled blind kids with AIDS and I'm gonna do it. And no fucking demon's gonna stop me."

I was impressed by that little speech. Not only by what he said, but the way he said it. This had become a guy with—as we used to say, back when I was a small Irish Cracker child growing up on the edge of the Everglades— sand in his craw. He still didn't have the F-word perfect, because he kept the *g* on the end, which made it sound a mite prissy. But he was headed in the right direction.

He got up, adjusted his pants, and walked me to my car. There he became somewhat emotional, wringing my hand and muttering, "Manny, I just want to say thanks. Thanks for—for everything."

I thought he was going to hug me. But he didn't, just gave me a blissful smile and turned back. And hey, I didn't mean to make a pun, but looks like I just made one, anyway. After all his troubles with Mr. Wrong, I really hoped that Ted had finally found Mr. Right.

Yet I was worried about him leaving his fortress, especially at night. So I rang Tony Dantoni over at Crocodile and asked if, as a fourth-generation Sicilian immigrant, he happened to have a *lupara* lying around the house somewhere.

He said sure. It was kind of a family heirloom.

"Well, how about loaning it to me tonight? Dance insists on going to this goddamn ball, and the guy who's guarding him might need a weapon with real stopping power."

He said no problem—great old piece, load it with buckshot and it would stop Godzilla. I asked him to drop it by Ted's mansion, a place he knew well, having killed Zane Cord in the patio. I did some desultory work, then went home, slept off the rest of the gin, and woke up in time to get dressed for the ball.

By then Shelley had arrived, lugging boxes. I was curious what she'd decided we should dress up as. Turned out I was a Spanish conquistador and she was an Indian maiden. "That means I get to rape, rob, and enslave you," I pointed out, while buckling on my armor. "That's the Florida story in a nutshell."

"You try it, Don Manfredo," she replied, testing the edge of her tomahawk, "and you'll be missing more than just your scalp."

At seven o'clock I guided Sacajawea through the back door of the museum, clanking with every step I took. The costume included a cape, so I was able to keep my Beretta concealed in a holster tucked in the small of my back. Generally speaking, I don't like getting nudged in the kidneys, but that night it felt fine. In the atrium, the caterers had finished loading up tables with every fat shrimp the Gulf Stream could spare, so we sampled them, plus oysters in little toasted shells and chunks of steamship round and crudités that made me feel virtuous and healthy while eating raw broccoli with ten thousand calories of garlic-mayonnaise dip.

We were still chewing when Jonas Whelk arrived, wearing an outfit that was supposed to make him look like Johnny Depp playing Jack Sparrow. The resemblance wasn't close, despite the cutlass banging at his knees and a wild bunch of fake hair on and around his sallow face. Ignoring Shelley, he told me the Governor and Dolly Lama and *Art News* had sent regrets, but he still hoped for Chelsea Varoom, who was more famous than all the rest put together.

He bustled off to greet some new arrivals, and Shelley asked, "Is that the scumbag you work for?"

"That's him."

"I never realized before what you go through to get me that M.A."

People began entering in a swarm. Their costumes formed a pretty good cross-section of Florida's last 495 years as a colony, first of Madrid, then of London, and finally of New York. I noticed Spanish grandees, women in spectacular hoopskirts, planters in white linen, Indian braves, and tons of conquistadors, so I didn't have to feel lonely in my aluminum armor. Confederate officers and their adoring Scarletts recalled the state's brief, unhappy fling with secession. Modern times were represented by people dressed as orange juice cartons and a couple of dozen Mickey and Minnie Mice from DisneyWorld. Astroguys and astrogals were all over the place, making sure Cape Canaveral wasn't forgotten.

I was watching Whelk gladhand the guests when somebody jogged my elbow. I turned and did a double-take, because Jonas seemed to be in two places at the same time. Then I saw that this time the guy with the leather britches and fake beard was Bliss. A wig of long greasy-looking black ringlets covered his blond hair.

"Howja like my getup, sir?"

"You look a lot more like a pirate than Whelk does. And that's weird," I mused, "because he really is a pirate, and you're not."

Bliss was wearing Tony Dantoni's *lupara* as part of his costume. The shotgun had a pistol grip and its sawed-off double barrels were only two feet long. Hanging by his side in a leather sling, it made a fairly convincing pirate gun, if you didn't look too close.

I asked, "Where's Ted?"

Bliss grinned. "Over there in the crowd, sir. See if you can spot him." I peered, but couldn't.

"At first Ted was gonna wear this outfit I got on," he explained. "But it's got bad memories, because Zane Cord picked it out for him last year when they were going to Mardi Gras. So he gave it to me and came as something else."

I was still staring at the throng, trying to find Ted. "He must be really got up. I've known him for over twenty years, and I don't see him."

"Took him like three hours to get dressed. It's something he said he's always wanted to do, but never had the balls before. He said when he realized he might die any day he began to figure, what the hell, it's now or never."

"Well, keep an eye on him. I've got the whole damn building to watch, and if the action at the bars is any guide"—there were five of them, spotted around the atrium—"I'll soon have a couple hundred drunks on my hands, too."

"Don't worry, Mr. Riordan. I been wanting to tell you, I'm resigning from Five Star at the end of the month. Ted's gonna be my meal ticket, besides everything else, so I'll watch him real good."

"You moving in with him?"

He nodded. "My wife won't like it, but that's tough."

"You got a wife?"

"And two kids. In Tallahassee. Ted's agreed I can spend a week every month with them. He says it'll give him a chance to get some work done."

"You're a busy young man, Bliss."

"It's a full life, sir."

At this point a Dixieland band that Whelk had stowed on the mezzanine broke into *Muskrat Ramble*, or one of the three hundred other tunes that sound exactly like *Muskrat Ramble*. Shelley emerged from the crowd, grabbed my arm and demanded we dance. I told her maybe later but not right now.

"This may be fun and games for you, Honey, but I'm on duty. Why don't you find Ted and dance with him? He's a helluva lot better at it than I am, anyway."

"I can't dance with him. Not with that costume he's wearing."

"What cost—"
I'd gotten just that far when the screaming started.

My right hand went to the grip of the Beretta, while my left was pushing Shelley behind me. Conquistadors, Scarletts, Indians, orange juice cartons, spacepersons, all began scattering like a school of mackerel before a hammerhead shark.

As the crowd parted I saw what had just come through the bronze doors. It wasn't exactly surprising, but by God it was appalling. Wrapped in a filthy sheet and preceded by a smell that could have tarnished silver, Zane Cord stumbled into the atrium. His skin was the oil-slick color of an old bruise, his face was starting to slide off its bony framework, and he had a black hole right in the middle of his forehead that appeared to contain maggots. But his boiled-egg eyes turned two shiny metallic-looking irises from side to side as if they could still see. Jonas Whelk was standing in his gladhanding position near the doors, lower jaw at half-mast, when the thing spotted his pirate costume and went for him with hands that were mostly green flesh and white bones.

Everything was happening quick, too quick—I had the Beretta out now and clanked a couple of steps forward, but Bliss got there first, pulling the *lupara* from its sling. It had double hammers and through the screams and the notes of *Muskrat Ramble* I heard the two sharp clicks as he cocked it. Jonas didn't hear anything, because Zane Cord had grabbed him by the throat and wrung his long neck like a chicken's and flung him aside with such power that his body slid across the smooth marble, dragging part of the red carpet with it.

Then Zane turned on Bliss, the next nearest guy whose costume meant he might be Ted Dance. By now everybody else was out of the line of fire, and the *lupara* let off two enormous echoing booms. The buckshot punched Zane Cord in the middle and he exploded wetly, screaming once as he came apart—the damndest noise I ever heard, like the shriek of a bandsaw hitting a knot in a pine log, then snapping with the twang of an enormous banjo string.

The echoes died away. Several people fainted, as they had every right to do. Shelley stayed upright, but leaned on my shoulder pretty hard, and since my own knees were feeling wobbly, we kind of propped each other up for a few seconds. We were still recovering when out of the crowd emerged a very tall lady of Spain—hoops, veil, silken mantilla—and circled the mess in the middle of the floor, somewhat wobbly on her clicking stiletto heels. She touched Bliss on the shoulder, raised her veil, and kissed him.

"You know," Shelley whispered, "I really think Ted's been wanting to dress up like that ever since the old days at Walt Whitman."

There was a messy aftermath to that messy night. The police were informed by the M.E. that at the time of his disintegration Zane had already been dead for quite a while. So who broke Jonas Whelk's neck? And why were a whole roomful of witnesses lying to them about what had happened?

Blah, blah, blah. Shelley and I and Bliss and Ted got out of it by telling the inquisitors, on legal advice, exactly what we'd seen and refusing to draw any conclusions whatever. Chelsea Varoom never had to testify, because she was stuck in rehab, and the Dolly Lama and the Governor, I'm sure, felt they were well out of it all. In time so were the rest of us—the incident went on the shelf as one more cold case among many, and we stopped being grilled every day and got back to real life.

It was maybe eighteen months later (Cinco de Mayo, I remember the date) when Shelley and I were invited over to Ted's for drinks. I presented him with Suzette the mastiff, who was getting old for guard duty and needed a good home. Of course she loved him—women *always* love Ted—and he scratched her ears while explaining that Bliss was away, indulging the flip side of his nature in romantic Tallahassee.

Then us old school chums settled in comfortable chairs and started bringing ourselves up to date on what had happened since the night of the ball. We had lots to congratulate Ted on, because the buzz generated by his new novel *Demon Lover* pointed to a spectacular success in the making. He said Clive Barker wanted it for a movie, adding that he'd need the money because when he took on Bliss, turned out he took on the whole family as well. So far he'd paid for orthodontia for the kids and a hysterectomy for Mrs. B, to say nothing of Bliss's new wardrobe and an '09 Infiniti for him to commute in. When he left us to fetch munchies for dogs and people, Shelley sighed and shook her head.

"Poor Ted. He always winds up getting exploited by those he loves."

"On the other hand," I pointed out, "he's rich and famous and lives exactly the way he wants to live. That's a lot more than most people can say."

Shelley nodded. "He's surprising, isn't he? Most terribly successful people are a bunch of jerks. But he's not."

Ted returned, carrying a tray loaded with caviar and Stolichnaya and a rawhide bone for Suzette. He explained that he'd given his staff the night off to go to the Latin festival, and anyway he always enjoyed serving his friends personally.

That started a train of thought I wouldn't have wanted to share with my wife. While he piled crackers with pearly Beluga roe, I recalled a tutoring session back at old WW, when my thick head, confronted by *Coriolanus*, refused to function at all. Eventually Ted said, "You're all tensed up, Manny. I know what you need." He did, too. Afterward, I went back to work a lot more relaxed and ready to learn. It was the kind of personal touch that made Ted a princess among men.

I raised my Stoli to him, and the three of us clinked our glasses. "Thanks for proving," I said in my warmest Father Flanagan voice, "that nice guys do finish first sometimes."

Ted looked embarrassed, but also happy. He lowered his eyes and blushed and licked his lips, and I figured he was remembering, too.

At Oxford, the oak beams in one of the halls need to be replaced about every 600 years, so the university plants a grove of oak trees every five or six centuries, just to make sure they'll have the necessary materials next time new beams are needed.

Herewith we meet a campus monster who understands and plays the academic game only too well.

THE WOMAN IN THE MOON

FROM HIS UPHOLSTERED BOOTH, Professor Threefoot gazed comfortably around the noisy hotel bar.

Outside, the Chicago winter was doing its worst, seventeen below with a sixty m.p.h. zephyr wafting gently over ice-clogged Lake Michigan. But here were warmth and cheer, aspiring youth mingled with contented age, all boozing, schmoozing, and gossiping at the top of their lungs. A dean entered, followed by a string of grad students in need of jobs. He nodded to Threefoot, who nodded back, as one Great Power exchanges recognition with another.

"That's Duggan," he told his young companion. "We were roommates at Slippery Rock."

Threefoot's latest wife had stayed home, remarking that only mad dogs and academics go to Chicago in the wintertime, so he was sharing a modest suite with his son-in-law, Adam Clarke. Adam was in a bit of trouble. He'd passed his comps but couldn't seem to find a dissertation topic. Kate was pregnant and soon would have to take maternity leave from her job. As an ABD—all but dissertation—Adam had so far failed to land a teaching position and had even begun talking about abandoning Academe for something he called "the real world."

It was time for an older, wiser man to intervene and put him back on track. Threefoot let a harassed-looking waitress deposit Walmart goblets brimming with cabernet in front of them, wet his whistle, and prepared to dispense wisdom.

"I remember when I was in your shoes, Adam," he rumbled. "Passed my comps in the spring of 2077. No idea what to write on. None. I'd become a father and a husband in that order, and had to support Chelsea and Kate somehow."

He paused, letting his memories assemble themselves into a coherent lecture. Threefoot always lectured, having forgotten how to converse.

"I began the miserable existence—I will not call it life—of a wandering scholar, lurching from one temporary appointment to the next. That September I arrived, along with my little family and the season's first blizzard, at the hamlet of Nyuknyuk, Alaska, and took up the lowly position of non-tenure-track instructor and faculty gofer at the Sarah Palin School of Mines."

Adam sighed. He'd come to Chicago in the hope that Threefoot might know somebody with a job to hand out. Instead, he was facing only another lecture, whereof he'd heard too many during his lifetime as a professional student. But he'd have to pay attention, for wherever the talk was headed, he felt pretty sure there'd be a pop quiz on it afterward.

So he tucked his upper lip into his wine, inhaled a goodly gulp, murmured, "That's fascinating, Dad," and sank into the brownish limbo, neither conscious nor unconscious, of the experienced listener.

"I found life in Nyuknyuk," Threefoot went on, "even worse than I'd feared. My colleagues spoke with scathing contempt of the Lower Forty-Eight, meaning the civilized portion of America, whilst my students were interested only in hunting what remained of Alaska's wildlife from helicopters with rocket-propelled grenades.

"I have been accused of prejudice against our nation's largest state, but those who have passed a winter there are likely to feel as I do. The weather was horrendous—in the profound and bitter darkness even natives sometimes froze to death on their way to the Student Union for coffee. My living quarters consisted of a bed-sitter in the faculty slums where Chelsea and I dwelt with a squalling, smelly infant who later evolved, rather surprisingly, into the lovely Kate.

"From the first moment, my sole aim was to get away. But that was far from easy. The campus Infocenter (formerly called the library) contained almost nothing but works on digging and smelting. Internet connections were off and on, due to the geomagnetic phenomenon that also gave us the mauve and sickish green splendor of the Northern Lights. Time after time I fished up some useful work from a great library on my Omnipad, only to have the text dissolve before my eyes when the face of our adolescent sun broke out in a new zit. I had no money for travel and research grants went only to established scholars who did not need them.

"The topic I chose to write on was 'Buried Treasure: Metallic Ores in the Development of Civilization,' which I hoped would bore my dissertation committee so intensely they wouldn't check the footnotes, most of which I had to fabricate for lack of sources. Many a time I was obliged to trust my memory, often citing a mythical scholar named Iris Bidrew whose name stood for *I read it somewhere, but I don't remember where.* Huddled in my carrel, wearing three sets of heavy underwear, two wool shirts, and a parka lined with faux sheepskin, I began tapping out Chapter One with frozen fingers, but also with the energy of desperation.

"Then disaster struck. To strengthen my professional standing, I'd joined the Society for the History of Industrial Technology, despite its unfortunate acronym, which provided my colleagues with an endless array of coarse jokes at my expense. I'd barely started on Chapter Two when I learned via the Society's *Journal* that a work on exactly the same subject, even with the same title, was soon to be published! The author was a plagiarizing bitch named Marsha Minor Hoots of whom I'd never heard, and such was the excitement among the six or seven scholars who'd read her draft that everyone in the Society was anticipating a masterpiece.

"In noontime darkness, I took the hardcopy version of my chapter outside and fed it to a snowbound moose, which needed all the sustenance it could get. A week later I set out for our annual meeting, vaguely hoping, like the fellow in *David Copperfield*, that Something Would Turn Up.

"As you know, Adam, scholarly get-togethers are always held when hotel rooms are cheapest, so that you see the sights of Quebec through a delicate veil of snow and those of New Orleans through a palpitating haze of heat. Our Society has a peculiar affection for the Second City in January, as witness the current meeting. Chelsea refused to accompany me, saying that she intended to stay under the bedcovers until the Fourth of July, when spring was scheduled to arrive in Nyuknyuk. So I was a temporary bachelor, and from that fact surprising results soon followed.

"The meeting's agenda informed me that the wretch who'd stolen my topic would chair an evening session titled 'Evolution of the Screw Pump: An Epoch in Hydraulic Engineering History.' I found each of the three papers less interesting than the other two, and occupied my time with hating Marsha Hoots, whose leanness of profile and nunlike preference for sable garb caused me to think of her as the Black Ironing Board. And yet, as soon as the session was thrown open—

"*Wake up, Adam!*" Threefoot almost shouted. "Pay attention! If you think that after thirty years of teaching I can't detect somebody sleeping with his eyes open, you're quite mistaken!"

Adam jerked upright as if he'd been goosed. Some of the wine meant for the inside of his abdomen splashed on the outside and began soaking through his shirt. The old bastard, he thought, was a lot like the Fountain of Youth— nobody else could so swiftly make him feel like a little child again.

"To repeat, then," the monologue resumed, accompanied by menacing twitches of Threefoot's unkempt eyebrows. "As soon as the session was thrown open to questions from the floor, I began to suck up to her without a particle of shame. Why? Because the First Law of Academic Survival counsels us to treat best the people we like least, in order to disarm potential enemies. After all, Hoots and I were in the same racket. The day might come when I'd find her sitting on my Dissertation Committee, and if I ever published a book, she might well be tapped to review it.

"So I raised my hand and asked a fawning question that enabled her to display her scholarship to great advantage. Then I waylaid her as she was leaving the room, begged her to grant a mere tyro her wise counsel, and invited her to join me in the dining room. Over a vegetarian pizza, I learned that she'd already received a tenure-track appointment at Tilton—then as now, a small college but well endowed and, above all, located in our continent's Temperate Zone.

"She was dissatisfied with a post I would have given my eyeteeth for, asking me repeatedly if I thought Harvard was completely out of her ballpark. I assured her that it was not; we retired to the bar, had a few drinks, and—to make a banal tale as brief as possible—hooked up for the night.

"For the rest of the meeting we were what professors emeritus sometimes still call 'lovers.' I found Marsha as intelligent as she was unattractive, and as unattractive as she was intelligent. Luckily, in associating with faculty wives I had become inured to dowdy women and did not hold her appearance against her. Indeed, I found her naïveté rather charming. Poor lady, I believe I was the first man who'd ever shown a romantic interest in her, for she soon began to exhibit the dreaded symptoms of first love. She had a fit of jealousy if I ordered a hamburger from an attractive waitress, woke me at two A.M. to whisper *je t'adore* in my ear, wept at any excuse, and gave me a sonnet of her own composition, along with a last tearful kiss, when we parted at O'Hare."

Now fully awake, Adam found Threefoot's tale astonishing. Could the large, rumpled, wattled, blotchy, and multi-chinned person seated heavily across the table really have had such an adventure, even in the distant past?

Like the rest of his generation, Adam felt instinctively that sex had been invented around the beginning of the twenty-second century, while those who lived earlier had reproduced by some kind of virgin birth. Yet, because Kate had flatly refused an abortion when she had the chance, one of these days there'd be a human person who looked on him as the older generation.

Adam shivered violently. Reality was kind of scary, wasn't it? What had he gone to graduate school for, if not to keep it at a safe distance for as long as possible?

"Back in Alaska," Threefoot went on, "I received intense messages from Marsha on my 'other' email account—the one I used for private purposes, which, I trust, need not be specified. I accessed her, not on my Omnipad where some trace would undoubtedly linger in a backup memory, but on the computer in my carrel, deleting her emails after, and sometimes before, reading.

"I would have liked to end our connection once and for all, provided I could do so without giving offense. Chelsea was growing suspicious, though she had not a thing to go on except a vagrant whiff of scent her Doberman nose had detected on my clothing. I was debating how to ditch Marsha in just the right way when, to my utter astonishment, she announced that she was going to the Moon!

"Metallic ores needed by industry were growing scarce on Earth, so the International Space Agency had launched a series of expeditions to comb promising parts of the Solar System for fresh deposits. I read of this venture in the *Journal* as one reads about, let us say, an earthquake in Kazakhstan—with dim awareness and no interest whatsoever. Marsha was different. She applied for the post of the lunar probe's historian and used the rep created by her forthcoming book to obtain it. How typical of her energy and resourcefulness!

"Aboard the Russian-built spaceship *Dmitri Ivanovich Mendeleev* she received a few cubic meters in which to live and work. Her mission was to record the expedition, detail its discoveries, and above all make sure that its commander, Captain Mako, won a footnote in the history of our time. But Marsha had a greater ambition than to be a mere official historian—i.e., a flack. She wanted to write a definitive account of off-world mining that would secure her place forever in the History of Industrial Technology cosmos—perhaps even win her the post at Harvard that she coveted!

"I congratulated her fervently, glad for her, glad also to see her go as far away as possible. It was high time, for by now Chelsea—exercising those arts of interrogation that detectives have to learn but women inherit in their DNA—knew damn well that *something* had happened in Chicago. I put on the usual husbandly show of injured innocence, and our nightly dialogues on the subject went on interminably whilst the deep snows of winter gave way to the muck of spring and eventually to the brief, mosquito-haunted summer.

"Then—startlingly, shockingly—our private soap opera vanished in a tsunami of excitement sweeping the whole Earth."

"I've read about that," murmured Adam in placating tones. "God, what a thrill it must have been for you, Dad—being in, so to speak, at the creation."

Threefoot, ever willing to accept appeasement sauced with submission, nodded gravely. "It was indeed an epochal time, my boy—a time matched in emotional intensity only by the funereal sorrow of a dark day later in the year, when all the world's joy turned to sorrow.

"Astonishing reports had begun to arrive from the *Mendeleev*. No useful mineral deposits had been detected on Luna, but unexpectedly something far more exciting had come to light. A new type of deep-penetration radar revealed an intricate cave system beneath the Sea of Tranquility, many of its pathways so straight as to appear artificial. Cynics scoffed, recalling a similar wave of excitement two centuries before, when astronomers claimed to have detected canals on Mars—a discovery that turned out to be quite false. But this time was different, for now people were on the scene to check the story out. Soon suited-up explorers broke through the lunar crust into the lightless caverns, and there discovered a whole troglodyte world whose existence had never before been suspected!

"And that world, though millions of years old, was almost pristine. The artifacts of the Selenite civilization—so named for the Greek goddess of the Moon in H. G. Wells's prophetic fantasy—had been kept safe from the aster-oids bombarding the surface, whilst extreme cold had preserved many Selenite bodies like mammoths in permafrost. The scene begged for scholarly study and Marsha was there—eager and knowledgeable, determined and utterly fearless in seizing her great opportunity.

"Like the rest of the world, I felt stunned and agog. Just imagine, I told my classes, who for once paid me some attention, an intelligent species whose existence had gone unsuspected since the days when our own ancestors were crawling out of the primordial ooze! There we and the Selenites had been all those millions of years—in cosmic terms, so close together, and yet so far apart—life-forms simultaneously arising, ultimately developing brains and building civilizations!

"Governments vied with each other to glorify their astronauts, their cosmonauts, or—a slang term that became popular—simply their Nauts. The Internet buzzed with the discovery and every moron on Earth had an opinion to offer. Skeptics claimed that the whole thing was a put-up job to get money for the Space Agency. Preachers divided into hostile sects, some welcoming this new sign of divine creative power whilst others held that the Selenites had been demonic beings rightly destroyed in their dens by a wrathful God. Children drew pictures of the Moonmen, enhancing the images sent back to Earth with ray-guns and whatnot. Rappers chanted about them. Private industry got into the act, as the Safety First Tokamak Company of Secaucus, New Jersey, contributed one of its newest fusion reactors to provide light and warmth for the explorers, and the Near Space Cruise Line, foreseeing a spike in lunar tourism, loaned a shuttle to haul it to the Moon.

"But of all humanity I was luckiest, for I had a front-row seat at the events transfixing the world. I expected Marsha to forget me, and was surprised and delighted when each rising moon brought messages from the *Mendeleev*, now resting on the surface of the Sea of Tranquility. She had not forgotten our tryst, and wanted me to share the excitement of her great adventure.

"She recounted seminars where experts from a dozen disciplines debated the meaning of newly discovered evidence, ultimately reaching the conclusion that life on the Moon, though long deemed impossible, had in fact been almost inevitable. Water had always been thought necessary to living things. Well, Luna turned out to have water in abundance, now frozen into deep permafrost beds, but ages ago, when its interior was still hot from the massive collision that created it, a liquid sea that filled its deepest caverns. With warmth, water, and minerals leached from the cave walls, the emergence of life was no more astonishing than those colonies of tube worms that cluster around volcanic vents in the lightless depths of Earth's oceans, drawing not a single quantum of their energy from the Sun."

"So that," murmured Adam in tones he hoped were full of awe, "was the origin of your classic *Moon Rise: The Tragic History of the Lunar Civilization*. An absolutely fascinating work, Dad. Absolutely. I've never enjoyed a book more."

Threefoot chuckled. "You forget, Adam, that I too was once a graduate student. I know that you have no time to actually *read* anything, only to give the impression of having read things. But don't think I'm offended by your little deception—no, no! The true charm of flattery is the fact of receiving it. Even if you know it's false, it means that someone feels the need to oil you up."

Beaming, he leaned across the table and patted the younger man on the shoulder. Adam managed not to flinch, even smiled weakly, as Threefoot returned to his lecture.

"That was only the beginning of the story. Over eons of geologic time, the Selenites emerged from the depths of the Central Sea into the dry upper caves. Many became amphibians, breathing an earthlike atmosphere sealed by the freezing of the lunar surface into immense subterranean bubbles, which were continually refreshed by the oxygen-rich exhalations of marine plankton.

"The Selenites continued to return to the water to breed, but otherwise spent their lives as dry as toads—toads that over the course of a few more eons developed complex brains. They began digging artificial tunnels to expand their living space, constructed crude stone dwellings, and later elaborated them into temples, palaces, and burial vaults of near-Egyptian grandeur.

"Hearing descriptions of these wonders, Marsha decided to cease being a mere recorder, and instead view them with her own eyes. She took lessons in wearing a space suit and working in low gravity, and as a scholar-adventurer descended into the tunnels. Now she gave me firsthand accounts of the endless caverns lit by flaring vapor lamps, of great temples carved, like Petra, from the living rock, of serried lines of frozen Selenites gathered in these holy places, perhaps in the last hours of their world, to plead for mercy from their gods!

"She described the strange and beautiful paintings that covered the temple walls, finding them hard to understand, since the Selenites apparently had lived in profound darkness. (One of the greatest differences between them and us was the absence of any evidence that they ever discovered or used fire. Apparently, like the thrifty Japanese, they lived on the lunar equivalent of sashimi.) She speculated—again following the lead of H. G. Wells—that the caverns had once been lighted by bioluminescent bacteria, fungi, or glow-worms. Later these living lanterns perished along with the Selenites themselves, as the Moon cooled, the temperature slowly but steadily declined, and air escaped through cracks opened by meteorite impacts.

"Thus, after sheltering life for countless ages, the Moon became—finally and eternally—the dead world we all learned about in school. What splendor, what tragedy had played out within the shining sphere that lighted earthly nights and haunted the dreams of poets and ordinary men. Good Lord, but it was grand stuff!

"To my great surprise, Marsha's prose proved equal to the story she had to tell. Sometimes she was still the chilly schoolmistress, spouting facts and data, but at others she became almost a prose poet, her words taking on astonishing verve and color. Perhaps, I thought, she had suppressed a natural flair for language, knowing how senior faculty members hate youngsters who write better than they do, but now had decided to let herself go. Her style lurched from formal to frenzied and back again, rather like her emotional state during our *nuits de Chicago*. And how I cursed the solar wind when it tore holes, gaps, lacunae in her narrative, like a mouse gnawing on a novel."

Threefoot signaled for more wine and when it arrived, submerged his upper lip in the crimson pool before continuing.

"To say that I was fascinated, Adam, would be a gross understatement. I felt reborn. During my years as a student, I'd majored in many things—in Chemistry, until I realized that my lab technique would embarrass a baboon wearing mittens; in Political Science, until I saw that my professors knew as much about real politics as I knew about Babylonian cuneiform. Unable to find my niche, I turned to History more or less in despair. A confirmed cynic at twenty-one, I ceased to care about learning. I wanted to win the degree that some call Piled High and Deep only for the comfortable life it could bring me—secure employment, limited labor, and the longest vacations known to humankind. But I fear this sort of talk may disillusion you, my boy."

"No, no, sir. Not a bit," Adam assured him.

"Then you must be less dewy-eyed than I imagined. My point is this: after being nearly killed by education, my once-passionate enthusiasm for knowledge rekindled. Again I felt the half-forgotten thrill of discovery—felt it all the more because I soon became, though in a very modest way, a part of the lunar adventure.

"You and I, Adam, know what a campus is like. In the academic ghetto, as in any closed society, small tensions grow into major storms of ill-feeling among people who see entirely too much of one another, and too little of the world outside. Well, the same was true among the Nauts aboard the good ship *Mendeleev*. They were a varied bunch of scientists and administrators, babbling the arcane lingo of their specialties in eight or ten different languages. To communicate they depended on new and still crude microtranslators that never seemed to get meanings exactly right. Quarrels began over nothing much and escalated into bitter feuds.

"Bureaucracy worsened the sorry picture. Captain Mako wanted to hog all the media attention for himself and demanded that expedition members submit everything they discovered to him. He had no hesitation in ordering his crewmen to search labs and even living quarters for information the scientists might have squirreled away. Marsha was his special victim. As the expedition's historian, her job was to balance and interpret everyone else's discoveries, and time after time she was obliged to watch her work being purloined for the benefit of a man she'd learned to hate.

"Hence she began to conceal her insights from him and entrust them to me. She begged me to keep her messages safe until she returned to Earth and embarked on her *magnum opus*. Of course I agreed. As her faithful Boswell, I accumulated box after box of memory cubes and through them gained ever more astonishing glimpses into the great human adventure she was sharing.

"She described the Selenites' freeze-dried corpses in clinical detail—their large hands with three webbed fingers and two opposing thumbs; their enormous eye sockets; their long legs and once-flexible knees, which had enabled them to sit comfortably on their haunches in a toadlike posture. Her grasp of their internal anatomy amazed me. The images she transmitted clearly had been made by a portable scanner using MUTT, or Multiple Undifferentiated Tomographic Technology, which had replaced CATs, PETs, and the rest of the radiologic zoo. But how had Marsha, a student of ores and smelting, learned to interpret the blobs and striations the machine produced?

"True, she was a quick study, absorbing information like the proverbial sponge. She mentioned spending many hours browsing the ship's collection of three-terabyte cubes, each holding the contents of an old-fashioned library. Yet her expertise still left me baffled, until—quite casually—she mentioned that the expedition's medical officer had become her lover and was giving her expert assistance! In another aside, she revealed that she had added the *Mendeleev*'s communications officer to her male harem, to assure that her messages came through to me as clearly as possible! She also had a geologist in her sights, just in case she needed him. Counting me, she had three men working for her and one on the string. Could this assured and competent adventuress be the trembling virgin I'd known in the Second City?

"I began to see Marsha winning well-deserved fame, not merely among members of the Society but among all people everywhere. Could I become her satellite, the Moon to her Earth? She wouldn't want the Tilton job now, and if she recommended me, I felt pretty sure of copping it. Such was my modest goal, until Destiny took a hand and did for me what I could never have done for myself.

"By now I was spending as much time in the dark depths of the Infocenter as she was spending in the tunnels of the Moon. My wife did not take kindly to my obsession. Chelsea's suspicions returned and increased—what was I up to, why was I never home, what had happened to our once nightly games of rummy? My restlessness and boredom grew in tandem. I couldn't help comparing the tedious shrew I lived with to Marsha, that incomparable mix of seductress, scholar, and adventurer—of Cleopatra, Barbara Tuchman, and Amelia Earhart! Chelsea's interrogations angered me, whilst her wifely chatter about an exciting new kind of diaper she'd discovered in the main igloo of the Polar Walmart bored me to death. Yet I still deplore with genuine anguish the end of our once warm and loving relationship.

"I hope, Adam, that Kate has long since ceased to blame her mother for eloping with Joe Mukluk, an Inuit seal-hunter. After all, I had little to offer Chelsea—neither money nor comfort nor prospects for the future. That does not excuse her for abandoning her daughter when Joe bore her away on the back of his Sno-Cat. Yet, if she'd taken Kate along to his North Slope hunting camp, the infant destined to become your wife and the mother of my grand-child might well have been eaten by the same polar bear that got the illicit lovers. Hidden blessings, Adam—hidden blessings!

"At the time, however, the shock of her desertion, followed by her grisly death, caused me no small amount of distress. Chelsea, despite all her faults, had made excellent waffles and kept our tiny quarters as neat as a pin. In her absence, Kate and I were left a truly odd couple, a twenty-nine-year-old ABD and his toddler, then passing through the emotional storms of the Terrible Twos. There we were, doomed to live together in ice and squalor, amidst a filthy midden of used diapers and empty pizza boxes. And discom-fort was not the worst of our situation.

"Between transcribing Marsha's messages and toilet-training Kate, I missed a number of my classes, which did not sit well with Dr. Chingatch-gook, the chairman of the department. His subtle hints and darting, malignant glances gave me the definite feeling that as soon as he could find somebody—indeed, anybody—to fill my shoes at the same pittance of a salary, my services would be dispensed with. Then how could I and my daughter live, with no money for food, for medical care, for Huggies? Like you, Adam, I had spent my whole life going to school and consequently was unemployable, except as a teacher.

"It was then, whilst our lives lay in their pit, perigee, and nadir, that I felt for the first time the stirrings of temptation. I had in my carrel an immense amount of material on the lunar civilization that was absolutely unique and eminently publishable—enough to vault my professional standing at a bound from the cellar to the sky! Yet if I naively lifted Marsha's work and called it my own, I would quickly be exposed as a plagiarist, and treated to the scholarly equivalent of tar and feathers.

"I felt like Ulysses bound to a mast, hearing the voice of the Siren yet unable to respond. On one side of my frail craft roared the Scylla of starvation, on the other the Charybdis of shame! Success lay within my grasp, yet I dared not seize it!"

Now Adam *was* shocked.

He'd always been taught that plagiarism was a sort of scholarly Sin against the Holy Spirit. Students were flunked out for it. Cases involving older scholars were spoken of in tones usually reserved for incidents of bestiality and child-rape. And here was the Grand Panjandrum of the Tilton campus confessing the regret he'd felt at not being able to practice it!

Adam opened his mouth to say something rather sharp about honesty and commitment to the truth. Then, just in time, he remembered a Latino fellow student who had described Threefoot in class as *el pomposo*. That guy had never managed to get his dissertation accepted, and was now selling vinyl siding. Adam also recalled an assistant professor who referred at a faculty gathering to the great man's "majestic super-eminent turkey-gobbler strut." He'd been driven from the campus by Threefoot's vengeance and wound up teaching on Guam.

No wonder Kate's dad thought of himself in Homeric terms—Ulysses, the Siren, Scylla, all that crap. Threefoot believed he was Zeus, his endowed chair a throne from which he hurled thunderbolts that made and unmade professional lives. Worse yet, that was exactly what he was, and what he did. *So maybe*, thought Adam, *I'd better not look* too *shocked.*

While (or *whilst*) Adam endured this crisis of conscience, before suppressing it as most of us do, the bass voice went rumbling along like a freight train with a thousand boxcars. Only now it had taken on a dirge-like quality appropriate to a tale of disaster.

"I have always," said Threefoot, "been a kindly, gentle sort of person, not given to rejoicing at the misfortunes of others. Especially not those of Marsha, for whom I had a ton of professional respect plus a soupçon of nostalgic affection.

"So you'll appreciate my complex feelings, Adam, on that grim day when shock and horror spread at light-speed across all electronic media—that day when the whole world went into mourning—that day when the Safety First Company's reactor exploded, ending all life on the Moon for the second time!

"Along with the rest of humanity, I grieved. Indeed, I wept—I am not ashamed to confess it. Yet my grief was not unalloyed with a sense of relief. Marsha was gone. The communications officer, the medical officer, all the members and prospective members of her harem were gone.

"The expedition was gone. The lunar civilization was gone, never to be seen again by human eyes, or any other. The frozen bodies, the temples, the artwork, all had been reduced in nanoseconds to their component quarks by temperatures more suitable to the surface of the Sun than the interior of the Moon. The tunnels compressed the force of the explosion, making it far more destructive than it would have been in the open, and then the expansion of suddenly heated rock shattered the floor of the ill-named Sea of Tranquility and blew it sky-high, destroying the *Mendeleev* which rested there. Along with the ship went Captain Mako and every record, memory cube, diary, and jotting the Nauts had made. Human memories were gone. Everything was gone—only I, and what I would later name the Marsha Minor Hoots Collection, remained intact.

"That night a spectacular meteor shower began arriving, as thousands of lunar fragments drawn by Earth's gravity plunged to fiery extinction in our atmosphere. And who could tell but that one of those coruscating flowers of light might be all that remained of my onetime lover? The Night of the Meteors put on quite a show, and we watched it together, Kate and I—she clapping her tiny hands and crowing in ecstasy, I shedding an honest tear, yet also secretly rejoicing that our dark prospects, like the sky above us, had suddenly been illuminated by an utterly unanticipated burst of light!

"The change in our circumstances became evident the very next day. Dr. Chingatchgook—his gray, damp, oysterlike eyes glinting with malice, as if they had secreted a couple of worthless seed-pearls—informed me that I would not be returning next year. I greeted the news with a broad grin and a chuckle that caused the oysters to look uncomfortable, as if suddenly threatened by a gourmet's fork.

"'I suppose, sir,' I murmured, 'you will not mind if I continue to use the resources of the Infocenter until the end of the term? I need to polish my dissertation.'

"His eyes opened wide and I realized they were more like gray-green clams than oysters. 'You've written a *dissertation?*' he gasped. 'How'd you manage that?'

"'Only,' I replied, 'by laboring through the endless days of summer and the still more endless nights of winter. As soon as it's accepted, I intend to apply for a position on the faculty of Tilton University, which I understand has an opening.'

"'Gawwwwd,' he muttered. 'And here I thought you was just one more a them Lower Forty-Eight fuckoffs.'

"'Give my regards,' I smiled, 'to the next polar bear you meet,' and left his office for what proved to be the last time.

"I deposited Kate at the campus daycare center to begin the process of socialization with her peers. Then I got down to the task of fabricating *Moon Rise*—intending, of course, to attribute Marsha's eloquent words to myself. Those who have never practiced the art and science of plagiarism, Adam, have no idea how difficult it is to do right. I could hardly claim to have been on the *Mendeleev* myself, so how had I come by my material? I decided to describe Marsha as a gifted, earnest, hard-working observer, a kind of research assistant. I recounted our many contacts, paid her courage the fulsome compliments she well deserved, and promised that a full text of her messages would one day be deposited in the National Archives for scholarly study. I need not say that the Archives are still waiting.

"The memory cubes themselves presented quite a different sort of problem. On rereading, I was distressed to see how incomplete they really were. Here I'd find a clear and detailed segment, followed by a garbled passage that appeared to be partly in English, partly in the unknown tongue of the Selenites. So I set about weaving the comprehensible parts together, like a museum conservator who draws upon his imagination to repair a tattered tapestry or show what Leonardo really intended when he painted the *Last Supper*. The resulting text may have drifted somewhat far from the original, but who could challenge it? Personally, I felt that my patching and darning helped to make the emerging work more truly my own—more, shall we say, *authentic*, whatever that may mean.

"Yet there was one hideously garbled cube that I felt a need to unscramble. It contained bits and pieces of purple prose, plus mentions of people I'd heard nothing about in any of Marsha's other messages—odd references, curious asides. I felt I must obtain a better picture of its contents, and at vast expense (well, what seemed like vast expense to me in my poverty) sent it to an outfit in Seattle that specialized in the recovery of lost computer data. The cube went by dogsled to the nearest landing strip, a bush pilot carried it to Anchorage, and from there it was flown by commercial carrier to SeaTac in the Lower Forty-Eight, whither I earnestly hoped to follow it in time.

"When it returned at last, I popped it into my machine, began to read, and made one of the most astonishing discoveries of my entire professional life. As Shakespeare remarked of Cleopatra, time did not wither nor custom stale Marsha's infinite variety. Until I die or succumb to Alzheimer's, scraps of her text will remain inscribed upon my memory, beginning with her startling first line: *I know, my dear, that this may sound foolish of me, yet I have such a great need to convey what I feel that I am now going to attempt fiction, even though I have spent my whole life striving after fact.*

"Yes, fiction. It soon became apparent that Marsha Minor Hoots, that cool and objective scholar, had celebrated her sexual liberation by sketching out a romance novel entitled *The Woman in the Moon*. In it, she recounted the impassioned love of a brilliant scientist named Vivian (Viv) for a mechanic named Declan (Deck), a sort of lunar *Lady Chatterley's Lover*, only with the hardcore material fuzzed and softened like an airbrushed nude to meet the conventions of romance.

"Both of these young people were slender and beautiful, Viv having taut breasts and eyes like profound pools of dark water. Deck was a veritable macramé of steely muscles and yet—the true chick-lit touch—so sensitive to a woman's needs that he almost lactated. *She woke and saw that he too had awakened. He turned on his side and lay with eyes open, yet distant and dreaming. Taking his powerful hand between her small ones, she murmured, 'What are you thinking of, dearest?' Instantly his gaze sharpened to the semblance of blue steel, piercing her to the very heart. 'What else but of you?' he asked in his deep, thrilling baritone voice.*

"I now understood why Marsha's messages had been written in two such different styles. She had intended to publish a scholarly study under her own name. But she also meant to vent her inmost feelings in a fictional work under a pseudonym—she tried out several, including Miriam Melmoth and Bruce Hardcastle—a work whose phallic symbolism, I must say, was sometimes shockingly crude.

"Hand in gloved hand, Viv and Deck stood gazing up at vast pillars that seemed to join stalactite to stalagmite in one towering structure. Yet these Pillars of the Moon were not the work of nature but of the Selenites, whose forms in blazing colors ascended the columns locked in amorous postures, like the figures on a Hindu temple. The visors of the lovers' helmets clinked together as they exchanged a kiss with their eyes, since their lips could not meet in the vacuous tunnels of the Moon.

"You see my problem, Adam. I could no longer tell what parts of the Hoots epic were factual accounts of the lunar underground and which were poetic effusions intended for the novel. Add my own emendations, and the portrait of the lunar world I meant to transmit to future generations bore, perhaps, only a shifting and ambiguous relationship to the real thing.

"Well, I knew how to deal with the offending cube. At Nyuknyuk's central flea market the preceding summer, Chelsea had bought—heaven knows why—a pair of smooth flat stones once used by an Eskimo housewife to pound blubber. I used them to reduce the fragile ceramic cube to molecules, then ground the powder further into atoms, which I disposed of in the toilet. When the MS was complete, I waited for a lull in the solar wind and sent it electronically to an agent in New York. He was enthusiastic, emailing me a standard contract and promising to get it published quickly. 'We got to act fast,' was the way he put it, 'while the Nauts are still hot from dying.'

"The reviews were the usual combination of snottiness, useful insight, and personal bias. Yet all admitted that *Moon Rise* would form the indispensable foundation for all future work on the vanished world of the Selenites. And that is just what the book became, Adam—to me and my present beloved wife, a meal ticket; to you, what I can only hope will be an inspiration. Be creative, my boy, be creative! That is the message I would convey to you. In the memorable words of Jesus, *Go thou and do likewise.*"

But Adam looked more bewildered than inspired.

"This has been truly fascinating, sir," he mumbled. "But, uh, when you invited me to this meeting, I'd rather hoped that you, uh, that you might, uh, uh, have heard of a tenure-track job available somewhere—"

"Oh, that's been taken care of," shrugged Threefoot. "Did you think I'd see my daughter married to a pauper? Good heavens, she might have wanted to move back home, baby, husband, and all! Lovely girl, of course, but—Ah, here comes Dean Duggan again."

The old gentleman was headed for the elevators, while his train of grad students stayed behind, all of them by now either drunk or getting there fast. Threefoot waved at him and when he approached, said, "Dick, this is the young man I was telling you about."

"Ah, Mr. Clarke," said Duggan. "I look forward with interest to reading your Curriculum Vitæ. We've been searching for somebody in what I'm told is your—er, er—specialty." He said good night, bowed a little tipsily, and departed with the small, slow steps of the aged.

"Better send it to him quick," said Threefoot. "I don't believe he'll last much longer. Strange to think what a rounder he was, back in the days when we'd escape the Rock for an evening of riotous living amongst the blowsy barmaids of Pittsburgh."

Incredulous, ecstatic, Adam tried three times to express his thanks, only to find his tongue tied in the proverbial knot. Meanwhile, Threefoot nattered on.

"Duggan's publishing his memoirs—*Molding the Young Mind: My Life in the Groves of Academe.* It sounds incredibly tedious, but I've agreed to review the hardcopy version, and I know as if by a flash of prophetic insight that the review will be a warm, nay, passionate endorsement. Of course, I'll only read the dust jacket and the first and last pages. Whilst preparing for my comps, I did that with *The Decline and Fall of the Roman Empire* and received compliments from the Committee on my profound grasp of all its major themes."

"Sir, I—I—I—"

"Don't try to thank me, my boy. Take Kate off my hands, be kind to her and my grandchild, and above all make a good job of your dissertation. You must establish yourself as an expert on *something*, you know. Duggan, for instance, has built a distinguished career solely upon knowing in detail what happened between ten and eleven-thirty A.M. on the second day of the Battle of Gettysburg."

"Oh," said Adam, thrown back into gloom. "The dissertation. I still don't have a topic, and Dean Duggan will expect me to include something about it in my C.V."

"Far be it from me," murmured Threefoot, "to thrust a topic upon a rising young scholar who might have other ideas. Yet I happen to know that the Tilton University Press would be delighted to publish a biography of myself, provided it were filled with the sort of warm, tender, intimate touches that bring life to one who might otherwise seem cold and distant, a mere Colossus of scholarship.

"But no debunking. No, no! The most successful biographers are those who leap like sprightly mountain goats from one sunlit peak to another, disregarding the dark valleys that exist in every life, or at least putting them in perspective as the trivia they are. Why, I could name a dozen distinguished bios, all Omnipad Reading Club Main Selections, that might serve as models for the kind of work the Press desires. Creativity, Adam, creativity! Reflect on what I did with the Moon, and do the same with me!

"I might mention, my boy, that I will retire in the next four or five years, and at that time the chair I hold will become vacant. No doubt some of my colleagues will want an older individual for the post. But I believe—I am quite certain—indeed, I am *absolutely* certain—that a young and vigorous scholar of demonstrated ability would be a far better choice."

Adam stared at him. *Why, the arrogant old bastard. He thinks he can plan my whole life for me! I should get up right now, tell him I'm not for sale, and stomp out into the—uh, the—*

The Chicago night? "I can't do better," he heard himself say, "than to follow your guidance, Dad."

Later, when Adam was in bed—actually, lying on a folding cot in the parlor of their suite, while Threefoot's snores echoed from the bedroom and hailstones rattled against the window—he called Kate on his Omnipad.

"So Daddy finally did what I've been after him to do," she said. "It's about time. I mean, what's the use of being a big wheel if you can't help your own son-in-law?"

"He seemed to be afraid we'd move in with him if he didn't."

"Move in with my stepmother? I'd rather share a bathtub with a barracuda. Well, Honey, I'm so glad it's all working out. Daddy terrorizes those academic wimps, but I've been wrapping him around my little finger ever since I was born, almost. Just don't forget," she added sweetly, "where the power lies."

Adam sighed. Threefoot's snores almost shook the walls, while (whilst?) his daughter's loving smile beamed from the Omnipad.

"I don't think I'll ever be able to forget that," he said.

A prizewinner from the haunted streets of (where else?) N'Awlins, home town of Anne Rice and a long line of witches—good, bad, and just plain.

QUEEN FOR A DAY

A SMALL MAN HASTENED down a corridor filled with the funk of cut flowers. His lips moved as he read the names on marble slabs. At last he found the right one and spoke to the chilly stone.

"Honeybunch," he whispered, "I couldn't get what you wanted, but I got you an absolutely beautiful copy... you in there?"

Silence. He repeated the question. More silence.

"Oh God," he cried, sending echoes through the mausoleum, *"where's she gone and what's she up to?"*

"Looka that goddamn king," growled Det. Alphonse Fournet.

"You in a mood," opined his partner, Det. D. J. Tobin. DJ was black and Fournet was white, but both spoke in the downtown New Orleans accent called Yat.

Traffic cops had shifted the movable barriers on Canal Street to let them through. But the parade had ground to a halt. On the royal float the bewigged king was drinking a toast to his queen, a pale deb shivering on the steps of the Posh Club. Just behind, the title float—THE BIBLE, with a wind-shaken, papier mâché Adam, Eve and serpent—blocked the growler's path.

"It's that crooked lawyer, Bose," Fournet bitched on, naming a lawyer famed for his almost magical skill in getting criminals off the hook. "Fuckin' king for a fuckin' night. Fuck him."

"Boy, you in a mood. Wife on your ass again?"

Fournet did not answer, for suddenly crystal goblets splintered on the tarmac, the Queen of Kronos raced inside to get warm, and the parade jerked to life. Space opened behind Adam and Eve, DJ hit the gas and the car slid across Canal into Bourbon Street, the crowd parting as reluctantly as the Red Sea probably had for Moses. Fournet rolled down his window.

"Outa the way, assholes!" he roared.

"Boy, you *really* in a mood," said DJ, shaking his head.

Spinning the wheel, he made the car climb onto the sidewalk. He nudged aside a garish party of transvestite hookers and came to rest under a polished brass plate engraved HOTEL ELEGANZA.

In the doorway the manager, Mr. Arcady, greeted them, wringing his soft hands and saying that he had never, never had a guest murdered before.

"Foist time for everythin'," Fournet growled. "You find the body?"

"No. The bellboy, Melvin Billups, found it. He's been throwing up in the men's room ever since."

"Well, show us where it's at."

The crime scene was a rose-hued room richly furnished with reproduction antiques. Fournet bent over a woman in a peach-colored evening gown. Her face was bluer than her hair and her tongue protruded.

"Name?" he asked Arcady.

"Anna Inverness of Philadelphia, Pennsylvania. Can I—can I go now?"

"Yeah, scram. Wait for me in your office. And tell Melvin when he's done pukin' I wanna see him."

Fournet took out a battered notebook and a pencil, licked the point and wrote, "Crime: Homacide. Victim: Anna Invoice. Motive: Robary? Perpatrater: Unk."

He was scribbling a description of the scene when Doc Pelf waddled in. "What, you all again?" he wheezed.

Despite his fifty-five inch waist, there never seemed to be any room inside the doc for a voice. He sank gasping to his knees and touched the corpse.

"I suppose you gonna say she was kilt by a grenade," suggested DJ, ever jolly. Pulling on latex gloves, he began to dust for prints.

"Nope. What you see is what you get. Old lady was garrotted."

"Ga-whatted?"

"Strangled with a cord. Wait a minute. See these little marks running along the line left by the ligature? Looks to me like she was strangled with a necklace."

"Wouldn't the string a broke?"

"This one didn't."

A wave of perfume caused Fournet to turn his head. Melvin Billups, a young man with a Brut addiction, had appeared at the door.

Fournet ordered him to lead the way to Arcady's office. There Melvin was happy to recount his finding of the body.

"She was gettin' dressed for the Kronos ball. She wanted a snack, so I brung her cheese and fruit. And there she was on the floor with her tongue stickin' out, like a dyke with a hard on."

"Door was open?"

"Nuh uh. I knocked, got no answer, so I used my passkey."

Fournet frowned. Instead of being greenish, Melvin's face was rosy with excitement and acne. Fournet sniffed but failed to detect any taint of vomit under the Brut.

"Huh," he said, puzzled.

But a non-sick bellboy seemed to have nothing to do with the murder. He asked Arcady about the necklace.

"As a matter of fact," said the manager, "I opened the safe to get a necklace for her about three hours ago."

"What was it? Dymunz?"

"No, it was trash. But good trash, if you know what I mean."

"That really narrows it down. This town is the woild capital of junk julery."

Outside, a meat wagon had arrived to collect the body. Fournet watched while Mrs. Inverness, wearing a plastic bag, slid into the wagon on a steel gurney with collapsible legs. A uniformed cop from the Eighth District stopped stretching yellow tape long enough to flash Fournet a big smile.

"Hell of a end for a rich bitch," Fournet muttered, and joined DJ in their car.

"She had $120 in her purse. Here's your half," said DJ, passing bills to Fournet, who pocketed them without a word. "So whatchoo think happened to the lady?"

"The bellboy says the door was locked, so she let the killer in herself. He seen her wearing what looked like dymunz, strangled her with the necklace, pulled it off and split."

"The old broad picked up the wrong kinda stud," opined DJ. "Happens alla time."

Fournet frowned. Something was wrong with this reasonable reconstruction, but what? He stared at a drunken seaman throwing up on the sidewalk; his shipmates had gathered around him and were chanting, "Go! Go! Go!" The little tableau made him think of something…but he couldn't remember what.

"Let's get the hell outa here," Fournet said, and the car bumped over the curb, crushing beads and beer cans as it went. On Canal Street the parade had passed, leaving a huge drifting throng, every member of which was wearing thick strings of glittering beads thrown from the floats by the maskers.

Fournet sighed. *Anybody* could be the killer, strolling casually homeward, wearing the murder weapon.

Arriving late at his house on Laissez les Bons Temps Rouler Boulevard, Algiers, Fournet picked up red beans and rice and pork chops his wife Alma had left steaming over pots of water in the kitchen. He grabbed a beer and joined her in the den, where she was watching a rerun of *Bewitched*.

Alma turned, a sour expression on her wide face.

"I just hoid today Lootenant Toussaint is gonna be King of Nero. Why dint you tell me?"

"It slipped my mind."

"Yeah, right. I hadda find out from his queen in the Piggly Wiggly. She's that big black gal from Sex Crimes. When she tole me I said, 'I ain't never seen a queen makin' groceries before,' and she said, 'Well, you seen it now, Honey.'"

The anecdote seemed to have no point except to underline the royal status of everybody except the Fournets.

"Someday I'd kind of like to be queen of Hecate myself. Someday before I'm dead, that is. How you think I feel when the annual Queen's Luncheon comes up and I don't never get to go, hah?"

"We ain't got that kind of money. I can't knock down like some people can. Whatchoo think I'm in, Narcotics?"

"So how come that gal in Sex Crimes can do it?"

"In Sex Crimes you loin a lot of embarrassin' stuff. You can knock down in Sex Crimes. Homicide's different. You ever try to embarrass a corpse?"

Giving a hearty sniff, Alma rose and headed upstairs to bed. Fournet poured himself a triple brandy and channel-surfed until he fell asleep in the chair, a common occurrence *chez Fournet*.

Just after dawn he woke up, showered the kinks out of his body, dressed in a $150 wash 'n' wear suit, white shirt and 1958-style knit tie, and headed for the bridge-and-freeway complex called the Crescent City Connection. The sun performed its curious local feat of rising over the west bank of the Mississippi and its reflection in his rear-view mirror seared Fournet's eyeballs. A blue mist of monoxide hung over the interchange. The traffic was horrendous. A new day had begun.

Homicide throbbed with its customary madness. For weeks life there had been a zoo. Bodies turned up in vacant lots, canals, sewers and public housing. Some were chalky, some gray as clinkers, some swollen and dark like overripe eggplants. Over all hung the morning-breath smell of unfresh blood and/or the stink of decay.

Modifying Chaos was Procedure. Day by day papers fluttered into in-boxes. The computer system flickered and beeped, or went down to a chorus of curses. Fournet and DJ looked at corpses, yawned, drank coffee to stay awake, questioned witnesses, scribbled in their notebooks. From an inner office Chief of Detectives Amedee Toussaint roared at his underlings, demanding they keep the media off his ass. Toussaint's normal voice sounded like a bass drum, but when he roared you could hear him from Westwego to Arabi.

And then, as if the normal Mardi Gras mess wasn't sufficient, the Times Picayune decided to make a big deal out of Mrs. Inverness's murder. VISITOR STRANGLED AT HEIGHT OF CARNIVAL SEASON, thundered the morning headline. The result was a spate of phone calls to the mayor's office from hoteliers who swung considerable weight.

Just past noon Fournet and DJ were summoned into Toussaint's office. They found him wearing pantyhose, rouge, a sequined cape, a wig, white vinyl boots, and a plastic crown. Zircons flashed from his scepter as he practiced waving to imaginary throngs. "So whatchoo think?" he asked.

"You some kinda king," DJ, ever the politician, assured him. "I never seen nobody look no better."

"I don't know," he rumbled, dissatisfied. "The outfit's okay, but it still needs a li'l sump'm to make it sparkle."

Then he got serious. "Now lissen. The Mayor called and he's shittin' green. It's this old broad moider in the Quarter, okay?"

"Okay," mumbled his audience. Toussaint tapped his scepter against Fournet's large gut to underline his words.

"You guys find the sumbitch done it and if you can't, find some other sumbitch and stick him with it. Now you know I never said nothin' like this, but that's where the fuck it's at, okay? I mean, we're talkin' *tourism* here, for Christ sakes. Don't let the door hit you in the ass," he concluded, "on the way out."

They left him parading up and down, waving his scepter.

"We gotta charge somebody," Fournet told DJ over coffee cups in the cafeteria downstairs, "or he'll have us ridin' scooters in the Desire Project. We need like a bone to throw the dogs to."

"How about Arcady?"

"Nuh uh. Guy's loaded. We grab him and that lawyer Bose'd land on us like a thousand-pound canary."

DJ frowned deeply with the effort of thought. Then Fournet slapped the formica tabletop with a sound like a falling gavel.

"That bellboy at the hotel. He lied about pukin'."

"Yeah, you right," said DJ, though he had no idea what Fournet was talking about.

"Let's go, then."

"Where to?"

"The hotel, asshole."

At the Eleganza a shock awaited them. When they cornered Mr. Arcady, he told them that Melvin hadn't come to work that day because he had been arrested.

"He was *arrested*?"

"Yes," said Arcady. "You know, Detective, I always imagined that Melvin was just acne on the hoof. But he gets around."

"He was *arrested*?" Fournet repeated. "For killin' Invoice?"

"No, the other one," said Arcady. "Didn't you hear? His girlfriend was strangled early this morning."

"Whoops!" said DJ.

Fournet was staring. "Where you hoid this at, smart guy?"

"Channel Four news."

"You mean he's the right one after all?"

"You some kinda detective," said DJ, slapping his partner on the back. "You had the right guy and dint even know it."

After making a call from Arcady's office, Fournet and DJ headed back to midcity and police headquarters. There a clerk dug out a cassette with Melvin's just-completed interrogation, and provided them a machine to play it on.

"I couldna done nothin' bad to my baby," the bellboy's nasal voice sobbed. "I love her, for Chrissake. That's why I took that dymun necklace to give her."

"Oh, yeah?" growled the voice of the interrogator, Det. Schlechter. "Now that's innerestin', Mel. Tell me all about that necklace. You gonna feel a lot better after you do. Also, if I hafta jump up and down on you, you gonna feel a lot woise."

After more badgering, Melvin admitted taking the necklace from Mrs. Inverness's body and hiding it in a toilet tank in a men's room off the Eleganza's lobby. Schlechter then booked him with Felony Theft, pending further investigation of the two murders.

Fournet and DJ left headquarters and crossed a narrow street to Central Lockup. From outside, the building looked like a large gray animal shelter. Inside, the smells of disinfectant, vile food and sour bodies confirmed the image.

Fournet and DJ passed through the metal detectors, waved at a couple of acquaintances, and headed for the Criminal Sheriff's office. Aided by a deputy, they extracted Melvin from the cell where he was awaiting arraignment and took him to an interrogation room decorated with peeling, gray-green paint.

In an ill-fitting orange jumpsuit, Melvin was a long way from the natty bellboy of the Eleganza Hotel. Instead of Brut, he smelled of jail and misery. He had been crying for hours, and now began again as he insisted that he hadn't killed nobody.

"Sure you did, Mel," said Fournet in a kindly tone. "You killed Miz Invoice to get that necklace for your girlfriend."

"No, no, no," Melvin wept.

"You tell the truth, we can get you life," wheedled DJ. "Otherwise, zappo—the lethal injection," and he mimed a needle jab into his left forearm. Melvin winced.

"Be nice to the kid," said Fournet. "He probably didn't know what he was doin'. Right, Mel?"

"Nuh uh. I never done nothin' like that before. Oh, I'm so glad Mama's dead and in heaven."

"See, DJ? Mel's a good kid, he wants to tell us the truth. Don't you, Mel?"

"Yes sir," sobbed Melvin.

Fournet slid a pad of yellow paper and a ballpoint pen to DJ. "Write down, 'I want to tell the truth. I didn't know what I was doin'.' What'd you do, Mel, pull on the necklace?"

"What?"

"Did you pull on the necklace?"

"Oh, yeah. Yeah. It was wound so tight. . . . "

"Write this, DJ. 'The necklace was wound tight around Miz Invoice's neck and I pulled hard upon it.'"

An hour later, the two detectives dropped into Toussaint's in-box a brief signed statement in which Melvin appeared to admit that he had panicked and killed Mrs. Inverness while robbing her. Then they went downstairs for more coffee.

"There, that oughta take the heat off," said Fournet as they stirred plastic cups with plastic spoons.

"I admired how you got Melvin to confess," said DJ warmly.

"It's like you got a rat in a corner," Fournet told him. "He goes left, you go left. He goes right, you go right. I just wish," he added, "that we could find that necklace. That'd really make Toussaint sit up and take notice."

"We'll find it. You some kinda detective. I loin sump'm new from watchin' you every day."

Suddenly Fournet jerked to his feet and roared, "SCHLECHTER! OVER HERE!"

A squarish man resembling an ingot of pig iron in a permanently unpressed suit made his way across the cafeteria to their table and dropped into an empty chair.

"Where y'at?" he asked, surveying Fournet and DJ with the illusionless eyes of a stray tomcat. He began to dunk a big sugar-crusted Danish into his coffee.

"Look, tell me about that necklace Billups's girlfriend got kilt with," Fournet said.

"Well, that's what her mama said. Me, I never seen no such of a thing. It was a ligature strangulation all right, but there wasn't no cord or nothin' in the vissinty of the victim."

"Goddawg," exclaimed DJ, "but that necklace gets around! Where's it at now? Whatchoo think, pardner?"

After deep reflection, Fournet answered, "I think I'll have me a Danish. That one Schlechter's got looks good and gooey."

—.——

Back in Homicide, Fournet and DJ were summoned to Toussaint's office and congratulated on their quick work in obtaining a semi-plausible confession.

"Not too bad," rumbled the great man. "I mean it's bullshit, but it's enough to where we can charge him with moider, and that'll kind of cool things off, y'unnerstand what I'm sayin'?"

Toussaint was back in civvies, except for his crown, which he'd forgotten to remove.

"Sometimes I almost think you guys ain't the total assholes you most generally act like. Look, try'n get this Melvin character to admit he done the young broad, too. Be nice if we could kill two boids, like."

Conferring with DJ over beers at Ya Mama's Bar & Grill on Tulane Avenue, Fournet decided to check the crime scene before trying to get Melvin to implicate himself a second time.

"Remember this, DJ," he said solemnly. *"It don't never hoit to look at evidence, provided you keep in mind that it ain't nothin' but evidence."*

Schlechter's report revealed that Melvin's girlfriend had been named Baby C. Motley. When Fournet and DJ arrived at the paintless cottage on Grand Trianon Street where she had lived, they found it overflowing with people bringing food and comfort to her mother.

"You watch the car," Fournet ordered, after viewing the rundown neighborhood. "Last time I had one snatched from under me, Toussaint was on my back for a month."

Mrs. Motley, an ample woman in pink plastic curlers and a spectacular orange kimono, was weeping and eating lasagna in the kitchen. The volume of sound was earsplitting. Forcing his way through the mob, Fournet was offered a chair at the table by Baby's brother, Ptn. Lester Motley, an Eighth District uniformed cop. "Detective Fournet," he said warmly.

Fournet frowned. He had a vague feeling he'd seen this scrubbed young face before.

"Do I know you?"

"Yes, sir, from the Eleganza Hotel. I know the names of every detective from Lootenant Toussaint on down. Now shut up, y'all!" Lester shouted. "And don't listen in, you hear? This ossifer's gonna talk to Mama like he has to, awright?"

Everybody fell back, creating a zone of relative quiet in which Fournet addressed the grieving mother.

"Baby was your daughter, Miz Motley?"

"Yeah, and she was so precious. I can't tell ya how sweet and dawlin' she was. She was never sick a day in her life until she met that boy. Then, right off, stuff begun to happen. Foist she got a yeast infection, then a urinary, and then she got killed with that necklace he give her. *Gawd*, I hate Melvin Billups. It's like he's coist or sump'm."

"Was Melvin with her when she died?"

"Nobody was with her at all. That's what I can't unnerstand. Baby always got up real oily for her job cuttin' meat at Swagman Giant Supermarket. She was all alone in her room gettin' dressed when I hoid her fall down and start threshin' around. And I never seen my…Baby…alive no more."

Her large face swelled dangerously and she dissolved into tears. Women rushed up, pressing wads of Kleenex upon her.

Fournet excused himself and rose from the table. Lester pulled him into a corner and handed him a drink that proved to be vodka and orange juice.

"Detective," he said respectfully, "I hope you don't mind me sayin' I gotta great ambition to, like, follow in your footsteps."

Fournet sipped the drink.

"Well, see can you help me out with this case. Your Mama says your sister was kilt with a necklace Billups give her. Was he around here? And where's the necklace?"

Lester shook his head.

"Baby had it last night. She really liked it; it was the foist nice thing Melvin ever give her. He went home about nine-thoity and never come back this mornin'. Mama was in bed in the front room and I was in the back and Baby's room is in between us."

His clean pink face was a study in puzzlement. "I just don't see how anybody coulda got at her. I just don't see it."

Fournet swallowed the last of his drink.

"You have you a great career in law enforcement," he said, and wrestled his way out of the house.

DJ was leaning on the car blowing smoke rings that drifted upward and dispersed against a cloudless February sky. A school band was marching by, headed toward some parade or other. Their brass instruments made noises like a herd of rutting gnus. Plump girls dressed entirely in purple sequins twirled batons and backsides. The sweaty bandsmen followed, bug-eyed and tootling.

"So, did Melvin do it?" DJ asked.

"He couldna. And neither could nobody else. Baby was like in a sandwich between her mama and her brother, who's a cop. The crime's physically impossible."

They stared at each other, baffled.

"Somethin' fuckin' weird is goin' on," DJ opined. "My grammaw, she runs a spiritual choich on St. Roch. It's kind of like Catlick voodoo. She been prayin' to the Voigin and sacrificin' a buncha chickens to get me promoted. We could get her to ask the spirits."

But Fournet wasn't yet ready to turn to witchcraft.

"Foist we try some more policin'," he decided. "If that don't woik, voodoo is next."

That evening life on Laissez les Bons Temps Rouler Boulevard was much the same as before, except that Alma hadn't turned the stove on under the pots of water and Fournet's dinner had congealed into a mass resembling rubble masonry. Stolidly, he ate it anyway while she berated him because she wasn't royalty.

"It's Mardi Gras and everybody in Noo Awlyunz is king or queen of sump'm," she pointed out.

"Them kings and queens ain't nothing but a bunch of assholes dressed up in fake dymunz, fake beards, fake everythin'."

"I swear to Jesus, you got no more ambition than a terlet."

After she went to bed, he poured himself a quadruple brandy and channel-surfed. The parade of Nero was being broadcast on Channel 4, but he flipped past it with a muttered curse. Finally he found a Stooge-a-thon on Channel 78 and settled down to enjoy himself. He was chuckling over the way Curly fell into a bandsaw when a news bulletin interrupted the show. A tragic fatality had occurred during the parade of Nero.

Hastily Fournet flipped back to Channel 4. Garishly lighted by flares and popping flashes, an immense crowd sluggishly gave way to an ambulance. Klaxon horns brayed and sirens whooped and whistled. A newsman shouted into a microphone, giving details.

Fournet listened, muttered "Key-rice," downed his brandy, hit the power button on his clicker, and headed up to bed.

"Anythin' happenin'?" asked his drowsy wife from a deep nest of bedclothes. She lay under a cloud of subtle odors rising from the salves and creams she put on at night.

"You might say."

After an irritating silence, Alma said, "So? What happened?"

"Toussaint fell offa his float and broke his neck is what."

Alma raised herself in bed like a surfacing manatee and stared at him, round-eyed.

"Noooooooooo shit," she whispered.

"You could say that, too," he said, climbing into bed in his XXL jockey shorts.

"If you was to become chief of detectives, we could afford me bein' queen of Hecate next year."

"I ain't gonna get Toussaint's job. The superintendent'll want somebody young and black and I ain't neither one."

"You solve that moider and you might get it."

"Fat chance. That necklace business is from outer space."

"Either you get me the money to be queen or you ain't never gonna have another peaceful hour as long as you live."

"Bitch!"

"Bastard!"

"Cunt!"

"Prick!"

Fournet got very little sleep that night. Neither did Alma, but she made up for it after he left for work.

—.—

At headquarters next morning, Fournet slouched wearily through pale corridors where a greasy brown streak ran along the walls at shoulder height and banged into a pasteboard office full of plastic-laminate-over-fiberboard furniture.

DJ was waiting for him, giving dislocating yawns and sipping a paper cup of machine-made coffee.

"Doc Pelf wants you should call him."

"What about?"

DJ shrugged. Fournet put in the call and when Pelf's wheezy voice replied, he asked, "Whassamatta, Doc?"

"The proper phrase is, 'What's up, Doc?'" said Pelf jocularly. "Hey. I guess you heard about your boss dying?"

"Yeah. He fell offa the float. So?"

"You want to guess how he died?"

"By hittin' his head on the pavement."

"Nope. By ligature strangulation. The hyoid bone was broken. He didn't die because he fell off, he fell off because he was being garrotted. Want to guess what with?"

"Four feet of coaxial cable?" Fournet suggested, hopefully. Pelf chuckled.

"Yeah, right," he said. "The necklace is back in circulation."

Fournet struggled to clear his head, which felt as if it was packed with plaster.

"Who was on the float with him?"

"Nobody except the Royal Cupbearer, who is eight years old and the mayor's nephew."

"Then it's impossible too. Like the other one."

He rang off and, pausing only long enough to tell DJ the news, headed for the Men's Toilet. There he selected a comfortable stall, sat down and put a roll of paper behind his head. Soothed by the murmur of water, ignoring the echoing voices and random explosive flushes, he fell asleep and snoozed for fifty-five minutes, awaking refreshed.

DJ was putting on his holster when he returned to the office.

"More meat," he said succinctly.

The address of the new victim lay west of the Quarter in the crime-haunted streets of Tremé. In a ratty old building layered with ochre paint, a shaky circular staircase led up to a cheap apartment. Guarding the door was Patrolman Lester Motley, Eighth District.

"Hey, Detective," he greeted Fournet breezily. "You and me only go to the best moiders, right?"

"Yeah, right," grunted Fournet.

The victim's apartment was a symphony of green-dyed ostrich plumes, flea market versions of African masks, moth-eaten potpourri, jars filled with dried pampas grass, and a six-foot papier-mâché rabbit from a Little Theater version of *Harvey*, attired in a sequined jockstrap.

The owner of all these riches was long and bony, bald-headed and boa-wrapped, lying separated from a red fright wig in the middle of the floor. Apparently he was a fanatic parade-goer, for aluminum doubloons from a dozen krewes were scattered everywhere. One doubloon attracted Fournet's eye as he bent over the body: stamped on its face was a fat drunk in a toga and the word *Nero*. The drag queen had been hustling the crowd during last night's parade.

Instantly Fournet was on his knees, pulling plastic beads, scarlet wig, and purple feather boa away from the victim's neck.

DJ asked, "Whatchoo find?" but Fournet paid no attention. He was staring at the now-familiar deep crimson mark of a ligature lined with tiny bruises and minuscule bleeding cuts from the beads of a necklace.

"Shit fire," seemed insufficient, and he could think of nothing else to say. He rose to his feet, staring at DJ, hardly hearing the shuffle and weighty creaking of the stair outside as Doc Pelf made his slow way upward.

Then he was squeezing past the Doc without a word of greeting, moving with a kind of elephantine speed to the head of the stairs, where he grabbed Patrolman Motley by the arm.

"Lester," he breathed, "you know what happens to a young cop goes to jail?" Lester stared at him.

"What happens is, he winds up with a butt looks like the back end of a Thanksgivin' toikey. Now gimme that goddamn necklace. Now! Give it to me."

Slowly Lester pulled a glittering object from his pocket and put it into Fournet's hand.

"It wasn't doin' Baby no more good when I took it the foist time," he apologized. "I hoid Toussaint was lookin' for nice stuff for his costume and I really, really wanna be a detective."

"So why you took it this time, then?"

"The fag musta stole it off Toussaint's body, right? I mean, he was a thief. I was, uh, gonna toin it in."

"Yeah, right," said Fournet, and rejoined DJ and Doc Pelf.

DJ was saying cheerfully, "I guess you gonna say the victim choked on a hairball, eh, Doc?"

"No such luck. It was the you-know-what again."

Fournet slipped into the bathroom, which featured a quadruped bathtub full of tubes and bottles of makeup and a cracked, clouded full-length mirror. He pushed the door to, and extracted the necklace from his pocket.

He was thinking of Arcady's description. Trash, but good trash. Good rhinestones, some dabbled with blood. No catch to break and a strong, tough cord. A garrotter's dream.

Experimentally he twisted the necklace around one fat hand, then suddenly tore it off and flung it into the bathtub. He stared in terror, first at the necklace, then at himself in the mirror.

"It couldn'ta," he whispered.

But it had. He'd felt it tighten on his hand.

Fournet slipped a ballpoint pen out of his shirt pocket, bent and lifted the necklace. He searched the litter in the bathtub, found a mostly empty face-powder box, dropped the necklace inside, fitted the lid, and slipped it into his coat pocket.

He emerged from the bathroom with mind made up. He said to DJ, "Where at you said your grammaw has that choich?"

"By St. Roch."

"Then that's where we goin'. Detectin' by itself ain't gonna woik in this case. We gotta call in the spirits."

—.—

The Divine Word Outreach Ministry Spiritual Church occupied a former chicken 'n' ribs outlet on a dusty stretch of St. Roch Avenue among a clutter of shotgun cottages.

DJ's grandmother had suede-colored skin and wrinkles like a mudflat baked by the sun. Dressed in jeans and T-shirt, she was pushing aside wooden and metal folding chairs to sweep the church floor and singing softly to herself, "Got my hand in the hand of the man from Galilee."

DJ asked her where she was at, got a vigorous hug and kiss in return, and introduced Fournet. "So what I can do you for?" she wanted to know. Fournet pulled out the box and exposed the necklace.

"This thing has kilt four people that I know of. I don't mean it was used to kill 'em, I mean it kilt 'em all by itself. Also, it tried to grab my hand when I was lookin' at it."

She frowned. "Prob'ly a snake spirit got into it."

"How that happens?"

"Who knows? The woild be fulla spirits and they got to go somewheres. Desiré, Honey, you know where everything is at, so you find your friend a beer while I gets ready to mess with this coise."

Fournet was stunned to learn that DJ's first name was Desiré. He'd had a vague idea it was Derrick, an impression DJ had done nothing to dispel. In a small, neat kitchen to the rear of the church they drank Turbodog beers, while Fournet explained how he'd come into possession of the necklace.

DJ was impressed. "How you knew that cop had taken it?"

"Who else? The foist time it was Melvin and the thoid time it was the drag queen, but who was the only guy around coulda taken it the second and fourth times? We was watchin' each other, and the necklace was gone before Doc Pelf arrived."

"Yeah, I see what you mean. You some kinda detective."

"Thanks."

DJ's grandmother returned, wearing purple robes and carrying a freshly cut branch of sago palm. She explained that ever since the first Palm Sunday in Jerusalem, palms had kept the memory of the Lord Jesus riding over them, and were blest.

"On the other hand, that tree they made the cross from, you know? It was coist, and so it died out. They ain't no trees like that no more. Desiré, look in the fridge, Honey, and bring me the blue fruit jar with the holy water in it."

She first led them in the Lord's Prayer, then dipped the frond into the holy water and extended it toward Fournet. He draped the necklace over the palm and watched—in a condition beyond disbelief—as the beads twisted back and forth, glittering.

"Yeah, sump'm mean be in here," said the priestess. She dipped the rhinestones into the jar and the necklace twisted more violently.

"Now, you all join in, you hear?" she said. "When I say sump'm, you say 'Amen!' And say it loud!"

She drew a deep breath and addressed the necklace. "Because thou hast done this thing, thou art coist among all cattle and beasts!"

"AMEN!" they roared.

"Upon thy belly shalt thou go!"

"AMEN!"

"Doit shalt thou eat all the days of thy life!"

"AMEN!"

"Come out, soipent! Come out, soipent!"

The exorcism went on for twenty minutes, until all three of them were running with sweat. The necklace continued to be agitated, but that was all.

"This here is a serious spirit," she acknowledged, wiping her brow. "This ain't no spirit just kind of casually crawled into these beads. Look to me like it's the woik of a witch."

"So what I do?" asked Fournet.

"Find out who owned it before it started killin'. That'll be the witch. You'll find a offerin' jar at the door, and Desiré, don't you and your friend just walk past it, neither. If it was just you I wouldn't charge nothin', but when I woik for the po-leece, I gotta right to be paid."

Fournet and DJ deposited ten dollars of Mrs. Inverness's money in a tall bell jar and returned to their car, where the radio was beeping steadily. Fournet answered.

"Yeah?"

"We just gotta call in," squawked the voice at the other end. "A citizen says she sold a piece of evidence to Miz Whatever—Inver—Inven—"

"Invoice," snapped Fournet. "Smatta, can'tcha read? What'd she sell the old broad?"

"A necklace. You innerested?"

From a moist flagstone sidewalk next door to a gargoyle shop, Fournet and DJ spent a minute contemplating the show window of Mardi Gras Memories, Marie LaMarie, Prop.

The clutter made the drag queen's apartment look neat. Engraved invitations, scepters dripping rhinestones, jeweled and feathered masks, caped sequined robes, a Mardi Gras Indian costume so complex the patterns bewildered the eye.

"They got 'em some of the real stuff," Fournet acknowledged, and pushed through the door.

A smiling, rotund Cajun woman approached, saying, "Bonjour." She had sun-tanned skin, shining black hair and dark, moist eyes like an intelligent ox.

"Where y'at?" said Fournet, showing his ID. "Look to me like you gotta great place here."

"Tanks. Me, I'm Marie LaMarie. Glad you like it. Ten year ago when I move from Opelousas wit' my hoozbond I figure, well, if I must live in the cité, I go whole hog. So I open up Mardi Gras Memories."

"What took you so long to call the po-leece about this necklace, Miz LaMarie?"

"I don' like crime reports, all 'at bloody stuff. I switch off sound when it comes on TV. But today somebody start talkin' 'bout the murder, and *toute de suite*—" She snapped her fingers. "Like 'at I reelize."

He showed her the necklace. She nodded.

"Yeah, 'at's it. An ole lady buy it. She love 'at necklace. I tole her it was favor for a queen, and 'at was true."

"Where you got it at, Miz LaMarie?"

"Estate sale. Come in my office and I check the records."

She led them on a winding path through heaps of musty costumes. Plaster heads modeled quarter-face masks, half-face, whole face, whole head.

Antique lithographs portrayed floats covered with jewels, insects, fairies, demons.

"I also gotta X-rated section in back," she said. "You gentlemen wanna to go in, it's okay, but I'm too embarrass to go wit' you."

Her office held a glass cabinet filled with favors from balls—glittering pins, cups, bracelets and, yes, necklaces. Fournet and DJ waited while she flipped through a shoebox full of 5x8 cards.

"Here. Owner died and her stuff got sole off. Necklace, it had a real frayed cord. Me and my hoozbond, we like to fish, so I restrung it on good strong fishin' leader, 200-pound test. After I sole it I gotta letter from a lawyer who offer to buy it back."

She dug into a second shoebox stuffed with bills and letters and extracted an envelope of thick cream-laid paper.

"Yes," she said, handing over the letter. "Guy name Bose. It was heirloom that got sole by mistake. I never answer him, so he phone me today. When I tole him it was gone, he sound kind of desperate, you know? He ask who buy it, I say a lady name Miz Inverness, and he say: Oh Jesus, not 'at woman who got kill? So I knew I must call cops."

She smiled, sentimentally. "He sound so sad, Mr. Bose. He must reelly love his wife, wanna get back her necklace so bad. I hope my hoozbond feel 'at way about me when I'm dead."

But Fournet had an idea Bose's emotion was something other than love.

The offices of Bose, Partridge, & Lemon occupied the top eleven floors of a skyscraper called the Place St. Georges. Fournet and DJ had to take three elevators to get to the eyrie where the senior partners dwelt.

The secretary of A.L.T. Bose III was an imposing woman whose helmet of blonde hair had apparently been turned in a machine shop.

"Whom shall I announce?"

"Detective Fournet and Detective Tobin, NOPD."

"May I inquire what your visit is in regard to?"

"Official business."

"Can you be more specific?"

"No."

"Please have a seat."

As she was vanishing into Bose's office, Fournet asked DJ loudly, "Just whom the fuck she thinks she is?"

Bose sat at a long, expensive mahogany table. His morocco leather chair just missed throne dimensions. A tall, ornate window opened on a bird's-eye view of the Mississippi River, of wharves and warehouses, gray streets and glimmering canals, all fading into a distant bluish horizon.

Despite the signs of prosperity and success, Bose did not look happy. His eyes had sunk into nests of dark bags and smudges and his pale, thin hands trembled like a victim of Parkinson's. The first word that came to Fournet's mind was "haunted."

"What can I do for you, Officers?" he asked in a weak, distant voice. His intonations were Garden District—a slight weary drawl, like a man on the verge of sleep.

Fournet pulled up an ornate chair, sat down and gestured for DJ to do the same. He extracted the face-powder box from his pocket and shook the necklace out on the table. Then he sat back and watched Bose's eyes grow big.

"You reckanize this?"

"Um yes. Um yes, I do. It belonged to my wife, Aloysia. It was, um, sold by mistake."

He sighed deeply.

"A great…big…mistake. She'd left specific instructions she was to be buried in the regalia she wore in 1963 as Queen of Medea. She was born, well, *downtown*—by the *Industrial Canal*," he whispered, as if still incredulous over his mesalliance—"and that one night of glory was incredibly meaningful to her. That's Aloysia," he added, pointing.

Fournet and DJ turned and stared at a portrait in oils of a woman in royal robes, glittering crown, scepter, and an all-too-familiar necklace. Her face was a clock-stopper and her small black eyes had the beady, fixed intensity of a king—or in this case, queen—cobra.

DJ leaned over and whispered in Fournet's ear, *"That ain't no snake in that necklace. It's the witch her own self."*

"Jesus X. Christ," Fournet muttered. "So that's how this guy got so goddamn rich. Whenever he went to trial, she put grisgris on the other side." Turning back to Bose, he asked, "Where's she at?"

"Evermore Mausoleum. At least, her remains are. Her spirit may be elsewhere. It would be nice," he said wistfully, "if…if I could take that necklace to her, uh, resting place. If I don't, who knows what she might do next?"

His voice trembled.

"Sorry," said Fournet, returning the necklace to its box and the box to his pocket. "This here's evidence. It might be released in a year or two, but even then it goes to Miz Invoice's heirs. I just hope it don't kill none of them like it did her, the drag queen, the lady butcher and the chief of detectives."

"Oh God!" cried Bose, plunging his face into his old spotty hands. Then, slowly, he looked up.

"But," he said.

"But what?"

"I happen—just happen—to have a copy of the necklace in my possession. You could turn that in."

He gave Fournet a significant look.

"It's a *perfect* copy. You'd be amazed, Officer, if you saw how much it cost me. Why, just look at this," he said, extracting from the drawer of his desk/table a checkbook in a long black tooled leather cover, stamped with his name in gold.

"Just look at what I had to pay," he said, handing the checkbook to Fournet, whose eye, possibly by accident, fell not on the amount paid to Goldmark Fine Jewelers but rather on Bose's current balance, which was more than merely impressive.

"If only," mourned Bose's elegant, die-away accent, "there was some way that we—'we' meaning, for the purposes of this transaction, you and I and your, uh, partner—could reach a meeting of minds."

Fournet looked at DJ. DJ looked at Fournet.

"It may be," said Fournet slowly, "that we can."

"So how's your home life these days?" asked DJ, when he bumped into

Fournet, both of them wearing rented tuxes, at the Hecate ball. All around them, dancing couples masked as beasts and beauties bounced and gyrated like a multicolored sea to the sounds of the New Leviathan Oriental Foxtrot Orchestra.

A year had passed and Mardi Gras had returned, as it tended to do. In answer to DJ's question Fournet gestured at the enormous, glittering figure of Alma on her royal throne, center stage at the Municipal Auditorium.

"When she's happy, everybody's happy," he said. "When she ain't, fuhgeddit. Right now she's happy. So how you like your new job?"

The Superintendent of Police had selected DJ to fill Toussaint's job, citing his success in solving the Inverness murder. Alma had wanted Fournet to file a reverse-discrimination suit, but he argued that it was better to keep DJ as a friend and anyway, you couldn't fight the spirits.

"It's hard," DJ answered soberly. "But I try to remember all the stuff you loined me. And Grammaw's helpin' me in her own way."

"She's some lady. You know, DJ, there's good witches, there's bad witches, and there's—" he gazed again at Alma—"just plain witches. By the way, whatever happened to Melvin Billups?"

"Judge threw out the moider charge. Lucky for me, it was after I was promoted. Melvin got two years for theft, less time soived."

"Fuckin' judges are all soft on crime."

Later that evening, Fournet danced with the queen. Alma flashed and twinkled in so many zircons that he wished he had dark glasses on. Her girdled waist felt like an oil drum and leading her was like steering a drug-smuggler's overloaded boat through choppy seas. But love flooded out of her like an aura.

"Sweetheart," she whispered, "this here's the best night I had since April 1, 1970, when you laid me the foist time in the Rubicon Motel on Airline Drive."

"Yeah, well I'm still the same guy done it way back then," he assured her gallantly. They leaned toward each other would have kissed, except that his gut and her bosom in combination held them apart.

So the dancers whirled on until the sun rose over the west bank of the river, and it was time for gleaming floats to turn into pumpkins, and kings and queens into housewives and cops and lawyers and veeps of middling concerns. Time also for all of them to begin dreaming up future fantasies to make tolerable the vile grind of existence.

Later that morning, in the Evermore Mausoleum, A.L.T. Bose presented a fresh red rose in a bud vase to Aloysia's marble slab.

"Honeybunch," he whispered, "Honeybunch…you in there?"

Out of the depths came a dark, whispery, sibilant sound like rough scales rustling over stones.

"Ssso, whatchoo think?" Aloysia asked.

For all you Trekkies, all you fans of Luke and Darth, here's a rousing tale of human chutzpah and native vengeance on a world far, far away.

THE TRIBES OF BELA

DOCUMENTS ASSEMBLED BY THE *Honorable Committee Investigating the Tragedy on Planet Bela, and JUDGMENT Thereupon.*

Item (1.) *Extracts from the Notebook of Kohn, Robert Rogers, Colonel, Security Forces.*

I feel like I'm diving, not landing.

Bucking headwinds, the freighter's shuttle fights wind and rain until we drop out of the overcast over a blue-black sea. We're heading for a small rocky headland that juts out of a dim coastline.

The green duroplast shuttleport looks like a large fake emerald set in a broken ring of foam. The retros sear the pad, and clouds of steam boil up. As the sole passenger, I'm allowed to exit the ship before its rusty handling bots begin loading. An army of shiny ingots—gold, titanium, metals I don't have a name for—stands to attention, scoured by rain, awaiting the outward journey.

Two moronic guards (male & female) named Vizbee and Smelt retrieve my luggage under the baleful eye of Julia Mack, Captain, Security. My local counterpart salutes and I say falsely that I'm glad to be here. Smelt comments, "You may be glad now, but you won't be for long."

Vizbee adds, "Oughta give this goddamn swamp back to the Arkies."

"*QUIET!*" trumpets Captain Mack, and without further comment, the guards stow my things in a little flyer waiting in a hangar with airfoils retracted. Climbing in, I feel the four or five extra kilos I weigh here—also taste a fizzy, champagne-like something in the air. Maybe the extra oxygen will help me carry the extra weight. Or maybe just make me drunk.

Welcome to Planet Bela, old man.

We're barreling toward Main Base over fog-shrouded cliffs, through a squall blowing in from the ocean. Mack thinks it's all beautiful.

"Born here," she proclaims, her voice overfilling the cabin. "Only human that ever was. Against company policy, of course; Mama was on the pill, but something went wrong. Folks died in a mining accident and the colony raised me. Now, with these murders, they're talking about closing down the mines. People say we're going home—but for me, this *is* home."

"If I can help you catch the killer," I tell her, "the mines will stay open."

The smell of disbelief mingles with the odor of mildew from her uniform and lacquer from her regulation black wig. Christ, what a huge woman—must weigh close to ninety kilos. Yet not flabby. Her haunch pressed against me is solid as a buffalo's.

We turn west—or is it north?—above the estuary of a wide river where it swirls into the sea, spreading crescents of foam. A pod of enormous sea creatures rises all together, like dancers, and submerges again. I spot the gleam of tusks. Then we're skating in toward a cliff covered with a cluster of domes, semiplast storehouses, and connecting corridors like chicken-runs.

Whoa…what the hell?

Beneath the clutter lie huge blocks of stone shaped and fitted together like a puzzle. Did I come four-point-something light years to find the Incas have been here before me?

"Welcome to Zamók, Colonel," says Captain Mack, expertly bringing us in to a landing on the gray circle of a rain-slick pad.

As a boy I loved listening to the adventures of old Navigator Mayakovsky—the Explorer of a Thousand Worlds, as one of my textbooks used to say in the clear neutral voice I still hear in dreams.

He named this one Bela, meaning white. When I saw it from space, I thought the reason was the clouds of water vapor that make it glow almost like Venus. But I was wrong.

"Some information for you," says Mack, handing me a memory cube as we stand at the Entries and Departures desk. I plug it into my notebook and listen idly while an autoclerk enters my essential data into the colony's mainframe.

The cube tells me much I already knew. About Bela's wildly eccentric orbit. About the 241 standard years it takes to make its awesome trek. About its endless seasons, whose radical heat and cold result from the orbital path, not the tilt of its axis, which is only about two degrees. Earthlike features: It rotates west to east and its day is 22.7 hours, which ought to be easy to adapt to, even for somebody like me (I have trouble with circadian rhythms).

Then the cube recites the text of Mayakovsky's original report. The great Russian arrived in late winter, finding the skies ice-blue and clear, the surface a white wilderness—hence the name. His scanners spotted an artificial shape and he investigated and found an abandoned city.

"Who could have built this huge stone platform and the lovely temples that bedeck it?" he demanded. "This world is dead. Beings like ourselves, alien wanderers, must have built this place. But why, in this endless Antarctic?"

He named it *Zamók*, the castle, and the unknown builders *arkhitektori*. Hence the slang term Arkies.

Exploring the castle led to a nasty encounter with carnivores laired in the temples. At first the species seemed merely interesting, a rough parallel to the Earth's polar bears—and what Russian doesn't like bears? So that was the name he gave them, *medvedi*.

"Their long fur changes from dark to white as they move from shadow to sunlight," murmurs the cube. "Tusks and claws are formidable."

Then a blizzard blew in. With complete white-out at seventy below and all bioscanners inoperative due to cold, the beasts ambushed an exploring party. "Two crewmen dead. Skulls crushed. Another vanished, probably eaten. A dangerous degree of cunning and intelligence in these animals."

That of course was a mere incident. The ores his deep metal-scanners found brought the mining cartel. The miners bulldozed off the lovely temples and built the current trashy hovels instead. Meantime winter had ended, and Bela turned out to be anything but dead. Thousands of species swarmed out of hiding and billions of seeds and spores sprouted, to thrive until summer arrived and turned the surface into a howling desert.

A banal thought: How fragile life is, and how tough. Once it gets started, seemingly it can survive anything.

At this point I have to turn off the cube. The local doc's arrived, a tiny energetic Chinese woman named Anna Li.

She puts me through the usual mediscan. Odd business she's in, meeting so many naked strangers—probably wondering later on, when she sees them clothed: Is this the guy with the birthmark on his butt?

I tell her I'm not bringing in any dreadful diseases, unless being over-the-hill is a disease. She smiles automatically, pays no attention.

"You're okay," she says, studying the printout, "but stay off sweets." Then dashes away.

When I'm dressed, Captain Mack takes charge again, leading me through bilious green corridors crowded with people in gray coveralls. Name tags echo all the tribes of Earth: Jiang, Grinzshpan, Basho, Mbasa, Jones.

To my surprise, my quarters are in the executive suite. A comfortable bedroom, an opulent private bath. On a broad terrace outside, the Inca-like stonework lies bare and gleaming in the rain. The view over the river valley to the distant mountains would be spectacular, except for a heavy steel screen that obstructs it. What look like maggots are inching their way around in the wet.

"Somebody'll bring your luggage," Mack tells me. "Security Central's right next door if you need anything. Like your suite, it has two doors, corridor and terrace. The Controller will see you in the morning after you've rested."

She turns to go. But I've got a question: "What's the screen out there for?"

Mack frowns. "Mr. Krebs used to sleep in here, until somebody fired a missile at him. Fortunately he was in the Security office chatting with me, and he wasn't hurt."

"A missile?"

"Just a shoulder-fired job," she says defensively, as if a small missile makes you less dead than a big one. "Some disgruntled employee. That's when we put the screens up. There's one in front of the Security office, too."

"Was the missile stolen from your armory?"

Mack glares and says, "Yes."

"And where does the Controller sleep now?"

"Someplace else."

She closes the door firmly, leaving me to rest as well as I can—in the middle of a bull's-eye.

Supper's in the dining hall. Mack guides me to the head table in a private room. I'm hoping to see Mr. Krebs. But the Controller dines alone.

Instead I meet a dozen or so executives and engineers. English is everybody's second language, and I listen to a babel of accents expressing fervent hope that I can find the killer. His current score is nineteen dead—almost two percent of the population of 1,042. Dr. Li again bustles in, wearing a laboratory smock, and tells me she has holograms of the bodies and all the autopsy data. I can see them after dinner.

"Hope you've got a strong stomach," says the senior engineer, a guy named Antonelli. Making a face.

"Actually, there's not much mess," says Li. "Always one blow through the top of the skull with a sharp instrument. Odd way to kill someone, but it's silent and effective."

REVELATION & Otηεr Talεs of Fantascιεncε

"Any particular sort of victims?" I ask. "Men or women, old or young, homs or hets?"

"No. If somebody was trying to wipe out a statistical cross-section of the colony, you couldn't get much more variety. True, they're nearly all young people. But that's just demographics."

Right. Mining colonies are like that: a few seniors to run the show, many young vigorous people to do what's often hard and dangerous work.

"There is one pattern. The crimes all happen here," puts in Captain Mack, who up to this point has sat silent, stuffing her face. "Never at the mining camp. For the first time, people are volunteering for extra duty at the mines."

A grim chuckle goes around the table.

When the meal's over, I ask Doctor Li to introduce me to the younger people. I stroll through the main dining room, shaking hands and gazing into a kaleidoscope of faces having nothing in common but under-thirtyish freshness. These youngsters probably all think of themselves as larval executives, here to punch their tickets, then home to climb the promotion ladder. I wonder how many will make it.

A few minutes later, I'm walking with Anna—we've quickly gotten on first-name terms—down a chicken-run leading to her clinic. When we're halfway through, she stops and says, "The first killing took place right here."

"Here?"

We're standing in the middle of a perfectly blank, empty corridor about twenty meters long—windowless, well lit and devoid of the slightest concealment. I ask about the victim.

"A woman named Cabrera. Athlete—good runner; life's so dull here that anybody who doesn't take to drink takes to athletics. She could've escaped, I'm sure of it, if she'd seen him coming."

"What was she hit with?"

"Probably a mountaineer's pickaxe—short handle, easily concealed. The point penetrated the longitudinal fissure of the cranium and sank about seven centimeters into the midbrain. Cabrera lived a few hours in a comatose state, then died."

"Does the killer have to be a man?"

"Not with all the girls who take martial arts classes. We're outnumbered by the men and there'd be a rape a week if we couldn't defend ourselves."

"You're implying that not all miners are gentlemen?"

"They're gentlemen in about the same proportion that cops are."

A woman of spirit, I see.

Item (2.) *From the Written Report of Anna Li, D.Sc., M.D.*

This person met Robert—Colonel Kohn—on the evening of his first day on Bela.

I remembered nothing from doing his mediscan except that he was uncircumcised. At dinner I noted that he was a large man with prematurely white hair.

Our initial talk was useful, I think, in helping him understand the situation here on Bela. He seemed interested in the data I was able to show him. Whether he was intelligent I could not at first decide, though he spoke like a cultured man. I admit that intellectual arrogance is one of my grave flaws. We professionals always look down a bit at policemen, whatever we may claim to the contrary.

When he left, I locked the laboratory door. I had begun investigating a common worm or larva, hoping that unraveling the structure of its genome might provide a model for later work on Bela's more complex and interesting creatures.

Wishing the colonel well in my thoughts, I settled down to quiet, enthralling work that took my mind far away from corpses and those who make them.

Item (3.) *From the Notebook of Colonel Kohn.*

The cool voices of clocks are announcing midnight, but of course it doesn't feel like midnight. I'm ready for bed but not, it would seem, for sleep. The old brain keeps cycling in the dry tedium of fatigue.

I'm glad I had this chip implanted in my larynx so I don't have to speak out loud to record my thoughts. You never know who's listening. The technique is somewhat like ventriloquism, and not hard to learn. All the rubbish from my stream of consciousness winds up in my notebook, buried deep in a coded memory.

Anna's pictures are moderately gruesome and not very helpful. Mack's notes on the murders are much the same. The killer's efficient. The MO's bizarre. The victims are anybody.

The crimes began in the corridors, shifted briefly to the hydroponics nurseries, then everywhere. Joggers were struck down on running trails, late workers in machine shops and offices.

Even after Mack issued orders that people were not to go anywhere without a companion, the killings went on. A woman was using a toilet stall while another stood guard outside. When she tried to open the door, it hit an obstruction that proved to be her friend's body.

Customary methods of investigation have failed. Tests for occult bloodstains, hair, and fibers turned up nothing. The colony lacks the equipment for sophisticated psych tests. Mack's methods have been rough-hewn; after the first crime she grilled everybody, eliminated those with solid alibis, then arrested three people who lacked them.

The results were not happy. After two more murders, the suspects had to be set free.

Now *everybody* has an alibi for at least one, and usually for several, of the crimes. No trace of the weapon has been found. Despite the prevalence of mining engineers, it wasn't standard issue; somebody whose hobby was mountain climbing might have brought it in their personal baggage. Mack's computers have searched personal-baggage invoices as far back as they go, but found no record of such an implement.

The stone platform under our feet is seamed with narrow passages. When stories sprang up about alien killers, the Controller first ridiculed the notion, then ordered Mack to explore. Almost any adult human would be too big to go down there, so she used a bot.

The memory cube contains a few images of wall paintings it found down below—the first ever seen of Zamók's Arkies, little hunchbacked brownish bipeds with three-toed feet and gourd-shaped heads and serious dental problems. But no sign of any recent presence except the scat and bones of small animals.

None of this surprised Anna. From the circumstances of the crime, she'd already concluded that the killer, like the victims, must be human....

Oh, hell. I'm still trying to sleep, but no luck. Just too tired, and the old brain keeps churning.

Seeking air, I put on a robe and open a thick transplast door onto the terrace and edge around the screen. A tremulous roar rises from the river. A few chilly raindrops are falling. Thunder grumbles among distant hills.

The air tastes good up here—phytoplankton in the sea and greenstuff in the jungle are hard at work excreting the poison gas we love to breathe. I can feel my heart beat a bit faster. I suppose when you're down in the jungle among all the rotting stuff, it stinks. Most jungles do.

My bare feet are cold—forgot to pack slippers. The blocks of stone are smooth and slick. Little worms squish nastily underfoot. I cross the terrace to a low parapet and look down. Lightning flickers on a dense black jungle lining the riverbank below. Then I smell something like the lion cage at a zoo—

Aghh!

Phew. Rude shock.

Let me catch up. Light was emanating from the Security office and I'd turned that way and was padding along toward it when somebody flung open the door, pointed an impact pistol at me and yelled, *"À bas!"*

I hit the wet stones just as a shot whanged by. I twisted around in time to see something big that had been coming over the parapet tumble back and vanish.

Feeling better now. I'm in Security and a young guy in uniform is offering me a towel, which I need.

"Sir," he says politely, "I don't think you ought to be outside at night. Wild ahn-ee-mahls sometimes climb the walls."

A skinny little watchspring of a guy with a blue chin and dancing black eyes. His English is fluent but sometimes original. He's Security Officer Lt. Michel Verray.

All around us monitors are blinking and humming to themselves. A voyeur's dream of heaven. In one bedroom, a tumultuous pile of bedclothes suggests a couple trying for a little privacy as they make love. One of the least interesting scenes—an empty bedroom—is my own.

Michel is Captain Mack's only full-time assistant at Main Base. He calls her, with ironic inflection, Maman.

"Here, Colonel," he says. "Let me give you a key to the security office. I'm sure Maman wants you to have one. And I'll sign you out with a pistol."

We chat while completing this transaction. I heft the pistol, check the load, press the recognition stud until it memorizes the pattern of capillaries in my hand. Hi, pistol. Hi, Colonel.

We chat some more. "I presume she's not really your mother?"

He makes a comical face. "Non. But I think she would like to be."

If he's right about that, it's the first sign of human feeling I've noticed in Mack. Michel shows me around, explaining that the monitors were installed after the early killings.

"We try to persuade people to keep to areas under surveillance. I wish we had more equipment. We don't have enough cameras and anybody could be prowling the dark areas, looking for a chance to attack."

"Do people complain that you're spying on them?"

"They did at first. Not so much now they are scared. Anyway, we spy on ourselves, too. There's my room, with my roommates. And in that one you will be thrilled to observe Maman reading in bed."

Mack has her wig off and her hair is close cropped. She looks like Picasso's portrait of Gertrude Stein. I ask if the dozen or so weapons in the rack are the only ones in the colony. No, of course not. The Security people—Mack and Michel and Vizbee and Smelt—all carry guns. So does Mr. Krebs and Senior Engineer Antonelli and one or two other top dogs. In fact, everybody wants one, but Mack's resisting and so far Krebs has backed her up.

Damn right, too. Armed civilians can be more dangerous than the murderer.

"How about the missiles?" I ask.

Michel grins, knowing what I'm thinking. "All five that remain are here locked up, and only Maman has the key."

"I suppose the attack on the controller made her look bad."

"The whole situation makes her look bad. She gets grimmer every day it goes on. She may look like Mont Blanc but actually she suffers from the stress. And refuses to take the medications Dr. Li offers her."

Michel fetches a bottle of cognac and two plastic cups from a supply room. The drink lights a welcome fire in my gut. We chat and soon get chummy. It turns out that Michel did the exploration of the subsurface passages.

"You built the bot?"

"Non. Miners already had them to explore places too narrow or dangereuse for people. Call them Spiders [he said speed-airs]—little guys, walk on three legs, carry a digicam and an HI-light. I guided it through the passages, made Maman a memory cube and sneaked a copy for myself."

He shrugs, rolling his eyes upward in comic alarm. "Boy, she'd be pissed if she knew that."

"Why?"

"Like many mamans, she's difficult. She thinks knowledge is power. Okay, she's right. She wants to know everything that goes on here. Okay, that's her job. But she also wants to monopolize information, store it up to use against her enemies."

"She has enemies, then."

"Mais oui," says my new friend cheerfully, tossing off the last of his drink. "Everybody but me and Krebs hates her comme la peste."

Like the plague, eh? Well, I never imagined she'd be wildly popular. Michel's becoming franker (and also Frencher) as he absorbs alcohol. While he refills our glasses, I ask, "What do you want the cube for, Michel?"

"When I get home, I want to get a degree in Alien Civ and start teaching. I've started going over the cube frame by frame, and I think I can get my whole tay-seize [thesis?] from it. Le bon Dieu didn't mean me to be a cop," he added, then blushes, thinking I may take this as an insult to my profession.

"I agree with God," I assure him solemnly, and say good night. Now armed, I cross the terrace without incident.

Good kid, I think, turning in. He's saved me a lot—my life, plus a ton of post-mortem embarrassment. Wouldn't that have been a fine terminal note in my personnel file? *On the first day of his last assignment, KOHN, Robert R., COL, SN 52.452.928, contrived to get himself eaten.*

Good night, all. And pleasant dreams.

Morning comes with rain, thunder, lightning, and a nasty shock.

Early on I'm summoned to Krebs's office. Captain Mack pounds on the door and, when I stagger out with eyelids still stuck together, leads me in grim silence through a labyrinth of corridors.

We're somewhere deep inside Main Base when we reach the new executive suite—so deep that the noise of the storm has faded into silence. Clearly, Mr. Krebs does not intend his quarters to be hit by any more missiles if he can help it.

His office is large, blank, and ugly, and so is the occupant thereof. Mack withdraws without a word and a spongy, grim-faced man leans forward in a tall executive chair and gives me two weak-feeling fingers to shake.

The chief feature of his face is a jaw like an excavator. His lower right canine sticks up outside. His gut billows over the edge of the desk, but his arms are thin and look unused. I typecast him as the perfect executive, a fat guy with a stone behind, good for nothing but giving orders to people smarter and stronger than he is.

"You'll be going in half an hour," is his greeting.

"Going where?"

"Why, to check the body," he growls, relapsing against the back of the chair. "Take Li with you. Third-rate doctor, but she's all we've got."

"There's been another killing?"

"Mack didn't tell you? Goddammit, I got to do everything around here. Yeah, it's at Mining Camp Alfa."

"The first at a mining camp."

"Right. Now these cowardly shits I got working for me won't want to go to the field at all. They all think they're here to eat company food and punch their tickets and do as little work as possible."

I begin to see why somebody might fire a missile at Mr. Krebs. He seems to have a similarly unkind view of me. He sits there glaring for a few seconds, then demands suddenly, "Are you piggybacking on my budget?"

Sticking his jaw out even further.

"No. HQ pays me and the mining cartel reimburses them."

"Well, thank God for small favors," says Mr. Krebs. "The dead guy was nobody special. Another small favor."

That ends the interview.

I collect my notebook, put in a new battery and meet Anna outside her clinic. She has an overnight bag full of specimen bottles and a medical chest, which I carry for her.

"I met your boss," I tell her as we hasten to the pad.

"To know him is to hate him," she says. "Hurry up, only one flyer's working and this is it."

Ten minutes later we're taking off into the very teeth of the storm.

What a flight. It lasts one hour or one eternity, however you choose to look at it. The damn black box piloting us has been programmed to take the most direct route—misplaced notion of fuel economy, I suppose—and that involves crossing a wide bay full of churning black water. A squall is barreling toward the shore, and we fly directly into it.

I feel sure the lightning's going to fry the black box and send us careening down into the sea. Haven't had breakfast, so there's nothing to come up except, of course, my stomach itself.

Anna takes all the pounding and shaking stoically, or seems to. Still, I notice she too heaves a sigh of relief when at last we leave the bay behind and bounce down onto another rain-scoured concrete circle near another clutter of domes and sheds.

"Well, here's Alfa," she says.

People come running with umbrellas—yes, real Earth-type umbrellas—but of course we get soaked anyway. Two dozen people are stationed here, but three guys are away fixing a slurry pump, whatever that is. So I get introduced to twenty live people and one corpse.

The latter is a young man named Thoms. He's lying facedown on the poured-stone floor of the machine shop. At first glance the only difference in MO was the fact that he'd been hit on the base of the skull instead of the top.

"Weapon appears to have penetrated the posterior median sulcus of the medulla," Anna tells her notebook.

But then she puts on a headset with a xenon lamp and high-power 3D magnifier, lowers the lenses over her eyes and kneels down, her nose almost touching the dead man's blood-stiff hair.

When I help her up, she's frowning. "The wounds at Zamók were punched through," she mutters. "But this time... the wound's not nearly so neat. As if the weapon flattened on impact. I'll have to check when I've got the body back at the lab. Help me turn him over."

Somehow, handling a dead body has a calming effect on me. When I first see a corpse I'm always shocked, even after so many years of looking at violent death. But when I handle the body and feel that special weight, especially—as now—with rigor setting in, I know I'm dealing with earth and stone, not a person, and I can treat it like any other forensic exhibit.

Superficial examination shows that except for being dead Thoms's body is not, as Anna puts it, remarkable in any way. After taking a bunch of holograms, we bag it and the miners help us put it in their freezer.

The rest of the day I spend in a small, bare office with a single monitor bleeping on a chipped duroplast desk. I'm sipping coffee, noshing on bad sandwiches covered with some kind of ghastly synthetic mayo, and interviewing survivors.

Nobody saw or heard anything. Thoms was well-liked, with no known enemies, and every single person at Alfa was under observation by others at the most probable hour of death, which Anna puts between 6.30 and 8.00. I reach the last name on my list before Madam Justice lifts her blindfold and peeks at me.

The witness—named Ted Szczech, pronounced Sheck—is a pale, twitchy, skinny kid who looks about sixteen and wears coveralls that could serve him for a tent. He shuffles into the room carrying an envelope.

"I've uh, uh, uh, got something for you, sir," he stutters.

"Oh yeah? What?" Bad food plus no progress has put me in a foul humor.

Ted spends the next five minutes tripping over his own tongue. The story gradually emerges that he worked with Thoms in the machine shop and so was the first to spot the body. Before sounding the alarm he ran for his digicam, rightly anticipating that everybody in Alfa soon would swarm in and obliterate every clue.

"Why didn't you bring me the pictures at once?" I demand in my growliest voice. Actually, I'm impressed by his initiative.

"I w-w-was w-w-w-waiting my turn," Ted explains. "And uh, uh, uh—"

"What?" I say, beginning to pull the printouts from the envelope.

"Well, you can see the f-f-f-footprints pretty clear."

"Footprints?"

"Yeah. They showed up when I used the infrared flash. Standard light don't show n-n-nothing. I never even knew they were there until I p-p-p-printed out."

I stare at dim little three-toed marks around a corpse so fresh that under black light it still glows with the warmth of life. In the early morning the stone floor was cold and the killer's body heat created just enough transient warming for the cam to register.

"It probably ran away when you started to open the door," I comment. That seems to scare Ted.

"You think so?" he asks, eyes bugging out. "You really think so?" Not a single stutter.

When I show the pictures to Anna, she looks ready to tear out her graying hair. "Oh, great Tao. We got it *settled*. The killer has to be *human*," she moans.

"Okay, a human did it. And then Threetoes walks in, trots over to body, trots away again and disappears into the jungle, and—"

My voice dies in midpassage. Anna looks at me. I look at Anna. We're both remembering where we've seen three-toed feet before.

"We'd better get back to Zamók," she says. "Now."

The storm's abated and the trip back is a bit tedious, which certainly was not a problem on the trip out. Lying behind us wrapped in translucent plastic the corpse reminds me unpleasantly of a giant fetus swathed in its placenta.

Back at the Castle we hump our gear across broad puddles and down gray corridors into Anna's lab. I retrieve my infopack and we check the pictures the Spider took underground. And yes, the Arkies have three-toed feet that resemble Ted's blurry images.

While I make tea on a hotspot under a vacuum hood, Anna calls Mack and asks for the memory cube containing the full exploration of the subsurface passages.

"You're not authorized to see it," that ungracious woman growls.

"What do you mean?" snaps Anna. "I've got top clearance. I need it for the work I do."

"You're a penis machinist, not a security officer. You don't have a security-type clearance."

At this point I step forward. "I'm cleared for everything you are, Captain, and a lot more. Send that goddamn cube and send it now."

That makes me feel pretty good. Pulling rank may not be nice, but it's effective.

We relax until Michel appears with a sealed container, for which Anna and I both have to sign. He gives me a wink, then heads back to his job. A couple of minutes later, she and I are head to head, staring into the image box of her computer.

The solid-looking forms jounce, steady, fuzz out, clarify. We're entering a narrow slot between two of Zamók's cyclopean stone blocks. We descend steep narrow steps. The high-intensity light swivels back and forth, its movement complicated by the robot's walk. Anna's forever freezing a frame here and there so we can get a fairly clear picture.

Along walls of smooth stone marches a painted procession of Arkies wearing fantastic outfits of skins and feathers. Projecting teeth give their heads a spiky appearance. At the foot of the steps a narrow corridor splits left and right and the robot begins to explore. Passages divide and subdivide and it pokes into small rooms covered with garish paintings that make me think of Mayan art at Tikal and Dzibilchaltun.

It's all quite fascinating and, as far as our current problems are concerned, absolutely useless. When the show's over, our tea has gotten cold. "So what's your conclusion, Colonel Sir?" asks Anna with ungentle irony.

"An alien—" I begin.

"The Arkies are natives," she corrects me. "We're the aliens."

"Okay, okay. First of all, you were right. An Arkie couldn't have done the killings at Zamók. You turn around in a corridor and see a strange creature, you run, you scream, you fight back, you do something the victims didn't do. The killings here were done by a human. So we have an anomaly."

We sit staring at each other. Feeling around helplessly in my empty head, I ask, "What do we know about the Arkies?"

She gestures. "What you've seen."

"I mean—" I don't know what I mean. "How'd they survive in this world? It's so bizarre, radical cold, radical heat, seasons that last for decades…how'd they get along?"

She sighs. "Nobody knows. We're like a pimple on the body of the planet. We came here with typical engineer's tunnel vision, to dig and smelt and ship the ingots home and follow them when the mines play out."

She spends a while reheating the tea, then goes on: "I'm as bad as the rest of them. Spend my days doing routine physicals and treating orthopedic injuries from the mines. That's where the crack about me being a penis machinist comes from. And there's truth in it. I try to do some real science after hours."

"Anything helpful?"

"For solving the murders? No. On the contrary—it's as far as possible from anything to do with them. I'm trying to get a start on understanding the molecular biology of—"

"Oh," I say. "Okay."

"Anyway, you asked me how the natives fit into their world. Answer: I don't know how anything really functions on Bela. We're all so busy being practical that we don't have time to be intelligent."

So we give up; I send Michel the info we gathered at Alfa, and then we go to dinner.

Replay of last night—Mack feeding her face, the engineers eyeing me, wondering if I know something they don't about the latest atrocity. To avoid questions I don't want to (meaning: can't) answer, I avoid socializing, say good night to Anna and as soon as possible drag my ageing butt off to bed.

Through the door to the terrace I see that another storm's moving in. The cube says the "spring rains" are scheduled to last about forty standard years. What would Noah say to that?

Hit the hay but again can't sleep, this time because the lightning keeps waking me up. Cursing, I get up and start searching for a way to darken the window.

Lightning flashes. Inside the screen a monster stares at me.

Lightning flashes. I stare back. Oh come on, it's only an animal.

But it's impressive. Standing upright, bowlegged, body covered with rough fur of indefinite color. It's a boar, by God—a huge two-legged boar. The hairy ears, the little red eyes with startling piggish intelligence in them— and the tusks, two down and two up, dirty orange but rubbed white where they cross each other—and especially the flat snout, quivering, with the hairy nostrils spread. . . .

And then, of course, I see it's not a boar or anything else I've ever known. Long claws instead of trotters. Muscled forelimbs adept for walking or climbing. Imagine a big bear crossed with a swine, crossed with…what? Something.

In the dark this triumph of natural genetic manipulation claws at the thick transplast with twenty-centimeter talons that make a nerve-jangling skreek. Lightning flashes. It exposes the full length of its twelve-centimeter tusks and turns away, frustrated.

Lightning flashes. The animal's gone.

Somewhat shaken, I continue my search, find a switch on the wall and touch it. Yes, praise whatever gods may be, the window darkens. I go to bed again and try to fall asleep.

Processions of feathered creatures march through my head, tracked by two-legged pigs and by Mayakovsky's *medvedi*, the bearlike animals that ambushed his people seventy years ago when it was wintertime on Bela. . . .

Why do all these strange critters seem vaguely alike?

Item (4.) *From the Written Report of Li, Anna M., M.D.*

I spent that evening in my laboratory, meaning to work on my project. But my mind kept drifting to the body in my freezer.

At length I gave up, dragged poor Mr. Thoms onto an examining table, and began to explore his wound. Almost at once I found something odd.

Perhaps I should have called the Colonel at once, but I decided he was probably asleep. So I promised myself to speak to him at breakfast, not realizing that tired as I was after our adventures of the day, I might oversleep and miss him in the morning. And that is exactly what happened.

Item (5.) *From Colonel Kohn's Notebook.*

"So," says Mr. Krebs, champing his jaws, "what've you learned so far?"

His windowless office gives me a feeling of premature burial. The man himself, with his piranha profile and billowing stomach and weak little hands, manages to look dangerous and helpless at the same time.

"Who do you think tried to hit you with a missile?" I respond conversationally. This is a question I (literally) dreamed up last night, when the old subconscious finally did something useful.

"I want answers, not questions."

"Well, I don't have any, yet. But you haven't just had twenty murders here. You've had that plus an attempted assassination of the colony's executive head. I'm curious as to whether there might be a connection."

He growls. Literally—grrrrr. Like a dog.

"Talk to Captain Mack," he says. "That's her department."

"I'm surprised you've kept her in such an important position after all the things that've gone wrong here," I say frankly.

"I trust her absolutely."

I take this as an admission that anybody appointed in her place might use Security's armory to try to kill him—again.

"Now, if you don't mind answering my original question, what've you found out about *the murders?*"

I open my notebook and set it humming. Briefly I outline the events of the day before. At the end I summarize, "The Arkies have joined the fun."

"But they're all *dead!*" he almost yells.

"No more than Mayans or Egyptians or Celts or Cambodians or any of the other builders of abandoned cities on the Earth are dead. They just moved away. Their descendents live on. Spring brought the Arkies out of hiding, and what did they find? Their Acropolis, their temple mount, had been desecrated by aliens—us. That pissed them off, and they've just killed their first human."

I think that's kind of a neat theory—much too neat to be true.

"You're saying none of our people killed anybody?"

Patiently I explain the difficulties in trying to blame the first nineteen killings on the natives.

"So you're telling me we've got two killers, in two different places, killing people in the same bizarre way, and one's a human and other's a whatcha-callit. That's the dumb-assedest notion I ever heard."

"Sir, you've summed up the problem," I tell him. "The evidence is unreasonable. *But it's still evidence.*"

The rest of the interview's a total waste of time. We just yell at each other, accomplishing nothing. A supply ship's due pretty soon and I guess he'll send me home, as he's authorized to do. That will make both of us happy.

Needing time to cool off a bit after the shouting match, I set out to find Anna's lab and promptly get lost.

I don't know if I've made this clear, but Main Base is a hopeless maze. The buildings were put up at different times for different purposes out of whatever materials were at hand. Meanwhile the population increased to a high of two thousand or so and then declined as mines were worked out and abandoned. Now a dozen buildings are permanently vacant, and a tangle of corridors lead here and there with no rhyme or reason, often ending in blank walls where an abandoned structure's been sealed off.

Adding to the general confusion, about half the people are absent at any one time. Some at mining camp Alfa—the only site that's presently active— the rest at the smelter, or exploring for new sites. Then they come back to work at administration or housekeeping. The idea is to train the youngsters in all phases of running a colony.

But that also means they rotate in and out, causing ceaseless turbulence. I've got a near-photographic memory for faces, and yet I've never seen many of the people I encounter.

Two I do recognize are Vizbee and Smelt, the guards from the shuttleport, who must have rotated back. Vizbee's as near insolent as he dares to be. "Enjoying Bela, Sir?" he asks with a nasty smile.

At least he's learned the word sir since I saw him last.

"You're looking a bit lost, Sir," Smelt chimes in, with a washed-out smile. Someday I will deal with this pair.

Actually, getting lost turns out to be one of the more useful things I've done. I've been dealing with facts, which are fine as far as they go. Now I'm getting the feel of the situation, too. The killer's been hunting his victims in a kind of indoor jungle. Add the fact that he doesn't seem to care who gets bashed as long as somebody does, and the bloody orgy becomes comprehensible.

I spend a couple of hours wandering, asking directions, finding the directions don't work, and getting lost again. Periodically I come across a sealed window and look out on the river valley. Or a landside enclosure with high fences and shrouded machinery on duroplast skids. Or a big cube sprouting thick cables—the main generator, a primitive fission-type reactor. Bela, I perceive, is run on the economy plan.

But I can't get out, and soon I'm wandering the maze again like a baffled rat.

Finally admitting I'm lost for the nth time, I ask directions from a pretty dark-haired engineer named Eloise. We chat, and she invites me to visit her room, explaining that she and her boyfriend are "on off-rotation"—awkward phrase—from the mines.

The boyfriend's named Jamal, and he's solidly built and dark and bitter as a cup of Turkish coffee. He and Eloise share a very cramped room, which they consider themselves lucky to get. I ask why space is so tight when, with all the empty buildings, it should be just the opposite.

"Mack says it's for security," growls Jamal. "Stay where the cameras can watch your every move, including when you shower and make love. I can just see her and Krebs lying in bed—incredible as it seems, a lot of people think they sleep together—and peeping at us like the swine they are."

My own impression is that Mack and Krebs are both asexual beings, but I don't argue the point. Instead I remark that morale in the colony is close to rock-bottom.

"It's dying," says Jamal, now sounding weary rather than bitter. "Everybody hates the leadership and everybody's scared to death."

I'm sitting with Eloise on the edge of their bed. Jamal is sitting on the floor.

"See, you haven't been here the last two years," he goes on. "You look at the number of victims and think, 'Oh, well, ninety-eight percent of the people are still alive.' But when you live through a campaign of murder, the effect is cumulative. I never leave El without wondering if I'll ever see her again, and she wonders the same thing about me."

She strokes his coarse black hair and nods. She has an inner stillness that he completely lacks, yet she backs him up.

"It's been hard," she says simply. "I'm sure nobody will want to come here again, and everybody who's here already is counting the days until they can leave. Bela will have to be abandoned."

She's less bitter than he is and makes an effort to be fair, even to Mack, whom everybody else blames for their miseries.

"She's in a terrible situation. If she's afraid of anything, it's having to leave Bela. I'm sure she's doing her best to find the killer, and I'm not sure anybody else could do any better. I mean, how do you catch somebody who doesn't care who dies as long as somebody does?"

"Some goddamn maniac," Jamal mutters.

"I don't think so," says Eloise thoughtfully. "The killing's random, yet at the same time it's calculated and deliberate. It's...cold. Somebody's aiming at something, and it can only be to drive us all away."

"Why would a human want to drive humans away?" asks Jamal, and neither of us has an answer.

There is, of course, the big exception—Thoms's murder. My hosts haven't heard about that yet. But the conversation starts me brooding about it once again.

Feeling a strong urge to revisit Alfa, I thank the young folks and ask them to show me an exit to the pad. They do so, and my luck's in, because on the pad the flyer's revving up. It's a dull trip, and everything seems normal until we arrive.

Then I ask for Ted Szczech, and learn that he won't be taking any more pictures. Ever.

—.—

No, he didn't die by the customary head-bashing.

Less than an hour before, something resembling a two-legged boar grabbed him when he was outside working on a stuck valve of a slurry pipe, and dragged him away—presumably to eat.

They're getting up a search party to try and recover his remains. I ask to go along and they say sure.

As I'm suiting up, a call comes in from Anna. She's been hunting me, called Michel in the security office and asked if I was on any of his monitors. He told her he'd seen me with Eloise and Jamal, so she called them and they told her they'd seen me catch the flyer. Then Michel called her back and said he needed to see me, too.

Funny, all you have to do to get popular is to go away.

Anna's full of her latest discovery. "Last night I found bronze fragments embedded in Thoms's skull. I'm not set up to do metallurgical analysis, so I asked one of our engineers to check the fragments out."

"Why?"

"I think the bronze was smelted by some very crude, primitive process. The alloy's soft and that's why the skull did almost as much damage to the weapon as it did to the skull. Or maybe it was meant for use on a softer, thinner cranium."

"In short, it was made by an Arkie to smack other Arkies and the hardness of the human head took its wielder by surprise."

"Something like that. When are you coming back?"

"They're sending out a party to search for Ted Szczech, and I'm going along. A wild animal got him."

"Great Tao. What kind of animal?"

I describe it.

"Oh, that's *Ursasus terribilis*," she says.

"Meaning?"

"Terrible bearpig. I started doing taxonomy on the local fauna, giving Latin names and so on. Then stopped, because it seemed so futile. Oh, poor Ted."

"We may find him yet."

Somebody's yelling for me. Michel will have to wait.

We put on transparent rain gear, the kind that breathes so you don't drown in your own sweat, and water-repellent goggles. We're all armed to the teeth. The flyer takes off to circle over the search area. Nobody's expecting it to find anything; the jungle's too full of big organic molecules that confuse the bioscanner.

Down below, it's exciting at first—walking in the deep wet woods of Bela. Up to now its green/blue/purple colors seen through misty rain didn't look especially strange. Close up it's a crawly place. Everything drips; every step squishes. Vines are in motion, like the hands of an antique clock; you can't see them move, but if you look away and look back, yes, they've changed.

The trees form short, twisty lattices of rope-like growths with trunks not much thicker than limbs. No large trees—there's been no time for them to grow yet. Leaves of all shapes stretch up and out toward the little light that's available, ruthlessly shading each other out so that the understory is choked with masses of dead and rotting vegetation.

No flowers. Everything in monotone. Things buzz around that look like flying crayfish. In glimpses of the sky, we see dashing small shadows that somebody on my intercom calls daybats. Hunting the crayfish, I suppose. Now and then I catch sight of an elaborately feathered creature crawling through the branches with its beak and talons, like a parrot. The usual little white worms are crawling around the wet ground, millions of them. My feet squash them at every step. I begin to feel like I'm walking through the innards of a dead, decaying beast. Even through the filters in my breathing apparatus I catch whiffs of decay, not quite like decay on Earth; a sharp touch of ammonia, stench of methane, a gagging bubble of—what? Chlorine? Plus that smell like a lion cage I sniffed before on the terrace at Zamók.

Lasers hiss in the murky air and slashed limbs fall smoking to the ground where the wet extinguishes them. The ground's like a spongy mattress and I sink knee-deep at every step. Soon my legs ache and my knees are quivering. We circle the whole camp, finding nothing.

Ted's just gone. Period.

Back at Alfa, I'm bushed. Fall on somebody's cot and snooze for about two hours. When I awaken, one of the guys tells me Zamók's been buzzing me.

"Why didn't you wake me up?"

"Easier said than done, old-timer. You were *out*."

First time anybody's called me old-timer to my face.

I stagger to the nearest monitor and press the return-call button. Michel's image says he'd like to see me as soon as possible. I call his code but get only his image again, promising to return my call at the earliest possible moment.

I have ersatz coffee and another plastic-mayo sandwich and think it over. If Michel wants to see me, why hasn't he called again and why doesn't he answer my call?

I call Captain Mack and ask if she knows where he is. She's looking, if possible, grimmer than usual. No, he's off-duty until tomorrow. Where's he sleep? Impatiently she gives me the code for the room he shares with two girls and another guy. I call and his roommates are there, but he isn't. I call Anna and ask her to look for him.

"I'm waiting for the analysis of the bronze."

"Look for Michel, please."

I go to Alfa's commandant and ask to borrow the flyer. No, he says, it's on a regular schedule.

When will it be going back to Zamók? Tomorrow noon, he says. Thank you, I say.

I walk out onto the pad and find a tech just finishing his service routine. I tell him Hi, and when he goes back inside, I climb in and tell the black box to take me to Zamók.

"Hearing and obeying," says the gadget.

"Accept no calls from any source until we arrive," I add.

"Hearing and obeying," says the gadget.

I settle back in the seat and wonder how I can explain snatching this machine if, after all, Michel meets me alive and well.

I needn't have worried.

—.—

239

By the time I arrive he's been found, and Main Base is in the state of an over-turned anthill.

As startling as the murder itself is the way it was done: Michel Verray has been shot in the back in the same chicken-run where Cabrera's body was found almost two standard years ago.

There was no approach, no hands-on attack. An impact slug was fired from the far end of the corridor. His beltpouch has been roughly opened, breaking the catch, suggesting robbery. His pistol's missing. Was he killed with his own weapon?

A scenario flits through my mind: Michel confronts the killer, draws his weapon, has it knocked out of his hand—maybe by somebody who's been taking those martial-arts classes Anna talked about. He turns and runs away, and the killer picks it up and coolly takes aim and shoots him. . . .

But I'm not even sure he was running when he was shot. Mack thinks so, but the holograms she took of the body seem ambiguous to me. A runner hit from the rear in midstride on a smooth surface slams down and slides. I think the abrasions on his face are insufficient for that. I'd say he was hurrying but not running, and Anna's inclined to agree.

In her clinic she starts crying, the first time I've seen her do so. She has Michel's body on her examining table, and it's a horrible mess. As usual with that type of ammo, the entry wound near the spine is the size of my little finger and the exit wound through the chest is the size of my head. The slug, of course, disintegrated as it's supposed to do, leaving no evidence.

"Even Mack's shaken up," she tells me when she's cried on my shoulder. "I saw her when they brought the body in, and she looked paralyzed. She kept saying, 'Oh no. Not him. Oh no.' He was kind of a substitute son, you know. Now she's really alone."

Well, murder gets to the toughest of us, sooner or later.

Anna washes her face at a laboratory sink and says dolefully, "I have to do the autopsy."

"Not now, you don't. Tomorrow's fine. Michel won't run away. Come on, I'll help you put him on ice."

I hate to touch the body, but as soon as I do, it's okay. Michel is gone; the good mind, the lively wit, the Gallic accent, the future he had sketched out for himself—none of that exists anymore. The corpse is merely evidence.

We wrap it up and put it in the freezer next to Thoms. We're getting quite a collection of dead youth.

Anna needs company, so I take her to my suite and, after I check my weapon—in case of bearpigs—we step out on the terrace.

Rain's falling in the distance, but a gap has opened in the clouds and pale sunset colors, lemon and rose, are showing. It's the first sunshine I've seen on the surface of Bela. I begin to see what this world will be like in those magical decades—between spring and summer, again between autumn and winter—when it's neither savagely cold, nor unbearably hot, nor a sodden mess. It'll be gorgeous.

For a while we stand there like a young couple holding hands. Anna needs distraction, so I begin telling her about the wet wild woods around Alfa, about the strange creatures and the restless trees. Her mood lightens a little.

"I want to do some real science here," she says. "I just won't let myself keep getting sucked into the routine. I've been doing a little work on these larvae."

She gestures at the worms crawling on the terrace. "They're all over the place and they're genuinely weird. A human has maybe forty thousand genes, but they've got five times as many."

"What, those little worms? Why?"

"I don't know. They're about as simple creatures as you could imagine—a kind of motile gut. And think about all the chances for genetic errors, for destructive variations—it's too much information."

She added, "Rather like the murders. Where we've also got too much information and can't make any sense out of it, either."

She's back on that subject now, and with a sigh I admit to myself there's no avoiding it. Now she's mourning Michel, who evidently had a gift for making older women want to take care of him.

"Such a nice young man. A little while and he'd have been headed home. It's terrible, all these young people dying."

She starts to cry again. I put my arms around her, and she's so small that for all the gray in her hair it's like holding a child. I'm just about to embark on some serious comforting when intuition—as usual—seizes an inconvenient moment to strike.

"Anna, listen. Tell me this: Why was Michel hurrying down that particular corridor?"

She looks up at me, eyes bleary, mind as usual clear. "Oh. Sure, it leads to my lab. You mean he couldn't find you, so he was coming to see me."

We stare at each other for a few seconds.

"Come on," I say.

"Where?"

"I just saw a ray of light. This time internal. I think I know what the killer was looking for in Michel's beltpouch. Let's go talk to his roommates."

Vengeance is on my mind.

Anna's an unusual woman. Asks no questions, just leads the way through the maze of shoddy construction. I stumble a few times because my mind's elsewhere, thinking of a lot of things that at last, dimly, seem to be making some kind of sense.

Michel's room is in an outlying building: large, clean, well-lighted; semiplast partitions between four bunks; a bouquet of artificial flowers lying on Michel's pillow.

His roommates are all drinking something with the sour smell of home brew and talking together in low voices. I ask to see Michel's belongings.

"Captain Mack took them all," says a young Eurasian woman named Jospin, who seems to be the spokesperson for the group. "She and those two characters Vizbee and Whatever practically turned the place upside down."

"She *said*," adds the guy, "that she was looking for evidence."

That starts an argument between those who say Mack was just doing her duty and those who say she was harsh and unfeeling. I short-circuit this argument.

"Listen. You all know who I am and what I'm doing on Bela. Now I need something and one of you may have it. I hope you do."

I explain what I think Michel has been killed for, and how much I need to see it if it still exists. Jospin looks steadily at me, then reaches into her beltpouch and takes out a pillbox.

"For PMS," she explains with a faint smile. She shakes out, not a pill, but a memory cube and hands it over.

"He asked me to hide it," she explains. "He said not to give it to anybody. He didn't say why."

"I don't know why either," I tell her. "But I hope to find out. Many thanks, and" (speaking as impressively as I can) "don't…say…*anything* about this."

In Anna's lab we play the cube and, yes, it's the copy Michel made for himself of the Spider's exploration of the subsurface passages of Zamók.

"We've seen this already," says Anna, disappointed.

"But perhaps not all of it."

As before, we settle down head-to-head to watch. Once again the little robot descends a slot half a meter wide. Once again pictures of garish creatures in bizarre attire wobble past. We enter familiar rooms, leave them, walk three-leggedly down corridors, enter other rooms.

I'm beginning to get worried. The trouble with intuition is that until you test it, an error looks just as convincing as the truth.

"I don't see anything n—" Anna's beginning when I yell something, maybe "Shit!"

We both stare breathlessly at the screen.

The Spider is entering a room we've never seen before. Slowly it pans the walls and ceiling with its HI-light. We're looking at a sacrifice. As with medieval paintings or comic strips, a series of scenes tells a story.

Unlike our Aztecs, the Arkies had metal weapons, the favorite being an implement with a long handle ending in a curved blade on one side and a spike on the other. With one of these gadgets a priest ceremoniously sacrifices one of his own kind to whatever gods he believes in.

The method is familiar; a fatal blow delivered with the spike against the back or top of the head. Only he does a follow-up, splitting the skull with the axe, after which the believers gather to eat the brain.

The victims don't seem to be resisting; light streams from their faces and rainbows encircle them with full-spectrum haloes. Above them god figures hover, radiating light; in the last scene, they welcome the sacrificial victim to Valhalla.

"Looks like a retirement dinner," I remark unfeelingly.

"No," says Anna. "They're not cannibalizing for food. It's magic. They're acquiring wisdom. They aren't murdering anybody, not in their own minds. They've sacrificed somebody they respect, made him a god, and now the tribe is sharing his knowledge and strength—oh!"

For the second time in a few minutes she's been interrupted, this time by herself. As for me, I am, as they say, struck dumb. Whatever I expected to see in the underground, it isn't this.

The Spider has emerged from the room with the images of sacrifice. In the corridor just beyond, a human child is lying against the wall—a tiny, an improbably tiny girl with golden hair.

For a moment I think I'm going mad. Then Anna says, "It's a doll," breaking the spell.

And with that, of course, the whole case opens before my mind.

Anna and I are outside in the rain. We stroll to the power station with its comforting roar of turbines and its EM fields to mess up listening devices.

We lean our heads together and whisper, reviewing the evidence.

A child can get down the steps into the underground, can take her doll and a flashlight, can see the paintings.

Perhaps, surrounded by busy adults who fundamentally don't give a damn about her, she spends a lot of time down there. She meets other small beings her own size. She plays with and loses her toy.

Mack grew up on Bela, the only human who ever did.

Mack is physically powerful. She's nobody's friend, yet she represents security. Somebody, turning and seeing her coming up from behind, would feel only relief—whew, I'm safe—but nobody would stop to chat with her.

They'd turn and walk on. And feel only one stunning blow before the darkness.

Anna talks about Michel, what a terrible thing it must have been even for a mass murderess to realize that for safety's sake she had to kill the nearest approach she knew to human affection.

I'm more concerned with how she caught on to him. "I bet the kid got careless, made a copy of his cube and left the images in a backup memory, where she found them."

"Mack's insane," whispers Anna.

"No," I say. "She's a native. Like the Arkies. She's helping them reclaim their world. When we go, she'll stay here with them. That's what she really wants—to be rid of us, and stay here forever."

The rain patters around us. It's getting dark, or darker. The power station roars and shakes. My imagination's doing acrobatics.

Suddenly I'm seeing in a whole new light that missile attack on Krebs, the one that conspicuously missed, while scaring the shit out of its target.

What if the whole episode was intended to make him feel surrounded by enemies, make him more dependent on her? And whose missile was it, anyway?

She said she was "chatting" with him in Security when it hit. She wouldn't lie about something like that—too easy to check. And I'm sure Michel wouldn't have fired it. Suddenly I'm remembering her other subordinates, Corporal Vizbee and Private Smelt.

Voilà! I think, in honor of Michel.

At last breathing all that oxygen is paying off—I'm in ecstasy, making connections, when Anna interrupts with a practical question. "What are you going to do?"

"Confront her, accuse her, arrest her. And I'm going to grab those two grungy enlisted people of Mack's. There's something I want to ask them."

"You won't get Vizbee and Smelt," she says. "They were just in to pick up supplies. Right after they helped her shake the place down, she sent them back to the shuttleport."

"Then it's Mack alone."

I'm a happy man. I'm about to crack my case and go the hell home and my ego's purring. When I get back to Earth, I'm thinking, I'll take a long vacation—preferably in Death Valley.

"You're really confident, aren't you?" she asks with an odd inflection. I peer at her, curious.

"Spit it out, Anna," I say. "This is no time to be feminine."

"Well, I think you're underestimating her. And this world. You don't seem to realize that she's not just a lone criminal. We've already had Thoms and Szczech attacked at an outstation. And think of *Ursasus terribilis*—what if the Arkies control the local carnivores? What if they've already used them twice to try to kill you?"

Goddamn women anyway. They have a gift for imagining worst-case scenarios. "If you're right, I'll have to move fast."

"When will you arrest her?"

"Now. Right this minute. Want to come along?"

As we hurry back into the maze, she's muttering, "There's something else. I know there's something we haven't thought of."

But I'm not really listening. First I use a public machine to call Jamal and Eloise.

"Do you feel energetic?" I ask.

Jamal looks baffled. "I guess so. Why?"

"I may need a little assistance. In my room. For something important and possibly a mite dangerous."

He looks at me with narrowed eyes, suspicious of anyone in authority. Eloise comes up behind him.

"We'll be there," she says over his shoulder. I break the connection.

"Don't hurry, just in case we're being watched," I tell Anna, and we move with what, I believe, is legally termed deliberate speed through the usual throng, anonymous in spite of their name tags: Ellenbogen, Menshnikoff, Nguyen, Rice-Davies.

In my bedroom we check the terrace outside, then exit and head for Security. I try the electronic key Michel gave me and it doesn't work.

"Shit," I profoundly comment. "She's changed the settings on the lock. Stand back."

The impact slug knocks out the lock and I kick the door open. The gun rack is empty. At the same moment my eyes fall on the monitor that shows Michel's room.

Oh, Christ.

So while I was busy solving my case, so goddamn sure of myself, she was watching us, changing the lock, removing the weapons.

Did she take the missiles, too? I check hastily. One's gone; the other four are still locked in. But she's removed the detonators so I can't arm them. Who's serving this match?

All things considered, Anna's voice is remarkably calm as she says, "Look outside."

My friend the bearpig—or his cousin—is coming over the parapet. He uses his claws like grappling hooks, climbs easily despite his weight of maybe three hundred kilos. As he moves into the light pouring from my quarters I see sticking through his coarse yellowish fur a million black spines, like a hedgehog's. The guy's armored as well as armed.

He rears up, freeing his forepaws for action. Then he moves bowleggedly yet with disturbing speed around the screen and a scream tells me that Eloise and Jamal have arrived there.

I fling open Security's door and run outside, Anna following. But before I can fire, the beast takes what looks like a tremendous punch from an invisible fist, right on the snout. He rears up, flops over and lies twisting on the Incan stonework.

The great skull is ruined. One eye stares at Anna and me with helpless rage before it films over. The body smells like the lion cage at a zoo—an acrid, sulfurous, somehow fiery odor.

I look into my room and Jamal's standing there in the approved shooter's crouch, holding a pistol in both hands, index finger on the firing stud.

"Where'd you get that?" I ask after we've all greeted each other.

"Swiped it from my boss's locker. I didn't see any good reason why the senior guys should have protection and El and I shouldn't."

"Good for you. Look, we have something of a situation here." I explain.

The four of us huddle. We've got two weapons. Each has fired once, leaving fifteen shots each. Mack's got a dozen weapons and all the spare ammo. She knows Main Base backward and forward, and however she calls her friends—those in the jungle, and those in the passages down below—she's undoubtedly doing it now.

Touching my forehead in salute, I tell Anna, "You were right. This is the worst-case scenario."

She's standing there as if in a trance, looking like a statue of Guanyin, the Goddess of Mercy.

"There's more," she murmurs.

So much for mercy.

"I've just realized," she goes on. "The larvae. Two hundred thousand genes."

I don't understand, even though I know what she's referring to. Eloise and Jamal are, of course, looking absolutely blank. But Anna now speaks with calm professional assurance, as if she's telling somebody they need to get their triglycerides down.

"The larvae must be the basic form. They must hatch from some kind of spore with a really tough capsule to survive the extreme heat and cold. Something triggers development into different forms—partly it must be temperature, but I'm sure it's more complicated than that. The Arkies are one form and Mayakovsky's *medvedi* are another and the carnivore Jamal shot is another. And there may be more.

"They're all cousins, so to speak. That's how they dominate their environment and survive the fantastic changes that happen here on Bela…."

Silence follows. Then the quiet voice insists, "Don't you see?"

"Unfortunately," I say, "yes."

We try to put out a warning.

Eloise has just settled down at the huge console in Security and spoken a first word of command when a sound of distant thunder comes through the shattered terrace door and the machine and the monitors and the lights all go out.

I step to the other door, the one leading into the corridor, and fling it open. It's dark inside Main Base, almost as dark as on the wet and dusky terrace outside. Battery-fed emergency lights are flickering on and beginning to glow redly. People are standing around, looking baffled, their faces purplish as if they had lupus. I turn back with my latest bad news.

"Mack just used her missile on the power station. Zamók's been shut down. All of it."

We head into the corridor and try to spread the alarm by word of mouth. It's not easy. The maze is more confusing than ever. Everywhere people are milling around, bitching about the power failure. Many were headed for the dining hall; complaining they'll have to eat cold rations tonight.

We try shouting, telling them an attack is about to begin, telling them if they've got weapons to join us, if not go to the dining hall and lock the doors. People crowd around us, trying to decide if we're crazy.

Some of them have never seen me before. Anna they know, but so what? She's just the doc. Jamal and Eloise are too young to count.

Where are their leaders? they want to know. Where's Krebs, where are the senior engineers—above all, where's Captain Mack?

"What does Captain Mack say?" a young guy demands. "I mean, she's in charge of security, right?"

"Captain Mack has already killed twenty people and is about to kill a lot more," I inform him, biting off my words.

The fact that I'm getting pissed off doesn't make this unpalatable news any more believable. Yet some people take alarm and start to hasten away. Even if we're nuts, the lights are out; something's clearly wrong.

Others stand around arguing. Some are belligerent—what the hell are we saying? Who the hell do we think we are? Are we trying to start a panic just because there's an equipment failure? Somebody will fix it. That's what engineers do, right?

Then comes a shout. "Doc Li! Come quick! The Controller's been shot!"

And that does it. Suddenly the *toute ensemble* gets to them. The shadows, the dim red lights, the air growing stuffy, the palpable anxiety, Jamal and me waving weapons and talking about an attack, warning them against Captain Mack—and now somebody's yelling that the Controller's shot.

So they hated him, and they hated her, so what, they're the symbols of command and control, right? If they're hostile or wounded or dead, everything's coming apart, right?

Suddenly they panic. And they bolt. They're like cattle scared by lightning. I see shadowy people caroming into one another, knocking one another down. Running into half-dark corridors, headed for I don't know where. Some for the dining hall, some bolting for cover in their rooms.

The guy who yelled for Anna fights his way to us where we stand together, waiting for the hall to clear. He's Senior Engineer Antonelli, and I met him

REVELATION & OTHER TALES OF FANTASCIENCE

for the first and only time on the day I arrived here. He's armed, and I'm glad to see him.

Anna asks, "Is it true Krebs has been shot?"

"Yes. I found him in his office and—"

He never gets to finish. Somewhere in the maze, people start screaming. There are roars and howls. People start running out of the corridors they ran into not five minutes ago. A chunky young woman trots up.

"Arkies are coming up through the floors," she gasps. "And there's some kind of big animal loose."

We hurry to the dining hall. About twenty people have gathered there, two with guns. They're using furniture to barricade the doors, of which there are four. The only light comes from the emergency system.

"Stay here," I tell everybody. I tap Antonelli. "You're in charge."

"I know that," he snaps.

"Where are you going?" asks Anna.

"To snatch a flyer if I can. The only reserves we have are at Alfa, and we're going to need them."

"I'm going with you."

"No, you're not. These people may need a doctor."

"You couldn't find your way with the lights on. How about with them off?"

Eloise steps up and says quietly, "I'll go with him."

To this Jamal objects so violently that I lose patience and, while he's ordering Eloise not to move a muscle, I give him a short left to the point of his dark stubbly chin. He drops like a stone.

I tell Antonelli, "When he wakes up, tell him we'll be back with reinforcements."

In the dark corridor, Eloise says, "I suppose you had to do that."

After we've walked a few meters, she adds, "He's such a dickhead, I've often wanted to punch him out myself."

Of course Anna was right. If I'd tried to find my way out of the maze I'd have gotten hopelessly lost.

Eloise, on the other hand, turns out to be one of those irritating people who always know exactly where they are and the precise azimuth to follow to get anywhere else. When I compliment her, she says, "I'm part homing pigeon."

There's a body in the way, the back of the head caved in. It's nobody I know, but Eloise gives a little muted cry before we hurry on.

"Know him?"

"Oh, yes. Before I…met Jamal."

Something roars up ahead. I'm smelling an odor like lions. I pull her into a dark doorway and we wait. Something big lurches past, making the floor creak, thick coarse fur and spines rasping the wall with a sound like a wire brush. Then a patter of footsteps, a chink of metal and a rapid warbling as varied as a mockingbird's song, only deeper.

Everything fades into the distance. A woman screams. There's a little popping sound—an impact weapon. A roar.

Eloise whispers, "You notice something? The Cousins—that's what Anna called them, wasn't it?—all smell kind of alike. The big ones and the little ones. Maybe that's how they recognize their own kind."

Right, they all have the lion smell, as penetrating as burning sulfur, and why not? They all must have the same basic body chemistry. An idiot rhyme runs through my head: If you stink alike, you think alike.

The birdlike voice of the Arkies fascinates Eloise. "Maybe there's only one 'word' in their language," she whispers, "that long sweet whistle, and the rising and falling tones make the differences in meaning."

"It would be nice," I say repressively, "to speculate about that if we had nothing else to do."

We venture into the darkness, turn down this corridor and that one. Under a red light the semiplast flooring's been burst out from below. I have no trouble recognizing the narrow slot in the stonework beneath, the steps leading down. I even catch a brief glimpse of painted walls.

"You know," Eloise tells me as we edge past and hurry on, "if circumstances were just a bit different, my sympathies would be with the Cousins. It's their world…turn here."

Suddenly we're slamming through a door onto the pad and the shuttle is sitting there, completely empty except for the black box that runs it. Standing in a hangar nearby are two others: one half-dismantled, one that looks service-ready. That fact may be important. Then we're inside the waiting flyer and I'm locking the door and shouting an order to take off. The black box is perfectly calm. "Hearing and obeying," it says.

Abruptly we're soaring into light rain, and as we tilt and turn, Main Base except for a few security lights is plunged in darkness as deep as the jungle below it.

Now we're over the bay, nothing to be seen below but faint crescents of white foam as another in the endless succession of squalls blows in from the ocean. Why do I have these repetitive nightmares, and why do they all turn out to be real?

Emerging from wind-driven rain, we see Alfa's lights still on. A valve is stuck open somewhere and the slurry from the mine—pollution, humanity's signature—is gushing downslope in an oily torrent toward the bay. Eloise makes a faint sound and points.

A guy and a young woman are sitting on top of Alfa's brightly lit power station. He's armed, and they wave at us. There's a dead bearpig lying below. As we bank and turn on our spotlight, something flickers, an arrow maybe, and the two flatten themselves as it flies over.

I doubt that our black box has been programmed for the current circumstances, so I wedge myself into the pilot's seat, hit the manual cutoff and take control of the flyer myself. It's a cranky little machine, and I have some trouble getting it under control. Meanwhile Eloise grabs the pistol and opens the right-side door. As I start swinging back over the power station she fires twice. There's a commotion in the shadows.

"Get something?"

"I don't know. I think there was a bunch of—of whatever, getting ready to attack."

I finally figure out how to bring us to a low hover. The attitude control's stiff—probably a long time since the machine's been on manual. We tip this way and that, then steady and move closer to the shed.

Over the whine of the engine I yell, "What about the others?"

Can the answer really be, "All dead."?

Item (6.) *From Doctor Li's Report.*

This person regrets intruding herself again.

However, I have a positive contribution to make, for Colonel Kohn's absence left him without knowledge of events at Main Base during many crucial hours.

I may state at the outset that locking the doors of the dining hall proved to be impossible. Regrettably, all the locks were electronic and failed when the power went down. How we longed for an antique mechanical bolt or two!

Fortunately the doors opened inward, and piling furniture against them provided a partial defense. Almost at once the doors began to move, pushing back the chairs, tables, etc. Our enemies had no machines but an abundance of muscle, and we were hard put to it to hold them out.

Then noises were heard from the kitchens. Antonelli led a small group of us to the source. When the tiles composing the floor began to shift and then to be knocked out from below, he was waiting.

An Arkie appeared wielding a bronze axe, and Antonelli's shot went through his body and killed also the warrior behind him, who was armed with a sort of barbed hook. Wild scurrying and scampering followed, leaving the mouth of the tunnel empty save for the bodies.

This gave me an idea. After the corpses had been dragged out, I found that I could just fit into the passage, being quite a small person. I asked to borrow Antonelli's weapon. Instead of waiting for a new attack, I proposed to drive back our enemies. And he agreed.

So for the first time I entered the subterranean world of which we had all heard so much and seen so little. I confess that my motive was far more curiosity than any desire to kill Arkies. I believed that the passages provided them protection from heat and cold, all-weather connections between the buildings that used to stand on the surface of Zamók, as well as storerooms and robing rooms where priests prepared themselves for public ceremonies. All this proved to be true as far as it went—which was not very far!

I carried a battery-powered lamp detached from the wall. It was dim and red, and I kept watching uneasily for side chambers, where anything might be hiding. But for twenty meters the passage ran straight and unbroken. It was profoundly silent, and I guessed that our enemies had abandoned any hope of getting at us by this approach.

Then I heard noises ahead, birdsong voices that sounded strangely in these caverns. I switched off the lamp, and stood for a time in profound darkness. Then I began to see very dimly, the way one does on a clouded night— peripherally, while the center of the retina registers only a blur.

This seemed strange to me, for of course the eyes do not work where no light at all exists. There was light, then, although very little, and I soon realized that microscopic fungi lived on the walls, emitting a dim greenish bioluminescence. Thus the lamp I carried had never been essential; but when we were looking down from the kitchen, the tunnel had appeared perfectly dark.

I placed the extinguished lamp on the floor, stepped over it with some difficulty, and moved on. The pistol was heavy, and I now held it with both hands, ready for action.

My next discovery was that my shoulders no longer brushed against the walls, though I still had to bow my head. The passage was widening, and I could see an opening ahead with something moving just inside it.

I stopped at once. When the obscure movement ceased, I advanced very, very cautiously, well aware that as the space opened around me I would be subject to attack. The tunnel widened into a broad room, where long slabs of stone stretched away into the dimness in mathematically straight lines.

On each slab lay terra-cotta trays a few centimeters deep, and in each the familiar larvae were swarming.

This was an impressive sight. Clearly, the Arkies no longer depended on the natural development of their kind in the forest. I heard whistling and movement toward the other end of this strange nursery, saw an Arkie emerge from the dimness and post itself beside a tray. Something began to trickle, and I realized that the adult was urinating into the trays, a few drops to each, and I caught the penetrating "smell of lions," as the Colonel called it.

No doubt, I thought, the urine contains hormones which speed the development of the larvae into the Arkies' form: a most fascinating achievement for a species that, so far as we know, has nothing that can properly be called science!

Well, and why not? I asked myself. Folk medicine gave us humans quinine for malaria and inoculation for smallpox. I was full of these thoughts when suddenly the Arkie spotted me and broke into a frenzy of birdsong.

Item (7.) *From Colonel Kohn's Notebook.*

We have them aboard now, the two Alfans, and yes, everybody else in the mining camp is dead.

The technique reminded me a bit of Ted Szczech's abduction. Something broke the slurry pipe, that set off alarms, and when a repair crew went out to fix it the Cousins ambushed them. The Arkies used poisoned arrows as well as bronze hand weapons, and with the bearpigs to aid them soon forced their way inside.

The Alfans say two species fight together like humans with war dogs or war horses or war elephants. Only here there's a family connection much more direct than ours with our symbionts. They recognize each other by smell, and seem to feel a kind of tribal loyalty. There may even be a telepathic bond—the Arkies seem to give orders at a distance. They're the most intellectual members of the clan, but even the ones we think of as beasts are—as Mayakovsky noted so long ago—disturbingly intelligent. In fighting, the bearpigs display initiative and cunning as well as savagery.

Down below, they're dragging the bodies out into the open, into the glaring lights. The bearpigs begin to feed and the scene is garish, horrible, a kind of Grand Guignol theater. The Arkies look on, but don't share the meal. Clearly, humans are not eligible for the company of their gods in Valhalla.

Watching the butchery, I know we've lost the war. Period. We have to assume that the four of us in this flyer and the people holding out at Main Base and *maybe* the guards at the shuttleport are the only survivors. So back we go.

—.—

Item (8.) *From Dr. Li's Report.*

As I retreated down the tunnel, I could hear and sense rather than see them following me, and I fired the pistol.

The place was so narrow that I did not have to aim. Of course, neither did they. Something came sliding and scraping along the floor and touched my shoe, and it proved to be a short throwing or thrusting spear with a leaf-shaped bronze point.

I fired again. There was no use trying to evade the necessity to kill or be killed. My heel struck an obstacle and I almost fell over backward, saved only by the narrowness of the tunnel. It was the lamp. I stepped over it and continued my fighting retreat.

The sounds at the end of the tunnel indicated that bodies were being pulled out of the way. I fired again, producing much agitated noise. My heel encountered another obstacle: the first step.

It is no easy task to retreat up a staircase that is both narrow and steep, at the same time keeping one's head down and one's guard up. With a metallic ping an arrow struck the riser of a step I had just vacated and the wooden shaft broke. Then friendly hands were pulling me out of the slot, into what seemed at first the blinding light of the kitchen.

I had hardly begun to tell the others of the mysterious world beneath our feet when a deafening impact rocked us all. We stumbled over one another rushing into the dining hall, now adrift in dust and shattered fragments.

The wounded, still shocked, had not yet begun to scream. One of the piles of furniture had been blown to bits and the door to the hall was a gaping hole.

Captain Mack had used another missile, and used it well. Our enemies were upon us.

Item (9.) *From Colonel Kohn's Notebook.*

I think the Cousins are awestruck—it's the only word I can think of. Stunned by Mack's demonstration of godlike power.

I left the Alfans at the pad with orders to rev up the other workable flyer to aid the evacuation. Then Eloise guided me to this scene of ruin.

In the dim red glow of the hallway outside the mess hall our enemies stand, small and great shadows under a forest of glinting spearpoints and axes with curved blades. Clouds of smoke and dust are billowing around them, masking shapes and distorting outlines. I bet their ears are deafened and ringing, just like mine.

For some of the animals it's too much. Frightened, they begin to lumber away, colliding with one another and the Arkies and the walls. The moment of confusion is perfect.

I can see Mack, wigless, with the missile launcher still on her shoulder. I take careful aim at her, fire, and hit a bearpig that lurches between us at the critical moment.

Then Jamal and Anna run out of the mess hall, both armed, firing too, and panic hits our foes. The coughing of the impact weapons is almost inaudible, and creatures large and small start falling over. Some scream, just like wounded humans.

Then they're running, fading into the darkness of the corridors, maybe some retreating into the underground passages until they can figure out what's going on. Mack's gone too—at any rate, I can't see her distinctive figure anywhere.

We stumble over bodies, shouting. Jamal hugs Eloise, glares at me. That left hook I gave him seems to have made me an enemy. Then Anna mistakes me for something hostile and almost shoots me before I yell at her.

The mess hall's in ruins, some people dead, some wounded, some stunned. We don't have a minute to lose, we grab the living and run. It's a total rout. We're like Spaniards fleeing Mexico City on the *noche triste*. Or like Americans fleeing conquered Saigon.

Eloise and Anna are leading the way through the corridors with their smears of red light, and I'm hearing our enemies roar and sing and reassemble for a new attack.

The walking wounded have to take care of themselves; the helpless ones are hauled and dragged by the shoulders or even by the feet. We've got four weapons but only about a dozen shots left, as near as I can figure.

Then we're out onto the pad. In the rainy dark the lights of the two functional flyers cast frenzied shadows everywhere. Those of us who are armed prepare to resist while the others are jamming people aboard. Two who died on the retreat from the mess hall get thrown aside like rubbish.

Anna has given her weapon back to Antonelli. She's in medical mode, doing a sort of instant triage. She orders the bad cases stacked like cordwood in one flyer so she can ride with them and try to treat them.

Meantime figures are gathering just inside the doors and arrows begin to flicker and ping. A young woman I don't know turns a frightened face toward the door of Main Base and takes an arrow soundlessly in her throat. It's short, about thirty centimeters, and it only pricks her, yet suddenly she's flopping helplessly on the ground, her face cyanosing.

We abandon her, too.

I don't really notice the last moments. All at once I'm hanging half-out of the door of a flyer, there's no room inside for all of me because I'm too goddamn big, and arrows with little barbed brazen points are sticking in the skin of the machine.

I hear the black box—so calm, so cool, a voice from another world—as it says, "Hearing and obeying," and we're lifting away from Main Base.

So slowly, so slowly. And I'm riding like that, arm crooked around a stanchion, and some friendly hand's holding onto my belt as we wobble and yaw out over the estuary and the white-crested black waves of the sea.

Item (10.) *From Dr. Li's Report.*

We were packed together like rice in sushi. At first I couldn't do anything for my patients, because I couldn't move.

Two of them died right there, and with great difficulty we extracted the corpses and threw them into the sea, making a little more room so that Colonel Kohn at last found a place to sit inside.

I discovered that eleven of us were on that little flyer, which was built to handle four plus luggage. That it stayed aloft at all was quite wonderful. I feared, however, that the excess fuel consumption might drop us into the sea before we reached the shuttleport.

It was the darkest part of the night, and I shall not soon forget the trip. Sometimes a soft moan, the rank marshy smell of human bodies that have been sweating with fear. The odor of blood. Fortunately, the wounded were in shock from their injuries and burns, and lay quiet.

Exhaustion was our great friend, and I suddenly opened my eyes to find that I had been sleeping, and that a pale gray misty dawn had begun to filter through the clouds.

Soon every eye was trying to pierce the veils of rain for our first sight of the promontory and the egg-shaped green dome. What we would find there no one knew—whether it had been attacked, whether its two guards survived—and I was thinking also of the months that must elapse before the next supply ship came.

It is no light thing to be at war with a whole world.

And then I saw something—I saw something—I saw a smooth geometrical shape rising out of the clouds and mist, and it was still there, the portal by which humans enter and leave Bela. I thought: Oh, that we may yet leave it alive!

Item (11.) *Extract from the Bela Shuttleport Log.*

7.56. Have spoted 2 flyers approtching. Linda and me didnt hardly have time to jump out the sack and put our draws on when they come boncing down on to the pad and a bunch of peple come spiling out. Memo: file complant with Krebs re (1) unskeduled flyte and (2) overloded flyers. (Singed) Cpl Vizbee, Securty.

Item (12.) *From Colonel Kohn's Notebook.*

Vizbee and Smelt are looking pretty sour and disheveled, and give us minimum help carrying the wounded. They keep saying they take orders only from Mack and I have to get a bit rough to convince them they now take orders from me.

We number twenty-two, of whom nine are too seriously injured to work or fight.

Brief tour of inspection shows a freezer stocked with foodstuffs for the guards and the loading parties who used to bring in the ingots. I ask

Antonelli to check it out. He says that if all the wounded recover, we'll starve before the supply ship gets here.

Medicines: the shuttleport has a small dispensary, but Anna looks grim when she inventories the drug locker. I suspect Vizbee and Smelt have been into it for recreational purposes, though of course they deny it.

The port contains about three hundred square meters of floor space. Walls and floor are thick translucent duroplast—solid stuff, nothing will break in. Power source: another antique reactor housed in its own dome and accessible by a protected corridor.

Escape possibilities: We now have three flyers, but the two we brought with us are almost out of fuel—that overloaded last trip, among other things. The flyer V&B came down in is usable, with enough fuel for a return flight to Zamók, where, of course, we don't dare go. One dismantled flyer remains there—I hope beyond repair.

Outside it is, surprise, raining. The pad is wet and shining. There's a bare space, maybe half a hectare in all, where everything except a kind of lichen has been killed off by the retros of incoming and departing shuttles.

Beyond are gray rocks and clumps of stunted trees. A neck of barren land connects us to the shore and the usual gray-green-purple wall of jungle.

Situation summary: We're in good shape, with ample space, bedded down warm and dry, with lights on and medical care and nothing to do but wait for the supply ship. It's due in about sixty-seven days—local days, that is. If it's late (and it often is) we'll be living on air and water. *Lots* of water.

The first need is to increase food supplies somehow.

I call on Jamal and Antonelli to help me search the peninsula. Jamal wears his patented scowl but obeys scrupulously, which is all I ask for. We take our weapons, just in case.

We complete our circuit in under an hour. It's not much of a place. I doubt it's more than a couple of square kilometers of volcanic slag. You can hear the sound of surf everywhere. The beaches are gray shingle or black sand.

We walk out on the rocky neck that connects us to the shore. The water's shallow on one side where the sand has built up, but deep on the other. Could be a fine fishing spot. I'm sure we can fabricate some tackle.

I've surf-fished on coasts like this, and for a moment it all seems halfway familiar—the sea air and the smell of the deep and the sting of salt in the flying drops of spray.

Jamal turns back toward the shuttleport, but I walk a few steps on with Antonelli. He begins to tell me something, shouting to be heard over the crash of the waves.

"Sometimes I dream about retiring to an island. Just me, a good library, a wine cellar, a bot or two to do the dirty work—"

Aagh!

The deep erupts and something huge and black falls with a weight that shakes the rocks.

It's big, big as an orca, and it has broad flippers in front and four huge splayed tusks. It takes Antonelli's whole head in its mouth and thrusts with the flippers and slides back into the water, dragging him under. The wind flings a geyser of foam into my face. I wipe my eyes and the last thing I see are the man's legs thrashing deep down like the arms of a squid.

Antonelli's gone. Just like that. The kelplike odor of the deep mingles for an instant with the fiery smell of lions. Then there's only wind and salt and Jamal is dragging me away.

Behind us something big roils the surface of the sea and there's a great bellowing roar, *Aa! Aa! Aa! Aa!*

Item (13.) *From Dr. Li's Report.*

Nothing of this tragedy was audible inside the dome.

I'd done what I could for my patients and was trying to comfort a young woman named Mbasa, concealing my fear that she might be permanently blind.

To treat this one injury properly, we needed a set of replacement eyes, fetal-monkey stem cells to regrow the damaged optic nerves, and the services of a skilled neurotransplant surgeon. We had none of the above. And there were other cases even more serious than this one.

Then Colonel Kohn appeared in the doorway, white-faced and soaking wet. He gestured for me to follow him. I gave him a blanket, made fresh hot tea and met him in the station's departure lounge. In one corner Eloise and Jamal were hugging each other as if they never intended to let go. The colonel sat hunched over, wrapped in his blanket like a beggar, and sucked greedily at the steaming tea.

"The Cousins have a cousin we knew nothing about," he said, and told me of Antonelli's death. "The trouble with the worst-case scenario is there's usually a worser one. How are your patients?"

I replied that at least four and possibly as many as seven would not survive.

"That's good," he said.

I looked at him and saw a man who was both familiar and strange. Despite his professional toughness, he had always seemed to me a humane man. Now I was seeing another side of him. Though he still trembled with the cold, his face was bleak and hard as the rocks of this nameless island.

"It's a good thing," he muttered, "that we have a big freezer. We're going to run out of food, Anna, and we're under siege and can't get any more. Once our supplies are gone, we'll have no choice but to eat our dead."

We sat quietly together, sipping tea, while the profound depth of our dehumanization sank in. Suddenly I knew that I could not face the coming ordeal alone.

I brought him another cup, plus fifty milligrams of Serenac, which he obviously needed. There was nothing else I could do for him, except go to bed with him and hold him and keep him warm. At that moment I resolved to do so, if he would have me.

Item (14.) *From Colonel Kohn's Notebook.*

I see it's been several weeks since I made an entry, so let me try to catch up. Much has happened, also little. Anna and I have become lovers—a development that was a surprise, at least to me.

By default we've also become the rulers of our tiny besieged colony. As Anna predicted, four people have died of their wounds and two more are moribund. With Antonelli gone, that leaves seventeen of us, soon to be fifteen.

In all we've suffered almost ninety-nine percent casualties. Even if some people at Main Base or the mining camp or the smelter have escaped into the jungle, they won't survive there long. They'll be killed, or they'll simply starve.

All the senior engineers being dead, I appointed Jamal as technical officer. His business is to keep the place working. I know he has long-term plans for revenge. I humiliated him in front of Eloise with that long-ago punch, and he's one of those people who never, never, never forget. Well, I need his brains, courage, and knowhow, and in return he can have his revenge.

Anna has the job of keeping the survivors alive. Eloise works under her and is rapidly turning into a capable physician's assistant. In bright people, on-the-job training produces quick results. I see to defense and discipline, make out and enforce the duty rosters, preside over the distribution of rations (about eighteen hundred calories for the healthy, twenty-one hundred for the sick) and act generally prickish. Like Mr. Krebs in his time, I am not beloved, nor do I expect to be.

The only serious violation of rules has been, inevitably, by Vizbee and Smelt. Ordered to turn over keys to all doors, cabinets and cupboards, they did so, but kept a duplicate set. When Anna told me that six vials of something called M2—a synthetic morphine substitute—had disappeared from the medicine cabinet, I staged a raid and found them in Vizbee's laundry bag.

The matter was serious, because we're low on painkillers and have a lot of pain to kill. In a container of Smelt's vaginal cream I also found the duplicate keys.

My first impulse was to shoot both of them. However, Anna spoke up for mercy and the general feeling in our community seemed to be that they were too stupid to be fully accountable.

So I held a private session with each of them, offering them life in exchange for some answers.

Both babbled freely. Each blamed the other for firing that missile at Krebs's quarters. Both affirmed that Captain Mack gave them the weapon and the order, which as good soldiers they had to obey, whatever their personal feelings.

"I'm sure you understand, Sir," says Smelt with her soapy smile.

"Only too well."

I had them sign confessions, and then I tied both of them up and put them in the freezer beside the corpses. Half an hour later I took them out. They emerged wrapped in spiderwebs of ice, and when revived seemed to have gotten the message. The next time they're going in for good, although the thought of having to eat Vizbee stew or Smelt croquettes eventually is pretty repugnant.

Aside from that, the time has been routine. We haven't been attacked. Those of us who hadn't already paired off are doing so now—most with the other sex, a few with their own. Everybody needs a companion here.

Recreation: Hidden away in cabinets we've found some chess sets, tennis racquets but no balls, a game called *Conquer the Galaxy*—excuse me, I'd rather not—poker and blackjack and Airborne Polo programs, and old sets of greasy playing cards, some of which are marked.

Daytimes we clean the place and tend the injured and service the machinery; at night we mark our calendars, make love and play games and gossip and feel hungry and bitch. And, as much as possible, sleep.

Between Anna and me there's a surprising amount of ardor, considering our mature age and marginal diet. Also a lot of caution. The conjunction of two loners of settled habits is dicey at best. And there are some physical problems, because she's so small and I'm so large. But—in sex as in life—where there's a will, there's usually a way. We've found privacy in what used to be a storeroom. I've locked the door with a confiscated key. At the moment, Anna and I are lying starkers on a pile of discarded shuttlecraft cushions, warmed by proximity and by some clean mechanics' coveralls she found in a bin and turned into bedspreads.

Now she turns to me with a smile and lets her tiny but very capable hand settle on my arm, like a dragonfly. I think this will be all my note-taking for tonight.

Item (15.) *Extract from a Letter of Eloise Alcerra to Her Mother.*

Dearest Mama, So many things have happened to us that I hardly know where to begin. First of all, there's been a war. . . .

—.—

So that's the story to date. Now I'm working in the hospital in the shuttleport here on Bela. We only have three patients left—the others have died or have recovered as much as they're going to here.

I'm doubly happy when Anna (Dr. Li) declares somebody well. I'm glad that I've been able to help them get better, but I'm also glad that they'll be going on the same 1,800 calories as the rest of us. That way we'll all last a bit longer.

I'm tired all the time. Yet when I lie down I usually can't sleep, and when I do I dream mainly about big dinners. Jamal's the same way. He works hard, much harder than I do. Maybe as a result he's less demanding about sex. I don't know whether I like that or not.

I dread the thought of our first cannibal feast. Yet it can't be far off. Will I be able to eat human stew? Yes, of course. When you're hungry enough, you'll eat anything.

Jamal makes ghastly little jokes about it. "You heard about the cannibal who passed his brother in the forest?" he asks, leering. Or pats my still ample backside and says, "Lunch. Hey, take that back. Lunch and dinner."

How, and above all why, have I put up with him so long?

At least once a day I sneak away and walk outside. I need to be alone for a while, away from the intolerably repetitive faces of my fellow prisoners. Needless to say, I stay off the beaches!

I don't feel so tired outside, I guess because of the enriched air, and I love the smell of the sea. Yesterday a sunbeam worked its way through the clouds and the seawind seemed to glitter with salt.

Yet today even my walk left me feeling down. I climbed, muscles quivering, up a pile of black rock and stood for a while looking out to where the horizon line ought to be. Only it wasn't, because the usual squalls were all around and as I turned, first the ocean and then the drenched jungle faded into the sky without a break.

The dome isn't our prison. This world is our prison, and I ask myself again and again if any of us will ever escape it.

Even if we don't, I'm sure people will come here again looking for us, and

I hope they find this. Meantime I hold to the thought of you and the Earth and its sunlight and blue skies as my lifeline.

Item (16.) *From Colonel Kohn's Notebook.*

The time until the supply ship arrives is getting short. If it's late, ciao, good-bye, sayonara. We're running out of food.

So today we eat human. Two of us do the butchering, I suppose to spread the guilt around. We rotate cooking by roster, and just as I won't name the other butcher, I won't name the cook, other than to state that (s)he doesn't turn a hair over the grisly task.

In fact, once the meat is separated from the frame, it looks just like anything else. We keep the head for decent burial on Earth, assuming we ever get back there. I won't give the name of the entree, other than to say it was someone I knew and liked. But once life has departed, we're all just meat and might as well feed our friends. Think of it as giving the ultimate dinner party.

The smell of cooking permeates the dome. People go about their usual duties, but they keep sniffing. Little groups talk together and I hear some high-pitched laughter. That worries me a bit. No hysterics needed here.

Then we sit down to eat. There are two schools of thought about our protein supplement: It tastes like veal; it tastes like pork. I belong to the pork school. After the meal, everybody's a bit frantic. Next day: We have leftovers. Nobody bats an eye, and two guys ask for seconds, which I have to refuse them. Cannibalism turns out to be like any other rite of passage. The first time's hard, the second time's a lot easier, and after that you don't think much about it anymore.

However, there's one thing we'll all soon have to think about, and I have to admit it's getting me down.

Item (17.) *From Dr. Li's Report.*

The problem facing us was this: When we had eaten the dead, what then? I began to hear jokes about "drawing straws." But was it a joke? Surely, I

266

thought, if the supply ship doesn't appear soon, we'll have to be killed one at a time, so that hopefully a few of us—or two of us—or even one of us can return to Earth to tell our story.

At dinner I saw Robert looking over our people with a curiously bleak face, empty of expression. I realized that he was mentally drawing up a new roster. He was arranging our people in order, from those who could be spared most easily to those without whom the whole colony would perish.

Others understood also. I began to miss Vizbee and Smelt, and realized that they were hiding from Robert's lethal gaze. How stupid! Surely the path of wisdom was for them to look as busy and useful as possible. But the poor wretches were just intelligent enough to realize whose names must head the list of expendables (I almost said "perishables.") And they remembered the freezer, and the shrouded bodies lying beside them.

Item (18.) *From Colonel Kohn's Notebook.*

I'm weighing the remaining rations for the umpteenth time when Eloise puts her head in the storeroom door. She's white as our last kilo of sugar.

Would I step outside with her? Well, sure. I don't ask why, because I know there'll be a good reason.

"Do you come out here alone?" I ask as we crunch through the lichen. "You shouldn't."

"I have to," she says. "I'd go nuts being inside all the time. Now stop being commander-in-chief for a minute, because I've got something to show you."

She leads the way up a black pile of—what do they call it—scoria? Broken lava chunks the sea will turn into black sand, and—

I only need a glance. "Go back and tell Jamal and Anna to join us."

"If Jamal's busy he'll want to know why."

"The reason is I want him now."

"Yes, sir," she says, and goes.

When the others arrive, I don't even have to point. There's only one thing to see.

A pod of the sea creatures is approaching, maybe twenty, maybe more.

They're gray, and close enough now that we can see irregular crusty white patches on their backs and tails—I guess the local version of barnacles. They're a ballet of monsters, rhythmically rising and sinking like the waves, all together.

"They can't come ashore, can they?" asks Eloise, hopefully.

Jamal and I look at each other. We're remembering the one that got Antonelli. The way it rose up on its flippers, the way it tossed its head back, the barking noise. Remembering the inevitable smell of lions. Sea lions. These things are pinnipeds that feed in the sea but drag themselves up on beaches to rest and fight and mate.

"Look," says Anna, pointing in another direction. "It took her a while, but she got it running. Clever lady."

Way, way off, a gray dot in the gray clouds darkens, takes shape, and turns into the last flyer, repaired and functional and heading our way.

Item (19.) *From Dr. Li's Report.*

Since we had no option but to resist or die, it was unnecessary to encourage the troops—we could rely on our enemies to do that.

As for myself, I put my hardcopy notes in order, wrapped them in plastic and hid them under loose ice in the freezer. Even if we are all killed, I thought, people sooner or later will come here looking for us, and with luck they may find this record. The last corpse that remained uneaten seemed to be watching me, and I came out shivering for more reasons than the cold.

Yet I continued speaking into my notebook, hoping to transcribe the rest of the story later.

Robert had deployed eight people, which was the number of weapons we had. Adding the shuttleport stock to our own slim armory, we had one hundred and eighty rounds, which was enough to do much damage, though not to drive off all our enemies.

I set up an aid station at the foot of the heap of scoria we had taken to calling the Black Hill, and filled a medical kit with M2, tourniquets, a few antibiotics, etc.

Then I climbed the hill to see exactly what was happening. The sea lions (as Robert called them) had vanished under the waves, meaning that they could reappear anyplace. The flyer had turned and was circling, perhaps a kilometer out. It passed over the shoreline, swung back. Wisely, Robert ordered his people to hold their fire.

I noticed that Eloise was standing beside Jamal. I called her over to help me at the aid station, and she had begun to approach with slow steps when in the corner of my eye I caught a flash from the flyer.

I shouted, "Down!" and she dropped to the ground just as the missile struck the Black Hill and exploded. The sound was loud enough to leave my head ringing. Then the sound *Aa! Aa! Aa!* from behind us warned that the sea lions were coming ashore. At the same moment the flyer veered and from an amplifier came a burst of birdsong so loud that it might have been the giant mythical Roc calling to its mate. At that, the margin of the jungle trembled and something roared in reply.

Item (20.) *From Colonel Kohn's Notebook.*

I can't say I ever liked Julia Mack. But I always respected her, never more so than now. She's got a very weird army, but she's doing first-rate command and control.

She's got an Arkie sitting beside her with an amplifier and she's got her goddamn launcher. Must be awkward—leaning out the pilot's port to fire it, so the backflash doesn't fry her. But she manages. A managing gal.

Okay, here come the lions from the sea.

Okay, here come the bearpigs from the jungle. There's more birdsong, this time from the line of trees, so Arkies are in the jungle as well, leading the troops.

The Cousins are closing in. If we make every single shot count, they'll still win. If panicking was any use, I'd panic.

Since it isn't, I'll have to try something else.

I cross over to Jamal and hand him my notebook. "Take care of this."

He raises black arched eyebrows.

"I have something to do. You're in command till I get back. If we live through today, you can sock me good and hard on the jaw."

That's sort of a good-bye.

Item (21.) *From Colonel Kohn's Notebook (continued by Jamal al-Sba'a).*

Kohn leaves the field of battle. Much as I dislike him, I don't think he is running away. He is a brave Jew.

May the Ever-Living One preserve him, for I hope to collect on his offer at the end of this day.

It's strange, I've never seen him talk into this notebook, yet he always has it with him. The idiot light goes on when I speak, so I suppose it's picking my voice up. I have no notebook of my own—all my stuff except my weapon was lost in the flight from Main Base.

All right, we have only eight weapons. We will soon be assailed from two sides. Do we fight out here in the open, or withdraw to the dome and try to defend it? This is the kind of decision a commander must make, and if he's wrong, everyone is lost. I've always longed for power, now I feel its crushing weight.

I decide that we'll retreat, for two reasons: first, Captain Mack and her goddamn missiles. She can kill many of us and we can't afford losses. Second, the Cousins can afford losses, so the damage we do to them is beside the point. The only strategy is to resist as long as possible and then accept our fate. I call Doctor Li and instruct her to move the aid station inside the dome. Eloise gathers up the medical kit and heads back, while Li waits to see if we take any casualties on the retreat. The Chinese woman appears perfectly calm.

Mack is coming round again in her flyer. The noise of the engine is lost in the volume of sound rising on all sides—the roaring, the warbling, the barking of the creatures from the sea.

And—*Inshallah!*—another flyer is rising to meet her! So this is why Kohn left us!

Item (22.) *From Doctor Li's Report.*

All my life I had struggled to attain the Buddhist ideal of non-attachment—maybe out of cowardice, because I feared the pain of loss.

Maybe this is why I fled from life into the laboratory—from the knowledge of passion to a passion for knowledge. Why, until Robert came to Bela, I was so much alone.

When I saw our one fully functional flyer take off, I felt as if I'd been stabbed in the heart with an icicle. Then I told myself that if Robert intended to crash into the other flyer, he would have said good-bye to me first.

So I comforted myself, thinking that, yes, he intended a dangerous game—to distract and alarm Mack, make her fire and waste her remaining missiles. He went, I decided, to court danger, not to seek death. Yet the flyer shot straight at her, moving far too fast for safety, and she must have been startled, for her craft yawed and for a wonderful moment I thought it would spin out of control and crash. But then she mastered the controls and the two aircraft began a twisting, turning ballet that I can only compare to the mating dance of mayflies.

Then our craft turned and fled, with Mack in pursuit.

I found myself again atop the Black Hill without any sense of how I got there. Looking down for a moment, I saw an incredible sight, the creatures of two worlds paralyzed by shared amazement and staring upward.

A sea lion had crashed through a barrier of stunted trees, and it rested propped on immense flippers with its tusked face in the air. Without the support of the sea its own weight oppressed it, and its great scarred sides heaved with the effort of breathing.

On the landward side, bearpigs standing on their hind legs moved their heads from side to side, following the action above like entranced listeners following the music at a concert. Arkies were pointing with their bronze weapons and exchanging wild and strangely sweet snatches of song.

I saw the launcher emerge from the pilot's port of Mack's ship, and an instant later came the blinding backflash. The missile burned a long twisting trail, and my heart stopped because I realized that it was homing in, that it was too swift for its target to escape, and then it struck our flyer, which exploded in a great orb of flame like an opening peony. Dark fragments floated downward like gull's feathers into the sea. From our enemies came a crescendo of sound that I can never describe—one world triumphant over another, howling its victory.

Next I felt a grip on my arm; it was Jamal and he said, "Come on, we're retreating to the dome. Save yourself."

I answered, "Why?" wishing only for my life to be over.

Item (23.) *From a Letter of Eloise Alcerra to Her Mother.*

We're all inside the dome together. There was one real shocker when it turned out the door to the hangar had been left open.

Something forced its way in, I didn't see what, but I heard an impact weapon cough and then a couple of guys slammed the door, I think pushing a body out. End of Crisis One.

I was looking for Doctor Li. I'd brought in the medical kit, but to be any good it had to be married to the one person who knew how to use it.

I found her looking awful and I said in alarm, "Are you wounded?" She said, "No, only dead," which I took to be some kind of weird joke— meaning, like, aren't we all?

Jamal was yelling orders, and I said to him, "Colonel Kohn won't like you taking his job away from him."

To my amazement, Jamal said, "Kohn's dead."

"No, he's not."

He ran off, saying he had to check the rest of the doors, especially the loading doors onto the pad, because they were big enough to let in an army if they'd been left open too.

Paying, of course, no attention to me whatever.

I went back to Anna Li, and she was preparing our hospital for new casualties. Her movements were strange, jerky like a marionette, and she hardly seemed to see what she was doing.

I said, "Anna, what's wrong? I mean, aside from the fact that we're all going to be killed, what's the matter?"

She said, "Robert's dead."

Second one in five minutes. Patiently I told her, "No, he's not, he's up on one of the catwalks under the dome, checking the air intakes."

She stopped and looked at me steadily. "I saw him die," she said.

"Well, he must've died very recently, because I saw him climbing a ladder when I was bringing in the medical kit."

"Inside the dome?"

"Of course inside the dome. He'd have to be nuts to be climbing an exterior ladder."

At that her face turned to parchment and she fainted. I caught her going down and laid her on an empty cot. The blind woman, Mbasa, was demanding to know what was going on, so I led her over and sat her down and gave her Anna's hand to hold.

Then I went looking for Colonel Kohn. As I pushed through the people milling around in the main lobby area, most of them were talking about his death. Apparently everybody had seen him die, and only I had seen him alive.

I suppose I should say I doubted my own sanity, but I didn't. What I doubted was everybody else's.

I found a metal ladder with its supports embedded in the duroplast and started climbing. I really don't like heights, but pretty soon I was twenty meters in the air and running along a metal catwalk, wondering where the damp warm air was coming from until I realized it was everybody's breath, rising and collecting up there.

I spotted him standing at the main air intake. He'd pulled off the housing and shoved back the big flexible duct and he was aiming his pistol between the metal louvers. He fired the way real marksmen do, touching the stud so gently that I could hardly see his fingertip move. The pistol coughed and something outside roared.

"One less," he muttered, and I didn't know whether he meant one less round or one less enemy, or both. "What are you doing here, Eloise?"

I told him that everybody had seen him die, including Anna, and he'd better show himself alive before she died of grief and before Jamal had time to make everybody hate him.

"You underestimate them both," he said. "Oh, oh. Step back and open your mouth and cover your ears."

I did and the catwalk jumped and I felt like I'd had an iron bell over my head and somebody had hit it with a sledgehammer.

"Oh my God," I was muttering. "Oh my God." He yelled something at me but I was almost deaf.

He walked me away from the spot. My ears were still ringing, but after a little while I could understand him. He talked like a lecturer.

"If that last missile had hit the grille we'd have a big hole in the dome. And it's accessible to an exterior ladder. But it just occurred to me that we ought to let them come in this way, because they'll be squeezed together on this goddamn catwalk and we can shoot them like rabbits. Or maybe just pry the catwalk loose and let them fall."

He told me to go see Jamal and have him order two people with guns up here. "And tell Anna not to wet her pants. I'm alive as I ever was. As soon as my two shooters get here, I'll be down."

Before going I asked, "Why does everybody think you're dead?"

"It's the flyer. I was going to take it up and harass Mack and see if I could get her to waste her last missiles. But somebody else got there first."

"Who?"

"Vizbee and Smelt, of course. I guess they figured they were on the menu and the battle gave them a good chance to escape. Though where they hoped to escape to, I don't know. Idiots. Now, scram."

Item (24.) *From Colonel Kohn's Notebook (Kohn speaking).*

Jamal tells me he's deferred the punch on the jaw until either the Cousins break in, or else we get away. That way if he knocks out a few teeth I can either have dental care or else not need it.

I've had some of the guys loosen the retaining bolts on the upper catwalk. A bearpig tore out the grille and louvers but nothing's tried to get through yet. I suppose they've figured out that it's like climbing into a bull's eye.

I wish I knew if Mack's got any missiles left. Let's see, there were six in the armory to start with. One fired into Krebs's quarters. One to blast the power station. One to open up the mess hall. Three fired here. Does that mean she's out?

I bet not. I bet she had a couple stored away in some secret place, maybe underground. This lady is daring but also careful. If she has more, they'll soon be hitting a door. Preferably two doors, one on each side. Then the big beasts will break down what's left, and they'll be inside.

We'll kill a lot of them but it won't make any difference, because, as Anna said, you can't fight a whole world.

WHAM!

Hear that? Just in case anybody gets to listen to this record. I wish I wasn't so goddamn right all the time. I wish I was dumber, so I couldn't see things coming. I wish Anna and I were anyplace but here.

It's the door into the hangar again.It's bent and bulging inward but still standing.

Lots of pressure against the outside. Nerve-shattering squeals of metal grinding on metal. It moves slowly, but it does move. *E pur si muove*—what Galileo told the Inquisition—but it does move. Meaning the Earth, which probably we'll never see again.

That noise like a very loud shot was a hinge breaking. If only these things were nuclear steel, but they're not; they're strong, but we need something indestructible.

I order four shooters to the threatened door. Order one guy to stand behind each shooter and grab his weapon if he's killed or wounded. Yell for the shooters on the catwalk to come down. Order one to join Jamal, the other to blow off the loosened retaining bolts if something comes through the intake, as of course something will. Order everybody to stay away from the area underneath. Order Jamal to watch the double doors that open onto the shuttlepad. If the Cousins break in there, we're seriously screwed.

Finally stop giving orders. I've done the best I can, now we'll fight it out and they'll win, as possibly they deserve to do. As Eloise said, it is their world.

On the way to her hospital, Anna gives me a blissful smile. She's actually happy to be dying with me—compared to living without me. In all my long life, nobody ever looked at me that way before.

Item (25.) *From the Letter of Eloise Alcerra to Her Mother.*

I feel like such an idiot, talking, talking to you across the light years at a time like this. But what else can I do?

It'll hurt you to know exactly how I died, but not as much as not knowing. And I want you to know my last thoughts are with you.

The expected blast just hit the double doors to the pad right in the middle and the metal snapped and bent. Then steady, unrelenting pressure.

All the usual sounds from outside. Warbling, roaring, barking. I hardly hear them, I'm listening to the outcry of the metal as it bends. A lot of muscle out there. An arm reaches through, one of the bearpigs, long claws scratching at the metal. Jamal yells *Hold your fire!*

And of course he's right, that would've been a waste of ammo. There's scrabbling around outside, more singing, more roaring, and then the pressure suddenly gets much, much worse. You can see the strong metal bulge, something snaps, something else snaps. Whatever's pushing is breathing in huge gasps.

We have to wait until the doors collapse, then shoot whatever's on the other side. Its body will block the opening, but not for long.

Mama, when I close my eyes for an instant I see your face.

Item (26.) *From Colonel Kohn's Notebook.*

The double doors to the pad burst open. One of the sea lions that's been leaning against them takes two shots and screams, screams like a wounded animal anywhere, only thirty times as loud.

Then with a huge metallic crash the catwalk comes down, carrying half a dozen bearpigs with it. I step up and shoot the one that's still moving.

Turn back and see that the body of the sea lion is blocking the double doors. It's like the hull of a boat, black and slick except for many white scars of past battles for mates and the two small entry holes left by the impact weapons.

Bearpigs are trying to pull him out of the way, and an Arkie scrambles over him, takes one look at what's waiting for him and scrambles back. But the body's moving now, and it's last-stand time in the old Beladome.

Item (27.) *From Dr. Li's Report.*

And then came a thunderous roar and such a collective scream as I never thought to hear even in hell.

Item (28.) *From the Letter of Eloise Alcerra (as dictated to Dr. Li).*

Jamal spun on his heel and picked me up and threw me out of the way before jumping himself.

I landed against the curved wall of the dome just as a long plume of fire licked into the doorway and the body of the sea lion burst into flame, all the layers of fat under its hide igniting like wax, melting, spattering here and there, burning gobbets flying. A guy who was caught in the blast was turning black and falling apart like a doll hit by a blowtorch. ·

If the Cousins hadn't been there to block the opening partly, we'd all have been fried. As it was, Jamal's clothes caught on fire and I threw myself on him and rolled, feeling the flame and not feeling it, until it was out.

And then people were grabbing me by the wrists and pulling me into the hospital, and somebody had Jamal too, and about the same moment the roaring stopped and I realized that the supply ship's shuttle was down and the retros had finally been turned off.

Item (29.) *From the Report of Doctor Li.*

I have never been busier than during the loading of the shuttle.

The surviving Cousins had fled for the moment, but of course they would be back. So time was of the essence, and we had serious burn cases. Robert had suffered compound fractures of the radius and ulna of his left arm. He had either been blown down or had fallen hard trying to escape the blast.

Fortunately, the shuttle was bringing in medical supplies among many other things, and we tore the boxes apart to find what we needed.

Jamal had severe second-degree burns on the torso and some charring on the hands. Eloise had painful but superficial burns on her hands, belly and right breast. A young man serving with Jamal had been burned beyond recognition, and died as we were loading him.

The shuttle pilot, a Lieutenant Mannheim, talked to me as I worked. He was still amazed by what he had found. He said the overcast had been unusually dense, even for Bela, and he was almost on top of the port before he saw that it was under attack.

Since the shuttle is unarmed, he did the only thing he could by landing in the usual way, using the retros as weapons. Robert praised and commended him, as indeed was only just, for this young officer—though suddenly confronted with an unimaginable situation—had saved all our lives.

At the earliest possible moment, we lifted off. I did not feel entirely safe until we rose above the clouds, into eternal sunlight blazing against the blackness of space.

Item (30.) *From Colonel Kohn's Second Notebook.*

Naturally, Anna wants to knock me out and put me in sickbay for the next six months. I tell her to give me a nerve block and splint the broken wing.

I also get a rest, which I need. Anna bathes me. I'm fed and allowed to sleep under sedation for twelve standard hours. When I wake up, I visit Jamal and find him encased in a kind of body suit that protects his burns from infection and promotes healing. Anna says he'll need a lot of grafting when we get home.

His hands are in no condition for punching me, but I renew my offer for whenever they are. He's wearing a blissfully silly smile, and I think is still too far under the M2 to hear me or care much, one way or the other. He's alive and loved and floating on a morphine cushion, and that's as close to paradise as any of us are likely to get.

Sitting beside him, Eloise is bright and talkative. She's wearing bandages soaked in a topical anesthetic, and when I ask how she's doing, says, "My right tit will look like hell for a while." She holds up her thickly wrapped hands and intones, "And never, never will I play the harp again." Funny lady.

Then I brief the supply ship's Captain Cetewayo (pronounced approximately Chetch-why-oh, with a click to start). He's a big guy with a polished bald head like a bronze ingot, which nods as I brief him. Fortunately he wears a uniform too, and I don't have to spell out the facts of life for him.

The loss of a whole mining colony is going to cause a stupendous stink back home. I expect to spend several years as a professional witness, being grilled by all sorts of people. I want everything done by the book before we leave Bela for good.

He agrees, collects my notebook and a number of other pieces of evidence and seals them in his safe. Issues me this new notebook. Orders Mannheim to start collecting statements from the survivors—all ten of us.

Since bureaucrats believe nothing until it's written down and all the signature blocks properly filled in with names and ranks, these statements will be collated and an after-action report prepared, signed and sealed.

Admittedly, this is a cover-your-ass operation. But there's one more thing. It's essential that we check the mining camp and Main Base from the air, to insure that there are no human survivors. If we had troopers with us, we'd have to physically go inside and inspect, whatever the danger. Since we haven't the people or weapons to do that, we must do what we can—or risk our careers.

That sounds cold, but I am metaphysically certain that everybody except ourselves is dead. We gotta do what we gotta do, but we will not save anybody by doing it. Cetewayo agrees and gives the necessary orders.

Then I join Mannheim in the shuttle. We strap in and drop off the underbelly of the ship, and all at once it's déjà vu all over again, as some ancient philosopher put it.

We're diving into the endless roiling clouds, rain hits us like surf and a huge crooked bolt of lightning flashes from cloud to cloud. I think how silly it would be, after all I've been through, if I get killed by a commonplace thunderbolt while performing a routine and essentially meaningless duty.

Instead we drop through the last and darkest layer of the eternal overcast, and we're flashing over the familiar blue-black sea. With a navigator disk in hand I'm directing Mannheim to Alfa. Soon we're viewing the familiar sheds and domes and chicken runs of the mining camp, and I ask Mannheim to drop down lower.

The jungle's closing in, preparing to erase every track humans ever made here. Only our machines are still alive, the power station chugging away, the brown stream of slurry gushing down the hill like a giant case of dysentery. The lights are long burned out, of course, and—

Something moving—

No! Somebody!

A little figure that's not an Arkie!

Standing in a doorway, waving!

We dip down for an instant, I haul him in with my workable right arm and we're soaring again. I look at him in awe, trying to imagine how he survived in an alien jungle this long—all alone!

He's even skinnier than I remember him, he's wearing rags, his pants are held up with a vine, he's got long angry scars on face and hands, and whatever isn't scarred is covered with some kind of insect bites. He smells like the whole rotten understory of Bela's jungle. He's beautiful.

"Ted," I tell him, "I'm sorry I missed you the last time."

"Well, here I am," he says, and starts to tell his story—without a single stutter.

How he wriggled out of the bearpig's grasp, leaving his oversized coveralls behind; how the beast wasted time trying to eat the coveralls, allowing him time to slide into the thickets; how he ran and hid; how he made himself a cape of leaves to keep warm and shed the rain. How he watched a wingless feathered creature like a parrot, and began cautiously eating what it ate. How in time he worked his way back to Alfa, found it deserted, scavenged some torn clothing and lived off the contents of a couple of sealed supply cartons until he heard the flyer.

"You weren't worried we'd go off and leave you?"

"No," he says serenely. "I know you're not like that," at which I have the grace to blush.

While listening to Ted Szczech, we've crossed the roiling bay and now arrive at the estuary of that river whose name I never learned—not that human names mean anything on Bela anymore. I suppose the Arkies have a musical phrase for it, as they have for everything else.

Zamók is rising before us, and I see that things have changed. It's no longer Main Base; the Arkies have already cleared some of the human hovels off their Incan stonework. Reconstruction of lovely temples to follow, I'm sure.

There's a crowd of them gathered in the cleared area, standing in circles, and they turn their heads when they see us. Some of them shake weapons, but most merely look once and then turn back to what they're doing. We don't count any longer, but a rite is a rite.

In the center of the crowd stands Julia Mack. I tell Mannheim to bring us to a low hover so we can watch. She completely ignores us, looking straight ahead, and she's wearing a gorgeous robe of some sort, and no wig, and she looks more than ever like Picasso's portrait of Gertrude Stein, or how Gertrude would have looked if she'd been wrapped in a Persian carpet.

Suddenly Ted's stutter comes back, and he starts sputtering, "Wh-wh-wh-wh-wh-wh-"

"I'll explain later," I murmur.

Now an Arkie steps up behind her and he's carrying—not the usual bronze implement—no, by God, it's white metal, it's the titanium mountaineer's pickaxe that Mack's parents must have brought to Bela so long ago. Only it's been fitted with a longer handle, so the little Arkie can reach her.

He swings it, and Mannheim exclaims something, I don't know what, and Ted gives a strange cry as Mack falls heavily with the point in her brain. Another priest comes forward, carrying the usual curved axeblade to complete the ritual.

Mannheim says, "We've got to stop this," and I say, "No, we don't."

This is her reward for all she's done for them—to become a god of the Arkies, to join their pantheon and live here forever. At last she's joined her true species, and she's no longer alone.

When it's over—all but the ritual meal—I have to jiggle Mannheim's arm to get his attention.

"It's their church," I tell him, "and it's their communion. We don't belong here. We never did. So let's go."

CONCLUSION AND JUDGMENT

KOHN, Robert Rogers, cannot be held legally culpable for the disaster on Planet Bela. However, as the only surviving senior official he must be held administratively responsible, since there is no one else left to blame. He is therefore involuntarily retired from the Security Forces with official reprimand and reduced pension.

PROTEST of judgment filed by Citizens Alcerra, al-Sba'a, and Szczech is hereby REJECTED.

PETITION of KOHN, Robert Rogers, and spouse to be allowed to live in retirement in an oasis of the Great American Desert is hereby GRANTED.

BY ORDER OF THE HONORABLE COMMITTEE

All aboard Mark Twain's riverboat as we head into a world that's gone with the wind for a tale of guilt and...redemption? Well, yes and no.

THE OVERSEER

T HOUGH APPROPRIATELY RUNDOWN, Nicholas Lerner's big house on Exposition Boulevard in uptown New Orleans was not haunted. The same could not be said of its owner.

That spring morning in 1903 the old man was getting ready for the day. Or rather, Morse was making him ready.

"So, Mr. Nick," murmured the valet, applying shaving soap to his employer's face with an ivory-handled brush, "are you writing a book?"

Damn him, thought Lerner. *He knows I detest conversation with a razor at my throat.*

"My memoirs," he muttered. "A few jottings only. Waiting to die is such a bore, I write to pass the time."

Was that the real reason he'd become a late-blooming scribbler—mere boredom? Most of his life had been devoted to hiding the truth, not revealing it. And yet now....

"I think you must be writing secrets," smiled Morse, piloting the blade beneath his left ear. "The way you lock your papers in the safe at night."

"I lock them up," Lerner snapped, getting soap in his mouth, "because they are *private*."

And had better remain so, he thought wryly. The other memorabilia in his small safe—an ancient, rusted Colt revolver; a bill from a Natchez midwife; a forty-year-old spelling book; a faded telegram saying RELIABLE MAN WILL MEET YOU RR LANDING STOP—would mean nothing to any living person.

Then why should he write the story out, give evidence against himself? It seemed to make no sense. And yet, having started, somehow he couldn't stop.

Humming an old ballad called "Among My Souvenirs", he pondered the problem but reached no conclusion. He closed his eyes and dozed, only to wake suddenly when Morse asked, "Who is Monsieur Felix?"

Lerner heard his own voice quaver as he replied, "Someone I...knew, long ago. Where did you hear of him?"

"Last night, after you took your medicine, you spoke his name over and over in your sleep."

"Then I must have seen him in a dream."

Shrewd comment. Morse knew that the opium he obtained for the old man caused intense dreams, and would ask no more questions.

Without further comment he burnished his employer's face with a hot towel, combed his hair, and neatly pinned up his empty left sleeve. He removed the sheet that protected Lerner's costly, old-fashioned Prince Albert suit from spatter, and bore all the shaving gear through the door to the adjoining den and out into the hall. Remotely, Lerner heard Morse's voice—now raised imperiously—issuing orders to the housemaid and the cook.

Good boy! thought Lerner, checking his image in a long, dusky pier glass. *Make 'em jump!*

He was rubbing his smooth upper lip to make sure no bristles had been left, when suddenly he leaned forward, staring. Then, with startling energy, his one big hand whirled his chair around.

Of course nobody was standing behind him. A trick of his old eyes and the brown shadows of his bed chamber with its single door, its barred and ever-darkened window. Or maybe a result of talking about Monsieur Felix, whom he would always associate with mirrors, fog, winter darkness, summertime mirages—with anything, bright or dark, that deceived the eye.

"Ah, you devil," he muttered, "I'll exorcise you with my pen. Then burn both you and the damned manuscript!"

Maybe that was the point of his scribbling—to rid himself of the creature once and for all. Smiling grimly, he trundled into his den.

Like its owner, his safe was an antique, the combination lock encircled with worn red letters instead of numbers. He dialed a five-letter word—*perdu*, meaning lost, a word with many meanings as applied to its contents. He jerked open the heavy door, drew out a pack of cream-laid writing paper and carried it to his old writing desk, a burled walnut monster honeycombed with secret compartments.

On the wall above, his dead wife smiled from a pastel portrait. Elmira as she'd been when young—conventionally pretty, not knowing yet that her short life would be devoted mainly to bearing stillborn children. On her lap she held their first boy, the only one born alive, but who, less than a month after the artist finished the picture, had suffocated in his crib, in the mysterious way of small children.

Bereft, surrounded by servants who did everything for her, idle, dissatisfied, Elmira had died a little too. Her husband had granted her everything she wanted except entry into his head and heart.

"Why don't you trust me?" she'd asked him a thousand times, and he'd always answered, "My dear, I trust you as I do no other human being."

She'd never quite found the handle of that reply. Morse's father and mother would have understood the irony—the fact that he really trusted no one—but of course they were dead too.

They saw into my soul, Lerner thought, *but it didn't save them, either one.*

He shrugged, dismissing Elmira and all the other ghosts. Time to introduce the Overseer into his story. But first he wanted to sharpen his unreliable memory by rereading what he'd written so far. He drew the papers closer to his nose and flicked on a new lamp with a glaring Edison bulb that had recently replaced the old, dim, comfortable gaslight. Squinting balefully at his own spidery, old-fashioned handwriting, he began to read.

CHAPTER THE FIRST
Wherein I Gain, Then Lose, My Personal Eden

As I look back upon the scenes of a stormy life, filled with strange adventures and haunted by a stranger spirit, I am astonished to reflect how humble, peaceable and commonplace were my origins.

My ancestors were poor German peasants, who in 1720 fled the incessant wars of Europe and found refuge on Louisiana's Côte des Allemands, or German coast, near the village of Nouvelle Orléans. Their descendants migrated northward to the Red River country, still farming the land but, like the good Americans they had become, acquiring slaves to assist their labors.

Here in 1843 I was born into the lost world that people of our new-minted Twentieth Century call the Old South. The term annoys me, for to us who lived then 'twas neither old nor new, but simply the world—our world. I first saw light on a plantation called Mon Repos, a few miles from the village of Red River Landing, and there spent my boyhood with Papa and Cousin Rose. Our servants were three adult slaves and a son born to one of them, whom Papa had named Royal, according to the crude humor of those times, which delighted in giving pompous names to Negroes.

Our lives resembled not at all the silly phantasies I read nowadays of opulent masters and smiling servants. Our plantation was but a large ramshackle farm, its only adornment a long alley of noble oaks that Papa had saved when felling the forest. Our lives were simple and hard; many a day at planting or harvest-time Papa worked in the fields beside the hands, his sweat like theirs running down and moistening the earth.

In our house Cousin Rose counted for little, for she was but a poor relation whose parents had died in the same outbreak of Yellow-Jack that claimed my mother. Ever pale and fragile as a porcelain cup, she spent most days in her bedroom, more like a ghost than a girl. The slave boy Royal, on the other hand, counted for much—at least in my life.

How I envied him! He never had to study, and went barefoot nine months of the year. I was beaten often by the schoolmaster, but Royal escaped with a scolding even when he was caught stealing flowers from the garden, or roaming the house above stairs, where only the family and the housemaid were allowed to go. Indeed, Papa so favored him that I came to understand (though nothing was ever said) that he was my half-brother.

Spirits, too, inhabited our little world. All who dwelt in that benighted region believed in divining rods and seer stones, in ghosts and curses, in prophetick dreams, buried treasure, and magical cures. Royal and I were credulous boys, like those Mark Twain so well describes in Tom Sawyer, *and we met often in the bushes near the servants' graveyard at midnight to whisper homemade incantations, half fearing and half hoping to raise a "sperrit" that might shew us the way to an hoard of gold—though none ever appeared.*

In these expeditions Royal was always bolder than I, as he was also in our daylight adventures. He dove from higher branches of the oak overleaning our swimming-hole than I dared to; he was a better shot than I, often bearing the long-rifle when, as older boys, we fire-hunted for deer. Ah, even now I can see and smell those autumn nights! The flickering of the fire-pan; the frosty crimson and gold leaves crackling under our feet; the sudden green shine of a deer's eyes, the loud shot, the sharp sulphurous smell of burnt powder, and the dogs leaping into the darkness to bring down the wounded animal!

Are we not all killers at heart? Scenes of death having about them a kind of ecstasy, however we deny it, greater even than the scenes of love.

Preceded by a clink of china, Morse spun the door handle and backed into the den, hefting a tray with a dish under a silver cover, a folded napkin, and a goblet of red wine.

"When," demanded Lerner testily, "will you learn to knock, my boy?"

"Mr. Nick, I ain't got enough hands to carry the tray, open the door and knock, too."

A doubtful excuse, thought Lerner; a table stood in the hallway convenient to the door, where Morse could have rested the tray. Frowning, he turned his pages face-down on the desk.

Morse set his lunch on a side table, moved the wheelchair, shook out the stiff linen napkin and tied it around Lerner's neck.

"Should I cut the meat for you, Mr. Nick?"

"Yes, yes. Then leave me alone. And don't come back until I ring."

"You'll be wanting your medicine at the usual time?"

"Yes, yes. But wait for my ring."

In leaving, Morse took a long look at the half-open safe, a fact that did not escape the old man. Lerner ate lunch slowly, pondering. His dependence on Morse reminded him all too clearly of how his father had become the servant of his own servant after Monsieur Felix entered Mon Repos. That had been the beginning of many things, all of them bad.

I will not suffer that to happen again, he thought.

Lerner had an old man's appetite, ravenous at the beginning but quickly appeased. Without finishing his lunch, he hastily swallowed the wine at a gulp, wheeled back to his desk, took up his manuscript and again began to read.

The Eden of my childhood did not last long. In the Fifties the world's demand for cotton soared, and Papa began to dream of growing rich.

He was not alone. The steamboats that huffed and puffed up and down the Mississippi began delivering carven furniture, pier-glasses, and Paris fashions to our community of backwoodsmen. Ladies—it seemed overnight—graduated from sun-bonnets to hoopskirts, and the men were as bad or worse, with their sudden need for blooded horses and silk cravats and silver-mounted pistols and long Cuban segars.

In this flush atmosphere, Papa borrowed from the banks and cotton factors and bought new acres, though land had become very dear. He made trips to New Orleans to barter for workers in the slave markets at Maspero's Exchange and the St. Charles Hotel, and he rebuilt our comfortable log house as a mansion with six white columns, which—like our prosperity—were hollow and meant only for shew. But he remained a farmer, not a businessman; he overspent for everything, and could not make the new hands work, for he was too soft to wield the whip as a slave-driver must. Soon he was in debt and facing ruin, and so in 1855, during one of his trips to the city, he hired an Overseer to do the driving for him.

'Tis hard for me to remember Felix Marron as a man of flesh. I see him in my mind's eye as the sort of shadow that looms up in a morning fog, briefly takes human form, then fades again into a luminous dazzle.

Yet when first we met, he seemed merely freakish. Royal and I were returning from a fishing jaunt when we espied him talking to Papa, and we stared and giggled like the bumpkins we were. I suppose he was then about forty, but seemed ageless, as if he never had been born—a strange creature, very tall and sinewy, his long bony face a kind of living Mardi Gras mask with grotesquely prominent nose and chin. Though 'twas August, he wore an old musty black suit, and I remember that despite the stifling Delta heat, his gray face shewed not a drop of sweat.

When Papa introduced us, he ignored Royal but swept off his stovepipe hat to me, loosing a cloud of scent from his pomade, and in a penetrating stage whisper exclaimed, "Bonjour, bonjour, 'ow be you, young sir?" Shifting an old carpetbag to his left hand, he clasped my right in his cool bony grip, causing a braided whip he carried over that arm to swing and dance. Then Papa led him away to view the quarters, and Royal and I laughed out loud—thereby proving that neither of us was gifted with prophecy.

Papa hired Monsieur Felix (as he preferred to be called) upon the understanding that he would have a free hand to extract profit from our people and our acres. At first the bargain seemed to be a good one, for the Overseer was restless and tireless, keeping on the move (as the slaves said) from can't-see in the morning to can't-see at dusk. He had a strange way of walking, lunging ahead with long silent strides that ate up the ground, and appearing suddenly and without warning where he was not expected. And woe to any slave he found idling! Not one escaped flogging under his regime, not even Royal, whose days of idleness and indulgence came to an abrupt end. Soon he learned to dread the hoarse whisper, "Aha, tu p'tit diable," the Overseer's sole warning before the lash fell.

At first Papa resisted this abuse of his darker son. But the Overseer argued that to favor one slave was to corrupt all by setting them a bad example; further, that Royal (then twelve years of age) was no longer a child, and must be broken in to the duties of his station in life. Finally, that unless he could impose discipline on all our hands, Monsieur Felix would leave Papa's employ, and seek a position on a plantation that was properly run. So Papa yielded, and by so doing began to lose mastery over his own house.

I watched Royal's first beating with fascination and horror. My own floggings at the schoolmaster's hands were but the gentle flutter of a palmetto fan compared to the savage blows administered by Monsieur Felix. Had I been the victim, I would have raised the whole country with my howls; but Royal remained obstinately silent, which the Overseer rightly saw as a kind of resistance, and added six more to the six blows first proposed, and then six again, leaving Royal scarce able to walk for three or four days.

Thus began several years of tyranny. Even when he grew older and stronger, Royal could not strike back—for a slave to assault a white man, whatever the provocation, meant death—nor could he flee, for the patterollers (as we called the cruel men of the slave patrols) scoured the neighborhood. And so he bore his whippings as the others did, and let his hatred grow. In my innocence I loathed the Overseer, for I was too young to understand that he flogged our people not out of cruelty, nor indeed of any feeling at all, but as an herdsman prods his ox or a plowman lashes his mule—to wring work from them, and wealth from his acres.

In that he succeeded. With the crops heavy—with the hands hard at work—with prices rising, and dollars rolling in, Papa felt himself no longer the descendent of Westphalian peasants, but rather a great planter and a member of the ruling class. He bought leather-bound books by the linear foot, and installed them in his den, though he did not attempt to read them; he drank from crystal goblets, though his tipple was corn whiskey drawn from his own still. He paid Monsieur Felix well, and built him a substantial house midway between Mon Repos and the slave quarters, which was where the Overseer himself stood, in the southern scheme of things. Papa thought he would be content to live there and receive wages that grew from year to year, and mayhap marry in time some poor-white slattern of the neighborhood. But in this he misjudged the Overseer's ambition.

Applying still more pomade to his lank black hair, he took to invading our house, supposedly to talk business with Papa, but in reality to ogle my cousin

Rose—then fifteen and almost of marriageable age. Though I was but a great clumsy overgrown boy with long skinny shanks and feet like keelboats, I well understood that the Overseer designed to marry into our family as the first step toward gaining control of Mon Repos. In a rage, I summoned up my smattering of French and called him cochon *to his face, for his English was so poor I feared he might misunderstand if I called him swine. I ordered him never again to set foot in the house, at which he laughed in his strange soundless way. He would have loved to give me a taste of his whip, but the caste system protected me, for only the schoolmaster was allowed to beat the heir of Mon Repos.*

To get rid of me, Monsieur Felix told Papa I deserved to finish my education in the North, saying how 'twould honor our family if I won a degree from a famous school. With money weighing down his pockets, Papa agreed, and in the summer of 1860 I was compelled to say goodbye to everyone and everything I knew, and set out for the land of the Puritans, as I imagined it. I wished to take Royal to Yale College as my valet, but Monsieur Felix warned Papa that he would run away, once in the free states. So he was doomed to stay behind, whilst I boarded a Cincinnati-bound steamer at Red River Landing for the first leg of my journey.

I was seventeen years of age, as fresh and proud as a new ear of corn, and as green. Wearing varnished boots and carrying my shiny first top hat, I stood upon the hurricane deck, gazing down at ragged and dusty Royal, who had come with the family to say farewell. We who had been playmates now were clearly master and slave. Yet we shared a secret plan, devised during many a night-time meeting at the graveyard. If, as I anticipated, Monsieur Felix laid hands upon Rose, Royal was to kill him, and give himself up to the sheriff without resistance. I would return post-haste and testify that he had merely obeyed my orders, as a slave should, to protect my cousin's honor. As his reward, when I inherited him I would set him free. Upon this understanding, I left my rifle in a place only Royal knew—wrapped in oily rags, and tied atop a rafter in the cabin of the slave quarters where he slept.

I raised my hand to him as one conspirator to another, and he nodded in reply, his face smooth and immobile as a mask of bronze. Rose wept, Papa honked into his handkerchief, and Monsieur Felix vouchsafed a thin arid smile, like an arroyo dividing his blade of a nose from his large blue chin. Then the whistle blew, the bell chimed, the gangplank lifted, and the muddy bank—like my youth—began drifting away from me.

Siesta time had come. Lerner returned the manuscript to the safe, closed the heavy door and spun the dial. He picked up a little silver bell, rang it briskly, and within ten minutes Morse appeared like a household genie. He removed the lunchtime clutter, spread and adjusted the old man's lap robe, put a pillow behind his head, and vanished again, quietly closing the door.

Since the back injury that had left him unable to walk, Lerner had needed such coddling to shield him against severe pains that otherwise spread up and down his spine. Yet he understood that his immobility was killing him. He could almost feel the systems of his body rusting in place, shutting down slowly. *How tiresome it is,* he thought, *to die by inches,* and with an effort of will concentrated his mind upon his story. He'd come to the end of what he'd already written; tomorrow he must carry the tale forward, weaving fragments of memory into a narrative.

He dozed until five-thirty, waking when Morse turned on the electric chandelier and set down his dinner tray with a folded evening newspaper beside the plate. Lerner ate while perusing the unexciting developments of the day—the end of the Philippine Insurrection, the galumphing of that damned cowboy in the White House. Then the long ritual of putting him to bed began. Morse worked with the deft expertness of a hospital nurse, and by seven-thirty the old man was resting in bed, propped up on a hillock of cushions and covered with spotless linen. He sniffed the penetrating, somehow frigid smell of grain spirits left by the alcohol rub Morse had given him, then folded his hands and smiled, awaiting the high point of his day.

"Come, come, Morse," he whispered.

The indefatigable one returned with a gleaming salver on which rested a sticky pellet of opium wrapped in rice paper, a crystal flask of amber bourbon, a shot glass, and a silver coffee spoon. Deftly he prepared the laudanum, dissolving the opium in the whiskey with ritualized movements, like a priest mixing water and wine.

"I need to go and buy more of your medicine, Mr. Nick," he murmured, presenting the drink.

"Why not buy it from a drugstore?" Lerner demanded. "Those neighborhoods by the docks are dangerous."

"Mr. Nick, I can do that, but it'll cost twice as much. The import tax alone is six dollars a pound, and I can buy decent opium from a Chinaman for five."

Grumbling, the old man extracted a few bills from a drawer in his marble-topped night table and handed them over. Then in three long sips he drank the draught that ended pain and summoned sleep.

His throat burned, he felt a sharp pain in his gut, then a banked fire that burned low, warming and soothing him. A delicious languor began to spread through his old body. He felt his weight lessen, then almost evaporate. He felt dry and light, like a balsa-wood doll floating high on still water.

"Ah," he whispered. "So good, so good."

Morse lingered, watching him, rearranging his bedclothes to make him even more comfortable and secure. When he felt sure that Lerner was asleep, he leaned close to his ear and whispered, "Father? I need to know the word that opens the safe. Tell me the word, Father. Father? What word opens the safe?"

Lerner grunted but slept on.

"Shit," grumbled Morse. "Old bastard, he don't relax even when he's snoring. I bet he keeps a bag of gold in that iron box of his."

From the cache of bills in the night table he took a tenner, added it to the five, thrust both into his pocket, and soon afterward left the house. He slipped away into the lengthening blue shadows, his mind perhaps on pleasure, or merely on escaping for a few hours the dull round of servitude to a dying man that defined his daytime life.

Lerner woke early, tasting ashes. Dun shadows filled the bedroom, but a thin white scar of daylight already ran between the red-plush window drapes, casting the shadows of iron security bars. He seized the silver bell and rang it loudly.

"Morse—" he began as the door opened. But instead of Morse, the yellow face of the housemaid—Cleo, was that her name?—intruded, anxious beneath a spotted kerchief.

"Oh, Mr. Nick," she burst out, "don't nobody know where Mr. Morse is at. I been up to his room to look, and his baid ain't been slep' in."

Lerner stared at her. If she'd told him the sun had failed to rise in the east, he could hardly have been more astonished.

With Cleo's help he wrestled himself painfully into the wheelchair, but there his abilities ended. A one-armed man with a spinal injury was close to helpless. A manservant had to be borrowed from next door to prepare him for the day. Lerner found the process distasteful; he hated to have a stranger see him unclothed or touch him; the fact that the man obviously disliked the work made it no easier to bear. In shaving him, the fellow nicked his face repeatedly, until Lerner sent him away with a miserly tip and a muttered curse. A barber had to be brought from a nearby shop, and he charged a whole dollar for the visit!

By then Cleo had brought him breakfast, and it was all wrong for a variety of reasons. Yet he failed to complain about the chilly toast, hard egg, and unsugared coffee. As he entered the den a good hour late and dragged out his manuscript, he was worrying over something much more serious: the possibility that Morse might *never* return.

As he'd warned last night, rough characters swarmed on the docks; the knife, the revolver, and the sling-shot were common weapons of choice; the Mississippi with its murky water, vast size, and hidden undertows was perfect for disposing of superfluous bodies—as Lerner knew well from certain experiences of his own.

"And without Morse, how would I *live*?" Lerner demanded aloud, and there was nobody to answer him.

From a desk drawer he took out a new gold-banded reservoir pen, uncapped it with fingers and teeth, filled it from his inkwell by pressing down an ivory piston, and tried to fix his mind on his story. From time to time as he wrote, he raised his head and listened. Despite the thick walls of the house, some street sounds intruded—the horn of a motor-car brayed; a seller of vegetables chanted "Ah got ni-ess al-li-gay-tuh pay-uhs"—and the house itself was never totally quiet, doors opening and closing for no good reason, a woman's starched dress (Cleo's?) rustling past in the hall.

And yet, despite his distraction, the new chapter began taking form. His thoughts might be elsewhere, but his hand traveled over the paper in a sort of automatic writing, like a spirit's message upon a sealed slate.

CHAPTER THE SECOND
Wherein I Encounter War, and a Spirit

Need I say that eighteen-sixty was a poor year for a southern lad to get an education? That winter a storm of rebellion swept the cotton states, and in the spring of '61 the country went to war.

For a time I dawdled, hoping that peace might break out. But after the affray at Fort Sumter, with the whole country responding to the call of the trumpet and the drum, I saw that I must go home. I took a train to Cincinnati, where the steam-packets were still running, war or no war; and after a week spent churning down the Ohio to the Mississippi, and down the Mississippi to the Red, stepped ashore at the same spot I had left a year earlier.

Already the Landing seemed to belong to another and darker age. The village was strangely silent; I learned that my schoolfellows had vanished into the Army, and two were already dead of camp diseases in Virginia. Mon Repos had never deserved its name less. Though I arrived at noon, I found Papa already drunk, and noted with disgust how he wobbled when he walked, like a goose hit with a rock. Royal and the Overseer both had disappeared, and when I asked Papa what had happened to them, he only mumbled and shook his head.

'Twas Rose—all atremble—who told me the story. Monsieur Felix had proposed marriage to her, and, when she declined, threatened to compromise her honor so that she would have to marry him, willing or not. This she took to be a threat of rape, and many a tear-stained letter had she written, praying me to return and save her. But because of the war, I received none of them. Then the war itself intervened. The men of the slave patrols joined the army and went east, and as soon as they were gone, Royal took down my rifle from its hiding

place, shot Monsieur Felix neatly through the eye and ran away, leaving the corpse lying spread out like a hog ready for flaying on the gallery of the nice house Papa had built for him.

At first I felt only pleasure in hearing this tale, and laughed gaily at the thought of being (as I imagined) rid of the Overseer forever. But after I spent a day tramping over our acres, I began to suspect that in reality his death had ruined us all. The crops of corn and cotton stood heavy but weed-choked and in need of hoeing; the hands idled about the quarters, and when I ordered them to work they went but slowly, with deep mutterings that boded no good.

Brooding over these developments, I turned my steps homeward, passing close by the Overseer's house on the way. I found it a scene of ruin, grown up with vines like a castle in a fairy tale, with cicadas droning in the trees and hot sunlight vibrating upon a weedy mound of earth where he lay buried. A pine board carven only with his name and the date of his death served as his headstone.

I was gazing upon this melancholy scene when something moved upon the vine-shrouded gallery of the house. I shaded my eyes against the fierce light, and espied through drifting red spots Monsieur Felix standing in the spot where he had died. His pale face seemed to float amid a dark wreath of cat's-claw, his left eye nothing but an oozing pit, his right gleaming like a splinter of glass. His blue jaw moved and his penetrating whisper etched itself upon my eardrums, saying, Tu, mon p'tit, serais mon vengeur.

I stepped back—stumbled over the grave marker—staggered, blinked away drops of stinging sweat, and an instant later found myself entering our house, with no sense of time elapsed nor memory of anything I might have seen along the way. Rose was fetching something for Papa, and she stopped and gazed at me, astonished. She brushed a strand of hair out of her eyes and said, "Nick, are you well?"

I answered without knowing what I said.

That night I drank with Papa, paying no attention as his slurring voice complained endlessly of his troubles, but instead thinking of the words of the Phantasm. I could make no sense of them: for what could be greater nonsense than that I (of all people) should become the avenger of my hated enemy, Monsieur Felix?

I went to bed more than half-drunk, and slept like the water-logged trees that river pilots call dead-men. When I wakened at first light, the house seemed uncommonly silent. For half an hour I lay at ease, waiting for the usual noises to begin, the murmur of voices, the rattle of pots in the kitchen, the creak of the pump handle. A summer wind passed across the world with a great sigh, and a light rain began to fall. Still I heard nothing from downstairs, as if the house had died overnight. Then my door opened and Rose slipped in, looking especially thin and pale in her cotton nightdress.

"Nick," she whispered, "where are all the servants?"

I jumped out of bed, threw on some clothes and ran outside. The brief shower having passed, I walked through the slave quarters, finding the cabins all empty, with doors hanging open on leathern hinges, and in the little fireplaces ashes that were still warm. The paddocks were empty, the farm animals all gone, driven into the woods and marshes by the departing slaves. I understood then that the slaves felt no loyalty toward Papa, who had never protected them from Monsieur Felix, whilst the Overseer's death had freed them from the fear that alone had made Mon Repos run.

I stood gazing at the overgrown fields, where little pines had already begun to spring up, whilst afar off, a church bell started to toll in dreary monotone—the notice of a funeral, whose I don't know: perhaps the funeral of our world.

So much Lerner had written, and was staring at an unappetizing lunch that Cleo had brought, when the door to his den opened suddenly and Morse stumbled in.

His hands were tremulous, his face yellow, his shoes muddy, his clothes mussed and odorous. In a hoarse voice he began to complain about the darkness of the house. In fact, it was no darker than usual; but as Lerner perceived, the pupils of his eyes had shrunk to pin-points that shut out the light.

If anybody knew opium's aftermath, that man was Lerner. Speaking firmly, he ordered Morse to go to bed and, when he sobered up, to return and explain his conduct. He slouched away, looking like some wretched Lascar who sleeps off his drug debauch under the wharves, while the old man, muttering a curse, returned grimly to telling his tale.

—.—

Well do I remember those late-summer days in '61 when, like a child, I imagined that the worst had already happened.

I knew that we must abandon Mon Repos, hoping to return in better days, should better days ever come. And yet for weeks Papa refused even to consider flight. Finally, in a rage I threatened to take Rose away with me, and leave him to manage alone. At last he yielded and we became refugees, an early rivulet of the great tide that would flow southward in years to come.

At Red River Landing we bought our way aboard a fishing yawl, for Papa had become very close with a dollar, and refused to buy us passage on a steamboat.

Mostly our fellow-passengers were ordinary country folk, but one caught my eye—a very tall, thin man dressed in black, who sat at the prow, stiff and unmoving like the dragon's-head of a Viking ship. 'Twas evening, and he was hard to focus on against the blaze of the setting sun. I looked away, blinked and looked back: a hefty woman was seating herself in a flurry of skirts; perhaps he was behind her, perhaps not. Intending to make sure whether he was what I feared, I rose to my feet. But the boat was now so crowded and the freeboard so small that the captain shouted at me to sit, or I should swamp her.

Night shut down, the sails were raised, and we began a ghostly voyage down a moon-haunted river, in company perhaps with a Phantom. Does this not sound like a poem by Coleridge, or a tale by Poe? Yet I remember chiefly the discomfort of the wretched craft. I dozed and waked a dozen times; a woman nursed a baby that cried often; some fellow who had managed to fall asleep snorted like a donkey-engine. Once a steamboat blazing with lights pounded by in midstream, and the waves so rocked our burdened craft that we shipped water, and had to bail with cupped hands.

Come morning, we landed at New Orleans, all of us stiff and soaked and blear-eyed. The levee swarmed with shouting laborers; barrels and bales and cannons and gun-carriages were heaped up everywhere, guarded by new-minted soldiers in fancy uniforms. I sought the man in black, but he seemed to have vanished in the confusion. We engaged a porter with a barrow, and traipsed behind him through the Old Quarter, which was saturated with the smell of roasting coffee and noisy as a parrot cage.

In time we reached a house on Rue des Bons Enfants, or Goodchildren Street, belonging to some of our cousins, and they bade us welcome, having plenty of room to spare. Their warmth was not entirely a matter of family feeling. We again had money, for the city banks were still open, and Papa insisted on paying all our expenses—as foolish in generosity as he had been in miserliness. From the same sense of pride, when I was commissioned a lieutenant in the Confederate Army, he bought me a fine gray uniform that did not survive my first and only battle.

That fall and winter of '61 I divided my time between Goodchildren Street and a training camp amongst the farmlands of Metairie, where I drilled men who knew as much about marching as I did, which was nothing. Passing through town one evening, I fell captive to the charms of a fair privateer, and caught the clap. 'Twas a light case that I got over in a week, but it occasioned much merriment in camp, where my fellow officers pounded me on the back and chortled, "Now Nick, when you have killed your first Yankee, you will be a real man at last!"

Whilst I was yet ill and feverish, I again saw the Phantom. Three or four nights in succession he rose in my dreams, fixing his one eye horridly upon me. One bright winter day I saw him gazing at me from the shade of an oak-grove hung with streamers of gray moss. Though daunted by the sight, I hastened toward him, but found nothing there. The figure had been only a compound of light and shadow—or at any rate, so I explained it to myself. Then I grew well again, and dismissed the Phantom as the trick of a sickly mind.

In plain fact I had no time for ghosts. The war was speeding up; we began to break camp and load our equipment. A thrill of excitement touched with fear ran through every man of us, for we knew that the day was nearing when at last we would see the Elephant, meaning combat. The order came in the first days of April, 1862, when the fields were covered with white and red clover. My company boarded a train to Jackson, and marched into Tennessee, where twenty-four thousand men were soon to be laid low in the great battle at Shiloh Church.

On the first day of the fight, I led a scouting party that blundered into an enemy picket. The Yankee sentry (a boy whose white, scared face will forever remain in my memory) instantly threw down his musket and fled; the weapon was on half-cock and discharged by itself, the ball smashing my elbow. Whilst *the battle raged, the surgeons chloroformed me and cut off all but about eight inches of my left arm. I was laid in a wagon amongst other mutilated bodies and hauled away to the rail-head, screaming at every lurch and bounce.*

So began and ended my acquaintanceship with war: but not with the Spectre, who soon seized upon my state of weakness to manifest himself again.

By the time I reached New Orleans, the stump of my arm had become infected (or mortified, as we said then), smelling foully and oozing unpleasant matter. Nursed by Rose, I lived through feverish days and haunted nights. Again Monsieur Felix ruled the dark hours, smiling horridly from amid great fields of corpses, where not one was whole—some torsos without arms or legs, some bodies without heads, some heads without bodies that glared from white eyes the size of walnuts.

Then my mind cleared, and I became able to understand the scarcely less frightening news that Rose brought me. I heard of the federal fleet appearing off the Passes, and of hard fighting at the downriver forts; of warships riding high on the flood-swollen Mississippi, with guns pointing down at the city's rooftops; of rioting mobs on the levee, burning warehouses and looting banks; of blue-backs filing ashore and deploying a battery of bronze cannon in front of the plush St. Charles Hotel, where Papa used to stay when he was bargaining for slaves.

At home on Goodchildren Street our cousins began to cast bitter looks upon us. Papa had run out of cash, and because the war had severed the connection between city and farm, food had become very dear and hard to come by. Our hosts begrudged us every mouthful we ate, as if we were taking it directly off their plates—as in fact we were. Indeed, we were no longer a promising or even a respectable crew. Papa was customarily drunk, and even when sober, more scatter-brained than ever; Rose was obliged to work as a house servant, but a frail one who never did anything right. As for me, the cousins thought that if I recovered, 'twould be only as a poor cripple who would continue to eat but bring in nothing.

So they moved me out of my comfortable bed-chamber, and put me upstairs in a store-room that held a clutter of retired furniture, broken crockery, and dusky mirrors. 'Twas stifling hot under the eaves, and no place for an injured man; but they thought it good enough for me, hoping perhaps that I might die and relieve them of a burden.

One summer morning I woke from a restless sleep. The arm I had lost was aching as no arm of flesh and blood could, every hair upon it like a burning wire. And yet, as the bright hot morning light grew, my eyes shewed me nothing, not even a ghost, lying on the ragged counterpane beside me. Rose slept nearby on a battered chaise, with a fine dew of perspiration upon her pale face, and though the pain of my phantom arm was such that I wished to moan or cry out, I remained silent for fear of waking her.

Restlessly my eyes wandered to an old dim mirror with an irregular dark shadow in the middle of the glass. As I gazed, the shadow began to take shape, like the sort of black paper silhouette that in those days decorated every parlor in the land. 'Twas Monsieur Felix—no, I could not have been mistaken! No man save he ever had such a face. As I watched in fascination, he began to turn slowly toward me, his features emerging like the image on a tintype in its acid bath, until his full face hovered in the glass, picked out in shades of glistening black and bone white.

Unable to bear the empty socket and gleaming eye fixed upon me, I stumbled from bed, my limbs rubbery as those of a new-whelped pup, and in one fierce motion turned the mirror and slammed it against the plaster. The glass shattered and Rose started up and cried out, "Oh Nick, you should be resting, not walking!"

"So should he who roused me," I answered, and her eyes widened in fear, for she thought that suffering had caused me to go mad.

The first sign that the household on Exposition Boulevard was wobbling back toward normal came when supper appeared at the proper hour.

Cleo carried the tray instead of Morse, but the meal was tasty and hot, with terrapin stew, warm bread, and a glass of elderly pale sherry. Lerner dumped half the sherry into the stew, swallowed the rest, and made a better meal than he'd expected.

After dinner Morse appeared, clean and silent, and went to work at the most intimate duties of a body-servant: setting Lerner upon the commode-chair, giving him an alcohol rub, putting his nightshirt on him and settling him in bed. Watching Morse prepare the laudanum, the old man found himself admiring the performance. Instead of making weak apologies, Morse was seeking to demonstrate how much Lerner needed him—and in that he succeeded, the clever fellow.

After drinking the potion, Lerner ordered him to sit down on the foot of the bed, and said quietly: "You know, my boy, this drug should be taken only to subdue pain and give rest, not for a doubtful pleasure that ends in a horrid slavery."

"I'm in pain all the time, Mr. Nick," he muttered, looking at the floor. "This stuff gives you ease, so I thought it might do the like for me."

"You're in pain? Are you ill, Morse?"

"No. Yes. My anger eats at me."

"Anger at what?" asked Lerner in surprise, for he'd always thought Morse very comfortably off, for a colored man.

"At *this*," he said, holding up his left hand with the dark back turned toward Lerner, then turning it over to show the white palm. "Wondering why I could not be like this. I have long known you are my father. If I were white, you would have loved and acknowledged me, and I would be a man among men."

For a moment Lerner was too astonished to speak. Unsteadily he asked, "Who told you that I am your father?"

"My mother."

It was on the tip of Lerner's tongue to say, *But you never knew your mother.* Instead he bit his tongue and said slowly, weighing the words, "I'm glad you've spoken out, my boy. Trust me, and I shall yet do you justice."

He sent Morse away, all his secrets intact. But when he was alone, lying in the dark on clean linen, Lerner found sleep difficult to come by. Maybe the laudanum was losing its effect. Or maybe he was finding it hard to grasp the fact that a Morse existed of whom he knew nothing.

What did the fellow do when he wasn't being the perfect servant? Did he read books? Practice voodoo? Engage in orgies with Cleo and the cook, improbable as that seemed? And how could he dare to live some other life, when he depended on Lerner for food, shelter, pocket money, everything? Wasn't that a kind of treason?

In time Lerner fell asleep, the puzzles of reality yielding to gorgeous visions of things that never had existed at all. And as he snored, the next day's installment of his memoir composed itself, someplace deep beneath the level of his dreaming.

CHAPTER THE THIRD
Wherein the Demon Saves and Enslaves Me

On that day, the day I saw him in the mirror, I dressed and went forth with sleeve pinned up, in search of work.

I found none. The city had always lived by grace of the river, but now 'twas blocked by warring armies. Everything had ground to a halt; the once-busy levee lay empty, save for a few Union warships and a graveyard of decaying hulks, and no work was to be had by anyone, much less a cripple.

After a week of useless tramping about, I turned the mirror in my garret around, for desperation had conquered fear, and I was ready to receive counsel from whatever source. Alas, the shattered glass shewed only fragments of my own gaunt and yellowed image, which I thought grimly appropriate. Gazing at that shattered countenance, I brought to mind a verse or incantation that Royal and I used to chant in the graveyard at midnight: Come ye, take me, lead me on/ Shew me gold, and then begone! *Very deliberately, I said it seven times, which was the magic number: but answer there was none.*

Yet that very afternoon, I saw—upon Levee Street, about half a square distant, amid waves of heat rising from the cobblestones—a thin, black-dressed figure loping with unmistakable gait through the trembling mirages. And as the strings of an harp will pick up and faintly repeat distant sounds, although no fingers have touched them, my heart-strings thrilled to a sense of hope and fear.

I hastened after him; he turned the corner of Gallatin Street, as did I a moment later: he had vanished, but in his place an amazing sight met my eyes. A file of colored men wearing blue uniforms were practicing the manual of arms. Royal was drilling them, and his strong nature had already asserted itself, for he wore upon each sleeve three broad gold stripes in the shape of spear-heads pointing down.

When the "Stand at ease" was given, I approached and spoke to him. He threw back his head, and laughed so loud that his men stared. We shook hands and spoke briefly of old times; he queried me about my missing arm, and briefly told me how he had enlisted in one of the new colored regiments. I admitted to needing food, whilst he revealed an ambition to sign the name he had chosen for himself—Royal Sargent—to the muster-roll, in place of an X. We struck a bargain: he promised to get me army rations, if in return I would make him literate.

That same evening he came to the house on Goodchildren Street, but was not invited in. The cousins pointed out that teaching him to read and write was forbidden under the state's Code Noir; *the fact that the black code was already dead they ignored, having no patience with mere reality. So Royal and I sat down on an iron bench in the patio, and for the first of many times bent our heads over a reading-book that some charitable society at the North had sent his regiment. When he went, he left behind army bacon and coffee and hardtack and cornmeal, which the cousins did not disdain to share that night at supper-time.*

When not working, he and I chatted about the past. I asked him how he felt after killing Monsieur Felix, and he answered solemnly, "I took my first breath when he took his last."

Hesitantly I asked if he thought the Overseer's spirit might walk, as those who die by violence are said to do. Royal laughed his loud laugh and said, "So many have died in the war, he'd be lost in the crowd!"

He inquired after Rose, and began to bring her small gifts, oranges and fruit pies and ices that he bought from the sutlers out of his pay of ten dollars a month. She received his gifts in the kitchen, the only room the cousins permitted him to enter. They stood by and glowered as she thanked him, saying how she rejoiced to see him a free man—at which they glowered more.

In this manner we all lived for a time, but had barely grown accustomed to regular eating, when without warning Royal's unit was sent down-river to garrison the forts at the Head of Passes. Then in quick succession fell two more blows: Papa died from a lethal mixture of whiskey and despair; and our cousins, in an excess of Confederate feeling, refused to take the oath of allegiance as ordered by the commanding general. Straightway they were branded Enemies of the United States and expelled from the city; soldiers seized their house as rebel property, and sold it at auction with all its contents.

Rose and I swore allegiance to the old flag, but it did us no good; we were driven into the street anyway, and a most difficult time began.

Ah, how fortunate are those who have never learned the awful truth taught by hunger: that a man will do anything, to live one single day more!

I tried hauling rubbish, but 'twas a two-handed job; I did poorly at it, and was laid off. I was for a time doorman of a brothel frequented by Union officers. One of them, a Major Wharton, was sufficiently moved by the plight of a Yale man to recommend me to a sutler, who sold food openly and bad whiskey secretly to the troops. I began keeping his account books, whilst Rose plied a needle twelve hours a day, repairing blue uniforms in a sweat-shop run by the Quartermaster.

Yet for all our efforts, we existed rather than lived in three poor rooms near the levee, beset with bugs of many species, but all equally blood-thirsty. I sought everywhere for my private Spectre, but found him not; at times my bizarre longing to behold again such an one as he made me wonder whether madness might soon compound my other troubles. And then, one night in January, 1863—I remember the rapid, mushy impacts of sleet against the shutters—I heard a shot in the street outside, and feet scampering away.

I tumbled out of bed, lit a stump of candle and hastened to the room's one window. A fat civilian in flash attire (probably a gambler) lay on the paving-stones amongst glistening pebbles of ice. Superimposed upon this image, I saw my own reflection in the dirty window-pane, and something else besides—a tall, thin, black-dressed man standing just behind me.

I whirled around, almost dropping the candle, and of course no one was there. But as I stood trembling, suddenly my confusion vanished and I knew what I must do. I blew out the candle, ran outside in my nightshirt, bent over the dying man and began rifling his pockets. My fingers slipped into something that felt like warm wet liver—'twas his wound—then closed upon his fat leather purse. Back inside, I hid the money (good greenbacks, near an hundred dollars!) in a knot-hole in the floor, and moved my bedstead to cover the hiding place.

I washed my bloody hand and went back to bed. Sounds came and went outside—a mounted patrol clip-clopping past halted, there was talk, and later a wagon clattered up to remove the body. Meantime I lay in bed, scratching my bug-bites, and resolved that henceforth I should take what I needed from the world by force. And though I had been law-abiding all my life, I knew exactly how to go about it.

Next day I used twenty dollars of the gambler's money to acquire an army Colt revolver (the famous model 1860) in the thieves' market that flourished in the alleyways near the Hospital Street wharf. I taught myself to load the weapon one-handed, clamping the grip under my stump, and using my right hand to tamp in powder and balls and affix copper caps to the nibs. That same night I ventured into the narrow fog-bound streets to try my luck. Guided by the glow of wide-spaced lanterns, listening always for the tramp of the provost marshal's guard and the clatter and jingle of the mounted patrols, I robbed two drunks. Though neither yielded as rich a haul as the gambler, I garnered enough to hand Rose money that would see us through a few more days.

"Where did this come from, Nick?" she asked, and I answered, "I prayed to Saint Dismas," meaning the patron saint of thieves.

Night after night I worked to perfect my technique. My method was to come up behind my victims and strike them down, using the heavy pistol as a club; then clamp it under my stump and search their pockets. 'Twas not an easy life, for others of my own kind were in the streets; we snarled at each other like dogs eyeing the same scrap, and twice I had to drive off my fellow jackals with bullets.

Yet these scavengers also became my new acquaintances. I met them in the cheap brothels I began to patronize, and the wretched saloons called doggeries, where I warmed my belly against the night air with dime shots of bad whiskey. From the garish crowd of whores, pimps and rogues who shared my perils and my pleasures, I learned that I was a knuck *or a* sandbagger *when I struck my victims down; that when I searched their pockets I was* overhauling *them; that my pistol was a* barking iron; *that when I tracked my prey in silence I was* padding my hooves. Yale had taught me none of these things.

There was also a Creole argot, of which I understood a few words: the women called me bras-coupé, *after a famous one-armed bandit of an hundred years before, or* bête-marron, *meaning a tame beast gone wild. I was struck by that term, because it reminded me that the Overseer's half-forgotten surname had also been Marron—as if we had been brothers.*

And brothers we might have been, brothers in crime. I saw his shadow often in the streets, slipping past a lantern, or sliding along a wall half-lit by a red-shaded coal-oil lamp in the window of a bagnio. I recognized him easily by his strange walk; I envied him his silence of movement, and soon learned to take him as my guide. He was clever at finding the staggering sots who remained my favorite prey, and the shadow of his long arm pointed them out to me. He also led me out of danger. One night, when the cavalry were so close behind me that I saw the sparks their horseshoes struck from the cobblestones, I spotted that angular dark form vanishing into an alleyway, followed it and found safety there.

Later—in that deceptive hour just before dawn, when the eyes cannot tell a cloud from a mountain—I saw him again, dimly through a bank of silver mist. With the mad aim of thanking him for my salvation, I shouted, "Monsieur Felix!" and sprang after him. The shadow turned, and like a razor seen edge-on, instantly disappeared. And later that day I started up in bed, awakened by my own screaming.

Those who never have been haunted can scarcely believe the power of a Phantasm. Soon even the full blaze of noon could not drive him off. Upon a crowded street my eye would fall upon my shadow against a wall, yet 'twas not my shadow but his; and if the shadow raised its arm, I would find my own rising too, as if he mocked me, saying by a gesture: You see which of us is real, after all!

In my dreams he appeared in many forms: as himself, stalking about in his old black suit, the whip over his arm; as the host of a costume ball, where at midnight the dancers all dropped their masks, revealing the faces of wolves, foxes and rats; as an idol carven of wood, to which dim crowds were bowing, myself among them. Awaking sweat-soaked from such visions, I began to comprehend that the Overseer was no mere ghost—no mere echo or reflected image of one who had lived. By giving himself up wholly to the insatiable passion of revenge, Monsieur Felix had become something stranger than that, more powerful and more utterly lost. And it was to this demonic power that I bowed down, for I needed to draw upon it to save myself.

One night in such a dream the idol's stiff jaw moved, and the well-known voice whispered, Tu, mon p'tit, serais le roi du coton! *At which, upon waking, I could not but laugh. For how should a one-armed knuck become King of*

Cotton? And yet that very day upon the street a Yankee officer with eagles on his shoulder-straps and a great clanking saber banging at his knees, called out to me, "Old Eli!"

'Twas my benefactor Wharton, now promoted to colonel. He asked if, as a onetime planter, I knew quality in cotton, and when I said yes, he intimated that a friend of his wanted to deal in Confederate cotton smuggled across the lines.

So I acquired a new profession, more rewarding than the old, though not less dangerous. Using my knowledge and my weapon and the wood-craft I had learned as a boy, I guided the dealer—a gross creature named Klegg, with especially foul breath—into the rebel-held regions beyond Lake Pontchartrain. There he bought cotton very cheap, intending (as he told me) to transport it to the city, ship it out and sell it very dear at the North, where the factories were starving for the stuff.

My spectral ally guided us well. Twice I saw him standing stiff as a scare-crow in an overgrown field, pointing a long finger in the direction we must take. Returning from our jaunt, I was poling our heavily laden bateau along the sedgy margins of Lake Maurepas, when I saw him again, this time a deeper shadow in the blue dusk, pointing directly at Klegg, who was seated in the bow with his fat back turned to me. Taking the hint, I silently laid down the pole, drew the Colt from the waist-band of my trowsers, and shot the dealer between the shoulder-blades.

This was my first murder, and as the reeking powder-smoke dispersed I was all a-tremble, gazing at the deep round oozing hole in the man's spine, scarce able to believe what I had done. But then I felt a great surge of power, as if now I could do anything. With some effort, I heaved the carcass into a slough, watched a drowsy alligator wake long enough to play sexton, and then, taking up the pole again, went my silent way.

After selling the cotton, I sought out Colonel Wharton, reported the dealer killed by bandits, and bribed him to select me as manager of a west-bank plan-tation the government had seized from its rebel owner. With free Negroes as workers and government mules to pull the plows, I was soon making cotton for thirty cents a pound and selling it in New York for a dollar-twenty—all without incurring any danger whatsoever!

Thus I attained the dignity of a war-profiteer, and the golden sun of prosperity began to shine upon me and mine. I freed Rose from her wage-slavery; I freed myself forever from the life of a scavenger. I cut Colonel Wharton a share of my profits, and was rewarded when he brought me—now that I had money to invest—into many a profitable venture. I invited him to the plantation, and visited his home; I came to know his dull wren of a wife, with her deplorable hats and her nasal midwestern twang. For the first time I laid eyes upon his daughter Elmira—then little more than an auburn-haired girl, but already giving promise of voluptuous beauty to come.

At first my mutilation frightened her—she thought me some sort of monster, in which she was more than half-right—but in time my ready wit, and the small presents I brought her, made me a great favorite, the more so as she came to pity me. I smiled at her and listened to her chatter, and told her closely cropped versions of my sufferings, for which she pitied me the more.

Elmira, of course, was a project for the future; 'twas pleasant to think that again I had a future. By the winter of 1864 I was back in town for good, and living in fair comfort with Rose in a pleasant cottage in the Third District. And the following spring, peace returned at last.

It had been a fine and busy day—wearying, but the kind of weariness that felt good. A whole new chapter completed, the household running like clockwork, everything normal again, just as it ought to be.

When evening shadows gathered, the old man lay at rest, lapped in clean linen, inhaling the smells of rubbing alcohol, bourbon, and the sour saplike odor of raw opium that lingered in the air. Before sleep took him, he again invited Morse to sit on the foot of the bed, and for a few minutes the two men spoke frankly—or at any rate, one of them did.

"I have no one to be my child save only you, Morse," Lerner told him, feeling a curious finicky unwillingness to call himself Morse's father in so many words.

Morse missed the distinction. "Yes. But because of my skin, you use me as a servant, not a son."

"When I die," said Lerner, "you will learn how much I view you as a son."

Morse gazed at him searchingly, as if to read his true thoughts. "Do you encourage me to have hopes, Father?" asked he, almost in a whisper.

"No," said Lerner. "I encourage you to have expectations."

Morse turned away, and a dry sob seemed to rack his chest. "I am sorry, Father, for the trouble I give you," he said humbly, then turned off the lights and left, closing the door to the den noiselessly behind him.

In the dark, Lerner lay back smiling, and played for a time with the thought of actually leaving Morse some substantial sum. How that would outrage the respectable white society of New Orleans! How it would kill them to see a Negro made richer than they could ever hope to be!

But was that really necessary? Lerner's will, after providing somewhat meagerly for his servants—Morse was down for a hundred dollars and his second-best suit—left most of his millions to found a library. A strange bequest for a man who'd seldom read a book since leaving Yale, but the point (as with the vaster gift made for the same purpose by Andrew Carnegie) was the fact that his name would be chiseled over the building's door.

Anyway, merely by giving Morse hope, which cost nothing, he'd safeguarded his own comfort. Truly, he thought, in walking with a demon one learns many things, including the fact that faith, hope, and love—those supposed virtues—may become chains with which to bind a spirit.

Still smiling, he fell asleep, and all the dark hours his next chapter wrote itself, ready to be transcribed in the morning by his hand.

CHAPTER THE FOURTH
Wherein I Triumph During the Reconstruction

One April evening, as I sat in the little courtyard behind our house, sipping a glass of tolerable whiskey and watching sunset streamers unfurl across the sky, the gate hinges creaked and a well-attired colored man entered and extended his hand. So quietly did Royal reenter my life.

Smiling at the stranger who once had been my playmate in Eden, I invited him to sit down and called Rose to bring a clean glass. When she saw Royal, she fairly ran from the kitchen, blushing and smiling in her pleasure. Then she recovered her customary demure ways, and asked him how he did. He said well, and she placed her small hand for an instant in his large one, before returning with a light step to making supper. I poured Royal a whiskey, he offered me a segar, and for a time we sipped and smoked, whilst covertly observing each other to see what changes the years had made.

"Nick, I hear you've become a Union man," he said at length, his voice strong and firm with the habit of command.

"Yes," I replied dryly. "'Twas conversion by the sword."

He laughed. "You were smart to make the change. Now me—I've been discharged from the army, and mean to enter politics as soon as my people get the vote. They'll need leadership, and I can supply that."

I said quietly, "Watch your back."

He leaned forward and peered at my face. "Nick, I hope you ain't like the Bourbons, who learned nothing and forgot nothing."

"You've been reading history, I see."

"Yes. And mean to make some."

"Royal," said I, "this city is full of people who have learned nothing and forgotten nothing. And most of them know how to shoot."

Indeed, they were returning every month by the hundreds—beaten soldiers, political exiles—like red-hot pumice stones raining down in the aftermath of an eruption. I saw them every day about the streets, people with pinched faces and missing limbs, the most desperate bending over garbage heaps behind the great hotels.

Royal was unimpressed. "Well, we'll have to work together to rebuild. I want to offer the former rebels the hand of friendship."

I smiled a little, thinking what was likely to happen to a hand so extended. But I said diplomatically, "Away with the past! Let us live for the future!"

Rose called out that supper was ready, we emptied our glasses, and Royal departed. When I went inside, I saw that she had laid three places at the table. She said in a disappointed voice, "He didn't stay to eat?"

"Why should he stay to eat?"

"Well, he was one of our people, after all."

"No longer," I answered, "now he belongs only to himself."

I piled into my food, still smiling at Royal's notion that Yank and Rebel could work together to rebuild our shattered world. Oh yes, my deals with

Colonel Wharton shewed that Blue and Gray could be brought together by the color Green. But well I knew that the spectrum of the time contained also a deep crimson stripe—the color of rage, of unburied hate, of blood-vengeance.

As if to confirm my belief, a few days later a strange man with a scarred face limped through our gate at sunset, when as usual I was drinking alone. He introduced himself as Brigadier General Eleazar Hobbs, late of the Confederate Army.

I said quickly, "I am a poor man."

"I haven't come to ask for money," he said with a grim smile. "I've heard that you too wore the gray."

This I acknowledged, and he invited me to join a club he was forming to discuss the current state of affairs in the city, the state, and the South.

For the founder of a debating society, he asked some odd questions. Eyeing dubiously my pinned-up left sleeve, he wanted to know if I were able to handle a weapon. I still went armed, the city being so disturbed; I had long since retired the old 1860 model revolver as a memento of difficult but exciting times, and replaced it with a new-model Remington, a sweet weapon that fired up-to-date brass cartridges in place of loose powder and copper caps.

I drew this gun, cocked it, took aim at a broken flower-pot against the garden wall and blew it to pieces. Hobbs nodded thoughtfully, and for a time we chatted, his preferred topic being the intolerable arrogance of the liberated slaves. When I told him frankly that I had taken the Iron-Clad Oath and knew a number of blue-backs, he was not disturbed.

"We need a friend in the camp of the enemy," he said, and I began to understand what he wanted of me. A new and secret war was beginning, and I was being invited to serve in it—as matters turned out, to serve on both sides!

I found it an odd sort of struggle. Brigadier Hobbs and his friends let strictly alone the blue-coated soldiers who once had been their enemies, for killing them would only bring down upon the South all the calamities of years past. Instead, they shot presumptuous blacks and Republicans of all hues. The Red River in particular proved to be well named, from the hundreds of bodies that floated down it.

'Twas my old neighborhood, its byways well known to me, and I had a ready-

made reason to go there, for I was attempting to regain control of Mon Repos, or what was left of it. The house had been burnt by one army or the other, or by bandits—I never learned which—but the land, with its alley of great oaks, remained. That summer, on a trip upriver I tracked and killed a man I did not know, nor why he needed killing: my sole motive being to prove my bona fides to General Hobbs.

Need I say that Monsieur Felix accompanied me? I first saw him on the boat, seated near the stern-wheel with sparkles of light gleaming through his shadowy form as he gazed at the frothing tumult of the water. A day later, when I had slain my man in a little wood near the levee, and was turning away, I saw him again, standing amongst the cottonwood trees with arms folded—looking on with great interest, but making no sign, like a wise teacher who lets an apt pupil learn by doing.

The thought struck me then that I was different, not only from the man I had been, but also from the man I might have become without his guidance. I might have been a good man; I might have been a dead man. Most likely I would have been both—good and dead!

In any case, why dream of what had not happened? With my latest victim lying at my feet, my whole being hummed with tigerish joy, for again I had broken the bonds of conscience and felt free to do anything. So I nodded to Monsieur Felix in a comradely way, and passed on.

All that busy morning, with the words flowing from his mind as smoothly as the ink from his reservoir pen, Lerner had nothing to complain of, except that Morse in performing his duties seemed a touch too familiar.

Give a nigger an inch, he thought, *and he'll take an ell*. At lunchtime he spoke firmly, saying that discretion was the first thing he would look for in any man who aspired to be his principal heir.

"In short," said Morse, his voice as pettish as a spoiled child, "despite what you said last night, in the sight of the world I am to go on being your nigger-man."

Hearing him use the same word, as if they shared a bond of mind as well as blood, gave Lerner an odd feeling. He answered almost defensively:

"I have never treated you so, but as a member of my household and as my right-hand man. Think about it, and see if I do not tell the truth."

Whether convinced or not, Morse apologized again, and after serving the meal and cutting the meat for him, departed as silently as an Arabian Nights servitor. Smiling, Lerner refilled his pen, set to work, and the tale emerged without a single deletion or correction, like the automatic writing of a seer.

Back in town, I began to find my true role in the Reconstruction. Not as a killer, of whom there were more than enough, but as a peacemaker—a reconciler of differences. Who could be a better go-between than I, who had lost a limb for the Cause, yet had sworn loyalty to the Union? I spoke to each side in their own language, and my tongue moved freely, as if hinged in the middle.

Without undue arrogance, I aver that within a few years I became an indispensable man. Most of my time was spent in the lobby of our statehouse—the pompous, gold-domed, elegantly decaying St. Louis Hotel—where blood enemies combined forces to build a new ruling class upon the ruins of the old.

Ah, I can see it now! The walls covered with stained and tattered silk; the floor scattered with spittoons, of which there never were enough, for the Turkey carpet was foul with spittle. I see servants hastening about with tall amber bottles and trays of crystal goblets that ping at the touch. I see the all-male crowd, smell the hazy bitter segar-smoke, hear the whispered conferences, feel between my fingers the stiff smooth rag paper as drafts of pending bills whisper and slide from hand to hand. And amongst the portly scoundrels with their embroidered vests and gleaming watch-chains, I perceive a rail-thin figure that flickers and comes and goes like a mirage, his one good eye gleaming like a splinter of glass.

One day when I was busy conniving, someone touched my shoulder. I turned to find Royal smiling at me. He was rising fast in the postwar chaos—a former slave who could read and write and knew how to exercise power. The tattered slave-boy had become a soldier, the soldier a state senator and a man to reckon with, through his influence over the Negro legislators.

"Nick," he said, "I might have known I should find you in a den of thieves."

"Come, Senator," I jested. *"Governor Wharton would not like to hear a fellow Republican so describe his friends and supporters!"*

He shook his head, smile broadening. *"Nick, there is something uncanny about you. That a one-armed Rebel should emerge as the governor's—what's a polite word for it—"*

"Legislative agent, shall we say?"

"Just so. The Master of the Lobby. You know, my constituents are all black folk, and from them I hear whispers that at night you transform into a Klansman—although that I refuse to believe!"

"I hope you disbelieve it, mon vieux, *for that is a vile slander put about by the envy and malice of my enemies."*

"I rejoice to hear it. Nick, I wonder…can you tell me whether the Governor has decided to sign my bill?"

"The one to legalize marriage between blacks and whites? I think he will swallow it, but only if sweetened with a spoonful of sugar."

He made a face. *"How much?"*

We quickly struck a bargain. The governor wished the Legislature to charter a rather improbable railroad, whose stock promised a handsome return from foreign investors ignorant of the fact that it was to run through a fathomless swamp. Royal agreed to swing the necessary votes in the Senate, and I guaranteed him a certain quantity of the stock to pass around.

He said with relief, *"Old Wharton is so greedy, I thought he would want a bag full of gold!"*

"No, there's more money in railroads. However, his daughter, the lovely Elmira, is soon to enter society, and a thousand dollars toward the cost of her ball and ball-gown would help to seal the bargain."

That was how things were done in Louisiana. But why do I say *were?* And why do I imply that things were done differently in General Grant's Washington, or Boss Tweed's New York? Yet some differences between North and South did exist: as was proved by a Mardi Gras ball I gave early in March, 1870, and the crisis that followed, making and unmaking so many lives.

Although my house now stands deep within the city, in those times it stood upon the Uptown fringes of settlement. I designed it myself, a place of stained glass and gables and towers and spires, all painted garishly as an Amazon frog, in a deliberate affront to the classical taste of the age I grew up in.

Within, gaslight glittered upon glass and silver, upon long tables piled with steaming food, upon champagne that flowed in sparkling rivers. The noisy throng was a patchwork of colors and a Babel of languages—a muster-roll of all who were corrupt, entertaining, and important in our world. How different from this dismal Twentieth Century, when white and black are hardly permitted to breathe the same air!

I took pleasure in inviting men of all races and factions, and women of all professions, including the oldest. I hoped they might amuse me by striking a few sparks from one another—little dreaming upon what tinder those sparks would fall.

At the time I was still a bachelor; Rose was doing the honors as hostess, and Royal asked her to dance. My dismay was great when I saw Brigadier Hobbs staring at them: they were a handsome couple, carven as it were of teakwood and ivory. But in Hobbs's scarred face burned the eyes of a crouching wolf.

I can hear the music now—a waltz called (I think) Southern Roses—*and the stiff rustling of the women's gowns like the rush of wind through dry autumnal trees, and the scrape of dancing feet. When the guests were leaving, an hour or two before dawn, Royal pounced upon me. He was in a strange mood, exalted and more than a little drunk.*

"Didn't I tell you that reconciliation would come? May our connection grow ever closer!" he exclaimed, almost crushing my one remaining hand.

"May it be so!" I replied, striving to retrieve my fingers intact.

"'Tis very late, Nick—or rather, very early—but I have a proposal to make. Could we speak privately for a moment?"

The word "proposal" passed me by entirely. I bowed him into my den—into this very room, where as a crippled old man I sit in a wheeled chair, writing. And here he rather grandly announced, in terms even then old-fashioned, that he desired to form "an honorable union" with Rose.

'Twas the worst shock I'd had in years. Rapid visions flashed across my brain of how Brigadier Hobbs and his friends would react, should a member of their society allow such a marriage to take place.

"Brother," I said, swallowing my feelings with difficulty, "I'm honored by your confidence. Of course, I must commune with my cousin. I fear that your proposal might place her in great peril."

"She is resolved to face it with me."

"That sentiment does her honor. But speak to her I must."

"Of course," said he, bowing like a dancing-master. "I shall return in—shall we say a week?—for your answer."

No sooner had he left than I confronted Rose, who met me with a face both scared and determined. I dragged her into the den and shut the door to exclude the servants, who were busy gathering up the fragments of the feast.

"How dare you connive at this lunacy?" I demanded, grinding my teeth.

"I dare, because it is time for me to be born!" she declared. "Here I am, twenty-six years old—almost too old to marry. And what have I ever been but an orphan, a poor relation, a seamstress to the Yankee army, and a housekeeper to you? I have never had a life! And I am resolved to have one now, ere it is too late!"

"This affair must have a long background!" I raged. "Yet you never confided in me, though I stole and killed for you."

"You stole and killed because you are a thief and a murderer!" she replied. "Royal is worth twenty of you. Did you know that long ago when we were children, he would risk a whipping to sneak upstairs and bring me flowers? That he would sit on the floor and tell me about his adventures, whilst you never talked to me at all, except to say good morning and good-bye?"

"What!" I thundered, "has it been going on that long?"

"He is a strong, wise man with a brilliant future. Have you forgotten that he killed that beastly Monsieur Felix to save me?"

It quite maddened me to hear that when I killed I was a murderer, but when Royal did the same he was a paladin.

"Royal shot the Overseer for his own revenge—you were incidental. You have always been incidental, Rose, a mere burden for others to carry, dead weight upon the road of life."

"Cochon!" she cried, and slapped me so hard my head rang. Then, weeping, she flung open the door and fled upstairs to her bedroom.

I closed the door again, took a dusty bottle from the tantalus and poured a *triple brandy. I had swallowed about half, when a movement in the corner of my eye caused me to turn.*

I can see the room as it was then—indeed, as it still is, save for the electric lights: the heavy red draperies; the dark crouching furniture; the small iron safe; the broad burled walnut desk; and the wavering shadows cast over everything by a gasolier's twelve flickering bluish points of flame. Against a wall covered with expensive French paper, something moved—a black shadow cast by nothing tangible.

"Well," I demanded, "what the devil shall I do?"

A very apt way of speaking, all things considered. And in that instant I knew—knew how to handle the situation—as if I had spent years and years planning every detail.

I finished the drink, climbed the stairs and went to Rose's room, where she lay sobbing upon the bed. Sitting down beside her, I spoke in the quiet, calm voice of a man who has regained his sanity after an emotional storm.

I reminded her that we were linked by blood, that we had been children together, that we had shared many perils and helped each other to survive terrible times. I lamented that we had both said things we should not have said. I said that she ought to have prepared me for Royal's proposal, which had come as a great shock.

"I ask only that you take a little time to be sure, my dear. I have but recently cleared the taxes from Papa's old land near Red River, and must take a brief trip there to get a new survey made. If, when I return, you are still resolved to marry Royal, you shall find me a champion of your right to choose him, and his to choose you. And you shall have a dowry proportioned to my wealth and your deserts."

We wept together; I begged forgiveness a thousand times. She called me her dearest friend, her other self, the best and most understanding of men. I have never known why women believe the things men tell them—or vice versa.

In my bedroom I smoked a last segar, smiling without mirth as I saw with clear, unimpeded vision how the demon had saved and shaped my whole life to this very end. "Damn it all to hell," I exclaimed, "je m'en fiche! I don't care!"

But in that I lied. I cared, but knew that I could no longer change my course, which was fixed for all time. And perhaps beyond time as well.

—.—

Next morning, without the slightest warning, after days of quiet, all the arrangements meant to secure Lerner's comfort broke down at once.

He woke from opulent dreams, as rich as those recorded in De Quincey's *Confessions of an English Opium-Eater*. Dreams of caravans pacing across deserts where the light was blindingly intense; of chiming camel-bells and wailing flutes; of dark-eyed houris glancing through silken veils that covered swaying howdahs; of Mameluke guards with crooked swords and prancing horses; of lavish pavilions where dancing girls twirled on rose carpets to the twanging of dulcimers.

And, yes, Monsieur Felix had been there, smiling his razor-thin smile and rubbing his hands like a master of ceremonies whose every gesture seems to say, "What wonders our performers will show you tonight!"

Then Lerner woke, tasting ashes as usual, and saw Cleo's scared face and chignon peeping around the bedroom door like a polka-dotted messenger of doom. He didn't even have time to ask what had gone wrong when she blurted out, "Oh, Mr. Nick, Morse he been arrested, him!" And burst into tears.

The rest of the morning was spent unraveling what had happened the preceding night. It wasn't easy. Two years back, with great reluctance Lerner had allowed a telephone to be installed in his house. But Morse had done all the calling, and when the old man wheeled himself into the hall to use it, he discovered that the box had been placed too high on the wall for him to reach.

So his questions had to be passed through Cleo—who was hysterical— and after he sent her away, through the cook, a sullen woman with the improbable name of Euphrosyne, an import from South Carolina with a Gullah accent as dark and impenetrable as a flagstone. The information from the other end of the line (first from Lerner's lawyer, later from a police captain named Hennessy) had to come back by the same cross-African pathway.

But the old man was persistent, and knew how to offer Hennessy a bribe without actually using the word. So he learned that what the captain called "your pet nigger" was the talk of Storyville, where—it now appeared—he'd been a familiar figure for years, known for dispensing money (*whose* money?) with a free hand, and for his rough way with the women in the cribs and colored brothels. A piano player called Professor Jelly Roll had already produced a "jass" composition in his honor, called *Mr. Morse's Blues*.

Lerner knew nothing of so-called jass music, except that it was said to be noisy. But as the story unfolded, he began to feel that Morse from his very conception had been headed for this reckoning. Apparently he began his evening with a few pipes of opium at some den near the docks that he'd discovered while procuring the drug for Lerner. Heading home, he entered a street-car while still befuddled and, finding it crowded, sat down on a bench meant for whites. The conductor and motorman ordered him to vacate it and stand behind a yellow sign that courteously stated THIS SECTION IS RESERVED FOR OUR COLORED PATRONS ONLY. Morse refused, and courtesy perished as the two men hustled him off the car and flung him into a mud puddle.

Considerably disheveled, Morse repaired to a saloon that served Negroes whiskey through a back window. He swallowed a few quick shots of courage and proceeded to a bawdy-house to seek further comfort. His choice of establishment was either deliberate arrogance or a grave mistake. The Madame, a fearsome mulattress who called herself Countess Willie V. Piazza, had built a fine business by providing handsome colored women to a clientele of white men only. She took one look at Morse—mahogany-hued, smelling of drink and much the worse for wear—and refused him admittance. When he forced his way inside anyway, she summoned the police, and Morse topped off a busy night by assaulting not one but two brawny Irishmen.

With Hennessy's assistance, Lerner's lawyer found Morse in a cell of Parish Prison, where the police had been amusing themselves by playing drum-rolls on his ribs with their billyclubs. Bribes were necessary merely to preserve his life; when he was dragged before a magistrate, the lawyer had to guarantee his bail. Prison remained a distinct possibility, only (the lawyer warned) to be averted by still more bribes. When Morse at length was returned home by cab, Lerner not only had to pay the hackman, he had to hire a doctor to tend Morse at two dollars a visit. By evening of a day of upheaval, Morse was lying in his room upstairs, the doctor had cleaned his wounds and strapped his ribs, and Lerner was in a greater rage than was safe for an elderly man.

Damn him! he thought. *Were he not a kinsman, I would let him sink or swim! Doesn't he know what can happen to a man of color in the grip of our police?*

Well, of course he knew. It was just that Morse, Lerner's pet from his birth, protected by the walls of this house, hadn't thought it could happen to him.

Next morning—sleepless, ill-shaven, nerves ragged for lack of his drug, back pains lancing him like sparks of pure white fire—the old man returned ashen-tongued and red-eyed to his task, under a compulsion made somehow worse by the events of yesterday.

CHAPTER THE FIFTH
Wherein the Demon Proves the Real Winner

As a burning sun rose over the Father of Waters, I boarded a steam packet on the levee at Felicity Street. I had already visited a telegraph-office, and sent two local wires, one to Royal and one to Brigadier Hobbs.

Whilst the shore fell away, I stood gazing upon the broad churning wake of the stern-wheel, and the wide, ever-busy river beyond. I watched the crowded riverboats; the sleek steamers from overseas trailing plumes of ash from their smoke-stacks; the sailboats with little patched sails, and the scows with men hauling at the sweeps; the green banks and the low, irregular levees; a party of church-goers clad in white gowns, being baptized in the shallows; and the floating and diving gulls that screamed in harsh voices.

Amidst all this busy life, I felt a strange loneliness, as if for all my wealth and influence I was but a gypsy and a wanderer upon the earth. My earlier homicides had been easy enough, for I had slain men who meant nothing to me. Perhaps I was not yet entirely what my master had designed me to be, for the thought that I must now play the role of Cain lay upon my heart like a stone. Somehow, through many years of dark deeds I had preserved the memory of my time of innocence, in which Royal played so large a part. Even if the tale told in the Bible be true, which I doubt, a vengeful God merely cast Adam out of Eden: he did not demand that he go back and befoul the very fountains of his former Paradise with blood.

Hoping to shake off my melancholy, I started to take a brisk turn about the deck, but stopped when I saw a well-known figure sitting at the bow, still as a carven figurehead. So the Overseer was coming along to see his revenge accomplished. I was not surprised—after all, the patient devil had waited nine years for it.

At Red River Landing, a tolerable inn survived, and I engaged a room. The town was muddy and straggling as in times gone by, but it boasted two or three steamboats tied up and unloading, with black laborers not unlike the slaves of yesteryear—indeed, they were the slaves of yesteryear—chanting work songs as they trotted up and down the gangplanks, with heavy loads miraculously balanced on their heads.

In my room, I laid my pistol upon the usual marble-top table, beside the usual chipped wash basin and flowered pitcher. Then I lay down to rest upon an ill-smelling featherbed, drawing a dusty musketo-net about me. My thoughts were sombre, but I did not have long to indulge them. Came a knock on the door, and the innkeeper—a huge man with smaller eyes in a larger face than I ever saw before—handed me two telegrams, and stood waiting whilst I read. I put the telegrams under my stump and began to fish in my waistcoat pocket for a coin.

"I'm not wanting a tip," he said in a low drawling grumble of a voice. "General Hobbs has contacted me. Where'd you lose the wing?"

"Shiloh. Better come into the room." He nodded and followed me.

"I was there too," he said. "I saw General Johnston killed. The minny-ball broke an artery in his leg; he turned white as cotton and bled to death in half a minute. Is this a matter of honor, or politics?"

"Both. You'll find that I know how to be grateful."

"I'm sure." Despite omitting the r, he made two syllables out of sure. "You want the nigger to go slow, or fast?"

"Fast."

"Night or day?"

"He's no fool. He won't go out at night. And you don't want him killed here."

"So it's daytime, then, which means masks and an ambush."

In whispers we completed our arrangements. After engaging his horse and buggy for the morrow, I explained that I had grown up nearby.

"I'm from Arkansaw, myself," he said. "You owned the nigger in the old days?"

"Yes."

"Ah," said he, sadly shaking his massive head. "They was happier then." He left the room with a surprisingly silent tread, for so big a man.

Everything was in readiness. I dined without appetite, slept poorly, but was waiting at the dock with the landlord's buggy when Royal strode ashore from the morning packet. As if impersonating himself, he was all strut and boldness, jaunty and dressed in flash attire—a claw-hammer coat and top hat—at which blacks and whites alike turned and stared. I hailed him, and he leaped into the buggy, which swayed under his weight, and gripped my hand.

"Nick," he exclaimed, "Never did I think we would meet here again, and for such a reason!"

I said, "Since you're a bird with two wings, perhaps you'll drive?"

He took the reins and snapped them with the casual ease of a country-bred man. The horse shook its mane and the buggy rolled with a jingle of little bells along the old familiar road that led to the ruins of Mon Repos. The day was fine, the ground dry and the spring weather cool and bright, with fair-weather clouds above, and great shadows flitting soundlessly over woods and meadows.

As we drove, I plunged into recollection, chattering nervously in a manner most unusual for me. Royal (a great talker) responded in kind, and soon we were pointing and exclaiming as if we were boys again. My school had been reduced to a few scattered bricks, and 'midst the ruins of the church I saw—fallen and rusting—the iron bell that once had tolled for the death of a world. We turned into a dim track, where tall grass brushed the underside of the carriage with the sound of rubbed velvet. Near the stark chimney that alone had survived the fall of Mon Repos, Royal tugged at the reins and we halted.

For a minute or so we sat silent. Then he said, "I was amazed at your tele-gram, Nick."

"I designed it to be amazing."

"Frankly, Rose and I were prepared to defy you, if need be. But how fine it is that you consent to our marriage—and that you intend this land to be Rose's marriage portion!"

"I could imagine nothing that would please either of you more than to own Mon Repos," I replied. "It's the logical dowry."

I watched covertly as Royal's natural wariness dissolved in the grip of irre-sistible emotion. "To own the land where I was once a slave!" he exclaimed, his voice choking midway in the sentence.

He gazed like one transfixed down the long alley of noble oaks, where gray streamers of moss floated on the breeze with the silent grace of shadows. I began to talk about the taxes, the difficulty of getting tenants to work the fields, and the need for a new survey, since most of the old landmarks had disappeared.

"Those were to have been my problems," I said. "Now I fear they will be yours. And you must be on your guard, my friend. The Klan's active here-abouts—you're safe enough in daytime, but a prominent colored man with a white wife should beware the night."

He grinned and raised the tail of his fawn-colored coat to shew a handsome silver-mounted pistol in a holster of tooled leather hanging from a wide cartridge-belt.

"I am prepared for anything," he said.

I shook my head at his fatal arrogance. How can a man be prepared for anything?

"Ah, look," I said, pointing, "do you remember that path? It led to our swim-ming-hole, did it not?"

He turned and craned, and as he did so a figure in robe and hood stepped from behind the chimney and raised a rifle. A shot exploded, and the round buzzed past me.

Frightened, the horse reared and whinnied. The buggy tilted; I grabbed at the reins and struggled one-handed to get the animal under control. Meantime, like a good soldier Royal leaped to the ground and rolled and fired.

His shot killed the idiot in spook attire, and the Klansman's hand, contracting in death, squeezed off a round that struck the horse in the brain. The animal crashed in the traces, the buggy overturned, and I was flung out and landed with a thump.

Well, the whole thing was a hopeless mess. I scrambled past a wildly spinning wheel, jumped to my feet, and found that I was alone amid the ruins of Mon Repos.

The assassin lay like a heap of soiled bedclothes on the ground. Royal had vanished into a nearby stand of trees, and I heard shouts and shots and the crashing of men plunging through the dense second-growth of pine and sweetgum saplings.

A shotgun boomed. Silence for six or seven heartbeats, then two revolver shots, Blam! Blam!

Desperate to learn what was happening, I drew my pistol and followed the sounds into the trees. The wind seemed to hold its breath; invisible birds were screaming, but the noise of the fire-fight had slain all movement save mine.

I paused and stood listening. The shotgun boomed again close by, followed by a revolver shot and a strangled outcry. I hastened through the blinding tangle, panting, inhaling the reek of sulphur mingled with the wine-cork smell of spring growth.

In a little glen I found a figure weltering in the grass—another hooded man, a big one. I lifted the hood and saw the landlord's broad face and tiny eyes. He had been shot through the throat, and his sharp little eyes turned to dull pebbles as I watched.

A new fury of shots broke out. A deathly pale young man broke from the thicket and ran past me, his breath rattling like a consumptive's. He ran like a hare, this way and that, either to make aiming difficult or simply in the madness of fear. Then he was gone, and I was alone with Royal.

I whispered bitterly, "You might have spared me this."

I had not forgotten all woodcraft, and slipped without a sound past slender pale trunks and rough pine branches, over thorny mats of wild grape and thick dying undergrowth. In the treetops strong sunlight vibrated, but down in the tangle evening colors—blue and bronze—enveloped me. Then I stumbled on a heap of dry wood, something cracked under my feet, and behind me Royal's voice said, "Hello, Nick."

I turned and faced him. He leveled his revolver and said, "Your weapon."

A smile of relief began to cross my lips, and he said more sharply, "Come, come—your weapon! And let me tell you, brother, you have but little to smile about."

In that he was wrong, for I was watching Monsieur Felix emerge from the ruins of his house. Then that unforgettable voice ground out, Aha, tu p'tit diable!

Royal turned his head, and looked into the one glinting eye and the one oozing pit. That was when I shot him down, and shot him again where he lay.

For a long moment the Overseer and I stood gazing at each other over the body. He smiled, that thin smile I remembered so well, like an arroyo between his blade of a nose and blue hillock of a chin. I hated him then, yet not half so much as I hated myself, for having sold my destiny forever to such an one as he.

Then, like a shadow struck by light, he vanished without a sound.

Strange, very strange, he thought, rereading what he'd written. After all, his tale was a confession. But who was he confessing to? God had long ago departed from his universe, and Royal and Rose already knew his guilt, assuming they knew anything at all.

The slow approach of shuffling footsteps in the hall interrupted his brooding. Hastily he locked up his manuscript and assumed the demeanor of a hanging judge. The door opened, and Cleo and Euphrosyne together helped Morse limp in to face the music.

His face was swollen, one eye was a purple plum, and he winced at every movement from the pain of his ribs, though the doctor had told Lerner that the bones were only cracked, not broken.

The old man greeted him with silence, then waved the women away. For several long minutes Morse stood before him, his one good eye fixed in contemplation of his toes. Finally Lerner spoke in what he hoped were the tones of Fate.

"I suppose you know that you might have been beaten to death."

Morse nodded.

"I can't prevent you from embarking on such adventures again. But I can withdraw my protection. Once more, and you're on your own. Then you'll either die at the hands of the police or else go to prison where, I promise you, you'll learn many things, but nothing to make you grateful to your teachers."

Morse nodded again. He already knew that he would be forgiven one more time. How else to explain the fact that he was here, rather than lying on the oozing brick floor of the prison, watching enormous cockroaches feast on spatters of his own blood? He also knew without being told that he'd reached the end of his rope, that he'd have no more chances, and that his hopes of inheriting a portion of the old man's wealth were probably over.

What he couldn't know were the thoughts passing through Lerner's mind. The old man was looking at Morse but, still full of the story he'd been writing, thinking not of him but of himself and Royal.

Well, we all come to it in time—we are broken down to ground-level, and must construct ourselves anew. If we survive, we become stronger: with few exceptions we do not become better. For most of us, when all else has failed, turn to the demon.

He drew a deep breath, said, "Sit down," and watched Morse relapse, wincing, into the same chair—now battered and dusty—where Rose had sat so long ago.

Opening the safe, Lerner took out a fist-sized parcel of rice paper. He unwrapped it, revealing a sticky dark mass of opium. The doctor had obtained it for him at a handsome markup; he used the drug in his practice, and made sure that it was legally bought.

From the tantalus, Lerner lifted a crystal flask of bourbon and two shot glasses. By now Morse had raised his one good eye and was watching as if mesmerized. Lerner prepared two shots of laudanum and offered one to Morse.

After they had both swallowed their medicine, and the mixture was spreading a slow fiery comfort through their veins, Lerner delivered his verdict: "Hereafter, Morse, you will use the drug with me in these rooms, and nowhere else."

"Yes," he mumbled. "Yes, Father."

"I take that as your word of honor," said the old man, noting wryly how odd the word *honor* tasted on his tongue. "If you break it, I will have no mercy on you. Now help me to bed. Tomorrow you'll do only what is most necessary, and otherwise rest."

The bedtime ritual that night was even slower than usual, with Morse wincing—sometimes gasping—with pain, and pausing again and again to recover. Lerner had plenty of time to think, and what he thought about was how, in one way or another, he'd lost everyone who had ever been close to him: Elmira, his and Elmira's children, Papa, Rose, and Royal.

All of them gone. Soon he would be gone too. But it was still within his power to save something from the wreckage, through a man of his blood who would live on after him. *He is, after all, the last of our family and, even if adopted, the only son I shall ever have. But if he continues the way he's going, he will die too, and nobody will be left at all.*

Old people have to decide things quickly, having no time for the long thoughts of youth. He resolved to act tomorrow—summon his lawyer and settle everything while Morse lay resting upstairs in bed. Lerner's old habits of deep suspicion didn't quite leave him, for he also thought: *Better not tell the boy. I know what I might do, if one old man stood between me and a great inheritance.*

He smiled craftily, thinking what a surprise ending he could now give his confession. Then leave it to be read once he was safely gone. Confession might be good for the soul, but if incautiously made public might be death to the body. After all, he reflected, his veins and Morse's held much the same blood.

No one instructed me as to how I should conceal my crime (he began to write next day, after the lawyer had come and gone). *Nor did anyone need to.*

I grasped Royal's hand, dragged his carcass down into the glen, and pressed my pistol into the hand of the dead innkeeper. Then I set out briskly enough, rehearsing my story as I went, and after disarranging my clothing, staggered into Red River Landing, crying out a shocking tale of ambush and sudden death.

All who saw me that day knew that I truly grieved, though they did not know why. General Hobbs, of course, knew what had happened, but my secret was safe with him. Rose (I think) divined the truth, but could do nothing, having no protector but myself, and needing one more than ever, because she was with child.

'Twas almost miraculous, how all the pieces fell into place. The hue and cry over the murder was great, for Royal had been a rising star of the Republican Party, and his death became a hook upon which President Grant could hang new and stringent measures against the Klan. In the months that followed, I traveled to Washington thrice to testify, and made (I may say without false pride) a good job of it: in lengthy testimony on the Hill, I never made a serious error; never was at a loss for words; most important of all, never told the truth.

Based largely upon my testimony, Congress concluded that two loyal Union men had been attacked by Klansmen, one being killed and other barely escaping with his life. The outrage led directly to passage of the Ku Klux Act, which caused so much trouble to General Hobbs and his friends: 'twas under that law he was later arrested for some trifling murder, tried by military commission, and sent to Fort Leavenworth, where he died.

Thereafter I was a marked man amongst his followers, as I was already a pariah to all who hated the Yankee occupation. Yet isolation was familiar to me, and I was not unhappy to be rid of so impulsive and violent a friend. For great changes were in the air, and a cool head was needed to take advantage of them. In 1873 a depression devastated the Grant administration, which was already falling by the weight of its own corruption. Another three years, and the Democrats seized power in Louisiana; Governor Wharton was impeached, and departed public life with a fortune (said to be in the range of two millions) to comfort his old age.

He paid me a handsome price for my land near Red River, and there built the grand and intricate monstrosity of a house he calls Réunion. He sited his mansion at the end of the great oak alley, clearing away the old chimney in the process, and the ruins of Monsieur Felix's house as well, which spoiled his view. 'Twas in this house, in rooms that were perfect symphonies of bad taste, that I courted his daughter Elmira, and won her consent to be my bride.

The marriage was sumptuous. Like the great slave-owners he had always secretly admired, the Governor displayed an instinct for magnificence. As the wedding day approached, he imported from South America hundreds of spiders known for the beauty of their webs and turned them loose in the oaks. When their shining orbs had taken form, with his own hand he cast handfuls of gold dust upon the threads.

Up this astounding aisle, more splendid than any cathedral, 'midst golden glitter and dancing sunlight he led Elmira, clad in ashes-of-roses chenille and watered silk and Brussels lace, to where I waited for her beside the soaring staircase of Réunion. There we were wed, and the parson prayed that our marriage might symbolize an end to the strife which had so long bloodied the State and the Nation.

After kissing my bride, I embraced my new father-in-law with one arm, whilst he hugged me with two. Tears leaked into his whiskers as he saw his family joined forever to what he liked to call, in hushed tones, "the old aristocracy."

Rose's story was less glorious. Eight months after Royal's death, she gave birth to an infant which she freely acknowledged to be his.

I was by then a busy man, between my Washington trips and my courting of Elmira, and was at some difficulty to cover things up. In the end I arranged for Rose to visit Natchez in the character of a widow, accompanied by a discreet woman of my acquaintance. There a hale and noisy male infant passed through the gates of life, and entered this world of sin. The final act of the tragedy came when Rose died of a hemorrhage resulting from a difficult labor. Well, she had always been sickly and frail—not a good candidate to bear a large and lusty man-child!

I was somewhat at a loss what to do with this new and (at first) unwelcome kinsman of mine. I expected to have children with Elmira. Along with the Old South had vanished those easygoing days when a large brood of varicolored youngsters, some slave and some free, some legitimate and some bastards, could all be raised together under one paternal eye. Since then a certain niceness and propriety had come into life, and appearances had to be preserved.

I named the boy Morse, an uncommon name for a black. At the time I knew not why I chose it, though I now believe 'twas a strangled echo of the remorse I felt over his father's death. I hoped that he might be light in hue and featured like an European, which would have made everything easier. But in a few weeks it became plain that—despite a double infusion of white blood, from his mother and his father's father—robust Africa was stamped firmly and forever upon his visage.

I put him out to be suckled by a wet-nurse in the Creole quarter, and this woman solved the problem for me. Recently she had lost an infant and been abandoned by her lover; she longed for a child, and she needed work. I took her into my household as a maid, where she remained until her death, representing herself to Morse as his mother. I believe that this woman, spotting a certain ghostly similarity in our features, decided that Morse must be my bastard, and in time passed on this bit of misinformation to her charge.

Yet he was my kinsman, and discreetly I watched over his raising, as in the past Papa had watched over Royal's. He grew strong and clever, learned to read and write and cipher to the rule of twelve, and in my service was trained to the duties of an upper servant. The walls of my house shielded him from much that was happening to his people in the outside world where, abandoned by the North, they were made into serfs by the South.

All unknowing, I was preparing a caretaker for myself. Ever since I had angered the Klan, a series of events had placed my life in danger: I but narrowly escaped two assassination attempts, and once had my house set on fire (though so incompetently that the blaze was readily extinguished). I hired Pinkertons to protect me, and for a time the attempts ended. But in '93, on busy Canal Street at noonday, an empty four-horse dray came careening around a corner and knocked me to the ground. The vehicle swerved around the next corner, and vanished: 'twas later found abandoned in a weedy lot near the river, the horses unbridled and peacefully cropping grass. The driver was never discovered—or so the police reported.

Thus by a spinal injury I became an invalid at the age of fifty, when otherwise still vigorous and in the prime of life. Believing that my former associates had forgotten nothing and forgiven nothing, I turned increasingly into a recluse, dependent upon Morse, the only caregiver I felt that I could trust. And so—

Unnoticed by Lerner, dusk had come, and with it came Morse, barging through the door with a touch of his old insouciance, despite his stiffness and the plum over his eye, carrying the dinner tray in which the old man felt no interest, and the drug he truly needed.

Lerner hastily put away his manuscript and closed the safe. Toward the

REVELATION & OTHER TALES OF FANTASCIENCE

food he made only a gesture, swallowing a forkful here and there and thrusting the rest away. After he had been settled for the night, Morse sat down beside the bed on a footstool, his head resting against the moss mattress, and they shared the opium.

As usual these days, one dose of laudanum wasn't enough for Lerner. The second put him into a state like the trance of a medium. He saw the specters of the past rising up about him, and whispered, "Look, look there."

"Where?"

"There, in the mirror. Can't you see him? It's Monsieur Felix! Look how his one eye gleams!"

"You're crazy, Father," Morse said, not unkindly.

"He wants me to come with him to his house. It lies halfway to the quarters, and once there I can never leave. Ah Morse, how can I tell him *No*, when I have so often told him *Yes*?"

"Rest, old man," Morse said, "for the past is dead and gone."

"No, no, 'tis a phantom limb that aches more than a real one, for there is no way to touch it, to heal it, to give it ease."

"Sleep," Morse said, and mixed him yet another dose. Lerner drank it off at a gulp, choked, gasped for a moment, then relaxed against his pillows.

Little by little the shadows of the room turned bronze, then brown. For a time the old man seemed still to be conversing with Morse; he heard voices, one of which sounded like his own, and unless mistaken he heard spoken the word *perdu*. But the voices became still; he found himself enjoying a brilliant scene of people waltzing at a masked ball. Then nothing.

Next morning he woke with his head, as usual, filled with ashes. For a time he lay in bed, unable even to reach for the bell. When his mind cleared, he rang as usual, but no Morse appeared. Nor anyone else.

After ringing again and again, Lerner, cursing, stretched out a trembling arm, drew the wheelchair beside the bed and despite a shock of pain, wrestled himself into it. Where the devil was everyone? He trundled to the door of his den and flung it open.

The safe door stood ajar. He rolled into the room and put a trembling hand inside. The manuscript was gone. *Well*, thought Lerner, *he was always a clever fellow.*

The house was utterly silent. Morse must have sent Cleo and the cook away. Lerner spun the chair this way and that. What to do, what to do? The telephone was out of reach, and anyway Morse might be waiting in the hallway. The old man peered back into the bedroom, but with only the one barred window it was a trap without an exit. He couldn't lock himself into the den, for the key to the hall door had vanished years ago—possibly removed by Morse, so that he could enter at will.

And he'd put his life into the hands of this man! Soon he'd be coming to accuse Lerner of murdering his real father. Coming with the razor, but not to shave him.

He turned to his desk, pulled out a handful of ancient bills that stuffed a pigeonhole, pushed aside a panel at the back and touched a hidden spring. A second panel opened into a dark recess. He thrust in his hand and pulled out the Remington. He clamped it muzzle-first in his left armpit, broke it open and checked the load of six brass cartridges. He snapped the weapon shut again. The hammer was stiff, but he cocked it easily with his one hand accustomed to doing the work of two.

He hid the gun under his lap robe and wheeled himself back into the bedroom. Closing the door to his den behind him, he waited for Morse—an old and crippled wolf, but not a toothless one.

Yet his first visitor appeared, not at the door, but in the mirror. Monsieur Felix couldn't bear to miss out on what was about to happen, and suddenly there he stood in the clouded pier glass—one eye gleaming, thin smile widening like an arroyo between the blue chin and the great blade of a nose. Perhaps he was too eager, for Lerner read his mind.

Why, he wondered, *did I ever imagine his vengeance would stop with Royal? Did I not call him swine, connive at his death, supply the weapon that killed him? Did I not write my confession at his command? In an opium dream, did he not cause me to speak the word perdu that let Morse open the safe? Is it not his pleasure now to destroy me and Royal's son at one stroke? For either I'll kill him and perish of my infirmities, or he'll kill me and go to the hangman for murder.*

At that moment the door slammed open and Morse entered, razor flickering in his hand. His face was swollen, his eyes drugged to pinpoints, his smile an arid duplicate of the one in the mirror. He whispered, "I've come to scrape your throat, Uncle."

Lerner pulled the revolver from under the lap robe. Morse halted like a man suddenly transmuted into stone. In the fearsome quiet that followed, Lerner spoke to him for the last time.

"Whatever else I've done in a long and mostly foul existence, Morse, remember how at the very end I saved you from the hangman's noose and gave you a new life for my brother's sake."

Two crashes of thunder. The shards of the mirror were still tinkling on the floor when Lerner slumped in his chair, the pistol slipping from his hand.

The smoke was dense, and through it Monsieur Felix, emerging from the shattered mirror, passed like a shadow seen in fog. He stared at Lerner, absolutely baffled. The vatic power he depended upon, the power that enabled him to plan his murders a decade or more in advance—why had it been blind to this possibility?

J'ai perdu son âme, he thought, almost in despair. *I've lost his soul.*

Then he turned his gaze on Morse. His trademark smile slowly rekindled, as he recalled the deepest secret of the young man's life: how, as a child, he'd entered the nursery in this house, turned Elmira's son over in his crib, and pressed the baby's face into the mattress until he suffocated—all out of fear that the white child would take his own place in Lerner's favor.

Now the poor devil needed help, which Monsieur Felix was always happy to supply.

Gradually Morse recovered from his shock. First he'd forgotten to breathe; then panted like a winded animal, heart thundering. Now his breath evened, his heart slowed to a regular beat. He folded the razor and put it into his trouser pocket, while cool thoughts seemed to rise from some unshaken region of his mind.

I must touch nothing. I must telephone the police. I must report the suicide. His illness and the drug will explain everything. And aren't the police identifying people by their finger-marks these days? Well, his finger-marks are on the pistol's grip.

But there was something else. *The police—suppose they decide to bury the evidence and hang me as they've hung other blacks, for the mere pleasure of it?*

A thought tickled the back of his mind. *There's something in the desk.*

He turned back into the den. Took the razor out again and threw it into the safe, so it wouldn't be found on him. He slammed the iron door, spun around, knocked the pile of ancient bills off the desk and reached his arm to the elbow inside the open hidey-hole. What was he touching?

He pulled out a leather purse with a string closure, opened it and grinned at the cylinder of gold double-eagles it contained. *Why, the old devil,* he thought. *Here's his secret cache, and all the time I thought it was in the safe!*

A few bribes would enable him to handle the police, and that was all he knew or cared about now. The fact that he would soon be rich—that he would have power beyond the imagining of ordinary people to exercise an appetite for cruelty that had grown up in him during a lifetime of stifled rage—all that remained to be discovered.

The Demon stood behind him, smiling, lending him useful thoughts, mentoring him, delighted as always to be the Overseer of human destiny.

Aha, le p'tit diable! whispered Monsieur Felix. *Him I won't lose.*

To a young man raised on the boiled dinners of New England idealism, it all seemed so obvious—to get rid of tyranny, you kill the tyrant. But is it really that simple?

THE ASSASSIN

CONNIE'S LITTLE GYRO WAS CROSSING the Blue Ridge when Andy began to shiver. The city where he'd spent some of the worst times of his life was fast approaching. That was how he thought about Washington—it was advancing on him, not the other way around.

The plane entered the Potomac corridor and the wilderness of red brick and eroded marble inexorably took form. On the right, the grim gray hulk of the Pentagon appeared, surrounded by the white teeth of missile batteries. After the War, Americans had talked of demolishing the Puzzle Palace, yet there it was, now the headquarters for the world government's Security Forces. *It's like the Sphinx*, Andy mused. *The ugliest things always seem to last the longest.*

His companions ignored the view. Connie was reading some sort of printout, while Gomez sprawled across three seats, snoring. Andy wished he could do the same. Instead, like a man reading Braille, he fingered the ridges of scars hidden by his poplin shirt. Astonishing to think that today he was wearing the same uniform as his onetime tormentors. Connie had checked every detail of their getups—their regulation haircuts, clothing, boots, insignia—before they left Tuamotu. Their ID badges displeased her, for they bore the Roman numeral IX. She'd wanted to get them Xs, which would have enabled them to go almost anywhere, but didn't try for fear of provoking an investigation. She, of course, had top clearance and wore it casually, as she wore her gold-washed name tag saying *Griffin* and the stars on her shoulder-straps.

The gyro banked and descended. The roof of the military terminal rose to meet them, displaying in giant white letters the slogan of the Security Forces, *To Serve All Humanity*. Andy wore the same words on a patch sewn to his right sleeve, and he remembered guards at the penal colony where he'd served his time who had it tattooed on their biceps, along with *Mother* and *Born to Die*.

With a small thump the gyro settled on the landing pad, the autopilot shut down, and Connie rose to her feet, stretching like a cat. Her skin had a yellowish tinge that sometimes made him wonder if she might be ill, yet her dark eyes glowed with all the old familiar fire. The waiting was over, the time for action close at hand. "Here we are, guys," she said. "Don't forget your weapons."

Better not, he thought wryly, considering that their mission was to kill the world's most powerful man—in Andy's case, to kill him for the second time.

Improbably, in view of what he had since become, Andrew Walden Emerson III had been a quiet boy, raised by his grandmother after his parents were killed when an errant missile landed on—of all unlikely targets—Great Barrington, Vermont.

In her quiet, ladylike home he'd become an obsessive reader, summoning books on his Omnipad from every surviving library. By the time Security reprogrammed the servers to filter out all writings on the Index of Subversive Literature, he'd already read such dangerous works as *A Tale of Two Cities* and *Les Miserables*, storing away old-fashioned rhetoric and quaint notions of honor and self-sacrifice he could hardly have learned from the world around him. *It is a far, far better thing that I do, than I have ever done*, young Andy liked to whisper to himself as he fell asleep. Yes!

But instead of going to the guillotine like Dickens's hero, he grew up and went to college. He decided to be a doctor, won a scholarship to New Yale, entered the pre-med program, and thought he'd found his calling. He was working hard, his fingers stained with chemicals from the labs, his life seemingly laid out before him, when he met an older woman—thirty at least—a blonde firebrand who called herself (revealingly) by the code name Faith.

He'd never known anyone like her, and went eagerly when she invited him to a meeting of a group she headed, Action for Anarchy. The members all had code names, which looking back was pretty silly, because the campus was such a tight community that they all knew each other's real names, too. The guys were Friedberger, Villeneuve, Swanson, Mbeki, and Nguyen, but at meetings they had to be called Karl, Max, Oliver, Mandela, and Minh. When Andy joined, he was assigned the name Thoreau, a man he resembled in little except a regional inability to pronounce the letter *r*.

Faith taught her boys that the politics of bygone times, like the faux-medieval towers of Old Yale, had been ground into rubble by the War. (They all capitalized the word, even in their thoughts, because to them it was the only war that mattered.) Under a dictatorship, she declared, death was the only way to get rid of a bad ruler, and that was why all politics had become the politics of violence. The first time she gave Andy this revelation they were in bed, and despite the place and the mood and the moment he retained enough New England skepticism to protest that he didn't really think people could live without any government at all.

Faith told him not to be so literal-minded. "We're not into fantasy," she said. "We want to tear down the monster the War created and see what emerges, once people are free." Then she became again a passionate and demanding lover.

Such horizontal lectures made her the inspiration of the young men of the AFA. She slept with each in turn, partly for the sex (good sex, they all agreed, was in itself an act of rebellion) but mainly to inspire them with her burning vision of a whole *planet*, for God's sake, set free by the death of World President Mahmud Alonzo Sol. When the War ended, exhausted humanity at last had formed a universal government with teeth, including nuclear teeth. Sol won the presidency by democratic means—a perfectly deracinated man, suave, eloquent, full of generous thoughts, not identifiable with any race or nation or creed. Then he used the newly formed international army (called the Security Forces to make it sound less threatening) to seize dictatorial power.

"It's like Caesar posing as the friend of the people, then overthrowing the Roman Republic," Faith declared. "It's like Napoleon coming on as the defender of the French Revolution, then making himself emperor. It's like Hitler getting power legally, then destroying free government in Germany. It's been tyranny's formula for 2,200 years!"

Exciting talk. The meetings of the AFA were noisy, fueled partly by cheap wine, partly by testosterone, but mainly by her fiery words. Her boys spread the message in every possible way, and yet they knew—for she had taught them—that words alone could never change history. Lanky, bearded Karl, a.k.a. Friedberger, liked to quote Goethe's line *am Anfang war die Tat*, in the beginning was the Deed. But it was Thoreau, a.k.a. Andy, and not his garrulous friends who finally volunteered to do what they'd all been talking about. That was when Faith became his alone.

Also when his life changed forever. He left the semiplast classrooms of New Yale, the crowded dorms, the smelly labs, the shoddy wards of not-yet-completely-rebuilt New Haven General Hospital, where he'd worked as an aide to gain practical experience. He really hated to go, and in cool moments wondered just why he'd volunteered to kill the President—how much was idealism, how much sex, and how much a yearning for action that had grown up inside him during his excessively quiet, bookish boyhood.

He told himself, *It is a far, far better thing that I do, than I have ever done*, but maybe didn't quite believe it, for the day he left Yale a blinding migraine came upon him, forcing him to hole up in a darkened room while Faith put compresses soaked in cold tea on his forehead. After twenty-four agonizing hours the pain faded, and he walked blinking into the sunlight of a summer day. He felt nervous as a young boxer before his first bout, but determined to fulfill the promise he'd made to her, to himself, and to the enigmatic force called Destiny that appeared to be urging him on.

In the Maine woods north of Bangor he practiced marksmanship, making the resinous green glades echo with shots from an impact rifle Faith had obtained on the black market. Every day they checked a website that reported the activities of President Sol. They thought they'd have to go abroad to catch him, and were debating how to obtain passports when his visit to Washington was announced.

That made everything simple. They plugged Faith's little electro in overnight to build up the charge, and next morning headed south. The old capital on the Potomac had survived the War under an umbrella of geosynchronous interceptor satellites that diverted incoming missiles onto Pennsylvania cornfields and the Virginia hunt country. Amish farmers and the horsey set—such as were left—didn't think much of the arrangement, but Washington was saved, alone of the cities in the onetime Eastern Megalopolis. Andy's first sight of it was a confused impression of brick and marble, tall quiet elms and broad acres of greensward badly in need of a mowing, for the War had left the American government too impoverished even to cut its own grass on a regular basis.

Faith knew the city well and led Andy via mysterious ways—a closed Metro station, abandoned service tunnels, a collapsed wall opening into a nineteenth-century cellar—until they reached a dusty cast-iron staircase corkscrewing up inside the two-centuries-old Executive Office Building. At the top lay a small loft whose single dirty window gave a slanted view of the White House lawn and the platform—still noisily under construction—where Mahmud Alonzo Sol was to address his American subjects the following day.

Andy was astounded at Faith's professionalism, her uncanny ability to find the aerie, then to slip him and the illegal rifle into it through a gauntlet of electronic sensors and armed guards. How, he asked, did she manage her miracles? "Better," she smiled, "that you don't know," and he accepted that, for he was about to put his life on the line, and had no time to think of anything else.

—.—

Today an older, wiser, weightier, and infinitely more cynical Andy exited a black limo at the Pentagon, and with Gomez followed Connie past sensors that blinked at their IDs and banks of lasers that withheld their fire.

The trio entered a concourse with milling uniformed crowds and shops selling goods not available to the general public. *To Serve All Humanity* was everywhere, in every language of the earth, as inescapable as Koranic verses in a mosque—chiseled into stone, cast into steel security screens, woven into carpets, stitched into uniform patches like their own. Connie ignored a rank of golf carts offering rides in plaintive small robotic voices—"E Ring, sir or madam, I will take you to any place on E Ring"—and led the way down kilometers of musty corridors, past cubbyhole offices where uniformed clerks bent over flickering monitors, and up ramps eroded by a century and a half of shuffling feet.

Soon he was hopelessly lost. Despite its logical form of five concentric rings and transecting diagonals, the Pentagon was hell to navigate. Here a wall had been erected for no visible reason, while over there a battery of lasers stood ready to fry anyone whose ID didn't give him right of passage. Everywhere, posted against the walls like caryatids, stood guards in the red berets of the *Spetsnaz*—Security's own security force—thick young men and hard-eyed women wearing X badges and carrying weighty impact pistols.

Connie threaded the maze without hesitation. Locked doors were no problem, for her palm pressed against glowing sensor pads opened them all. Twice she made Andy try the same trick, for she'd entered his print into the system, and was pleased that the computer remembered it. Everyone was so indifferent to their passage that he began to feel like a ghost moving unobserved among the living. Or maybe the other way around. On Tuamotu he'd become used to ghosts, which the villagers saw everywhere and accepted as a part of life, and he began to wonder if the crowds were the ghosts of the men and women for whom the Pentagon had originally been built—fighters in a war against genuine evil that now seemed as remote and fabulous as the Crusades. Then Connie murmured, "Here we are," and all his fancies vanished.

They halted in a corridor outside a conference room. Twenty or so guards were lounging around—not *Spetsnaz*, just ordinary enlisted people with IX tags—peons assigned as personal aides to serve, protect, and grovel to a general officer, the same role that Andy and Gomez were enacting. All wore empty holsters and Andy learned why, when a sergeant wearing a red beret gave him and Gomez each a chit and removed their guns for safekeeping. "God, they're so *paranoid*," Connie muttered, reminding him of the old saw that paranoid people sometimes have real enemies.

The double doors to the conference room stood open and the interior was banal, with a speaker's dais and lectern and metal chairs that were clamped to the floor so they couldn't be used as weapons. Only Xs could enter, and even they had to pass through still more sensors able to detect the different kinds of plastic used in bombs, nonmetal weapons, and exploding bullets. Connie tucked an earbud under her short, dark regulation hair to catch the simultaneous translation, and walked past the gadgets without a glance to join the staff members already seated inside.

Gomez and Andy lingered, surrounded by a hum of gossip. The enlisted people all used the f-word as noun, pronoun, adjective, adverb, preposition, conjunction, and interjection, sometimes with comic results. "I told that effin' effer, eff you, Jack, that's what I effin' told him," said a guy, and his pal replied, "Effin' A."

Then a tall, pale, blunt-featured man wearing multiple stars entered the conference room from a door outside Andy's range of vision, mounted the dais, and took his place at the lectern. Instantly the hallway quieted down, for the Chief of Security had appeared. The general officers inside applauded politely, and at the same time the doors—steel, Andy noted, and thick at that—closed slowly, like vault doors controlled by a timer. But before they clicked shut, he spotted an iridescent shimmer in the tall man's uniform, as if his gray tunic were woven not of cloth but of oily metal wires.

"We have our work cut out for us," he told Gomez in the nearly imperceptible whisper he'd mastered while in prison. He realized now that this plot might turn into a fiasco as total as the last one.

For a year or more after it happened, Andy had been able to remember his attack on Mahmud Alonzo Sol only in bad dreams.

Then, little by little, during his life with Esperanza on Tuamotu, he'd become able to remember it, though not with pleasure. Sometimes he lay half the night in her arms, shaking with sobs, while the baby Corazon slept peacefully in the crib he'd made her. Now he lived it again, the flashback signaled by an olfactory hallucination, the dry reek of the old mouse droppings that had littered the floor of the loft.

He could almost hear Faith pleading to stay with him and share his fate, and his own voice telling her no. She'd confessed to being pregnant with his child, so how could he allow her to run such a terrible risk? She dropped her clothes on the filthy floor and approached him, holding her little breasts in her hands like pomegranates on a plate. He pressed her back against the wall, all thought swept away by the rising of his own hot seed, and they coupled a last time, his hands holding her under the butt, her legs wrapped around his waist. She uttered a little mewling cry, and when he released her, wept like an abandoned child.

She dressed and left him, and the endless night began. While sunset faded slowly from the window, he sat with his back against the door, the impact rifle lying across his lap, the greasy magazine inserted and the first round already chambered. He kept checking his watch, but it appeared to have stopped, and after a while he gave up in sheer frustration. Instead, he closed his eyes and began writing the history of the assassination, like a scholar of the future looking back.

Boldly Thoreau struck the blow, and the President fell dead. Beginning at the White House and spreading outward like ripples on a pond, chaos enveloped the city. The brave assassin discarded his weapon and silently retraced his path down the spiral stair to the cellar. He climbed over the collapsed wall and entered the Metro tunnel, feeling his way in the darkness down the long-disused tracks, guiding himself by the cool and rusty third rail. He reached a station that had become a dormitory for the homeless, edged silently through the crowd of shadowy, ill-smelling forms, climbed a frozen escalator, and reentered the chaotic world above.

Dodging through alternations of flaring searchlights and pitchy shadows, he worked his way down alleys, hastened across streets and squares, and at last escaped from the city. For a week he hiked the open countryside, moving at night, pausing only to steal food from a kitchen or take a day's rest in an abandoned barn. He crossed parts of four states, all the way back to New Haven where his friends greeted him with cheers, tears, and embraces. Hidden in a safe house, he assisted Faith at the birth of their son (daughter?), and with her watched the child grow up, an inheritor of the new birth of freedom that her vision and his courage had brought to the whole world!

Maybe he fell asleep and dreamed part of this fantasy. Anyway, he awakened suddenly, propped in an awkward position with his neck wry and all his muscles stiff. When he stood up and tried doing deep knee bends, the cramps that shot through his legs almost made him cry out. That terrified him, for muffled sounds began to echo in the old building and he wondered if guards might be giving it a final search. But the sounds died away, silence returned, and he relaxed and touched his watch. After all, it *was* running, just very, very slowly. The green display said 0001—one minute past midnight—and he still had half the darkness to endure.

Dozing, stretching, shivering—however the building was heated, none of the warmth reached the loft—he endured hours that had lost all semblance of time, had become downpayments on a bad eternity. Shortly before dawn he had to take a crap, really *had* to, and the loft became more fragrant than ever. By the time faint daylight returned to the window and random noises outside the building told of a crowd gathering, Andy wanted to kill Mahmud Alonzo Sol, not so much for enslaving humanity as for making a boy gently raised in pristine Vermont spend the worst and longest night of his life in a closet that stank of rodent shit and his own.

Finally a wave of cheers announced the President's arrival. Carefully avoiding the deposit he'd made on the floor, Andy stretched out on his belly with his face to the window and used one sleeve to clean a spyhole in the dirty glass. Far below, a few faded-looking American dignitaries were taking their places on the first row of seats facing the speaker's platform. As a recording played the Grand March from Aida, the nation's honored guest appeared, a large smiling man with olive skin and glistening black hair, who moved confidently from the rear of the speaker's platform to the front.

Andy flexed his stiff fingers and used the rifle barrel to knock out a window pane. The breaking of the glass sounded very loud, but he never heard the tinkle that followed, because the shards had such a long way to fall. He wrapped the rifle's sling around his left wrist, put his right eye to the scope, tapped the aiming stud to enlarge the image, and centered the red dot of the laser on the third button of the President's dark double-breasted suit. He touched the firing stud, and the stock thumped the hollow of his shoulder in a muffled drumroll until the clip was empty.

And then—exactly *then*—the whole thing turned to farce. Andy's aim was good, a big black electronic module behind the President disintegrated into bits and pieces. *But that was all.* The speech went on, as if the President didn't choose to dignify with his notice anything as trivial as sixteen exploding bullets. Andy was still gaping when thunder resounded outside the loft, only it wasn't thunder but steel-toed combat boots echoing on the wooden floors. The door burst in and men with big hands dragged him out like dogs pulling a badger from its hole.

Andy's interrogation took place in the old prison on Hoover Square, in a fetid vault of stained concrete. The big guys stripped him and took him on in relays, like tag teams at a wrestling match. When beating and kicking failed to make him name names, they shoved a cold metal electrode into his anus and hit him with jolt after jolt. Every time they did he passed out, and the EMT required by regulations to be present at such sessions revived him to be jolted again. In time he broke, confessed everything, betrayed everybody—gave real names, Friedberger, Villeneuve, Swanson, Mbeki, and Nguyen—all except Faith, whose real name he also knew, yet managed to sew up in a place his tormentors couldn't reach, perhaps in a chamber of his heart.

For weeks afterward he lay in a crowded ward in the prison dispensary, shackled by one ankle to the frame of a steel cot. The nights were the worst, for then every man lay alone amid the wreckage of his life. During the day the chatter of the others and the restless jingling of their chains distracted him, while a wall monitor brayed continuous propaganda interspersed with martial music and weather reports.

One day a talking head announced a rare piece of reality TV—the confession of the would-be presidential assassin, Andrew Walden Emerson III. His black eyes had pretty well gone down by then, so he was able to watch as well as listen when Virtual Andy appeared in three glorious dimensions—four, if you counted time. The simulacrum looked pale but in good health, its boyish face perfect in every detail, right down to an enlarged pore in its nasal cartilage left by a zit Andy had popped at the age of fourteen. Speaking in tones that any voice-analysis software would have recognized as his, the image told its story and begged for death as the only proper punishment for its crime.

Meanwhile, Real Andy—the one with the sore bones, the scarred rectum, the broken nose, two missing molars, and skin a Jackson Pollock of varicolored bruises—that Andy started cursing as loud as he could with his lower jaw held together by screws and wires. A memory from his days at New Yale had come back to him, an after-midnight bull session with other science students, their tongues liberated by cheap wine and the fumes of *Cannabis sativa*. Some physics wannabe was boring him with news of a new system for projecting 3-D images in real space, and complaining bitterly because the technique ("*really* interesting, you know, Emerson") hadn't been licensed for production. Instead, Security had hauled the inventor off to a Preventive Detention Center to continue work under official supervision.

Andy knew then that he'd sacrificed his friends, his freedom, his youth, and his future to shoot a conglomeration of pixels. And now, standing beside Gomez in the Pentagon hallway, he felt the old humiliation and despair return, because that brief chromatic shimmer in the tall man's uniform had told him that *his target wasn't real this time, either.*

He whispered the news to Gomez. But that dark scarred man—older than Andy by ten years and even more experienced in disaster—only shrugged.

Something would turn up. Gomez had learned that long ago, growing up in the dusty streets of Laredo where he studied the secrets of crime and survival. He remembered a thousand fights, a hundred burglaries, and a dozen stays in jail. He'd lived like a stray dog, every man's hand against him, yet something had always saved him from death. Even when a weary judiciary sentenced him to Tuamotu Penal Colony for life as a habitual criminal, Destiny had given him the means to survive. Even to triumph.

By then he was a professional prisoner, what one of his judges had called "a perfectly institutionalized man." He knew the ropes and quickly became a snitch, alerting the prison cadre to fights and rapes and riots before they occurred, in return for food and favor. He wasn't surprised when his contact, a guard whose unique aura had won him the nickname Stink, pulled him out of the chow line one day and took him to a storeroom, ostensibly to clean it but really to receive a new assignment.

Stink told Gomez that a guy called Emerson had tried to shoot President Sol, had been condemned to death but later reprieved and his sentence commuted to life at hard labor. That hadn't ended the President's surprising clemency—an order had come down from HQ instructing the warden to make sure that Emerson survived in prison.

"Easy to say," Stink shrugged, and Gomez nodded.

They both knew the score. To the criminals, Emerson would be fresh meat. To the politicals, he'd be the fool whose ill-considered attempt on Sol's life had gotten them arrested during the worldwide roundup of subversives that followed. Because of the roundup the prison was jam-packed, with endless opportunities for somebody to plant a shank unseen. The crowding forced two men to share every futon, and Stink instructed Gomez to become Emerson's bunkmate, watch over him, and preserve him from harm.

"You can screw him if you want to," he added generously. "Just don't hurt him none."

At first glance Gomez saw that he could do as he pleased with Andy. The guy was small, skinny, badly battered, and so new to the system that he still wore a bandage on the back of his neck where his ID chip had been implanted. To judge from his collection of half-healed scars, he must be pretty dumb, too—probably tried to be a goddamn hero when they were using muscle on him, instead of saying whatever they wanted to hear at the beginning, and saving himself grief.

Gomez had no objection to prison-style sex when nothing better was available, yet didn't do what he could so easily have done. He had an abstract hatred of big shots, all big shots everywhere, and looked with something like awe at this skinny kid who had tried to kill the biggest shot of them all. So instead of raping Andy, he adopted him—called him Li'l Brudda, stuck close by his side, and warned anybody trying to mess with him, "Bet I pull your effin' heart out and effin' feed it to you."

Andy was surprised and grateful—becoming some guy's punk was the only humiliation life had so far denied him, so he'd rather expected it to happen—and he worked hard to learn the lessons Gomez taught him. They weren't easy to master. Gomez told him to watch out for a guard the cons called Sneak, but Andy was used to solitary musing and had to learn the hard way how the man got his name. One day when he was with a gang working in the cornfield, instead of pretending to hoe weeds like the others, he sat on the ground in a posture resembling Rodin's *Thinker*, brooding about the mysteries of life and fate.

That was when Sneak materialized out of the tall green stalks and used a bamboo cane he carried like a swagger stick to beat him bloody. The cons wore only straw hats, khaki shorts, and flip-flops cut from old tires, so he had a lot of skin to work on, and made the most of it. Andy was sore for a month, sorer because he'd burned in the tropical sun and already resembled a medium-rare steak when Sneak attacked him.

But he'd learned the hard way to stay alert every waking moment. Other useful lessons followed. Keeping the cons half-starved was the cadre's simplest and cheapest method of maintaining control, but Gomez taught him how to steal handfuls of food without getting caught when he was on kitchen police. Working in the rice fields gave him a condition called paddy foot that made him feel as if he'd been walking all day on hot coals instead of cool slimy mud. But Gomez rubbed his soles with an antibiotic ointment he'd scrounged from a trusty who worked in the dispensary, the skin healed, and in time Andy's feet toughened and became as insensitive as a pair of boots.

The rest of his adaptation to prison happened just because it happened. His sunburn peeled and healed, and all the skin not covered by his shorts turned to a kind of leather resembling cordovan, save for the white scars memorializing his past. They never changed color, as if the story of his life were written on him in cuneiform, like a stele. He often told Gomez that he hated prison and wanted to die, but he only shrugged. Andy was a survivor—Gomez recognized the breed, being one himself—who just couldn't release his grip on life, even if he wanted to.

By the end of his hard first year, Li'l Brudda had turned from a college boy into a creature of bone, sinew, and cordlike muscles, a sort of hairless two-legged coyote, wary and silent and almost unkillable. His gray eyes gazed out of his sun-darkened face as if through a mask, and when he needed to convey a message he did it with lips unmoving, like a ventriloquist. He began fighting his own battles, winning some and losing others, but gaining respect in a world where respect was everything.

Gomez felt pride at the transformation. His own life had been mostly cruel and selfish, and he felt an unfamiliar glow because for once he'd done what was right, helped a dumb kid survive until he was ready to get along on his own. Improbably, the Yalie and the Latino burglar bonded and became brothers—the only kind that matter, those who stand together as allies against fate. And so they remained.

One day Stink took Gomez aside and gave him a new and unbelievable order—so unbelievable that he made the guard repeat it twice, to make sure he'd heard it right. Yet it confirmed his feeling that there was something uncanny about Andy, something exceptional, *raro, extraordinario*.

For the time being he said nothing, because a secret known to two people is a secret no longer. When Stink passed over several cons with more seniority to select them for a gang working outside the wire, he merely remarked *bueno, bueno*, that meant they were now trusties and would get a little more food. About that he was right, for next day at the predawn shape-up they received a breakfast of beans with shreds of real pork in it. Andy and the others ate like dogs, eyeing each other with suspicion, swallowing quickly and licking their plastic bowls clean. Then they fell into line and marched to the camp's Sea Gate, flip-flops crunching on ruler-straight streets of red gravel that other cons had pounded from lava.

On the way they passed rolls of razor wire threaded with sensors and a gleaming catapult with a drone whose missile, everyone knew, homed in on the ID chips in their necks. They crossed a three-meter death zone where the earth had been plowed and raked to show footprints, and at last reached the electrified perimeter fence. Military lasers craned down at them from ten-meter watchtowers as they passed one by one through a narrow postern. Sneak counted them out, his clipboard beeping when he touched it; he was chewing something and his bluish lower jaw moved slowly, like a ruminant's.

Then, wonder of wonders, Andy was outside the wire, and gaping at the amazing fact that the world was *still there*. Beyond a white line of foam at the coral reef, the Pacific glimmered bluely, the same ocean that touched America, Asia, the world. The air blew fresh and salty, and he was inhaling it in gulps when Gomez spotted Sneak sidling up, poked him in the ribs, and saved him from another caning.

They set about the day's work, unloading supplies from a freighter at the dock, cleaning the warden's house and the barracks in the cadre's compound, sweeping the blinding white concrete of the gyro landing pad and hosing it down with seawater. They ate lunch on the quay and at sundown shuffled back to camp—stick figures, all burned mahogany except the Africans, who were burned ebony. In the latrine they showered in seawater, wearing their shorts to wash them, too. Finally they marched damply to the mess hall where they ate standing up, scooping dollops of brown rice and boiled cabbage into their mouths in handfuls.

Back in the barracks, Andy collapsed on the futon, too weary to gamble or quarrel or gossip or anything. But when the lights dimmed, Gomez pulled their thin cotton blanket over their heads and began to whisper. In the confined space Andy wondered why after all these years Gomez smelled peppery, as if all the chilis he'd ever eaten were still working their way out through his pores. It took him a while to realize what his bunkmate was telling him—they were going to escape. Remembering the wire, the sensors, the death zone, the drone, he wondered what the joke was supposed to be about, and in his minimal Spanish replied, "*Absolutamente loco.*" He turned his back and in ten seconds or less began to snore.

Meanwhile Gomez meditated. He'd rejected his first idea of escaping via the Sea Gate, even though the dense jungle lay down the beach only a hundred meters from the dock. But they'd have to swim, and the goddamn sharks nosed up close, hoping for a handout of mess-hall garbage, or maybe for an edible con. *It's the Mountain Gate* then, he thought, and fell asleep with a crescent of white showing beneath each eyelid, for even in dreamland Gomez never felt safe with both eyes completely closed.

A few days later, he and Andy were once more assigned to work outside the wire. On the camp's landside, jungled slopes rose to the heights of Mount Tuamotu, the extinct volcano that long ago had created the island. The peak above the treeline wore a small, neat cap of snow, and Andy gave a dry sob at the sight, for it reminded him of other snow-capped mountains near his lost home and vanished youth. Today's job was to clear a thirty-meter field of fire between the perimeter fence and the jungle. The gang received weed cutters—archaic buzzing devices with little hydro engines and spinning lengths of tough plastic—and moved west across the narrow neck of land that connected the prison to the body of the island. Then back east, toward a black-sand beach where the sea growled at boulders of broken lava.

There a con working in a patch of weeds suddenly screamed and vanished to his waist. Gomez grabbed the man under the armpits and Andy helped wrestle him out of a fumarole—once a vent for an ancient lava tube, but now invaded by the ocean and filled with its distant surge and murmur. Andy was staring into it when a sudden wasplike sting set him doing the dance the cons called the Bamboo Two-Step.

"Wake up, scum!" Sneak shouted, and swaggered away, a thick bandy-legged man, making his cane whistle through the air.

That night Andy didn't fall asleep as quickly as before, because of the still-burning line across his calves. Gomez was wakeful, too, but for a different reason—he had a message to deliver. After lights-out he turned on his side, again pulled the blanket over their heads, and whispered that Andy should prepare himself, for their escape would have to come soon. Andy replied concisely, "*Merda*," and after a few more curses, this time in English, grumbled his way into slumber. Gomez lay awake for almost another hour, watching everything come together in his mind. After all, it was merely a question of the weather, and in the tropics the weather is nothing if not predictable. *Bueno*, he thought, *está bien*, and went to sleep as usual with half-closed eyes.

Tuamotu had two seasons, wet and dry. The wet was beginning, and the weeds outside the Mountain Gate grew a lusty thirty centimeters a day. So a week later, another party set out to cut them—ten cons to do the work, with Sneak and Stink to supervise. The guards stood in the shade at the edge of the jungle, watching them labor in the sun, and the lasers on the watchtowers turned back and forth, guided by biosensors, like spectators at a very slow tennis match. Andy went rhythmically about his task, mesmerized by the heat, the roar of the little engines, the steamy odor of fresh-cut greenstuff. He felt like a Whirling Dervish at his dance, for once totally mindless and at one with the universe.

Then during lunch break the intense yellow sunlight abruptly faded. Gomez stopped shoveling kidney beans into his mouth, nudged him, and nodded to the west, where a Himalayan sky—mountainous purple clouds, peaks of shining white—had silently taken form. A cool damp gust whipped by, driving a locust swarm of cuttings before it. Andy shivered, met Gomez's gaze, and shivered again for a different reason. He knew that they were about to run, lasers or no lasers, drone or no drone, and all he could think of was the old New England motto *Live Free or Die*.

Sneak shouted, "Okay, scum, fall in!" and just then the squall arrived. First came a barrage of fat droplets, and then a gray wall of rain bellying out like the spinnaker of a racing yacht off Nantucket, only thousands of meters high. In an instant, guards and cons alike turned from men to shadow-puppets. The world darkened, the noise of the storm rose to a drumroll, and when a violet-white flash of lightning split the sky, distracting the lasers, Gomez clamped a big hard hand on Andy's upper arm and yanked him head-long into the jungle.

After three steps, Tuamotu Penal Colony and everyone in it ceased to exist. The tangle blinded them, vines clutched at their legs, branches lashed them as they ran, and orchid-wrapped boles rushed at them like tacklers on a gridiron. They were both gasping for air when Gomez called a halt in a clearing, and they slumped side by side on a log cushioned with red fungi and emerald moss.

Here the rain beat down with buckshot force. A siren wailed distantly, and Andy blinked at the rags of gray sky beyond the threshing leaves, awaiting the drone, the missile, and death. Gomez had picked up a papaya downed by the storm and begun to eat, when something like a silvery fish flashed overhead. An eternal moment passed and the missile exploded in the distance with the deep, expansive note of a bass drum.

It missed us, thought Andy, and turned with a smile of incredulous joy. Gomez handed him a chunk of the sweet mealy fruit, spat out a barrage of round black seeds, gave a gap-toothed grin, patted him on the back, and finally told him the whole secret.

"Dat guy you shot at, Sol? He don't want you dead. Dis escape, it's wired, it's fixed. Stink set it up. All we hadda do was make it look good. Now dey gonna say da drone got us, and we gonna go in da records as dead. So how it feels, hah? What's it like to be alive and dead at the same time?"

He threw back his head and laughed, gulped a mouthful of cold rain and let it wash the pulp from the gaps between his teeth and go sluicing down his throat.

Here in the Pentagon corridor, recalling that sweetest of moments, Gomez smiled wolfishly. He'd never forget Andy's expression, as his lower jaw fell halfway to his chest. *Muy dulce,* Gomez thought, *muy dulce.* After all, Li'l Brudda wasn't the only one who was full of surprises.

Andy couldn't imagine what in *hell* he had to grin about. Personally, he felt merely ridiculous, an assassin without a weapon and nobody to shoot if he had one. When white-jacketed stewards set up a coffee machine, he nodded at Gomez and they joined the line for simple lack of anything better to do. They filled Styrofoam cups and strolled down the corridor, sipping and looking for anything that might give a hint of how to proceed. Pentagon décor didn't help—blank walls, a metal trapdoor covering a trash chute, *To Serve All Humanity* here and there and everywhere. Gomez opened the trapdoor, listened for a moment to the distant roar of an incinerator, and shrugged.

They moved on, turned an obtuse angle, and halted. The connecting corridor was blocked by the usual bank of sensors and lasers, but—two heartbeats suddenly quickened—*this* barrier bore a sign saying X.

Behind the gadgetry stood a massive, red-bereted guy with a concrete jaw and either a head too small for his neck, or a neck too wide for his head. His badge also said X, and an impact pistol filled his holster. Beyond the *Spetsnaz* the corridor stretched away between blank mahogany-paneled walls, like a study in perspective. Andy was eyeing the scene, while trying not to eye it too obviously, when a general officer brushed past him. Ignoring the enlisted men as if they were furniture, he passed between the lasers, stepped to a paneled wall, and pressed his palm against a sensor pad set in a recess. A concealed door opened, he walked through like an actor going backstage, and the door closed and vanished into the woodwork.

Huh, thought Andy. He suddenly realized the importance of where they were—A Ring, where the brass worked—and the significance of the paneling. To rate mahogany in the Pentagon, you had to, well, *rate*. There were more invisible doors here, and behind one of them worked somebody important.

A glance passed between him and Gomez. This was something they needed to check out. Andy was wondering exactly how to manage it when he became aware that Gomez had left him, returned to the coffeemaker, and was filling the biggest available cup, a half-liter monster. He returned holding it with both hands, raised it to the *Spetsnaz*, and said, "Figgered you might need it, Brudda."

The guard managed a smile, or at any rate a slight elongation of the lips, reached past the lasers, and took the cup. "Effin' A," he said, adding with an effort, "Thanks."

Contact established, Gomez asked, "Where dey keep da shithouse at, round here? I gotta go."

"Thataway," said the guard, pointing, and returned to his post, noisily gulping coffee.

Inside the enlisted men's head, Gomez first took a wad of toilet paper, wet it in a basin, and glued it over the lens of a security camera on the wall. "Prob'ly," he muttered, "all dis brass aroun', nobody be watchin' da peons piss. But who knows?"

He took Andy into a stall, flushed the john repeatedly, and under cover of the little Niagara explained his plan. In any security system, said Gomez, the weak point was the human. In his days as a burglar, he'd seen big shots pile a fortune in gadgets onto a warehouse, then hire a minimum-wage *cretino* to

355

watch the monitors. Maybe the plan he'd formed wouldn't work, but at least it was simple and wouldn't hurt anything if it failed. "We can't get da bugga dis time, we get 'im da next," he promised, and sent Andy out of the stall while he lingered inside.

During the next forty minutes, Andy bellied up to a urinal at least six times when other enlisted men—always the wrong ones—visited the head. Fortunately, the Chief of Security must have been verbose, for at last the guy with the red beret ran in, gasping, "Gimme room, I'm about to bust."

He'd hardly opened his fly when Gomez stepped out of the stall and rabbit-punched him with a sound like a football being kicked. The guard's forehead whacked the wall and he rebounded, fell on his back, and lay there imitating a whale.

His beret had fallen off, so Andy scooped it up before helping Gomez drag him into a stall. They propped him on the commode and Gomez pulled his pants down, while Andy took his pistol and ID, both of which he donned along with the beret. He noticed that their victim was wearing an earbud, so he took that too. Finally, he pressed a thumb against the guard's columnar neck and felt the carotid artery throbbing deep inside. *Probably a concussion*, he thought. But the guy had a hard, thick skull—he'd live.

They left the stall, closing the door behind them. From the outside, two large feet in combat boots were visible, trousers bunched around the ankles—not likely anyone would barge in *there*.

"Good luck, L'il Brudda," said Gomez when they were back at the barrier. "You find 'im, give 'im one for me."

"I will," said Andy.

He took a deep breath, put up one hand as if to adjust the beret, and with face momentarily obscured, silently said good-bye to Esperanza, to Gomez, to everybody he knew and loved. Like a suicide stepping from a high ledge into midair with no hope of ever going back, he walked between the lasers.

Gomez, too, felt a painful tug at his heart, *atormentado por la pena*, as he watched Andy press his hand to the sensor pad in the paneled wall and pass through the hidden door.

Gomez's home was gone, the first real one he'd ever had. His woman was gone. And now Li'l Brudda was gone, too, and might not come back. Life was hard, Gomez had always known that, and the demands of honor and vengeance were harder, yet had to be obeyed, for without honor a man was nothing. How many had he killed because of some insult to his honor? And now he could only wait helplessly and curse the cold witch Destiny for granting him happiness, then snatching it away again.

The good part of both their lives had begun on the slopes of Mount Tuamotu, at the moment when the missile detonated. For days afterward they trekked through the jungle. They climbed into open woods swept by chilly breezes off the snowcap, then descended into the familiar green tangle on the other side. Fallen fruit sustained them, flights of noisy green parakeets kept them company, birdlets peeped from the leaves and spoke to them in tiny voices. Wild pigs were enjoying the feast the storm had brought down, and boars with orange tusks and sows with broods of piglets gave them warning glances from small red eyes, but kept on eating.

On the third morning, Gomez stopped and sniffed the air, smelling woodsmoke. Half a kilometer farther, and they emerged into a clearing with a village where dark-skinned people turned to stare at them. He and Andy did not yet know that the place was called Hilo, or that two of the women in the little crowd that soon gathered to view the newcomers were Esperanza Aquiño and her confidante and adopted aunt, one-eyed Susan Kapingama-rangi.

Susan was the most accomplished gossip in the village, and later, when Gomez settled down with her, she told him everything about everybody, whether he wanted to know it or not. So he learned that a shark had killed Esperanza's husband, and that she had lived the last year with only her infant daughter Corazon for company. She'd spent a lot of time saying No to bachelors who were trying to nudge her into choosing a new mate and starting her life over. But she wanted something new, something—well, she didn't know exactly what. Maybe a man who wasn't totally *Hilo*.

She told Susan that she felt like a spider on a twig, letting threads of gossamer drift out and hoping one would catch. But everything was at the mercy of the wind, or chance, or *Destino*, and a year passed while whoever she was waiting for failed to appear. Then one day when she and Susan were tending the baby and exchanging gossip, people came running past her little house. Susan needed only a minute to learn that two guys had escaped from the prison and that George Satawan, the town's Big Man, was deciding whether to let them stay or drive them back into the jungle. So Esperanza hefted Corazon onto one hip and they hurried to join the gathering crowd, because when would anything this exciting happen again in dull little Hilo?

When they arrived, George—a Samoan, a short, weighty man wearing a scarlet lava-lava—had already made the decision to let the newcomers stay. Without asking her permission, he pointed at Susan and said, "You will take this one," meaning Gomez, then at Esperanza and said, "You will take the other."

Susan had learned long ago not to quarrel with Destiny, and merely looked at Gomez with interest, while he looked at her and wondered what it would be like to wake up next to a one-eyed woman. Esperanza was young enough to resent being ordered around, yet didn't protest because—well, because, speaking of eyes, Andy's were gray, something unknown in dark-eyed Hilo. The eyes proclaimed him an outsider, maybe the one she'd been waiting for.

"You will work for these ladies," said George Satawan to Andy and Gomez. "They need a man around. They will cook for you. What will happen between you, only God knows, but if you use force on them, I will kill you. Welcome to our town."

That night Gomez and Susan made love, for they knew by long experience that time is the only kind of wealth which, if you fail to spend it, spends itself. In the next house but one, Andy didn't try anything, and Esperanza— as she told Susan next day—wasn't sure whether she liked that or not. Yet it was nice to have a man snoring under her roof again. He slept in an old hammock, while she slept with Corazon on her marriage bed of wide boards. Heavy rain fell in the darkness, veritably the sound of silence, and all three rested well.

Next morning, George put Gomez and Andy to work in the town's communal garden. Except for the absence of guards, they might have been back in jail, hoeing weeds among a mixed botany of string beans, musk-melons, casabas, pineapples, and growths resembling alien beings that turned out to be adolescent artichokes. That afternoon, Esperanza visited the garden to gather a few things for dinner, and Andy walked her home. Once again nothing happened, and yet everything happened, too, for while waiting for his dinner, he took the baby on his lap and let her wrestle his fingers with her tiny hands. That was when Esperanza decided to keep him.

Susan repeated this story to everyone in town, leaving only Andy in the dark about his future. On Sunday she joined him and Esperanza in church, a large thatched house with pews of split coconut logs. Gomez stayed home, but heard what happened from his usual source. The Kahuna was a Fijian, an ebony statue except for a mane of coarse white hair, and Andy understood not a single word of his sermon except Jesus, amen, and "numba five," which turned out to be a hymn. There were no hymn books (Esperanza explained that they'd been eaten by ants) but everybody knew the words by heart and sang very loud, accompanied by gourd drums and a four-string ukulele strummed by a young woman in a gaudy skirt and much-mended bustier.

Other hymns followed. Andy finally recognized one and was caroling "Just a Closer Walk with Thee," when—observed by Susan, who was standing just behind them—Esperanza quietly took his hand. At the end of the service, she turned Corazon over to her friend, while she and Andy ducked into a thicket of fire ginger and made urgent love, flattening the stalks and crushing out the flowers' honeyed attar. She whispered to him that before they became lovers, she'd first wanted to make sure he believed in God.

"People like you," she explained, "sometimes be too damn smart for their own good."

"Actually, most of my life I've been too damn dumb for my own good," he said, and she smiled.

That night they waited until the baby was asleep, then made love twice more. The next day Esperanza had a long talk with Susan and told her almost everything about the experience, including the odd fact that Andy was circumcised. By noon the whole story, including the circumcision, had become public knowledge. Except for the bachelors Esperanza had rejected, everybody smiled at the new couple, and Andy, relaxing for the first time in a long time, smiled back until his face hurt.

In the days that followed he was so happy that Gomez enjoyed being near him, just for the glow he put out. After many false starts, Li'l Brudda had found a life, or rather had one presented to him on a plate, and he made the most of it. He worked and loved and played with the baby, made new friends in the village and with them caught fish and hunted pigs and swam in a nearby lagoon. He even found a use for his aborted education. Esperanza spread the news that he'd trained to be a doctor, and people started asking him for advice about their aches and pains. Most of his patients recovered simply because they were healthy and strong and had vigorous immune systems. But Andy got the credit, and his practice grew.

He and Gomez were becoming villagers, and little by little the life of the place absorbed them. The original Hilo had stood on the big island of Hawaii, but after a tsunami destroyed it some survivors came to Tuamotu, built a new town, and named it for their lost home. *This* Hilo was a jumble of small houses, some with wooden frames and clapboards, others with thatched roofs and no walls at all, for the sake of coolness. The fifty or so residents formed a Pacific medley of islanders with a few Africans, Orientals and Haoles thrown in for flavoring. Most appeared to have clothed themselves from a shipwreck in faded shirts and shorts, but small children ran naked and some older people wrapped themselves in lava-lavas like George's. Some women went about modestly in flowered print dresses, while others left their breasts bare—especially the ones with good breasts, as Gomez and Andy both noted. Everybody, old and young, male and female, decorated their hair with scarlet and yellow hibiscus flowers.

Though the villagers were mostly self-sufficient, they got things they couldn't make for themselves—toothbrushes, mirrors, aspirin, and so forth—from the prison staff. In return they provided the guards with fresh fruit, fresh fish they caught out by the reef, and fresh meat from feral porkers they trapped in the jungle. Some guards visited Hilo, including Stink—that was why he'd been able to give Gomez directions for finding it—while others met the locals in a jungle clearing near the perimeter fence called the Trading

THE ASSASSIN

Post. The guards paid willing women for sex, giving them colored beads and cheap watches that decorated wrists and necks all over Hilo.

Living in a place where food was abundant and work far from excessive, Gomez developed a bit of a paunch, while Andy turned robust and chunky for the first time in his life. He began to love the island that had been his prison and told Gomez he never wanted to leave. Daily rainbows came and went, sometimes three or four at a time. Prevailing westerlies had carried most of the volcanic ash toward the east coast, forming the peninsula where the prison stood, but elsewhere near-vertical cliffs plunged into the cobalt sea. Their rough slopes bore forests of man-high ferns, like a cloak of green feathers that glistened with rain or dew and rippled in the gentle trade winds.

Esperanza showed Andy a path that twisted through the woods, climbed a spur of the mountain, and dipped into a narrow valley. It was a mysterious place where shade lingered even at noon, and a tiny silver waterfall left pearls on spiderwebs before cascading through a fissure into a cavern below. Strange sounds rose from the old fumarole, sometimes a booming like iron bells, sometimes cries as of animals or men. The Kahuna disapproved of all magic but his own, and declared the place taboo. But Andy loved it, and often walked the path with Esperanza, or with Gomez, or alone.

One day when the two friends were together, they topped the spur and paused to catch their breath on a rocky shelf. The sheer cliff rose on one side, the fern forest fell away on the other, and they were about to move on when Sneak stepped as soundlessly as ever into the path ahead of them.

He wore a holstered pistol and raised his hand to signal Halt. The ex-cons were standing paralyzed when a small woman wearing a Security Forces uniform emerged beside the guard, and Andy whispered, "Faith."

She told Sneak, "I have things to talk about with this man. Give us some space, and take the other guy with you."

As ordered, Gomez fell back a couple of meters, wondering if he should attack while the guard's pistol was still in his holster. Then he decided to wait and see what happened between Andy and Faith. You share a futon with a man for a year, you learn a lot about him, and Gomez knew that a woman named Faith had been Andy's lover, back in the days when he was getting ready to shoot Mahmud Alonzo Sol. He sensed a tale of betrayal and waited with ears twitching, hoping to learn more.

She led Andy down the path, and he stumbled twice, as if unable to control his feet. He couldn't speak either, and found himself listening to Faith—*Oh hell*, he thought, *why think of her by that so-called secret name?* Even back at Yale he'd known her real name was Constance Griffin.

"I know this must be a shock," she said, inadequately.

When he still couldn't find words, she explained, "I wanted to make sure those idiots at the prison really had arranged your escape." She seated herself on a boulder of eroded lava and gestured for him to sit beside her. But he preferred to stand.

"I'm not a complete monster, you know," she said.

He couldn't stop staring. Her face both did and didn't belong to the woman he'd known. Her hair was dark now instead of blonde with dark roots, as it had been. She still had a spark in her eyes, but the fire was different, he didn't know how. Three years had passed since they'd parted in the loft in Washington, yet she looked older by a decade. Still the lecturer, like Miss Birch his fourth-grade teacher imparting knowledge, she explained herself in tones that reminded him of the days when she was recruiting him for the AFA.

"I was working undercover when I set you up," she said, quite calmly, as if such betrayals happened every day. "The world government was having problems, still is. Security wanted to provoke an act that would justify a general crackdown, and they were looking for somebody to put on the kind of spectacular but harmless show they needed. Provocation is a very common ploy in my line of work, but it has to be done exactly right. The fake assassination was the first big action I was completely in charge of, and I owe my meteoric rise in the Service to doing it right."

She paused to take a small white regulation handkerchief out of her sleeve and wipe her eyes with it. "What I didn't count on was the way I started to feel about you. You were such a child, Andy, so helpless, such a—"

"You can skip that," he said, suddenly finding his voice.

"Sorry. It's not easy, you know, talking like this, as if I'd been the one in the wrong. There's no natural right to be a fool, and really, with your education, you had no excuse."

He looked away from her. Ferns, bird-of-paradise flowers, heliconia, fire ginger, all were growing nearby. For some reason, it suddenly felt important to call everything by its right name.

"I was shocked when I heard those bastards at Hoover Square had worked you over. I mean, I knew the whole story from the inside. They didn't need to get a single thing out of you, but sometimes the left hand doesn't know what the right hand is doing. I suppose it was pretty rough."

Again he said nothing. She frowned at the weighted silence, as if he'd accused her of something.

"Well, I'm truly sorry. But I *never* intended it to happen. After that I tried to look out for you, I really did. I got your sentence commuted, also those of the other boys. I saved your life, not that you'll ever thank me for it. When I had a chance to come to Tuamotu on official business, I jumped at it. There's a dirty job underway—ironically, it's called Operation Clean Sweep—but at least it gave me a chance to make sure you'd been released and see you one last time. I found you by that chip in your neck."

She dabbed her eyes again, and her voice changed from a somewhat strident major to a minor key. "You were kind of...oh, I don't know. My fling at passionate faith and youthful enthusiasm, all those things I'd never had, never really wanted to have in my own life. I'd never met anybody like you, ready to die for your beliefs, and now I never will again."

Andy had to ask her one question, even though he already knew the answer. "What about our child?"

"Well, of course there never was one. Getting pregnant would've been strictly against the regs. Anyway, I had my tubes cut long ago. You've never held a real job in your life, so you don't know the kind of things people have to do when they're fighting their way up in the world. Especially women— it's always harder for us. There's nothing like a pregnancy to take you out of the loop long enough for your enemies to knife you."

Finally he understood the fire in her eyes—it was the glowing coal of ambition. She got up and they started back.

"Do you have a girlfriend?" she asked.

"Yes."

"Is she sensible?"

"Yes."

"That's good. You really need somebody to take care of you. You're looking great, by the way. You must be eating right. Well, here's my escort. Good-bye, Andy. Stay on your tropical island. You need a place away from the real world, while I—"

"While you go on serving Mahmud Alonzo Sol."

"Not really. He dropped dead twelve years ago. The fat old fool was partying with hookers and coke and brandy, and it finished him. There was talk about replacing him, but the technology's gotten so good there's really no reason to have a President any longer."

"Then who in hell's been running things?" he demanded, feeling new outrage because he'd not only shot an image, he'd shot an image of a dead man.

"You're not authorized to know. Good-bye, Andy. We won't see each other again. I don't think I could take it."

She and Sneak reentered the fern forest. A few minutes later a silvery gyro lifted, briefly backed up in midair, then spun, banked, and vanished. Andy watched it go, and Gomez, though palpitating with eagerness to learn what had happened, had the good sense not to ask. That was why, in his own good time, Andy told him everything.

Back at home, Esperanza took one look at him and demanded to know if someone had died. He answered that in the secret valley, the ghost of a dead lover had appeared to him and confessed that she had once betrayed him.

The lie—maybe because it wasn't *all* a lie—worked remarkably well. It was exactly the sort of romantic fable Esperanza loved and she swallowed it whole, including the ghost. Ghosts were common in Hilo—she often saw her deceased Mama, and every night put a small plate of fruit outside, in case the old lady felt hungry and wanted a snack. Of course she told Susan about Andy's encounter, and Susan told everybody else, so that his ghost became a part of village lore.

Next day he was called to assist the local midwife, and went willingly, hoping that work would help him forget. The birth was a breech presentation that went on for hours, and left three adults and a sore, squalling, purplish baby boy all smeared with blood and smelling like the bottom of a swamp. He was going home when Hilo's best fisherman—a thick-muscled man named Joe Aiaiea—passed him, a beautiful big tuna slung over his shoulder. Joe said he was headed for the Trading Post, because his girlfriend wanted a nice mirror and he hoped the tuna might get it for her. Andy only grunted, returned home, had Esperanza pour a bucket of water over him by way of a shower, fell on their bed, and passed out.

By the time he woke from his siesta, Joe had returned and so had the fish. That night he and his girlfriend baked it in a pit with sea salt and peppers and limes and other good things, invited the village, and served the food on chipped dishes and fresh-cut banana leaves. At the feast Andy learned that no bargaining had taken place, because no guards had appeared at the Trading Post. Puzzled, Joe had crept to the edge of the jungle, risking the lasers to find out why.

"Dey breakin' up da camp," he said through a mouthful. "Alla guards runnin' round like crazy. No trade for a while, damn shit."

That news was enough to send Andy, Gomez, Esperanza, and Susan next morning on a long walk up the mountain, to heights where the trees thinned out and winds blew cold off the snowcap. He and Esperanza shared the work of carrying the baby, until they reached a vantage point where part of the mountain had crumbled, leaving a sheer cliff. On the verge they rested, gazing out over the whole eastern end of the island, forest canopy and coves and inlets, beaches of black and white sand, the foaming reef, the encircling sea.

And the prison—an alien intruder on its promontory, the only place on Tuamotu where all lines were straight and all angles precisely ninety degrees. Cons were shuffling like columns of ants through the grid of red streets toward the Sea Gate. Offshore lay a missile cruiser gently rocking on the waves, while an old rust-bucket of a merchant ship towered over the quay. Even at this distance, flaking white letters that said *Pelican* were visible on the bow. The big portside cargo doors stood wide and the prisoners inched down the dock into the dark, cavernous opening.

Did the authorities, Andy wondered, intend to jam all those hundreds of men into that one ship? He tried to recall what Connie had said about Operation Clean Sweep. A really dirty job—but why was closing the prison and shipping the cons someplace else a dirty job? It sounded complicated, a problem in logistics, but that was all. Or—the thought came to him suddenly—could this be the reason Connie had arranged his escape? Did she want him out of the prison before something bad happened?

His head began to hurt as if another migraine were coming on. Some part of him already knew the score and Gomez knew it, too, for his face settled into grim lines and he began to mutter curses under his breath. Esperanza looked merely baffled, for she had lived her whole life among decent people and found acts of great cruelty unimaginable. But Susan was as old as Gomez, and—Andy noticed for the first time—her blind eye, an opalescent globe like a milky opal, had the thin pale scar of a razor slash leading up to it. This lady had lived hard, which might be one reason why she and Gomez got along so well. She sat tensely watching the scene, one hand over her mouth, the other closed in a fist between her scrawny breasts. Like the men, she knew what was about to happen.

Sunset was stoking a tropical effusion of red and yellow and green and purple fire in the west when the merchant ship left the dock. But not under her own power—the *Pelican* was under tow by the cruiser. About a kilometer offshore, the hawser either broke or was released, leaving the rust bucket to wallow helplessly in the waves. Andy could imagine the men in the hold, thrown this way and that, puking with seasickness and terror, maybe raving and fighting in the claustrophobic darkness. By now even Esperanza understood what impended, for she turned her back to the sea and lowered her face until her nose touched Corazon's belly. The others went on staring, unable to look away.

The first missile struck the old ship at the starboard waterline, causing it to shudder, list, and spin slowly around. A few seconds passed before the sound of the blast reached the watchers. The second missile hit astern on the port side, leaving the *Pelican* mortally wounded and settling fast. No more firing followed—missiles cost money, and the job had been done.

Punctured on both sides, the ship filled more or less evenly, the only drama coming when a hatch cover blew off amidships. For an instant the heavy metal square hovered like a kite, sustained by a geyser shooting up from the flooded decks below. Then it turned sideways and fell like a guillo-tine blade into the ocean. Within minutes the ship followed, its rust-stained sterncastle vanishing last of all. A whirlpool formed, then broke up into random turbulence, waves foaming and dashing and parting. Gradually the Pacific erased the maelstrom, and with it the last traces of the men who had lived and suffered in the penal colony.

Esperanza bent over folded hands, muttering prayers in Tagalog, her childhood tongue. Susan wept from both her live eye and her dead one. Gomez sat rigid, trembling with fury. Andy's head stopped hurting, but his heart turned to something much harder and colder than mere ice. All the failures and humiliations and agonies of his life fused into a single need to find vengeance, to strike back, to kill. He pronounced sentence in the tones of a hanging judge.

"Somebody will pay for this," he said, and Gomez growled, "*Sí*. But who?"

Well, obviously, the man whose name Andy wasn't authorized to know, the name only Connie could tell him. He and Gomez kicked the problem around but reached no conclusion. How were they to get hold of her? And how could they make her talk?

For some reason, the fisherman Joe Aiaiea had been tapped as Fate's messenger. Two days after the *Pelican* incident, Andy was shelling beans for supper when Joe entered his house, bearing in his arms the stick figure of a man. He'd carried his burden all the way from the reef, yet wasn't even breathing hard as he laid him gently on the plank bed. "'Nother con like you," said Joe. "Damn shit, but he in bad shape, him."

He explained that when the hatch cover blew off the *Pelican*, the geyser must have thrown the man into the sea and the sharks, busy with the other bodies, hadn't wanted him. So he drifted with the onshore current and got caught on the reef, where Joe had been casting his net and found him.

"Enda da story," he concluded, shrugged, and walked away, leaving Andy to stare aghast at the dying man, his fellow conspirator Karl, a.k.a. Friedberger. He must have been serving time in the same prison, only in another barracks. The two had spent more than a year close enough to yell a greeting, yet like corpses buried in adjoining tombs, had never seen one another.

Andy dripped cool water into his mouth, watched him try to swallow but fail, and shook his head. Esperanza used a clean rag to wipe his eyelids, inflamed and crusted with salt, and then his bristly face. When his cracked lips moved, Andy put his ear down to listen. It was hard to tell what Friedberger was trying to say, maybe, *They killed them all.* What Andy heard was *kill them,* and he promised, "I will."

An hour later the man was gone. Andy called Gomez to help, and they buried him in the village graveyard. The Kahuna delivered another of his incomprehensible sermons, and the townspeople sang "Just a Closer Walk with Thee." Afterward, Andy went home and slept and slept and slept, as if he could put off the demands of Destiny by remaining unconscious. But his sleep was uneasy, beset by restless dreams, and he woke suddenly, smelling a goat.

That seemed odd, for Tuamotu had plenty of feral pigs, but no goats he'd ever seen. He raised his head from the bed of boards, and there in the brown shadows stood Stink, with George and Joe holding his arms. "Dis guy say he know you," said George. "We was gonna break his neck."

"It's okay," said Andy. "Let me have a word with him."

Stink sat down on the ground, holding a small paper-wrapped bundle in his lap and wiping nervous sweat off his face. For the first time in their long acquaintance, Andy took the trouble to read his name tag—Fowler. So the guard had a real name, possibly even a real life. When he spoke he sounded shaken.

"What'sa matter with these guys? I know 'em, we trade together, I get 'em things, they get me things, but today they wanna kill me."

"They blame you for the *Pelican.*"

"Why blame me? I didn't have nothin' to do with it."

Andy nodded. Of course that was true. To calm Fowler down, he summoned his bedside manner and asked about his family. Fowler had been born in Wyoming but grew up more or less everywhere, for his father had been in the American Marshal Service and the family moved often. "Law enforcement," he said proudly, "it's in my blood."

That was why he'd entered the world government's Prison Service, which paid better than anything impoverished America could offer. He took pride in his job. Guards were role models, he said, teaching cons by discipline and example how to live upright, honorable lives. Andy found this astounding. Sneak and Stink as role models? But Fowler was serious, and anger darkened his face when he spoke about the massacre.

"Here we take care of these guys, try to point 'em the right direction, give 'em some discipline, whack 'em when they do wrong, get 'em shaped up. Then somebody comes along and kills 'em. Without even a warrant! How can you execute somebody without no warrant or nothin'?"

He started to denounce Connie. "The one in charge was a little bitch come out of HQ. But when she's watchin' it happen, I look at her face and I know she's made a mistake. She did it, but she hated it—drownin' all those guys like rats! That takes somethin' she ain't got. I figure that was why she went and cut her wrists afterward."

For a few seconds the dim interior of the house spun slowly around Andy's head. "She's dead?" he whispered, filled with a complex of emotions he couldn't have named.

Fowler shook his head. "No such luck. Somebody found her and called the medics. Sometimes I wish those guys would just leave well enough alone, you know? Pretty soon she'll be fixed up and ready to kill a bunch more people, I guess."

"So she's still on Tuamotu."

"Yeah."

At that point, Andy's mouth opened and he heard himself make a request to which Fowler, though looking baffled, agreed. Then the guard picked up his bundle and stood, casting a nervous glance at the doorway of the hut.

"All I want is a nice fish, so the cook can fix it for dinner. I wonder if those guys gonna try and kill me again."

"They won't now," Andy promised, walked him outside, and nodded to Joe, who nodded back. Relieved, Fowler shook Andy's hand for the first time in their long acquaintance. A guard couldn't shake the hand of a prisoner, but the gesture was permitted with a man who was both free and—officially at least—dead.

"You look like you doin' good, Emerson," he said. "Funny, I never figured you for a survivor. It's hard to tell, sometimes. Big guys croak and little guys go on forever. It's really hard to tell."

He started unwrapping his package, which contained the usual mirrors and whatnot. Joe approached, and they squatted on their haunches and started to bargain, all thoughts of killing forgotten.

But Andy's thoughts were of nothing except killing. He'd finally accepted the harsh demand of Destiny, to leave a woman he'd come to love and a life where he was happy and content, in order to kill a man he'd never met. He could curse the burden, but he couldn't shift it.

When he told Esperanza, she surprised him by understanding. She'd seen the *Pelican* sink, washed Friedberger's face, sung a hymn over his grave. Like all her people she believed in honor and vengeance, so she wept but didn't try to stop him. As for Gomez, there was never any question that he would stand beside Andy if he could identify the target and find a way to reach him.

They met Connie together, choosing the tabooed valley because it was remote and private. Again Sneak accompanied her, and he and Gomez stood back to let the others parley head to head. But something in the atmosphere—maybe the way Gomez looked at him, as if he were personally responsible for the Pelican—made Sneak edgy, and after fidgeting a few minutes, he muttered, "You stay here," and followed Andy and Connie, maybe concerned for her safety as well as his own.

As ever, the valley was shadowy, lush with tropical jungle, blazoned with strange flowers, filled with the sound of rushing water and the echoes rising from the fumarole. Today they sounded sometimes like thunder, sometimes like cries and distant laughter. Connie's long-sleeved uniform shirt gave Andy only glimpses of the bandages around her wrists. She was pale, her face lined, her eyes enormous. She looked years older, and the first thing she said was, "I didn't give the order."

"No?"

"You've got to believe that. I was sent here as an observer, to make sure Tomsky's instructions were carried out. I had to do it. He's like Stalin. You have to become an accomplice in his crimes or he gets rid of you."

"Who's Tomsky?" Andy had never heard the name before.

"The Chief of Security. His name's an open secret, one of those secrets that everybody who's anybody knows."

"Why did he have them killed? Those guys were helpless, totally helpless. They couldn't have hurt him."

She sighed and sat down on the same boulder as the last time. She looked thin, weary, tallowy, used up. Either she was suffering from a wasting illness or she really had hated watching the prisoners drown. Or maybe both. More important, he saw that she hated the man who'd forced her to become his accomplice.

"It comes down to fear," she said. "All the worst things people have ever done have been caused by fear. They burned witches for fear of the Devil. They burned heretics for fear of new ideas. Hitler killed the Jews—well, I don't know *why* Hitler killed the Jews, but I bet fear was at the base of it.

"As I told you, the world government's in trouble. Rebellions are breaking out on every continent except Antarctica, and if anybody but penguins lived there, they'd probably be rebelling, too. And it's a shame, we really do need a government to prevent another war. But first Sol with his stupid dictatorship and then this fool with his policy of terror have messed things up so badly that it's going to fall. Tomsky's afraid of the future, he knows he'll be held accountable for his crimes, and the prisoners were the only enemies he could get at and destroy. It wasn't a rational action, but whoever said that people are rational?"

"Somebody did," muttered Andy. Somebody long ago, for whatever reason, had called the species *Homo sapiens*, rational man.

"Well, he must have been an idiot, whoever he was." She opened her hands and looked at the palms as if something written there could explain it all. "What's happened to my life, Andy? There I was, trying to do my job and get ahead, and first I lost you and then I lost my soul. God damn this island," she said with sudden violence. "For me it's the Isle of the Dead."

"Finished whining?" he asked.

"I suppose so, but—"

He wasn't conscious of hearing a sound, yet suddenly he spun on his heel and there was Sneak close behind him. Without a thought, Andy swung the heavy hand he'd developed during years of manual labor and wrestling fat infants out of tight wombs. His knuckles connected with Sneak's left ear and the guard's eyes spun around in his head. As he fell, Andy caught him by his uniform belt, dragged him a few steps, and threw him headfirst into the fumarole. He leaned over, rubbing his knuckles, and waited for the splash, which was a long time coming but came at last.

Connie was shocked. "Andy, he was just making sure I was okay!"

She'd risen, but he pushed her back down. For a few seconds he stood quietly, thinking of the man he'd turned into. Then he dismissed his first homicide with a shrug and got back to business.

"Let's," he suggested, "discuss the assassination of Tomsky." She continued to stare, said nothing, waited for him to go on.

"Think about it. You can arrange it—you're on the inside and he trusts you because you're his accomplice. Killing him will make the rebels love you, you'll be Lady Liberty who freed the people, and when they take over, you can move from the old government to the new one without a bump on the road. How's that sound?"

Slowly she loosened the fastenings on her cuffs, opened them, and looked down at the elastoplast bandages binding her wrists. So she *had* wounded herself, but whether her suicide attempt had been real or intended only to leave a scar, he couldn't tell. Maybe she'd felt real remorse; or maybe she'd merely been covering her tracks, preparing evidence in case of future need. With Connie, how could you be sure?

"It's an interesting concept," she murmured. "Actually, there's already a cabal inside the Forces that wants to get rid of him. But they need...well, they need somebody to do the dirty work. How'd you come up with the idea, Andy?"

"I didn't. It's what has to be."

She looked him over thoughtfully. "I'll need to find a uniform for you. And shoes." She shook her head over his dirty bare feet.

"You'll have to find disguises for two," he told her. "My friend's coming with me. He's a good man, wants revenge for the *Pelican*."

"You trust him?"

"More than I trust myself."

She sighed. "In an action like this, there are always a million details to work out, and every one has to be done just *exactly* right, or the whole thing fails. It's not easy being a cop, Andy. You'll find that out."

"It's not easy being a con, either. But I survived."

She looked at him, really *looked* at him, maybe for the first time in their long, complicated relationship. Not as somebody to be loved, or betrayed, or protected, or destroyed, all the things he'd been to her in the past. Finally she was seeing him as just this . . . incomprehensible . . . *other*.

"You'd survive anything, wouldn't you?" she murmured. "If there's another nuclear war—which is possible, the way things are going—when it's over, there'll be nothing left but cockroaches and kudzu and Andrew Walden Emerson III."

Suddenly she jumped up, all her weakness gone, her eyes blazing at the thought of action. She'd already forgotten Sneak, as if he never had existed at all.

"'A good plot, good friends. An excellent plot, very good friends!'" she cried. "That's in Shakespeare. Give me your pal's name. Both of you were cons, so your vital statistics should still be in the computer—probably in the backup, since you're both supposed to be dead. I'll get the info out, enter it in the military records, create new identities.

"Isn't it nice the world's gotten so abstract? Anybody can fake anything, if they know how. And I know how."

While Gomez loitered in the Pentagon corridor, remembering and fretting and hoping for the best, Andy had already passed through the hidden door in the paneling, and begun exploring what lay beyond.

He stood in a narrow passage with three other doors, the first labeled MEN'S TOILET—OFFICERS ONLY, making him smile at the crudeness of Destiny's excremental joke. If the toilets hadn't been segregated by rank, the *Spetsnaz* guard could have relieved himself right here, and the whole plot would have come undone. The next door was unlabeled and opened into a storeroom full of quaint metal filing cabinets with rusty steel rods inserted through the handles, secured by padlocks that were also rusty. *God knows*, he thought, *what war these date from.*

Behind the final door, a voice muttered, becoming clearer when he opened it a crack. Inside was a darkened studio filled with formidable gadgetry. Bored-looking techs perched on metal stools, watching the tall man's image on three screens. Each showed him from a different angle, and Andy understood that when the images were fused by some digital process and projected in real space, they formed the walking, talking hologram that ruled the world.

But where was the man himself? The studio was a dead end, with no exit but the door where he stood. Maybe, he thought, Tomsky lived in a space warp inaccessible to the real world. He turned back into the passageway and was scratching his head when a voice—he was alone, so he thought at first it must be God's—commanded in harsh, emphatic tones that made his head ring, "Guard, get your ass down to the front office soonest."

Andy had forgotten the earbud. He returned to the hallway with the paneling and started down a deep-pile carpet with interwoven medallions showing the triumphant eagle of the Security Forces and their inescapable motto. *Pour servir tout l'Humanité. Der ganzen Humanität zu dienen.* Besides the English, these were the only versions he could read, and the odd thought occurred to him that maybe Destiny had sent him here for exactly that purpose—to serve humanity, whatever language it spoke. But even its plans would hit a snag unless he could find the front office, for the hallway was as blank as an elevator shaft turned on its side.

Of course the office found him—that was Destiny's way. When you were playing its game, things came to you. A door appeared in the paneling, one that had no keypad and couldn't be opened from the outside at all. A frowning colonel standing in the aperture said, "Come in, Sergeant. I've got to leave, so stand at attention and wait till I come back."

Even the outer office was palatial, with a wide desk and all the usual equipment, including a document vaporizer to dispose of inconvenient memories. Andy assumed a ramrod stance by an inner door of creamy paneled wood until the officer, after gathering hardcopy from a file, left without ever actually seeing him. Something with a red beret and a X clearance and a standard-issue weapon had done what it was told, and for the colonel, that was sufficient.

Beyond the door a voice was speaking a language rich in consonants. Andy cracked it and peeped into a truly vast office, the biggest he'd seen in the Pentagon, or maybe anywhere. It lay mostly in darkness, except for the man standing at the center in a blaze of light. Andy had found his target at last.

Drawing the heavy impact pistol from its holster, he studied the man minutely, as curious as a lover studying his love. In the studio images, Tomsky had looked unlined, healthy, almost youthful. But those were corrections made by the software. Under the merciless lights he looked old, weary, and stiff as a creature of wood. Power wears out its human receptacles, Andy reflected, remembering how Connie had aged a decade in a third that time.

Directly in front of Tomsky stood a black module gazing at him with multiple eyes, like a spider. Shadowy people lounged here and there—techs, it appeared—plus two aides following the speech phrase by phrase on a green-lit prompter. Their concentration gave Andy his chance. He sidled through the shadows to the edge of the glare. Then, his whole body turning somehow dense and metallic, he slipped off his weapon's safety and with one long stride stepped in front of the transmitter. Tomsky blinked, seeing only a shadow emerge through the blaze of light.

"This is for the *Pelican*," Andy said, and shot him point-blank in the face.

He stepped from the dazzle into the darkness, fired again at someone blocking his way, slid through the door and crossed the outer office. In the paneled corridor everything looked phenomenally peaceful. He holstered the pistol, returned to the barrier, stepped though, and changed caps and badges. The trash-disposal chute he'd noticed earlier now seemed to be there just for his benefit. He discarded his surplus equipment, and as the first signs of confusion began to spread—people yelling, answering, nobody sure yet what had happened or where—he rejoined the crowd outside the conference room.

Once again he was only a uniform among other uniforms, a IX among other IXs, an Invisible Man among the other invisible men and women. He felt his pulse and found it elevated, but not by much. His calmness at first surprised him, but then less so, as he reflected on what he'd done. He'd killed the most powerful man in the world, yet that was a mere anticlimax to the years of adventure and suffering that had preceded it. He'd avenged the dead, expunged his shame, rid himself of guilt—wiped his slate clean, in short. But something newly wise at the center of his heart told him that nothing really mattered now, except what he would write upon it in time to come.

He winked at Gomez, who gave him a nod, and together they waited for Connie and the rest of the staff to emerge. Through the steel doors came sounds of shouting and disorder, and Gomez gave him an evil grin and whispered, "You shook 'em up, Big Brudda."

Andy smiled at that, grateful for the only commendation he either needed or wanted.

An hour later he sat in Connie's office, having a drink—her big office on the A Ring, overlooking the five-sided patio with shade trees and jonquils in the garden beds spelling out *To Serve All Humanity*.

She gave him her version of what had happened in the conference room. How the general officers at first sat in stunned silence, watching the virtual back of a virtual man in uniform emerge from nowhere, shoot virtual Tomsky and make his virtual head virtually explode. Collectively the room gasped, and then came panic.

"Sound the alarm!" shouted somebody, "we're under attack!" Others yelled, "Lockdown! Catch the assassin! Make him talk!" One small plaintive voice was heard asking over and over, "Vhat is *Pelican*? Please, does anybody know? Vhat is *Pelican*?"

That was when Connie spoke up, her clear, sharp tones cutting through the noise.

"The assassin," she said, "is already in custody. He's made his confession, and he'll repeat it to the whole world on the evening news."

Some people weren't quick-witted. A baffled voice queried, "But who captured him? And how'd we get his confession?"

"It's a virtual assassin, you idiot," said somebody who'd been part of the plot against Tomsky. "His confession's in the can, been there for a week. You're out of the loop, that's all."

"Sometimes," Connie went on, in her lecturing voice, "the effect precedes the cause. It's unusual, of course, but it happens. Especially nowadays. Can we get down to business? A new situation has arisen and I suggest we consider how best to deal with it."

"Griffin is right," said another member of the cabal. "Tomsky's dead, he can't hurt us now, and he can't help us either."

"It's time to think about the future," she agreed. "Specifically, how to blame everything bad that's happened on him alone."

Anyway, that was the way she told the story to Andy. Meanwhile Gomez waited in her outer office with a driver she'd assigned them. She wanted them out of Washington quick, but at the same time she wanted Andy where she could find him again, in case of need. "I may have more work for you," she explained. "As I once told you, today all politics is the politics of violence. And you're so *good* at it."

He sipped his drink—how long had it been since he last tasted scotch?—and wondered if he should lunge across the desk and kill her. God knows, he had motive enough and opportunity beckoned. But then he and Gomez would never get away. So maybe he'd better just go home, kiss Esperanza, and let Corazon wrestle with his fingers again. That felt like a much better plan.

He finished his drink and left, saying he knew she must have a lot to do, now that she'd be helping to run the world. Within an hour he and Gomez were on a military flight to ruined and half-rebuilt Honolulu, and from there they flew on to Tuamotu. The whole journey took fourteen hours, and they slept through most of it.

At home Esperanza was nursing the baby, wincing occasionally when Corazon clamped down on her nipple. She smiled a greeting and wept when Andy kissed her. He tried to persuade the baby to grip his extended finger, but her tiny hands were far too busy clutching the breast. Warm milk was leaking from Esperanza's other nipple, and she caught the ooze on her thumb and held it out for him to lick. She asked how things had gone with his mission of vengeance, and he said well.

"So you killed that bad man?"

"Yes."

"Good. I'm glad he's gone. Will there be another war?"

"Maybe not. Everybody's terrified of the nukes, so the peacemakers have fear on their side. Maybe things will get better. But it's all up to Destiny."

"Destino, Destino," she murmured. "Isn't it funny, it governs our lives, yet nobody knows what it means or where it's headed."

Andy, not knowing either, only watched the baby and smiled.

He expected to see Connie again—speaking of destinies, theirs were tied in so complicated a knot that only death could undo it. Yet two more years passed before the inevitable happened. By then many things had changed. Corazon had given up her all-milk diet and learned to walk, then to run with the other kids, all the time babbling freely and endlessly in a way that her mother considered *maravilloso* for one so young. With her nursing duties over, indications had appeared that Esperanza was pregnant again.

That was when Connie came back to Tuamotu. Not because she wanted to, but because her habit of playing both ends against the middle had finally caught up with her. When the new world government launched its great Justice Commission to ferret out the crimes of the past and punish the evil-doers, the massacre that Tomsky's agents had carried out in prisons around the world was the first item on the agenda. What had happened on Tuamotu became a kind of poster child for all the atrocities of the old regime, and Connie—despite every handful of dust she could throw in the eyes of the judges—received the blame for it.

Her colleagues in the Security Forces made sure of that. To save themselves they needed a scapegoat, and since Tomsky was dead, she was elected. Yet for all the political byplay, the verdict was just. Contrary to what she'd told Andy, she *had* given the order to drown the men, though only under protest and with feelings of guilt that might well have been deep and genuine. The court weighed the question of her remorse—had her suicide attempt been real or not? On that point there was conflicting testimony. Prosecution doctors said that her wounds had been superficial, while defense doctors said the scarring reached the bone. In the end it didn't matter—the world needed a villain to punish, and she filled the bill only too well.

Condemned to death, she spent a year in the old prison on Hoover Square, most of the time in the dispensary where Andy had recovered so long ago. Then, in consideration of her failing health, the new World President reduced her sentence to exile on the same island where she'd committed her crime.

Since the penal colony had long since been closed down and demolished, she had to live in the village. Joe Aiaiea had recently succeeded the aging George Satawan as Hilo's Big Man, and he reluctantly allotted her a small house to live in and ordered her to work in the communal garden. She was not popular in Hilo—everybody looked at her but no one spoke to her, so that she moved about in a bubble of silence. Even Susan refused to gossip about her, for she said that Connie was nothing, and what nothing did was not worth discussing.

Andy saw her in his capacity as Hilo's general practitioner. He needed no complicated tests to conclude that she was suffering from widely metastasized cancer, probably originating in the ovaries but now invading blood, bone, and brain alike. He asked her why she didn't have the trouble taken care of, back when it was new and curable, and she said that her job always got in the way. Suppose her enemies had found out that she had a serious illness? She'd never have gotten another promotion—never!

Andy went to see Fowler. Not only had the guard survived all the upheavals, but his long, devoted service had won him promotion to the post of resident commissioner for the new world government. He lived in what used to be the warden's house, married to a village woman who made him wash every day in coconut milk to moderate his unique aura. He was friendly with Andy, allowing him to use the official computer to study for his medical degree on the recently restored Worldwide Web. But when Andy informed him that Connie must be evacuated for treatment, he flatly refused.

"I got my orders," he said. "You know, Emerson, I always do my duty, and my orders say she ain't never to leave this island."

"Then she'll die."

"Most people do, sooner or later. That's probably what the big shots want, anyway. She knows too much."

"I don't have modern painkillers. Her death will be slow and agonizing. At some point she'll become demented. It'd be kinder just to execute her."

"I can't execute nobody without a warrant. That's illegal. She'll just have to die the way nature wants, and if it hurts, that's tough shitsky. I don't have no pity for her. Nobody does, except you."

Andy returned to Hilo, sought Connie out—she was doing her washing—and suggested they take a walk.

For an hour they strolled along jungle trails, talking of small matters, jokes they had shared when they were young, people they remembered at New Yale. He asked if she'd ever read *A Tale of Two Cities*, and she said no, she'd never cared for fiction. So he kept to himself the amended line that was passing through his head: *It is a far, far better rest that you go to, than you have ever known.*

When they reached the spur of the mountain and began to climb, she panted and leaned on his arm, yet still had to halt every few steps to catch her breath. "Don't worry," he told her, "it's all downhill from here."

The cliff towered to the left of them, the forest of giant ferns bowed and murmured on the right. Showers of gemlike droplets fell. When they entered the tabooed valley, with its little waterfall and the sounds like cries and laughter rising from the ancient fumarole, she whispered, "Do you have to?"

He said, "It's better this way," put his heavy arm around her thin shoulders, and urged her on.

Alas, poor St. George! If this tale were an ancient map, it would have to be marked "Here Be Dragons."

THE LORD OF RAGNARÖK

S IR RICHARD DE COUDRAY stood in the pitching bow of a Viking-style longship, clinging to a guyline of the mast and shouting conversation with his young squire, Gorand. The fourteen-year-old's squawky, seabird voice penetrated the roar of the wind, asking, "Are there truly dragons, sir?"

Now what, wondered the knight, *brought that on?* The ship's carved figurehead? Rumors Gorand might have heard about *les isles occultes,* the Hidden Isles, where they were headed? Or maybe he'd been browsing Father Joseph's "other" book—the illuminated Bestiary he kept chained to his desk beside the Bible.

Confirming that guess, Gorand explained, "There are dragons in the priest's book. There's Leviathan who lives in the sea and Crocodilus who lives in Africa, wherever that is. But maybe they're just pictures."

"No," the knight replied, "they're not just pictures."

"The Prophet Isaiah called Leviathan 'that crooked serpent, the dragon which is in the sea.' I read that in the Bible all by myself. Father Joseph said he couldn't have done better."

Gorand knew perfectly well that Richard had trouble reading anything except the motto on his shield and writing anything more than his name. Yet the knight let the boasting pass without the sharp cuff on the ear that it deserved. If Gorand lived long enough, he'd inherit the fief and become Richard's master. So, with an eye to the future, he replied, "Since we're on the ocean, perhaps you'll see him."

"Oh, that would be *fantastique*," squawked Gorand, causing Richard to smile grimly. He knew what lay ahead in the Hidden Isles. The boy didn't.

The crew—all Breton sailors hired for the voyage—began concocting the evening meal in the stern, making the inevitable mutton stew in an iron pot set over glowing coals in a box of sand. Everyone ate from clay bowls, then washed them by leaning over the side and trailing them in the sea, for the freeboard was no more than the length of a man's arm. Afterward they prepared for bed, stretching extra sailcloth over the gunwales like a tent, rolling themselves up in coarse blankets, and lying down on the rowers' benches to avoid the ankle-deep bilgewater sloshing beneath.

By then Richard and Gorand had moved to the stern. The air under the tent had a dense smell of onions and armpits, so they slept in the open, the boy wrapping himself in a wool cloak and lying down at his master's feet like a faithful dog. The steersman stood with his back to the tiller, both arms crooked around it, and said something in Breton, whose liquid Gaelic l's made it sound to Richard like the language of birds, not men. But he nodded *oui, oui*, anyway and settled down against the port gunwale in a cloak lined with wolf's fur that Lady Matilda had given him.

Except for the gentle slapping of waves against the hull, the night was as silent as the sky. The men had set the single square sail and a following breeze, perhaps sent by the Master of Tides, pushed the ship steadily toward the Seven Stars marking the north. Richard had lived his whole life in a crowd—in the peasant village where he was born, in barracks, in the castle— surrounded always by the smell and bustle of men and animals. He valued all the more being alone with the sleeping boy, the incomprehensible steersman, and the night. Alone with the memories that came to him at such rare times—especially the ones he couldn't share with any living soul.

He often felt that his real life had begun, not at birth but on the day when he first met the Crusader. Astride a big, rangy horse, the stranger paused at the edge of the field where Richard—still a peasant, still a boy—was digging turnips with a pointed stick.

He felt a stab of fear at the dirty white cross on the man's surcoat, for veterans of the failed crusade in the East were anything but welcome. The peasants called them *écorcheurs*, flayers, and saw them as dangerous riffraff with empty saddlebags, sharp swords, and a defeated soldier's resentment against the whole world.

Even so, when he gestured with a big, dark hand—imperiously, like a man accustomed to being obeyed—the boy dropped the stick and began to shuffle toward him. Something drew him like iron to a lodestone, though what he saw close up was not encouraging. The green eyes gazing from the man's leathery face looked somehow odd, and his black beard bristled like spines. The backs of his hands were rough and scaly like the skin of a garfish, and the boy thought, *Bon Dieu, in the East he caught leprosy, just like in the Bible!*

Hastily he bowed, pulled off his woolen cap, and touched his forelock. From on high, a voice like summer thunder growled, "Where can I find the Countess Matilda? I have a gift for her."

Ah, that was an easy one. "Through yon woods, sir knight—it's a tangle, don't lose your way. Beyond it, you'll see the shore, and a crag rising out of the sea called Michael's Mount. Her ladyship's castle stands atop it."

"What's the village back there?"

"Coudray. Hazelgrove."

"I saw burned-out cottages. What's going on?"

"We are much harried, sir knight, since his grace the count went to the Holy Land. He took the men-at-arms with him, so we have no one to defend us and no weapons to defend ourselves."

"Ah," said the stranger thoughtfully. After a moment he went on, "I see. Want to earn a penny?"

"Oh yes, my lord." Cash in any denomination was enough to promote the man from a knight to a lord. Among the peasants most business was done by barter, and many lived from one end of the year to the other without ever seeing money.

"Then guide me through the woods."

The horse moved at an easy canter and Richard trotted beside it, left hand on the stirrup. They slowed to a walk in the wood, a dark, entangled place where the peasants came only to gather mushrooms, or hide out when raiders descended on them to rape and plunder. The knight remained silent until they emerged on a bluff that overlooked the glimmering sea at high tide. A floating bridge connected Michael's Mount to the land and small, distant figures were passing over it.

"If your father asks where you've been," he told Richard, "say you were aiding Sir Drangø of the Hidden Isles." He clucked to his horse and seemed about to ride away.

"Oh, sir knight," cried Richard, clutching the stirrup, "my lord, your excellency, wait, wait! Let me lead you to the castle."

Drangø tugged the reins and stared down at this village lout, this shit-kicker in his peasant smock, leggings, and *sabots* or wooden shoes. Already deformed by hard labor, Richard's back was humped, his chest bent a little inward. His hands were big, the knuckles swollen, the fingers thick and splayed. But he wanted that penny, and would stick like a burr until he got it.

Half-smiling, Drangø took the coin from a leather pouch and handed it down. "I don't need a guide anymore. I'm on the right track now. And so are you, my lad—in this world, you must always take what you're owed, and a little more if you can get it."

He spurred his horse and started down the long slope toward the sea. Neither of them expected to see the other again. But both were wrong.

They met again—if it could be called a meeting—half a year later, on the terrible day when the master-at-arms appeared, roaring like a lion, in the village at dawn and dragged Richard from his parents' cottage by the scruff of his neck. Outside sat Drangø on his horse, his strange eyes devoid of either recognition or pity.

That night on Michael's Mount, the boys taken in the sweep were thrown into the barracks beside the stables, where the men-at-arms spent the dark hours kicking them around for mere amusement. Long, hard days followed, days that began even before the false dawn, when Richard and the other recruits learned the basic lessons of combat to the tune of incessant beatings when they did anything wrong.

How often he'd wanted to die and get it over with! Yet in the end, as he now recognized, it had all been for the best. War was men's business, and learning how to fight was the first and highest step to take on his way up. In time he was made a man-at-arms, and then by energy and daring became sergeant and second-in-command under his old enemy, the master-at-arms. But when Matilda's fief was invaded by Grimoire, Count of the Dry Hills and Dusty Valleys, Richard's urge to distinguish himself almost brought him a painful death.

Foolishly, he volunteered to lead the rearguard and hold the enemy off while axmen destroyed the floating bridge. He was knocked out by a glancing blow from a mace, and woke with a blinding headache to find himself lying on the round stones of the beach, trussed up like a chicken for market. One of his captors sat beside him, sharpening his knife. When he saw that Richard was awake, he began to tell him precisely how they planned to skin him alive.

"We want to see if you can live raw," the gap-toothed fellow explained, winking. *Whet, whet, whet,* said his blade as he rubbed the edge with a stone. "We'll start with the soles of your feet. You look tough, so you'll probably last a long time. When you're dead, we'll throw the meat to the dogs, stuff your skin with straw, and use it as a target for our arrows."

Richard turned his aching head to the side—about the only movement he could make—and gazed longingly at the enemy leader a bowshot down the beach. *He can save me,* he thought. But saving people was not what had given Grimoire his fearsome reputation.

At the moment, he was discussing his next move with his entourage. No, that was wrong—they were listening while he discussed it with himself.

"*Now* what do we do?" he queried, but his knights and courtiers, shivering in the raw wind, said nothing. Their heads were still on their shoulders and they hoped to keep them there.

Instead, they gazed at the endless, sodden, dun-colored plain of sand and silt where the sea had so recently been. The granite pile of Michael's Mount thrust out of the muck some five or six bowshots offshore, topped by its towering castle. They viewed the dark walls and grim battlements with foreboding, wondering how they could ever take the place, and how many of them would die trying. Most wanted only to bale up their loot and return home. They'd made a profitable raid on the rich dominions of Countess Matilda, so why risk it all now?

Their leader had other ideas. Turning to his chamberlain, he demanded, "What's the rank of that prisoner we took?"

"Sergeant, my lord."

"Bring him here. I want to question him."

The chamberlain got to Richard just in time. A few moments later, he was lying at Grimoire's feet, mumbling his name.

"Of what degree are you?" the count demanded, meaning what class.

"I was born a peasant, my lord. My father was a tenant of Lady Matilda. Lord Drangø began to recruit new forces, so one day the master-at-arms came to our village and took the biggest and strongest boys away to train as soldiers."

"Well, Richard, you've gotten yourself into a bad spot," said the count. "But perhaps there's a way out. You must know the castle well, so tell me this: How am I to reach it now that the bridge is gone? If you find a way, you can keep your skin. Otherwise my men will flay you like a pig."

Richard frowned. At heart he was a peasant still, and thus a realist. He'd done his best for Lady Matilda and Lord Drangø. Now it was time to save himself, and if that meant betraying them—well, so be it.

"You can't just march across the flats," he muttered. "There's quicksand everywhere, and soon the sea will come back. You can try to starve the castle out—it's crowded, too many mouths to feed. But that would take a long time, and you haven't got time. When you invaded, Milady dispatched a fast boat to summon Lord Drangø. Soon he'll return with ships and men, so you must have the castle by the time he arrives."

"Drangø's gone? Where?"

"To the Hidden Isles where he was born, to pay his respects to his father, the Master of Tides. But your scouts must have seen that the *serpent de mer* wasn't flying, or you wouldn't have dared to attack us."

The sea serpent was Drangø's personal flag, flown only when he was in residence. Grimoire gave a laugh like the neighing of a horse at this unaccustomed candor. "This hick tells me the truth, which is more than any of you cowards do. Untie him and send for a ram's horn of beer."

When the prisoner had refreshed himself, Grimoire said, "So he's gone to the Isles. But why? Merely to bow to the old man?"

"No, my lord, it's more than that. The last time he came back, I was still a common pikeman. Everybody gathered in the Great Hall to welcome him. Countess Matilda's ladies had sewn a new tapestry of Saint Michael with his sword, and we hung it on the wall above the high table. Servants set out food and wine, and I listened to my belly rumble and hoped we'd be allowed to eat the leftovers of the feast. Then came a great booming note—the Tide Horn, which usually sounds a warning when the sea is coming in. But the ocean was already at high tide, so we knew that this time it meant Lord Drangø had been spotted by the watch. Lady Matilda led the way into the tunnel that goes to the Sea Gate, and—"

"Ah, so there's a Sea Gate," Grimoire interrupted. "What's it like?"

"Great wooden doors, heavy and thick, but rotted by dampness and salt air. They were wide open, and when we followed Milady I saw a stone ramp leading down into the water. The sky was dark because a storm was coming, and a minstrel began to strum his lute and sing 'Night gales darken, it snows from the north.'

"Suddenly a boat with a prow carved like a dragon appeared out of the murk, then another, and another. I was craning my neck to see when the master-at-arms ordered us back into the Great Hall. A fight had started, people wrestling for the best places, so we were knocking heads to calm them down when a cheer came from the tunnel, and I knew he'd arrived. Soon all the people of quality returned, with the count leading them. He was taller than the sons of men and he carried a casket bound in iron. He opened it and poured gold and silver and jewels on the high table."

"Ah, now tell me about that," said Grimoire, greed flaring in his eyes.

"The best jewels he gave to Lady Matilda, and then his chamberlain distributed the rest so that everyone received a gift according to his rank, even the soldiers. My share was a silver coin with words on it that Father Joseph told me were written in runes. Someone asked, 'My lord, where did this wonderful treasure come from?' and he answered in a voice like distant thunder, 'From the floor of the sea, from the bottom of the monstrous world.'"

Grimoire frowned. "How does a man get treasure from the floor of the sea?"

"Some say the Hidden Isles are surrounded by reefs. The Master of Tides is a great magician, so he raises storms to drive ships onto the rocks. I believe that, for even common witches can cause thunderstorms, as all men know. The islanders are descended from the Vikings, and they row out to loot the wrecks and pay him tribute. So the Master is richer than all other men, and he shares with his son."

Grimoire turned to his courtiers, smiling. "See how much I've learned from this fellow? And the men wanted to take him out of his skin! What's inside him is far more valuable than what's outside. Skin is only skin, but knowledge is power."

To the prisoner, he said, "Will you swear allegiance to me, Richard, become my servant, and fight for me as bravely as you did for Drangø and Matilda?"

"Right gladly, my lord." At a gesture, he approached on hands and knees and kissed the toe of his new master's boot.

"Take him away and feed him," commanded Grimoire. "And you, my servants, gather near, for now I know how to take the castle and all its treasures for ourselves. As for that peasant, he's the key to my plan, so he must live for the time being."

For the time being. Sitting apart from Grimoire's men, Richard devoured bread and cheese and pondered what still looked to be a short life. He'd heard the count's last words and thought, *What'll happen to me when I'm no longer useful?*

He recalled a story of his father's about a peasant sentenced to be hanged for poaching. The rope was already around his neck when the king galloped by on a great black stallion.

"Your majesty!" the peasant cried out. "Spare me! Spare me, and I'll…I'll teach your horse to talk!"

"H'm," said the king, reining in. "I'd like to hear what Prancer has to say. He has more sense than any of my sons. Take this man to the royal stable," he ordered. "Post a guard over him. You have one year," he told the peasant, and galloped on.

"Are you crazy?" asked the hangman as he removed the noose. "You can't teach a horse to talk!"

"Listen," said the peasant, "in a year the king may die. Or I may die. Or the horse may start to talk!"

That was wisdom, Richard reflected. In peasant stories, the rabbit always outwitted the fox, sly weakness always overcame foolish strength. He was safe for tonight, anyway, and what happened tomorrow would just happen. He borrowed a bloody cloak from a corpse that didn't need it, lay down on the stones, and instantly fell asleep, ignoring the bustle and movement that filled the camp.

The noise didn't mean a night attack. The Tide Horn had boomed, clearly audible ashore, the sea was returning, and soon Michael's Mount lay secure behind a broad moat of salt water. But in the darkness, Grimoire sent raiders with torches fanning out to scour the countryside for captives. What finally woke Richard were the lamentations of the men and women the soldiers brought in.

Groggy with sleep, he sat up and peered around him. The sun hadn't yet risen, but the sourceless light of early morning already suffused the sky. A dense, low-lying bank of mist covered the sea, and beneath it he could hear the tide beginning to withdraw again, sounding like a gargoyle rainspout in a storm. And as the water left, Grimoire's men began prodding their prisoners with pikes and swords out onto the mucky plain it left behind.

The peasants held hands like frightened children, for they knew the "boils" or quicksand pits were there, but not how to spot them. First one, then two, then three became trapped and sank slowly out of sight, struggling and screaming. That showed the soldiers what to avoid, and they drove the diminishing crowd onward until the dark mass of Michael's Mount took form in the mist. The sentries on the walls saw them, drums beat, arrows and crossbow bolts started to flicker and twang. The attackers cheered, trumpets brayed, serfs manhandled ladders forward, and the assault began.

By now, Richard was wide awake. He'd saved a chunk of black bread for breakfast and munched it while listening to the progress of the fight. With four years of soldiering behind him, he thought, *They'll never get over the wall. It's highest and thickest on the landside, and when they try to climb, their ladders will sink in the muck. So this is a diversion. The real attack will come elsewhere.*

The count's chamberlain appeared and grunted, "He wants you." Richard swallowed the last crumbs of breakfast and joined forty or so men-at-arms in mail shirts and conical helmets who were gathering at the shoreline. Six serfs wearing yokes like oxen carried an iron-tipped battering ram between them on leather slings, and they stood waiting like patient animals, breath smoking in the chill.

Grimoire arrived in hauberk and breastplate, sword at his side, and growled at Richard, "Now, *paysan*, lead me to the Sea Gate. And make it quick, before this fog disappears."

They set out over the sodden plain, zigzagging to avoid the boils, whose smooth, glistening surfaces Richard pointed out to his new master. "No ruts, no stones," he explained. "They're like death—cruel when they stifle you, but soft once you stop fighting and just sink down."

The farther from shore, the thicker the mist. They entered a horizonless world where nobody could see more than three or four paces in any direction. The fog distorted the sounds of combat, so the fighting seemed sometimes near, sometimes distant. Now and again, a sudden cry or brazen clang rose above the clamor, only to die away. But mostly they marched as if in a dream, hearing no sound but the squelching of their mucky boots. The rising sun shot gleams of silvery light through the grayness and flickers of color appeared, like the mother-of-pearl inside an oyster shell.

Richard sensed Grimoire's tension. The count was brave to a fault, but he was in a world absolutely strange with nobody but a former enemy to guide him. "Don't worry, my lord," counseled Richard. "Many a training march have I made here, and even when I can't see Michael's Mount, I know where it lies."

Grimoire shot him a bleak glance that promised instant death if he wasn't telling the truth. But then something huge and dark began to solidify ahead of them. Slowly its edges sharpened, shadows became walls, and they could make out the base of a tower whose conical roof was still invisible in the mist. When a ray of sunlight touched the seawall, Grimoire gave a rare smile, for the battlements were empty of defenders. A murmur of admiration ran through his men. Their boots were lumps of sticky clay, cramps in their thighs felt like barbed arrows, but labor and pain were now forgotten. The count's daring maneuver had achieved perfect surprise.

Straight ahead stood the ramp, just as Richard had described it. Slime, seaweed, pale barnacles, and the brown shells of mussels covered the stones to the high-tide line. But above that they shone smooth, even began to glitter as the fog dispersed and the early sunlight gilded them. The double doors of the Sea Gate stood massive and dark and might have looked impregnable, except for white ridges of salt staining the oak and streaks of rust eating at the hinges.

Grimoire shouted an order. The serfs began to climb with the heavy ram, grunting and cursing as their wooden sabots slipped in the sea-slime. At the top they took a breath and swung the ram backward and then forward, crashing its iron head against the place where the doors met—once, twice, three times. For what seemed an eternity the pounding went on, as monotonous as a hammer on a blacksmith's anvil or flails on a threshing floor.

Then, without warning, metal snapped. The rusty bolts holding the hinges of the right-hand panel to the stonework had given way, and slowly a couple hundredweight of oak folded back, sweeping serfs and ram off the ramp into the muck below. Grimoire roared, "First man inside wins gold and a knighthood!"

The soldiers cheered and their boots crunched the seashells as they swarmed up the ramp. The count was in his element now and Richard could see it, for there was a look about born fighters that he knew well. The man loved war—many people said it was the only thing he *did* love, though some charitably believed that his young son, now safe at home in Castle Grimoire, was another. "I should have brought the boy," he muttered, "and given him a lesson." He laughed to see his men scrambling over the wreckage, and followed them with Richard at his heels.

But at the tunnel entrance they were met by a sudden fury of clashing metal, and Grimoire stopped, looking utterly astonished. For a moment Richard, too, was baffled. The landside attack was supposed to have drawn all the defenders away, yet sounds of combat resounded in the tunnel, made louder by echoes. Cursing, Grimoire plunged headlong into the dark interior, shouting orders and beating the backs of his men with the flat of his sword. Richard stumbled after him blindly. At first he saw only struggling shadows and sparks flying as steel met steel. Then amid the din of battle, a woman's strong contralto voice cried out, "Saint Michael! Saint Michael! Kill them all!"

Richard knew that voice and what it meant. Alerted by the pounding of the ram, Countess Matilda had brought her bodyguards into the Great Hall and stationed them in the narrow archway leading into the tunnel. Richard had drunk beer with those massive brutes and knew them well—they numbered only a dozen but were giants, top-notch fighters carefully chosen to protect her, and they blocked the opening as a cork plugs a bottle.

Peasants, when not being scorned for their stupidity, were famous for their low cunning. Richard's low cunning now told him it was time to go. If Matilda spotted him among the attackers, she'd know him for a traitor, with a traitor's fate to look forward to if she won. And he already knew that if Grimoire won, he'd be discarded as no longer useful—probably handed back to the troops to be killed for their amusement. His skin prickled, as if warning him that he might yet lose it, and he turned to escape, hoping to find a hiding place where neither army could spot him.

He trotted down the ramp, turned shoreward, and set off, threading his way among the boils, skirting the crags and boulders of Michael's Mount. He was searching for something he'd noticed one day when he was doing sentry duty on the castle wall, and suddenly he saw it—a narrow defile leading crookedly upward. He forced his way between two slimy boulders and began to climb, paying no attention to the sharp-edged barnacles that cut his hands and scraped his knees. Finally he reached the square-cut blocks that formed the foundation of the castle, and sank down in the shadow of the wall to catch his breath and think.

There were some advantages to his lowly birth. He'd spent a great part of his boyhood waiting—for winters to end, for crops to grow, for rain in a drought—and waiting was the only thing he could do now. Let the fighting sort itself out, he decided, and only then consider what might come next. Meanwhile, he did something that no one but a peasant would have done in the middle of a battle—he crossed his arms on his knees, put his chin down, and took a little nap.

At once he began to dream. He seemed to enter his parents' cottage, back in Hazelgrove. He kissed his mother, who smelled like baking bread, then his father with his briar-like whiskers and perpetual barnyard aura of sweat, earth, and dung. The walls of wattle and daub dissolved and Richard found himself outside in the mild glow of an autumn evening. The reaping was over, the men had laid aside their sickles, and the women were swinging flails in rhythm. Clouds of golden dust rose from the threshing ground, and he heard the twittering of barn swallows and the bells of cattle shambling home. His little brother had starved to death during a hard winter ten years ago, yet in the dream he lived again, riding by on the back of a cow and giving him an impish grin in passing.

Richard awoke weeping. He yearned so desperately to go home that he almost leaped up and ran down Michael's Mount, as if an enemy army didn't lie between him and Hazelgrove, as if the village wasn't smoking ruins, as if his parents weren't as dead as his brother. He'd known the cruelty of life from his earliest days, yet sometimes it still had the power to unman him, and for a while he sat with his back against the stones, sobbing like a child.

Then reality intruded. He wasn't dead yet, so he wiped his tears and began to study the world around him. He was seated high above the plain of silt with a wide view of land and water. Out to sea, a storm cloud gathered above the northern horizon. Ashore, he could see a corner of Grimoire's camp with its piles of loot, tethered horses, stragglers and doxies and other hangers-on.

Cook fires burned; a large woman was stirring a pot. He couldn't see the combat along the landside wall but he could hear it, and cupped his hands behind both ears, trying to judge who was winning. As if in answer, a wave of cheering came from above, followed by a roar from the master-at-arms, "The oil! Give 'em the boiling oil!"

As Richard had foreseen, Grimoire's men were having a hard time trying to climb out of the muck into the face of everything the defenders could throw at them or pour on top of them. Yet they might triumph anyway. If the count won the fight in the Great Hall, if he seized the castle keep and displayed his banner from the battlements, even the stoutest defenders might decide they were in a trap, lose heart, and stop fighting. The battle was at its turning point. What should he do?

Once again a woman's voice told him. Matilda had sent one of her ladies to raise the alarm, and over the clamor of battle he heard her shriek that the master-at-arms must send men to the Great Hall, or all was lost. Instantly Richard leaped to his feet and began shouting, "Saint Michael! Saint Michael! Brothers, throw me a rope!"

A head appeared between two crenellations and someone cried, "By God, it's the sergeant!"

A rope came coiling down. He looped it around his waist and scrambled up the wall and through the gap between the stones. Father Joseph, Matilda's chaplain, stopped feeding the fire under a fresh cauldron of oil to greet him with the sign of the cross. The master-at-arms, massive as a bull in armor, lurched up and thundered, "So you escaped, Richard! Good man! What about the others in the rearguard?"

"All dead but me, sir."

"All heroes, all dead! Well, that's war. How'd you get away?"

"They had me tied up. They were planning to skin me. But when they left this morning to attack the castle, I wriggled out of the ropes and escaped. It took me a while to get here, for I had to make a long detour over the muck to avoid them. But here I am."

"God must be with us, to send me my sergeant just when I need him! Grab a weapon from one of these dead fellows and take these bastards along—I mean *you* bastards, standing there with your thumbs up your arses!

Take them to the Great Hall, Richard, and see what her ladyship's cater-wauling about. Women!" he added, and turned back to his own battle.

Richard stripped a corpse of its shirt of greasy scale armor and shrugged into it. He rejected the first helmet offered him, choosing instead one with a half-visor that would partly hide his face. He buckled the chin guard, selected a sword with a counterweight on the pommel for balance, and set off at a run with eight men following him. His plan was simple and direct—everyone in Grimoire's party knew him for a turncoat, so every one of them had to die.

The castle was part fortress, part village. Behind its walls, a tangle of narrow, dark, twisting alleys housed blacksmiths' forges, pawnbrokers, sellers of wine and beer, bakers, cookshops, even a brothel at whose mullioned window three slatternly women stopped catching lice in each others' hair to cry invitations. Richard threaded the maze by instinct, turning this way and that, taking flights of wet stone steps at a bound. Finally he spun on his right foot and dashed down a passage so narrow that his shoulders brushed the walls. At its end, across an open space that once had held a food market, the huge tower of the castle keep soared into the air.

A moment more and he and his band erupted into the shadowy, high-ceilinged Great Hall. How well Richard knew it—the smoke-darkened beams, the long refectory tables and narrow benches, the rush-strewn flag-stone floor, the raised platform where knights and nobles ate at the high table under tapestries portraying hunts and battles. Above them all, the warrior archangel hefted his sword in garish colors undimmed as yet by smoke and grease.

Grimoire's men were hewing down the last of Lady Matilda's guards, but they'd taken losses, too, for bodies choked the archway into the tunnel and others lay sprawled across the floor. Facing his first foeman, Richard well remembered the gap-toothed fellow sharpening a knife, threatening to peel him like an onion. "Saint Michael!" he thundered and split the caitiff's skull with a downstroke, cleaving through his helmet and his face, whose look said more clearly than words, *So now you're back on their side?*

The sword stuck in the vise-like grip of steel and bone, and Richard was wrenching it free when another enemy came at him with teeth bared and mace upraised. But before he could strike, his armored head flew off and went clattering across the floor, spraying crimson as it went. Richard turned to find Lady Matilda, sword in hand, completing a swing like the vane of a windmill. She gave him a triumphant smile, pointed at the head and cried, "Faith, 'twill reach hell before the rest of him!"

After that the fight was still brisk, but Grimoire's men had lost heart—the more so as they began to realize that their leader had deserted them. When all were down, Richard walked among the bodies, hewing off heads like a peasant cutting cabbages from their stalks. Those who begged to surrender died too, for he wanted nobody babbling unwelcome truths to Matilda. But the man whose death he most desired was not there. Had the count made his escape when he saw the battle turning against him? And if so, where the devil was he now?

Followed by the countess, he made his way into the tunnel and over the wreckage of the shattered Sea Gate. From the top of the ramp he searched the dun-colored plain but saw no one. Had Grimoire used his knowledge of the boils to make it back safely to shore? Was he, at this moment, rallying his men for a new attack? Or was he still in transit, hidden from sight by the rocks or an angle of the walls?

A blast of cold wind turned Richard's gaze to the north. Far away—perhaps over the remote Hidden Isles—the storm he'd noticed earlier had become a vast and growing cloud shaped like an anvil. Lightning flickered like sparks from a blacksmith's hammer, and the horizon appeared to be in motion. The sight held him spellbound for a moment, utterly confused. Then he understood—the Master of Tides had raised a great tempest and the storm-surge was driving back the sea before its time!

The sun vanished like a quenched candle. The wind strengthened to a steady gale, and the first waves of the tidal bore swept foaming up the gentle slope of the shoreline. Steadily their onset strengthened, the sea rushing across the flats, rising as if it never intended to stop, dashing against the boulders of Michael's Mount and flinging spray a bowshot into the air. Then Matilda pointed and cried, "Drangø comes! Saint Michael preserve him!"

Yes, now Richard saw the little fleet, mere dots in the distance, but growing under the impetus of wind and tide into long, low ships like those the Vikings had made famous in the last century. The masts were bare, for the sails had been lowered or had blown away, and hard-laboring seamen rowed mightily to prevent the ships from broaching—turning sideways to the wind and getting swamped. The dragonhead prows rose and fell in a steady rhythm as shorebound waves rushed under the keels. At the stern of the flagship, a big man wrapped in fur stood beside two seamen wrestling with the heavy beam of the tiller.

"He'll see the broken doors, he'll think we've been conquered!" cried Matilda. "Richard, do something!"

He hastened back into the reeking slaughterhouse of the Great Hall, wrenched down the tapestry of St. Michael, bore it to the Sea Gate, and with the aid of two of his men raised it and clung tight as the wind tried to tear it away. The message was received, for when the little fleet swept by, Drangø took off his helmet and joined his crew in a cheer that went unheard amid the tumult of wind and waves.

The next act played out far from Richard's sight. But he heard the story so often—heard it told, heard it sung, heard it every possible way—that sometimes he almost believed he'd been present at the moment when Drangø arrived. With no way to anchor on a lee shore in a gale, he beached his fleet. One by one the ships grounded on the shingle, striking with violent shudders that made their timbers groan, canting over and spilling men into the surf like wheat from a gleaner's apron.

It was a disorderly invasion. Some fighters stepped into quicksand. Some drowned in their armor. Some swallowed seawater and came ashore puking, not fighting. Disciplined defenders could have cut them to pieces. But the leaderless enemy was already in flight from the onrushing sea, obeying no command but *sauve qui peut*, every man for himself. Some fugitives paused to retrieve their loot and were hewn down and left lying among their stolen treasures. Some jumped on horses and galloped away. Most merely ran for their lives, and the storm gave them cover as wave after wave of rain swept in, followed by an avalanche of hailstones.

All that night the wet, wild darkness—almost as dense as the nighttime sea—covered the shattered enemy like a cloak. But next morning the sun rose on a glistening world spangled with ice, and Drangø reorganized his men and began the pursuit. This part of the victory Richard saw with his own eyes, for by then he and the master-at-arms had reached shore in a small boat. Soon the soldiers were joined by hundreds of peasants, who came crawling out of their hiding places in woods and caves to hug their saviors and join the hunt for their beaten foes.

They were deadly at the game, for they knew every fold and thicket in the countryside. When they found an enemy in hiding, the men-at-arms stood back, grinning, and let the peasants attack him with their sickles, clubs, and reaping hooks, striking from every side like crows mobbing an owl in daylight. Those so unwise as to surrender were bound, dragged back to the sooty walls of still-smoldering Hazelgrove, and imprisoned in rabbit hutches. All day the village children tormented the captives, poking out their eyes with sticks, and that night the grown-ups piled firewood around the hutches and burned them alive.

They were still screaming when the revel began. Matilda sent bread and beer from the castle and all night the peasants and soldiers ate, drank, and danced to the beating of drums, the hollow whistling of panpipes, and the wailing of two-string viols. Wooden *sabots* pounded the earth, cries of laughter could be heard as far away as the walls of Michael's Mount, and many a child was begotten among the ruins to fill the places of the dead. That was peasant justice and peasant joy: *My enemy is dead, I'll live on, I'll see another day.* Could anybody ask for more?

Richard didn't join the common people in rejoicing. Indeed, by the time the party started, he was no longer one of them. Puzzled and anxious, he was standing on the beach at sunset, wondering for the thousandth time where the devil Grimoire could have gotten to, when Drangø approached with bloody sword in hand.

There had always been something strange about his eyes, and they had never looked stranger than now, the green irises almost lost in pupils that were wide and shining black. The skin of his face was still like leather, his beard like spines, his huge hands scaly with leprosy acquired in the Holy Land. He looked like Richard's image of Death, and his guilty conscience told him that Grimoire had survived long enough to be captured and tell of his treason. His fear became a certainty when Drangø growled, "Kneel!"

Richard sank to the stones and bowed his head, grateful that his death would at least be quick, instead of the long, slow exit usually accorded traitors. He was waiting for the blow when Drangø struck each of his shoulders with the flat of his blade and roared, "Rise, Sir Richard, for I dub thee knight!"

He was so dazed that he remained kneeling until Drangø extended a hand burned brown by the fierce sun of a distant land and raised him to his feet.

By mere accident—by being first loyal, then disloyal, then loyal again—Richard had achieved more than he'd ever dreamed of. Perhaps destiny was like the *serpent de mer*—it twisted from side to side, and you had to stay loose to follow its many turnings.

At the victory feast in the hastily scrubbed Great Hall, he sat for the first time at the high table—at the far end, to be sure, not beside Drangø and Matilda, which might have created dangerous envy among the knights of good family, who looked at this jumped-up intruder with astonishment and anger in their eyes.

Yet there he sat, elevated above the heads of common folk, wearing a pair of spurs that Matilda had given him for saving her during the fight in the Great Hall. He was too ignorant to realize that nobody wore spurs to dinner. Indeed, he didn't yet know how to ride a horse, for common soldiers walked everywhere and his nearest approach to equitation had come as a peasant boy riding an ox on his way to plow a field.

But one thing the new-minted Sir Richard did know—he knew how not to be a fool. Instead of boasting, instead of saying that the castle would have been lost but for him, he sat quietly, ate and drank sparingly, and if questioned about his part in the battle, answered in deferential tones, "I did what I could to help." He addressed ordinary knights as "My lord," and called Father Joseph, who sat beside him, "Your holiness," until the priest gently reminded him that he wasn't Pope, at least not yet.

That night, instead of demanding better quarters, Richard slept as usual with the soldiers in their barracks next to the stables. Next day he worked with them to inter the bodies of friends with prayers and incense, and burn those of enemies with dung and toss the ashes into the sea. Then he assisted the carpenters, whose hammers resounded from dawn to dusk, rebuilding the bridge and repairing the damage to the Sea Gate. Out on the water, fishermen cast their nets and hauled in loads of squirming cod; on land, peasants hastened to rethatch their huts before the winter set in, and to plant root crops that could survive the coming frosts.

Finally, Matilda remembered her new knight, called him inside, and assigned him quarters appropriate to his rank—a pallet bed in a room with sixteen other bachelors. The keep was thronged and hallways had yet to be invented, so the low vaulted chamber served also as a passageway, with people constantly going back and forth on errands of their own. The rushes that covered the floor were infested with mice, and a nearby latrine added to the gamy fragrance of unwashed bodies, especially after the shutters on the single small window were covered with stretched pigs' bladders and shut tight against the autumn cold. But at least Richard was *inside*.

He kept to his well-tried strategy of silence. He could have drunk too much, boasted, mocked the minstrels who attributed the victory solely to Drangø (*great knight, who rode the horses of the sea*) and Matilda (*stern lady, who with sword in hand, slew the foul wretch and all his band*). Richard could have laughed, said that she and her guards were already defeated when he arrived on the scene, that Drangø really did nothing but pursue an enemy already beaten—but he didn't, and as a result kept his cool head on his thick shoulders.

Instead of complaining about his noisy, smelly quarters, he made friends with his new roommates—especially with Drangø's squire, a red-bearded young man named Fulk de Vere. They began to exercise together, wearing leather helmets and quilted jerkins while pounding each other with wooden swords. Fulk came of good family, had been brought up to ride, and taught Richard how to stay on horseback by knocking him off every time they jousted. They worked hard at these impromptu battles, for the count and countess were already plotting vengeance on Grimoire, his lands and people.

At night, while their roommates gambled or snored, Fulk and Richard chatted over a jug of wine. Both enjoyed these bull sessions, though for different reasons. Fulk simply loved to talk and give advice, while Richard hoped to learn how to play his new role as knight. First of all, said his coun-selor, he must take a surname and rid himself forever of the lowly, one-named peasant he had been.

"Don't matter a bit what it is," Fulk added, "just so long as it has a *de* in it. What's the name of that village where you were born?"

"Coudray. Hazelgrove."

"So call yourself that. Sir Richard de Coudray—it's got a ring to it!"

Matilda had begun to create a little court made up of her minstrels, her ladies, and male favorites who were young and pretty. She also ordered the priest to make her knights literate—no easy task. Richard complained to Fulk that all the letters looked to him like arrowheads and axes, and his pal commiserated, saying that reading and writing were monkish pursuits unfit for one who wore the spurs of knighthood. But to please the countess, he advised Richard to learn how to write his name, so he mastered letters to that extent. He spelled his name seven or eight different ways, but that hardly mattered, because everybody's spelling was free-form.

As Sir Richard de Coudray (Coudraie, Codrai, etc.), he made himself a fixture of castle life by volunteering for jobs that nobody else wanted. He took command of the sentries and walked the circuit of the walls day and night, even in the snowstorms of a long and bitter winter, to make sure the shivering men stayed awake and alert. He borrowed money from Fulk, acquired arms and armor, and began looking for a symbol for his shield. Richard already had a head full of strange creatures—angels that lived in the sky; devils that resided underground; earthly beings like elves that tied people's hair in knots while they slept; trolls that hid under bridges to attack the unwary.

But the animals in the priest's *Bestiary* were new to him. He studied Leviathan, River Horse, Crocodilus, and Cameleopard, but the one that caught his eye was Chimera, whose name Father Joseph taught him to pronounce (incorrectly) as she-*mair*-ah. It was a curious compound, with the head of a roaring lion, the body of a goat, and a serpent for a tail. An ancient Greek could have told Richard the creature was meant to be female, but ancient Greeks were in short supply in medieval France, so he had the lion painted on his shield with a full bristling mane, and the goat with the underpinnings of a billy. Why he liked Chimera, he couldn't have said—perhaps because, like himself, the creature was made of many contradictory parts.

At his request, the priest wrote out the motto he chose—*Esclave du Devoir*, Slave to Duty—and he had it painted under Chimera. Day by day, Richard proved himself worthy of both the monster and the motto. With the men he commanded, the roaring lion was most in evidence. When the goat rose rampant, he satisfied his needs with the gaggle of pliable wenches, doxies, drabs, trulls, bawds, strumpets, and whores who infested the Mount. But the snake with its seeming lowliness and its cool, sly wisdom prevailed whenever he served the count and countess.

He studied them carefully, listening as usual to Fulk, a born gossip who liked nothing better than showing off his knowledge of the great. Matilda, he said, had come to Michael's Mount a generation past from her birthplace in Caen to marry the count of those days, whose name had possibly been Guillaume. Of their five children, one son survived to adulthood, which was about average. When news came that the Muslims had retaken Jerusalem from the Christians, the Pope preached a new Crusade and father and son went to the East, whence like many others they failed to return.

Matilda was left struggling to defend her fief against an array of enemies—not only her lawless neighbors, but the *écorcheurs* drifting back from the Holy Land. Then one day, a different sort of veteran rode across the floating bridge and asked for an audience with her. He shocked Matilda with his ugliness, yet won her favor with a remarkable gift—her husband's seal ring, taken from his finger when he was dying. That night he sat beside her at the high table, telling stories of the failed Crusade, of Ascalon and Acre, of battles he'd fought, of Christians dying by the thousand under Muslim arrows on the burning field of Hattin.

Now fascinated by her strange guest, Matilda gave Drangø comfortable sleeping quarters, and loaned him a ship to carry him home to the Hidden Isles. When he returned bearing a casket of gold coins as a gift from his father, the Master of Tides, she made him her seneschal or chief steward. He took on the task of defending the fief against its many enemies, and did it well. Instead of fighting the *écorcheurs*, he recruited them with money and the promise of land, and used them to crush first an invasion and then a rebellion. Again and again in battle he proved himself *un chevalier sans peur et sans pitié*, a knight without fear or pity, a rough man made for a rough time, and his harsh measures gave the immense gift of peace to Matilda, her lands, and her people.

He became indispensable, and she no longer shrank from his leprosy (if such it was), for his scaly skin condition appeared to do him no harm and did not spread to those he touched. They became lovers, and in time married. He remained only her consort until the Duke of Normandy (who also happened to be King of England, as if that mattered) accepted a handsome gift of gold to award him the title of count. Thus the veteran of a lost war became Sieur Drangø des Îles Occultes, Comte de Mont Saint-Michel, and the sheer orotundity of his name—two *de*'s instead of one!—caused common men to fall to their knees in awe when they heard it.

All through Fulk's flood of talk, Richard kept his own counsel. He never repeated what he heard, fearing it might echo around the whispering gallery of the castle and lose him the favor of his masters. Perhaps his good sense came from his peasant background, perhaps from the anxiety he lived with, for he knew that if his old treason were ever discovered, the count and countess who today showered him with honors would send him without hesitation to torture and the ax. In bad dreams he attended once again an execution he'd seen as a boy. A man of his village had stood between two soldiers, trembling and white-faced after a night on the rack, mumbling plaintively, "Before God, I swear I didn't do it." Do what? Nobody knew. But he was hanged anyway.

Fulk had no such fears, and loved gossip far too much for caution. He often acted as Drangø's valet, assisting him to robe and disrobe, and told Richard with a theatrical shiver, "You should see *le Chef* with his clothes off. The Boss is quite a sight, *mon ami*, quite a sight! The leprosy's all over him in spots. Ugh!"

"I hope you don't say things like that to anybody but me," murmured Richard, looking over his shoulder to see if anybody might be listening.

"Who cares? If we lived in Paris, everybody would gossip about the king. Out here in the sticks, everybody gossips about the count. It's expected."

Richard shook his head and decided that his friend—like so many of the well-born—thought himself invulnerable, and for that reason was a bit of a fool. *He'll never wear a gray beard*, he thought, but kept that opinion, like so many others, to himself.

With the approach of spring, Drangø prepared to visit the Hidden Isles to bend his knee to his father, whose magic had done so much to save Michael's Mount from the enemy.

He fitted out a small fleet and chose two dozen men-at-arms to go along in case of pirates. He ordered Fulk to accompany him, leaving Matilda to rule in his place, and naming Richard—a new sign of his favor—to command the Mount's permanent garrison until he returned.

Fulk was pleased to have the Boss all to himself, for he hoped to marry one of Matilda's ladies. He had his choice all picked out—she was of good birth, he said, and she'd bring a handsome dowry. Richard congratulated him on his expectations and helped pack his gear into leather bags oiled for protection against salt water and air. Together they carried the luggage through the Sea Gate and down the ramp. The evening was brisk and bracing with the smells of tar and cordage, and the green and crimson pennon of the sea serpent swelled and fluttered at the flagship's masthead. The friends embraced, and Fulk stepped over the gunwale where—to the sailors' great delight—he promptly fell flat on the pitching deck.

While he scrambled up red-faced and began looking for a spot to stow his bags, Richard returned smiling to the castle. He too had his ambitions to consider, and if his pal now had Drangø to himself, he had Matilda. That evening at dinner, he carved her mutton for her, a lowly task that most knights would have scorned for fear of getting the name of *flagorneur* or toad-eater. Richard could not have cared less, for becoming her carver meant that he sat beside her—indeed, she invited him to take Drangø's big chair, which fit him pretty well.

She was a good trencherwoman, piling into her food with energy, but continuing to talk between mouthfuls. "See your friend off?" she queried during such an interlude.

"Yes, milady."

"Nice boy, but not discreet. It's not enough to know secrets, you must also know how to keep them."

"He's entirely loyal to you."

"Of course he's loyal. What else could he be? The de Veres think they're special, but really they don't count for much. They were lucky to get their son into Drangø's service." Richard must have shown his surprise, for she added, "It's being born between the cabbage-rows, my lad. You still don't know how to distinguish between different shades of prominence."

"I learn every day how much I've yet to learn."

That made her chuckle, and a quivering blancmange deposited before her put her in an even better mood. "Ever think about marrying?" she surprised him by asking.

"Often," said Richard, who had never thought about it at all.

"Anyone special?"

"I mean to seek counsel from some wiser person."

She polished off the dessert, licked her fingers, and laughed aloud. "You are clever," she said. "I'm so glad I told Drangø to knight you. Well, I'll pick somebody you'll like. She'll be low-born, of course, but she'll have wide hips, be a good breeder. You need to leave the whores alone, get some savoir faire. Your friend Fulk could use some, too. How'd he look when you saw him off?"

"Delighted to be going with the count."

"He may be less delighted when he meets Drangø's father. I've never seen the Master of Tides, and I don't want to. Some doors are best left unopened, as the wife of Comorre the Cursed discovered too late."

Richard knew what she meant. Like other peasant children, he'd been brought up on tales of the cruel Breton count of the Dark Ages, not yet called Bluebeard but already famous for his way of solving matrimonial problems.

No such clouds hovered over his own wooing when, a few days later, he began to court the girl Matilda selected for him. Barbeau, Cornflower, was the only daughter of the master-at-arms, whom Richard called Lucas nowadays. (Lucas called him Sir Richard, instead of such earlier names as You

There or Shithead.) Barbeau was a bit overripe at the age of sixteen, but she was handsome, rubicund, and agreeably curved, with the promised wide hips and an abundance of hair like the golden awns of wheat. She favored the color blue, and Richard assured her that in her best gown she reminded him of *ciel d'été sans nuage*, a cloudless summer sky.

Her father watched them like an Inquisitor to make sure her honor was not compromised, but he thought Richard a good catch, the one chance his daughter would ever have to become a knight's lady. After some coquetry she agreed, and the three quickly reached an understanding that the marriage would take place as soon as Drangø returned and gave his approval.

So began an unusually peaceful time in Richard's life. With its master gone, the castle was a quieter place, but still orderly, for he and Lucas kept the sentries at their duty and the countess was a strong ruler who let nothing escape her. Taxes were collected, masses said, the stableboys fed the horses and mucked out the stalls, and the charwomen every day spread fresh rushes on the floors and threw the old ones into the sea. Evenings brought the usual dinners in the Great Hall, where entertainment meant jugglers tossing balls in the air, minstrels singing to the tinkle of lutes, and acrobats doing cartwheels or standing on their heads. Richard and Barbeau spent the gentle days together like the young lovers they were—they played games, ate and drank, and basked in Matilda's glowing approval of the impending match she'd made.

The count arrived at the beginning of summer with a chest of rare jewels and coins, some still encrusted with limestone and little shells as if they'd lain long on the bottom of the sea. His men were all safe and sound, except for one—Fulk de Vere was missing. Richard grilled a couple of the men-at-arms about his friend but they professed ignorance, saying only that Fulk had followed the count into "a cavern" and not returned. At the homecoming feast, Richard occupied his usual modest place at the end of the table and when someone mentioned Fulk's name, he noted Drangø's frown and decided to delay asking questions that might be unwelcome.

He didn't, however, stay silent about his marriage plans. When Drangø appeared next morning looking well-rested and approachable, he fell to one knee and asked permission for the match. When that was granted, he requested a place to live with his new bride, since she could hardly join him in the men's dormitory.

"That Barbeau's a fine-looking wench," mused Drangø. "She deserves a decent home. You can have the Little Tower."

Richard was delighted. An afterthought sprouting from the huge body of the keep, the Little Tower was hard to reach but as private a place as anything the castle could offer. Steep stone steps spiraled up to a small circular room with a single slit window covered by a thin, translucent sheet of vellum. More steps set into the wall led to a trapdoor opening on the tower top, an aerie with breathtaking views. Richard hired a carpenter to build a wide bed ("Your workbench, sir," said the fellow with a leer), Matilda contributed bedding and a square of Saracen carpet, and Barbeau brought samples of her needlework. Suddenly Richard had a home, the first he'd known since the far-off day when Lucas had hauled him, a terrified boy, out of his parents' cottage.

It was time to visit Father Joseph and—with a bellyful of butterflies he'd never felt in time of battle—avow his wish for lawful marriage. The date was set, the banns followed, and Barbeau went into seclusion in her father's quarters, surrounded by women friends who spent whole days giggling. The ceremony in the chapel was brief but the banquet that followed was long, with much drinking and endless coarse jokes. Finally, Drangø rose and led the guests through the vaulted chambers of the keep and up the spiral stairway to the tower room. He put his personal seal of approval on the marriage by laying one leg on the bed and taking it off again, thus asserting his *droit du seigneur*, his right to sleep with the bride on the first night, but also his decision to forego that right.

Applauding this chivalrous act, the guests urged the newlyweds to "do the two-backed beast," and counseled Richard to "break his lance many times" and "make her squeak." While leaving, one knight fell off the spiral stairs but luckily was too drunk to kill himself. Richard closed the door, embraced his bride, unlaced his codpiece, and swiftly got down to the business of the night. Just before dawn, Barbeau rose and sprinkled a vial of pig's blood on the bed, for she wanted the washerwomen to report—wrongly, since Lucas hadn't seen everything—that she'd been a virgin. So the wedding and bedding were completed in the best of taste and tradition, and everyone agreed that when it came to *politesse*, the famous court of Camelot could have done no better.

As a married man, Richard began to create his own small world within the vast hive of the castle. The Little Tower became his refuge both from his duties and from the anxiety that continued to beset him. Every night one of his men slept just outside his door, sword lying beside him. Yet Barbeau noticed that Richard suffered from unspoken fears, slept restlessly, and sometimes cried out, "Grimoire, Grimoire, where are you?" She wondered what dark secret he was keeping from her—then thought of a dark secret she was keeping from him, and decided not to ask questions that might lead him to ask questions of his own.

Both of them felt most secure atop the tower. The stone circle with its knee-high parapet formed a kind of crow's nest from which they could look out over their whole world. Together they watched the changes of the tides, the passage of ships, the pristine dawns, the flaming sunsets. The sea had many colors, from the deep dark blue of Barbeau's gown to meadow-like green to quicksilver under a full moon. One quiet evening on the cusp of autumn—they'd been married three months or so—Barbeau found the courage to tell him about a visit she'd made to the midwife, then turned sideways, and held her gown close to her belly to let him see the small bulge. He broke into a boyish laugh, they submerged into a deep embrace, and were whispering to each other with the tips of their noses almost touching when an uproar began in the castle below.

Richard hastened down, sought out Drangø, and learned that after a lifetime of many centuries the Master of Tides was dying. By some means known only to great magicians, he was calling his son home across the width of the sea, and this time Drangø ordered Richard to leave his new wife and go with him.

As usual, he bowed his head and prepared to follow his master, though with many misgivings. He hated leaving pregnant Barbeau, and the night before he departed they clung to each other and Richard wept as he hadn't done in years, drying his wet face on her hair. Next day she followed him to the Sea Gate, then hastened back to the Little Tower to watch the fleet grow small in the distance, and wave her handkerchief until it vanished in the horizon haze.

Richard, trying to stand on the pitching deck, feared also for himself. He'd never been out of sight of land, couldn't swim, and trembled when he thought of the mysterious being at the journey's end. Would the magician look into his soul and reveal the secret of his old treason to Drangø? Then, like Fulk, Richard would not return from the Hidden Isles and no one would dare even to ask what had become of him.

And there was the sheer discomfort of life aboard the longship. The deck was the bilges, or vice versa, and a catwalk mounted above the keel rose only a handsbreadth higher than the rowers' benches. Within an hour of departure, Richard was seasick, and learned a basic lesson of seamanship by puking into the wind and getting his last meal back in his face. The Breton seamen roared with laughter, and Drangø smiled and said, "The lee side, *paysan*, the lee side."

He spent three days in misery, then acquired his sea legs and began to keep down the mutton stews that formed the main item of diet. Yet he was cold and stiff all the time, for autumn had begun to ruffle the open sea, and the wind was bitter and edged with ice. When the sailors were forced to lower the square sail, break out the oars, and mount them in the creaking tholes, Richard took his turn rowing like a commoner, not because he had to, but simply because he needed the exercise to get warm.

By the seventh day, he was almost enjoying the voyage. With the cramps gone from his muscles and the sickness from his belly, he strode the catwalk inhaling the cold salt air and told himself, *I can do this, too.* By then, he and Drangø were chatting more like comrades than like lord and vassal. Richard even tried a peasant joke, the one about teaching the horse to talk, and won a neighing laugh for his trouble. Drangø told him stories of the Crusade, and—his voice growing harsh and bitter—his anger at the priests whose lies had sent so many brave men on a fool's mission.

"They said Christ rules the world and would give us victory," he growled. "*Merde.* My father told me long ago not to trust the Christians, but I had to find out the truth for myself."

Richard replied, "I listen to Father Joseph and don't say anything, but I think that if God is good, He has strange ways of showing it. This world's a cockfight, and dead birds are lying everywhere with feathers full of blood."

"There are only three truths, Richard—the truth of pain, the truth of triumph, and the truth of death. Everything else is the chatter of fools."

Toward the end of the voyage, the wind came around to the south, so the seamen raised the yard and unfurled the single square sail. They spent the rest of the voyage doing little but managing the tiller, pulling at lines, and carving strange figurines of beasts and men in a smooth white stuff they said came from the horns of sea-unicorns. An experienced seaman now, Richard slept well wrapped in his cloak, and on the last day woke to find the sky already light.

He rose quickly, for he was curious to see the fabled Hidden Isles. A tiny mound like a pimple on the horizon grew slowly into a cone of jumbled rock, which in turn became a hill where gray stones mingled with green growth. Creamy breakers encircled the shoreline, and a village of small thatched houses came into view, huddled in the lee of the hill. By evening, he could make out small figures moving across a patchwork quilt of gardens and dark fields. Smoke rose from chimneys of baked mud, and now and again a vagrant breeze brought the harsh smell of burning peat. Wooden racks along the beach displayed the sleek bodies of drying cod, and in the distance Richard saw small boats with fishermen pulling at long sweeps.

Was this commonplace scene the lair of the mysterious Master of Tides? The island looked like any place where people lived by hard work. Otherwise he saw only barren islets, and instead of being misty they were all as clear and sharp as black letters on a vellum page.

When sunset reddened the sky, the seamen trussed up the sail and rowed until they caught a powerful wave that shot them through a foaming gap in the reef line to the quiet water inshore. Landing was by the usual method— everybody jumped over the side and waded on the bottom of firm, clean sand through icy, knee-deep wavelets. Women and children ran from the village to greet Drangø as he emerged dripping from the sea. They did much bowing and forelock-tugging, and he responded with a few words in a harsh, guttural language that might have been Norse.

Richard followed him, looking about with the curiosity of a man who'd never in his life been more than a league from home. One oddity of the village struck him—a wooden cross stood in its center, but hanging from it, instead of Jesus, was a face made of twisted branches entwined with ever-greens and mistletoe. Dinner was mutton stew—again—served in wooden bowls by the village women, and he and Drangø spent the night on a fir-bough platform in a log cabin whose cracks had been stuffed with moss and mud to keep out drafts.

At first light, Drangø shook him awake and they stumbled outside into a world as gray and chilly as the sea. They were relieving themselves against a fence of pale driftwood when the count startled Richard by saying, "Today we visit the house of my father."

Suppressing a sudden stab of fear, Richard cleared his throat and asked with apparent calmness, "Is the Master's castle on the mountaintop?"

"No. This island is his castle. It's all seamed with caverns and he lives inside it."

"I see," said Richard, who did not see at all.

When the sun rose they set out, riding small horses with rope bridles and long white manes and tails. As they trotted up a winding trail, Drangø explained that the mountain once had been a vent into the underworld, like Etna, which he'd seen in Sicily on his way to Palestine. For ages now it had been asleep, its crater filled with seawater that poured in through openings where molten rock once had flowed out. It was called Ragnarök, after the pagan Apocalypse—that day when the titans of the Earth will rise up, over-throw, and annihilate the gods.

"For the gods are only dreams," he said, "while the powers of the Earth endure forever."

He fell silent when the mouth of a cave appeared, half-hidden by a thicket of vines and a jumble of porous boulders. They dismounted, tied their reins to a wind-bent sapling, and entered the dark tunnel. Richard stumbled after Drangø, nearly falling three times before he began to see by the dim, greenish light of countless glowworms hanging from the ceiling on sticky white threads. Then the light strengthened, and soon he was blinking again as they emerged onto a shelf overlooking a blue crater lake. The rock walls shut off the sea breeze, and though the water was perfectly still and clear in the bright sunlight, Richard could see no bottom at all.

Drangø began to speak again. "My father takes many shapes. The pagans called him the Old Man of the Sea, and in that form he lay with my mother and begot me, as he did many another in his time. But when I saw him last, he looked as he does when he dwells alone in his castle. Fulk de Vere was with me and became frightened, so he drew his sword, and that was the end of him. Help me off with my clothes."

Now it was Richard's turn to play valet, and as surcoat, habergeon, shirt, and leggings were removed in turn and laid in a pile, he grew ever more astonished at the strange being that had gone about the world for so many years muffled in cloaks and leggings, presenting himself as a man. Under his clothing, Drangø's leathery skin should have been lighter than his face and hands but instead was darker, with more and larger scaly patches. His back was armored like the beast Crocodilus, and when he met Richard's stare the strangeness of his eyes was explained at last, for he had slit pupils, like a cat.

Richard stopped breathing, then began again, very quietly. When his lord stood naked—or rather, clothed in his native garment of gleaming scales—he tapped Richard on the chest with a sharp black claw that pierced his shirt and pricked his skin. In a voice growing ever stranger, as if throat and tongue were changing shape, the half-transformed being—no longer *he*, not yet quite *it*—gave him three commands in a voice descending from bass to tones so deep that Richard felt them as a tremor in his breastbone.

"Guard this place till I return. Care for the child Barbeau will bear. Take vengeance on Grimoire's lands and people, as I meant to do." Now almost incomprehensible, the voice added something that sounded like, "In time, every man becomes his father."

Then he—it—began inflating and emptying its lungs with a sound like the panting of a blacksmith's goatskin bellows. It turned, and in one quick motion slid into the lake as silently as a water snake. Ripples spread and vanished and the surface became absolutely still once more. The sky was just as blue and deep, so that (thought Richard) the crater looked as the whole world had on the first morning of creation, when the waters above were divided from those below.

Time or perhaps timelessness passed, while he folded his arms and waited with the dumb patience of a peasant. Then the surface roiled and heaved. He bent and saw something huge and dark rising from the depths. Remembering Fulk, he hastily unbuckled his belt and let it fall with sword and dagger to the ground, so that he stood defenseless when the reborn Master of Tides rose streaming from the depths. It towered above him; its crimson scales glinted; its whiskers had become long, trailing spines, and its huge green eyes fixed him with unwinking gaze.

In awe, Richard fell to his knees and beat his forehead on the ground until it bled, overwhelmed by the sudden insight that whatever gods might rule elsewhere, this was the true and only god of the harsh world he knew.

He returned to the village riding one horse and leading the other. The people he met looked him in the face, noted the bruise and dried blood on his forehead, and dropped their eyes. On the voyage home he hardly spoke, except to give orders that were instantly obeyed. When he addressed a seaman, the man would make a strange gesture with one hand, and none would look him directly in the face.

When they reached Michael's Mount, he stepped from the prow to the ramp—swaying on his feet, because he'd grown used to the movement of the ship—and found Matilda awaiting him amid a crowd of torch-bearers. He climbed to the Sea Gate, sank to one knee, and with eyes grave and face drawn, said, "My lady, I bring you a message from my lord the count. His father is dead, and he has stayed to take his place and rule over the Hidden Isles."

For a long time Matilda stood as if turned to stone, while everyone else stared and crossed themselves. Then she sighed and murmured, "I'm unfortunate in my loves." While the bustle and confusion of unloading began, she led Richard through the tunnel, across the Great Hall, and into her dressing room. She sent her ladies away, remarking, "I'm fifty now, an old woman, and I can receive a man without fearing the tongue of slander."

After a long silence, she said, "I wed twice, but both my husbands are gone. I bore five children, but they're all dead. Well, that's life and life is cruel. I've been caring for Barbeau because Drangø told me to adopt her firstborn and make it my own. He must have known that he wouldn't be coming back, and I'd need someone to comfort me.

"It'll be nice to have a child again. If it's a girl, I shall bring her up to be one of my ladies and marry her off to a man of quality when she's fourteen and ready to bear children of her own. If it's a boy, you shall see to his training as a knight, and if he proves worthy I'll make him my heir. You can't become a nobleman, Richard, because you're the child of peasants, but he'll be the son of a knight, so he can. That's the way people rise, in two generations or sometimes three. You've climbed a long way in this world, but you'll go no higher.

"What I can do for you is this: I'll give you land and serfs and you'll become my seneschal and learn the management of a great estate. Did Drangø have any final commands for you?"

"To care for the child and to ravage the lands of Grimoire and slay him," said Richard, adding *slay him* because that was what he wanted most.

"Then do so. I have not forgotten or forgiven what the men of the dusty hills did to my land and my people. Call on Saint Michael to give you strength, call on Satan to harden your heart, call on anybody you please, but leave not one man living in the enemy's country, nor one ear of wheat unburned, nor one stone of Castle Grimoire standing upon another. But now, go up to Barbeau—she's waiting for you in the Little Tower."

Richard bowed again and left. He found his wife propped on pillows on their bed, and she held out her arms to him. The child was growing inside her with uncanny speed; already she was shaped like a fat pear, her breasts great, her eyes shadowed, her nipples dark and swollen. He sat beside her on their bed, held her hands and said gently, "My love, I must tell you that the countess means to take our child and raise it as her own."

She stared at him, moaned like a dying creature, then wept on his shoulder. "They do what they please, the wellborn. What were their ancestors, anyway, but common folk who happened to get lucky? Yet they expect us to give them our service, give them our bodies, give them our children, give them our lives. All in return for a smile and a promise—if that."

Gently but firmly, Richard put his hand over her mouth, for such talk was dangerous. Anyway, what was the point of complaining? She'd have to yield the babe regardless, and in time there would be others. He stayed with her that night, and in the morning set out to learn the duties of a seneschal, and to gather an army.

Through the rest of autumn, his days were more than merely full. He familiarized himself with the whole fiefdom—the people, the houses, the pigs, the sheep, the goats, every cabbage and stalk of wheat—so that taxes could be levied with accuracy. Father Joseph rode by his side on a white mule, carrying a sheaf of vellum and an abacus, a Saracen invention that Drangø had brought back from the East. He made a written record of everything they found, a kind of Domesday Book like the one Duke William of Normandy had made for the same purpose after he conquered Britain.

At the same time, Richard put together his invasion force, intending to strike as soon as the harvest had been reaped. Recruiting was no problem, any more than it had been for Drangø a generation earlier. Warfare in Europe was more or less chronic and left a detritus of masterless men and so-called free companies, soldiers of fortune ready to fight for whoever could pay. The old feudalism based on loyalty was fading out, and a new one based on money was taking form.

The armed mob he accumulated weren't easy to handle, not even for Lucas, who took charge of them. Richard established a camp on the border of Grimoire's domains, moved his mercenaries into it, and paid them small sums on account so they could buy food and drink and the services of a regiment of camp followers who appeared as if by magic. The men called their camp the Village of Bitches and it became a rowdy, dangerous place, with tents and lean-tos for sleeping, stalls for peddlers of beer and food, a field for jousting, a smithy that doubled as an armory—a transient city, noisy at all hours, with a daily quota of fights and stabbings. The surrounding landscape served as the common latrine, so the place could be smelled long before it could be seen.

On the first morning after the harvest, when hoarfrost whitened and stiffened the few remaining stalks in the fields and gleaners blew on their fingers for warmth, Richard rode across the floating bridge into a blood-washed dawn. He wore hauberk and helmet, and his long sword and his shield painted with Chimera hung by his saddle. At the camp he waked Lucas and ordered his men to arm, mount, and form a column. He put himself at their head and they set out at a slow trot, the metal they wore clinking like cowbells as they rode past fields where the gleaners paused to give silent thanks that such dangerous guests were going.

What followed in the enemy's country was less war than slaughter. The dry hills at best were poor in men, and the losses of Grimoire's failed invasion hadn't yet been replaced. The survivors were mainly old people, women, and half-grown children. The invaders killed the dotards, raped anything female they could catch, and set fire to the hamlets and the fields of wheat, which were only half-reaped for want of men to wield the sickles. When at last a small force appeared under Grimoire's banner of nine black toads on a field d'or, the engagement was quick and decisive, with only one major loss—a crossbow bolt felled Lucas.

Richard hardly noticed the death of his father-in-law. His attention was fixed on the enemy leader, a tall figure armed *cap-à-pie* with face concealed by a visored helmet. *So Grimoire escaped after all!* he thought, then kicked with his sharp spurs and his steed leaped forward as if touched by fire. Man, animal, and lance fused into a single missile flying toward the enemy like a bolt hurled from a mangonel. His men broke into a cheer and plunged after him into combat, for what was life that they should cling to it? What was death that they should fear it?

The crash, the clangor, the roiling dust, the pounding of hooves, the scream of a wounded horse, the hammering of steel like twenty smithies—through all the noise and confusion, Richard steadily hacked his way toward the enemy leader. He reached him at last, and for so celebrated a fighter he proved strangely inept and clumsy. Richard went at him like a woodsman felling a tree, and when he toppled from his horse, sprang down to deliver the traditional coup de grâce with a dagger.

He struck open the helmet's visor and beheld the face of a boy no more than sixteen. Grimoire's now half-grown son had taken what was left of his father's forces and led them against the invaders—a child facing a pack of wolves. Utterly helpless, his conqueror's knee on his chest, he gazed up with dark eyes wide open, not pleading, just awaiting the blow.

"Lucky is the father of such a son!" Richard exclaimed in admiration, then in one quick motion cut the boy's throat from ear to ear.

After the battle he had Lucas buried secretly, his grave hidden under brush to protect it from postmortem insult. He interred young Grimoire with every honor he could provide: Father Joseph was far away, but one of Richard's most savage fighters had been a monk—a Templar, no less—before turning freebooter after the loss of the Holy Land. He said the necessary prayers in Latin, right down to the last in *sæcula sæculorum*, meaning forever and ever.

Then Richard interrogated the prisoners taken in the fight. They expected to be held to ransom and killed if they couldn't find the money, but— perhaps remembering the time when he'd been a prisoner himself—he paid the debt for them, and invited them to swear fealty to Matilda and join his forces. Without exception they did so, for the whole House of Grimoire was now extinct, and no one could accuse them of disloyalty. In like manner, he took his enemy's castle not by assault but by offering the garrison money and their lives to open the gate. He gave his men three days to loot the place and they got a good haul, for Grimoire had been a rich lord in his time, and the booty he'd gathered in many battles now passed into their hands.

Afterward they set the place afire and Richard watched the rafters burn, the towers become torches, the slate roofs collapse, and the fortress turn to smoke-blackened ruins whose thick walls and massive keep alone remained standing. When the first storm of winter arrived and extinguished what was left of the blaze, Richard took it as a signal from the Master of Tides—for didn't he speak in the language of storms?—that the campaign was at an end.

His army gathered its winnings and set out for home. In rebuilt Hazelgrove, the peasants turned out to cheer the victors and offer them gleaming apples, fresh-baked loaves of bread, and wreaths made from golden leaves and frost-burned autumn daisies. Father Joseph appeared on his white mule to sprinkle them with holy water, so that grinning rapists and killers rode the last league munching sweet fruit and sour rye, with garlands on their horses' necks and crowns of flowers on their greasy hair. All were happy men, shouting back and forth the most obscene jokes they knew, laughing loud and agreeing that the campaign had been *une p'tite guerre très splendide*—a very fine little war. And now for blazing fires, tankards of beer, cups of wine, roast *cochon de lait*, and all the festivities of Christmas!

Reaching the sea, they found the gray-shingled beach littered with wreckage. The storm had cast all sorts of remnants above the high-tide line— white bodies of cod, bits of sunken boats, a head-sized glob of spermaceti, many-armed cuttlefish, and a jawbone so huge it could only have belonged to the beast Leviathan. The place stank of decay and a cloud of gulls circled overhead, quarreling in harsh voices. Some fishermen who were trying to refloat their stranded boat stopped working long enough to seize Richard's stirrup and lead him—pointing and gabbling excitedly—to the greatest marvel the beach could show.

A merman's corpse lay like a big, dark leather doll among the other detritus.

Richard dismounted, bent over it, and instantly recognized his old enemy and sometime master, Grimoire. He knelt beside the body and prodded its stiff, salted flesh with his fingers. The lower jaw had fallen, so he put two fingers into its mouth and felt impacted grit. After all Richard's years of worry, he knew now that Grimoire had died long ago in one of the boils, gulping down quicksand and salt water as he struggled to breathe. But why? Hadn't Richard taught him how to avoid such traps?

He closed his eyes and thought back to the day that had remade his life— to the battle in the Great Hall, the cloud shaped like an anvil, the flicker of lightning, the rush of the tidal bore surging in before its time. Then he began seeing things he'd never known—things he could not have known.

He saw Grimoire hastening shoreward to rejoin the part of his army that had not been defeated. Around his feet the water rose swiftly, hiding the bottom so that silt and quicksand looked the same. Suddenly his right foot met no resistance and he toppled over. He struggled in something like cold, gritty porridge, sinking deeper the more he tried to escape. He cried out for help, and when his mouth and throat filled up, he swallowed and swallowed, but could never swallow enough. He choked, his body bucked and twisted, salt water ran into his lungs and turned to fire, and suddenly everything was over.

Truly, thought Richard, *I serve a great magician.* With one storm the Master of Tides had destroyed Grimoire and with another had scoured out the boils, disinterred the corpse, and flung it on the smooth round stones for him to find. He opened his eyes and looked out to sea, where waves moved endlessly in gray ranks toward the shore like armored men under white plumes of foam. The light of an ice-blue sky illuminated the north, and for a moment more he lingered, wondering why the Lord of Ragnarök had troubled to save him and slay his enemy. Did the dragon need Richard to carry out some secret purpose? But what could the purpose be?

He rose to his feet, thanked the fishermen for showing him the marvel, and gave them a handful of coins. Then he set off with his men, hurrying now to get home. They were nearing Michael's Mount when a hard-riding horseman thundered across the floating bridge and galloped toward them. The rider was one of Matilda's favorites, a pompous youth of noble birth who fancied himself a herald in the making. Reining in, he cupped his hands around his mouth and intoned, "Sir Richard, your lady wife begs you to return, for her days are accomplished and the pangs of birth are upon her!"

The soldiers roared at that. Their term for giving birth was "shitting a kid," and they sent their commander on his way with catcalls he would have punished if only he'd had time.

At the door of his bedroom in the Little Tower, Matilda's ladies stopped him from entering. He stood outside like a mendicant, listening to Barbeau's screams until they ceased and fainter cries in another voice began.

When at last he was permitted to enter, he found her lying naked on the stained bed, her eyes surrounded by dark bruises as if she had been beaten. The midwife was washing a boy who was purplish, noisy, and astonishingly big—that was why he'd caused Barbeau such great pain. He already had two tiny front teeth and a curl of wet black hair. What would become his navel was still a bloody cord, tied off with gold thread. But the sight that drew and held Richard's eyes was the nap of soft small scales, faintly iridescent as if oiled, that covered his lower body like mail.

While Father Joseph baptized the child in case he died—most infants did—one of the ladies whispered to Richard that, of course, the countess would select the baby's name, but if he had a preference she would gladly mention it. He muttered, "Suggest that she call him Gorand."

When Matilda saw the infant, she would know him for Drangø's son, and—bastard or no bastard—the predestined inheritor of the fief. Hadn't William the Conqueror himself been a bastard, begotten when his father, Rollo the Norseman, impulsively raped a peasant girl? Had that stopped him from being Duke of Normandy and King of England? The boy's future was secure—he would rule, and Richard would serve him whether he wanted to or not. Utterly helpless, he watched the ladies wrap his stepson in clean linen and bear the bundle away. The *serpent de mer* had him in its coils, and he had no way to escape the destiny the God of This World had assigned him.

The midwife washed Barbeau and covered her with a felt blanket and a quilt, under which she lay trembling with cold and weariness. The room was growing dark, so the woman left a rushlight in a saucer on the floor before shutting the door softly behind her. By its dim glow, Richard watched his wife until she fell asleep, then climbed to the top of the tower. He stayed all night in the open, despite a brief, cold rain that tapped his face with fingers of ice. Next morning he brought porridge, fed Barbeau with a spoon, and asked when Drangø had begotten the child.

She whispered, "When I was in seclusion before our wedding. He sent my father and the women away and took me. It was his right, his *droit du seigneur*. Did you expect me to say him nay?"

No, Richard did not expect that. Then why, all the past night, had he felt dark fury building inside him? Was this how Joseph, the stepfather of Jesus, felt when he realized he'd been cuckolded by the God he served? And if the God of This World wronged a man, could he do anything but bow down and submit? No, of course not. Yet Richard knew that he would be revenged on *someone*.

He ordered servants to care for Barbeau and spent the day working at his many duties. All the time he felt that people were looking at him with hidden, sardonic smiles, knowing him for a cuckold. That night, instead of returning to the Little Tower, he went to the town brothel. He chose a peasant girl newly arrived from Hazelgrove, who reminded him of the ones he used to ogle as a boy, watching them turn hay with long-handled rakes or dance at a harvest festival in their clumsy *sabots*. He took her quickly, like an animal, and went to sleep beside her.

At some time during the dark hours, he had a nightmare of falling and woke to find the girl shaking him. He shrugged her off, dressed, and returned to the keep through dark alleys slippery with ice. Guards saluted and stood aside for him. He trekked through warrens filled with recumbent bodies and climbed the spiral steps of the Little Tower. As usual, a soldier slept on the landing, but Richard kicked him awake and sent him away. That was all anybody knew until dawn, when he appeared at Matilda's door.

One of her ladies opened it, and he heard the child crying lustily inside. The crying ceased, a gentle cooing began, and over her head he could see a peasant woman seated beside the cradle, giving young Gorand suck from an enormous breast.

"Yes, Sir Richard?" queried the lady, softly. "The countess is still sleeping, you know."

"When she wakes, tell her there's been an accident. My wife has fallen from the Little Tower."

"Oh, how *terrible*. The countess is so *fond* of her. Indeed, we *all* are. How did it happen?"

"I blame myself. She wanted some air, so I carried her to the top of the tower. She tried to walk, but stumbled and fell over the parapet."

"I'll tell the countess the sad news as soon as she awakens."

"How's the baby?" he asked, turning to go.

"Ah, that's something to comfort all of us, Sir Richard. He's as healthy as the devil."

Gorand was four when Richard and Matilda married—a coupling that caused some heartburning among the nobles of Normandy. They talked for a while of invading her fief and dividing it among themselves. But they'd have to fight Sir Richard, as the low-born fellow called himself. They'd heard tales of what had happened to Grimoire's lands and people, and . . . well, none of them were quite ready to risk that. Anyway, they told one another, the countess was beyond her child-bearing years, so there was no danger of

421

peasant blood being infused into a noble family. Their threats passed off in grumbling, and the boy grew and flourished in the shelter of a long peace maintained solely by the neighbors' healthy fear of his stepfather.

As for Richard, that slave of duty provided Matilda the comfort that only a younger husband can give an aging woman, and compensated for a less than passionate marriage by exercising his own *droit du seigneur* with the women of Hazelgrove and other villages. He'd lost his virginity on a haystack when he was twelve or thereabout, and such natural beds with their rustling, prickly softness and harvest redolence remained his favorite coupling spots. In that respect, he was a peasant still.

Children bearing a marked resemblance to Matilda's consort grew up all over the countryside like fresh grass, and Richard kept an eye on them, giving his daughters small dowries when they wed and taking the strongest boys into the castle to be trained in the profession of arms. Someday, those who survived the hard course of instruction he marked out for them would become young Gorand's men-at-arms, and he would lead them in wars that were yet to be.

The boy was twelve when Richard made him his squire, but two more years passed before he took him to the Hidden Isles. Until then he went alone every spring, sometimes staying a whole day and night in the cavern before he emerged, always carrying new wealth. Did he and the Master of Tides have a language in common? Did the Master speak silently to his thoughts? Nobody knew, and the people of the Isles were far too wise to speculate, except in whispers.

At last, when Gorand was old enough, his voice beginning to change and the first down growing on his spotty face, Richard took him to meet his father. He watched the boy endure seasickness and cold, as he had done so long ago, and at dawn on the last day of the journey, shook him awake, saying, "Up, lad, come to the bow and see the Hidden Isles."

The sailors were stirring, taking down the tent and rolling up the thick sheets of striped wool. Looking gummy-eyed and ratty, as all newly awakened people do, they lined the lee gunwale to add their own water to the sea, then went about their duties stretching and gaping. Gorand, his eyes clotted with sleep, collected two bowls of the inevitable stew and brought Richard his breakfast in the bow. Peering at the tiny mound on the horizon, the boy pointed with his spoon and asked, "Is that where the Master of Tides lives?"

"Soon you'll see."

"Is it where the count my father died?"

"Now, Gorand, no more questions. Pay strict attention and do everything I tell you, for the Master is a great magician, a raiser of storms and a slayer of men, and even if you feel fear you must not show it."

They slept that night ashore, and in the morning made their pilgrimage up the slopes of Ragnarök. When they were standing together beside the crater lake, Richard repeated his warning, laid a heavy hand on the boy's shoulder and said, "Be brave, for in this place, fear is death." So they waited in silence, until the Master of Tides rose streaming from the depths to tower above them.

That night they slept inside the mountain. Next day the boy emerged with a haunted look that caused the people of the Isles to cluck their tongues, nod to one another and say, "So young, yet now he knows who rules this world, and how this world will end."

On the voyage home, Richard stood beside him in the bow of the flagship, both clinging to guylines of the mast. The gray-green waves rolling under the keel heaved them up again and again into the sky, only to drop them into the deep trough that followed. The day was splendid—the cold sun sparkled, wind strummed the lines, flying droplets of brine stung their faces, and grinning porpoises kept them company.

Since his night beside the crater lake, the boy had been mostly silent, but now he said something the wind whipped away. Richard placed one hand on his shoulder and lowered his head, like a priest listening to a penitent whisper a secret into his ear.

"I don't *want* to become a monster," squawked Gorand, his breaking voice full of childish petulance and pathos.

Richard felt tears spring to his eyes. The biting wind instantly dried them to flakes of salt, yet when he searched his hard heart stained with many crimes, he found a thin stream of hope still flowing among the stones. Maybe in time the God of whom Father Joseph talked so much would finally assert himself. Maybe the world would become a gentler place. Maybe people would grow kinder and more just. Maybe—but on the other hand, maybe not.

"You'll become whatever life makes of you," he told the dragon's child, and slapped his face gently, like a bishop giving confirmation.

ACKNOWLEDGEMENTS

ABOUT THE AUTHOR

ALBERT COWDREY HAILS FROM New Orleans, Louisiana—fantasy town, USA—and was educated in its schools and at Johns Hopkins University in Baltimore. Like most young men of his time, he served a stint in the US armed forces, returned home to cop a Ph.D. from Tulane, and after some years of wandering found thirty years of satisfying work in teaching and writing history, the writing done mainly in Washington, DC, where he worked for the Army staff.

His life's been obsessed with words, also with trying, via Zen, to escape from words. He's been blessed with more ideas than he can ever put on paper, also with friends he needs all the more as a practicing and compulsive loner. When he began spinning these fables, his mantras were Science fiction is what we live in, an insight that every day's news confirmed, and Fantasy is the mind made visible. He was lucky enough to find in *The Magazine of Fantasy & Science Fiction* an outlet for his work, in Gordon Van Gelder a gifted editor, and in time he added an award from the World Fantasy Convention to another he'd received years earlier from the American Historical Association. Really.

Nowadays, a certified Old Guy, white-bearded, flatulent, lurching, full of sleep, he looks over his weighty shelf of published histories, scholarly articles, two novels and array of short stories, and finds in them the same sort of mélange étrange he's found in life, filled with blood and laughter and misery and whatnot. Maybe laughter more than anything else. Did he really write about soldiers and scientists and demons and witches and find them all, in some weird sense, perfectly real? Well, yeah. But as Nabokov said, "reality" is a word that means nothing unless it's between quotes.